<u>JEWFISH</u>

A novel

Andrew Furman

A

LITTLE CURLEW PRESS

TRADE PAPERBACK

Jewfish

ISBN: 978-0-9960825-4-9
Library of Congress Control Number: 2020932873

Cover Design: James Knake
Cover Image: David Tripp

For my son, Henry, in his twenty-first year

And upon all that are lovers of virtue; and dare trust in His providence; and be quiet; and go a-angling.

> Izaak Walton, *The Compleat Angler*

He loved to think about the power of the sun, about light, about the ocean. The purity of the air moved him. There was no stain in the water, where schools of minnows swim. Herzog sighed and said to himself, 'Praise God—praise God.' His breathing had become freer. His heart was greatly stirred by the open horizon; the deep colors; the faint iodine pungency of the Atlantic rising from weeds and mollusks; the white, fine, heavy sand; but principally by the green transparency as he looked down to the stony bottom webbed with golden lines.

> Saul Bellow, *Herzog*

\

Book One

Chapter One

Nathan Pray pulled the Tacoma gingerly onto the street. A too-small truck for a too-small skiff, but he could get away with it. No gradients in south Florida, its humble topography fairly leveled within Nathan's lifetime, frosted with concrete and asphalt. Hills or no, the trailer groaned and bucked at the insult, the only noise shattering the blissful quiet of his little burg at night. Scarcely a soul about.

He lowered the window and jutted an elbow into the surprising cold. My town, Nathan mused, then checked himself. My town. A quaint notion. Who cared about hometowns anymore?

He rolled the window back up. The entire planet had been set to boil, yet what a winter this season in the subtropics! The snook had disappeared from his immediate fishing grounds. Purged. A few more degrees south, one more cold snap, and the few likely survivors at this northern fringe of their range would perish too. The last cold front pretty much did in Florida's linesiders. Polar vortex, they were calling these strange episodes. Water temps plunging from 75 degrees to 54 degrees overnight. Too abrupt a shift. The extreme low of snook tolerance, in any case.

A rare fox darted across Nathan's illumined field of view and flicked its ridiculous bottle-brush tail above the asphalt. The actual fox ushered phantom creatures to his mental screen. Land crabs scuttled across the sandy two-lane road, disappearing beneath the palmetto scrub; armadillos wandered blindly, nose to the air, fragrant with wax myrtle; gopher tortoises lumbered below ground into their burrows; a scrub-jay pair, wearing their gray backpacks, hopped follow-the-leader across the tattered bark branches of a slash pine.

So long to all that.

Some beauty remained, though. And so Nathan stayed too. For what remained.

**

The fisherman pulled up beside his fishing partner's house, the roadside dust and shell-bits crunching beneath the tires of his truck and trailer. He cut the headlights. It felt like a stealth mission, which it wasn't. Camilla had always been good about letting Terrance fish with Nathan at night. Nathan couldn't think of many wives–certainly not his own; that much was clear–who'd abide these twice or thrice-weekly fishing excursions late into the morning. Terrance, just a step slow for a football scholarship at U of F, FSU, or Miami, had met his wife at Alcorn State. That Terrance had known him longer than Camilla worked to Nathan's advantage. The longstanding tenure of their relations somehow mattered to her, and Nathan wasn't above exploiting this curious deference.

He gazed toward the front door, the matching light fixtures on either side, burning. He didn't want to honk, or knock on the door, and risk waking one of the little Stillwaters. Terrance usually sensed his arrival, somehow, heard the groan and rumble of the trailer, maybe, or glimpsed the flash of headlights against the window treatments. And here Terrance was, opening the front door now, throwing the hood of his sweatshirt over his mostly shorn pate, turning back to say goodbye, or maybe something else, to Camilla, whom Nathan couldn't see.

Terrance swung his oversize canvas duffle (which held too many plastic tackle boxes) over the gunwale onto the skiff's deck along with three fishing rods, and then joined Nathan in the cab. He smacked his palms once and then rubbed them together, as if it were much colder outside than it actually was. "Woo-ee!" he said, then with open knuckles tapped Nathan's thigh. "Evening, cap'!" Terrance declared, half-facetiously, then rubbed his hands again. Nathan smiled. Only Terrance tapped his thigh with his open knuckles to greet him and called him cap', half-facetiously. It was a gift. Others had less.

"Evening, T."

**

Before long, they were on the water.

"Slow it down a bit, Terrance, will you?" Wielding an inshore rod, Nathan hopped up on the bow's casting deck. He tugged his line taut above the bail, testing the drag, and savored the reassuring *zzzzzp* in his ear. Next, he popped a Lemonhead into his mouth. Cherry Chans he had liked too, but it seemed they stopped making those a while back, maybe on account of the impolitic name, the slant-eyed portrait on the cardboard package. Well fine. The candy itself, though, he missed.

"Just cut the motor, T. I'll use the trolling."

Terrance, Nathan was certain, rolled his eyes behind the console as he turned off the ignition. It burned him up that Nathan insisted upon wasting time inshore alongside a few lit docks and here, beside the crusty pilings of the inlet bridge, with his spoons and homemade wooden lures before heading out to the reef lines, where they actually stood a chance of filling the coolers with snapper using frozen pilchards, sardines, and slimmer silversides.

"Plan on casting anytime soon up there?"

Nathan raised a hand to quiet his companion, which didn't work.

"It ever occur to you, my brotha', that you done chose the one path you least cut out for?"

Terrance usually didn't talk like this. He had started out as an English teacher before scaling the administrative ladder. Yet his street diction, syntax, and timbre rose proportionately with his vehemence.

"Take a look at yourself, man. You've got options. With your B.S. from U of M I can get you a provisional teaching certificate, lickety-split. English teachers, dime a dozen. But science, math"—a rhetorical burst of air fluttered between Terrance's lips—"can write your own ticket, homeslice. When are you going to give this up and teach science for me?"

"Soon," Nathan replied, smiling at "homeslice," tasting the sweet lemon ball dissolve, turning tart. "Real soon, T."

"You can blow it off all you want, but face facts, Nate. You can't handle the sun, you don't like getting wet, you're not into social media or any self-promotion at all far as I can tell–heaven forbid you answer or even carry your cell phone–you don't really like people very much. . . "

Terrance was right about most of this, especially the sun bit. Nathan could scarcely bear the subtropical afternoon rays, lacking the olive Pray hue. Pink craters of various circumference and depth dotted his forearms, his nape, his sloping forehead, remnants of Dr. Krauss's scalpeled defense against squamous cell incursions. But Terrance wasn't finished. . ."You're out catching colorful fish all day but you're color-blind—"

"It's an advantage, I keep telling you. Being colorblind. I see my grays better down under the surface. Come on, now, T. You've seen me spot tarpon down there."

A bird bleated from the bridge scaffolding somewhere low. Green heron, probably.

"Just you have to see things as they are, Nate? Not how you want them to be. How many times we been through this? You want to fish, fine. But we ain't fishing for croakers out the El Rio no more. You gotta ditch this skiff." Nathan glanced back to see Terrance gesture downward with an open hand, dismissively, as if the twenty-two foot skiff were an inner tube. "Get yourself a center console, something with a decent-sized V, take folks out to the Gulf Stream for dolphin, wahoo, marlin, sailfish. That's where the Benjamins are. That's what all those dumb clucks at the dock are doing. They ain't got half your smarts, a Jew like you, so why you letting them make off with all the charters?"

A Jew like you. Terrance used the expression from time to time to leaven his chastisements with humor. All the same, it seemed to Nathan that his friend ascribed too much validity to certain notions. What did smart mean, anyway? Sure, Nathan had earned solid grades and scored well on the SAT (a performance he might have curbed had he known his mother would hassle him these many years for his squandered intellect), he still preferred the quietude of books to the dizzying array of visual media enticements. But a smart person, it seemed to Nathan, would have figured out how to hold on to his family. A smart person would have figured out how to make a respectable living. Perhaps he was only a high-IQ moron, which was much worse, somehow, than being a plain-old moron.

"I'm not nearly as smart as you like to believe, T."

"There! There! Don't you see? Just saying something like that proves the point. You feel me?"

Nathan didn't "feel" him—Terrance's street voice again!—and confessed as much. "Besides," he added, "you know I'm not into that sort of thing, Terrance. The blue water stuff. Next you'll be telling me to fish with kites or balloons."

"Well, what's so wrong with that?"

"It's not angling, Terrance! That's what's wrong with it!" It was Nathan's turn to grow exercised. "Playing with your food is what that is. . . . Want a Lemonhead?" he abruptly proposed, in a spirit somewhere between peace offering and taunt, rattling the cardboard box.

Terrance, frustrated by the inscrutable terms, elided the offer. The heron bleated again. Vehicles groaned overhead as they crossed the bridge.

"You and your rules, Nate." Terrance plopped heavily down on the cooler seat. "Not sure if you've noticed, but you're pretty much the only one anymore who cares about these rules of yours."

His fishing partner was right. The waters had shifted over the years, the fish stocks had depleted—climate change disrupting eons-old patterns of migration and provoking ever more erratic spikes and dips in the air and water temps, the sugar and cattle industries releasing their tonnage of "nutrients" into the estuaries, exacerbating the toxic red tides that were once more local and short-lived, plus the plastics and sewage from too many Floridians ravaging the reefs. The commercial and charter community had recalibrated, harnessing every conceivable advantage to locate and land these ever-dwindling creatures. 3-D sonar, 32-megabyte GPS, newfangled baitcasting reels boasting unprecedented torque in complex ratios and variable-speed retrieves, 12-volt electric reels for deep-dropping on the swords miles offshore, a plethora of glimmering, mass-produced stick-baits and plugs, and now these scented plastics, dangerously blurring the live-versus-artificial boundary. And live bait had always been anathema to Nathan. Any moron could catch a snook throwing live pilchards, pinfish, or mullet. The only thing that mattered anymore, it seemed, was the bottom-line. The fish landed.

No boundaries. No shame.

Nathan, for whatever reason, couldn't adjust in kind. More and more, it seemed to him, he had become a person who didn't do, who wouldn't do, any number of things that most people would do, and did do, as a matter of course. There were innumerable overpriced lures that Nathan refused to tie to his leader, or to the leader of any of his char-

7

ters, no matter their earnest protestations. The skitterwalk, the skitter-pop, the top dog, the popa dog, the popa pup, the shad rap, the jitterbug, the chug bug, the bomber long-A, the hula popper, the zara spook, the thin fin, the spot, the Rat-L-Trap. Anything made by Parabola. Those fuckers.

Nathan outright refused to rig any number of set-ups too. The chicken-rig, the fixed float, the sliding float, the stinger rig, the knocker rig. Anything with wire, balloons, kites, pyramid sinkers, bank sinkers, or pencil sinkers.

Nathan's preferred angling methods comprised a much shorter list, methods faithfully adherent, he felt, to the venerable principles of angling. Ten-pound test. Maybe twelve in a pinch. A medium-weight spinning rod and reel. Artificial bait to match the hatch. He handcrafted his own plugs from dogwood or cedar using a lathe and gouger. He also used bucktail jigs and gleaming spoons, secured all these go-to baits with a trilene, palomar, or loop knot, depending on conditions. He used a few soft-plastics, too, mostly at night, and partly to appease Chad at Swallow Artificials, his sponsor. None of those funky hues and patterns–electric chicken, mango tango surprise, green eggs and ham, drunken monkey, watermelon blaze, psychedelic Chernobyl. . . Natural presentations only. He rigged them weedless or on a jig–eighth ounce, quarter ounce, half ounce–sometimes below a popping cork that splashed and gurgled and clicked. More often, not. Braided line and 1-aught or 2-aught circle hooks (kinder to the piscine creatures) represented Nathan's only bows to modernity.

Nathan fished the way he fished because it was the right way. The way he believed one should fish. Because fishing this way silenced the deafening roar dockside rather than contributed more noise to this strange new world—a world in which everyone seemed angry at everyone else. Because it was called fishing, not catching. This was what he endeavored to impress upon his charters. That landing fish was only a small part of the larger picture. The water. The air. The heady odors of marine organisms, living and dead. Your perfect breath. The wetted line against your finger. Contact!

Nathan believed all this. At least he thought that he did. But perhaps, he considered, still reading the current from his perch on the bow, it was mostly his belief in the belief that held fast after all these years. He breathed the briny air, spiced here so close to shore by restaurant foodsmells and vehicular exhaust. Perhaps, as Terrance suggested, he was just unwilling to face facts. Ah, it had been his wife's favorite chastisement too. Perhaps he was merely stubborn.

"Look around you, Nate. Look," Terrance urged. Nathan complied with a weary exhale, lifting his gaze toward the wide expanse of ICW. The natural inlet, he knew, had been at the north end of the lake, just yonder. A rat's mouth. No more. The Army Corps of Engineers, for whatever reason, had dredged this alternative inlet long before the war, this inlet that looked only like the manufactured inlet it was, and then stoppered the natural channel. The war was pretty much the only reason they completed the intracoastal waterway, a protected passage up and down the eastern seaboard safely beyond the German U-boats' field of view.

"Where do you think you are, Nate? The Mosquito Lagoon? The Ten Thousand Islands? Flamingo? Biscayne Bay? You want to be an inshore snook guide throwing plugs, plastic, and spoons with ten-pound mono, you're in the wrong place. Face it, Nate. They're gone."

"There's still snook here," Nathan declared, softly, not altogether convincingly, reading the water still from his perch on the bow's deck. He spotted the bird now. A green heron, yes, stalking minnows, crouched on the lowest plank of the channel wall beneath the bridge. A sizzling bulb under the bridge, a few feet above the high-tide line, washed the heron with its urine light.

"Jimminy-Crickets man," Terrance squealed in falsetto. "Are you going to cast or not, Nathan Herschel Pray?"

"Now now, Terrance."

"Might as well give me some of those Lemonheads!"

Nathan grinned as he underhanded the cardboard box behind him toward Terrance. *Jimminy-Crickets*. His God-fearing friend cultivated a whole lexicon of non-curses, which sounded downright babyish to Nathan's ears. Such practiced restraint. Need Terrance deprive himself a full-throated *Jesus Christ* once in a while?

"I'll cast . . . I'll cast . . . I'll cast," Nathan assured his partner softly, reading the dark water beside the bridge piling once again, its ripple illumined by the sizzling bulb. Outgoing tide. Yes. Good. The heron was here nabbing outgoing prey from above, the snook (hopefully) snatching whitebait and such from below. Gripping the cork handle lightly, he flipped the bail, felt the textured braid lay across the uncalloused crease along his index finger's first joint. The first cast. It wasn't something to attempt, casually. The second, third, fortieth cast, fine. But there was only one first cast, one chance to set his homemade silver mullet down in the drink just beyond the ocher O edge, where bridge light gave way to darkness, where the snook lurked, if any had survived the last freeze. His carefully weighted and contoured wooden plug would inspire an underwater wave hewing to the precise real-mullet signature, offering its eons-old come-hither tickle across the snook's lateral line. He crunched down with his teeth on the sour-sugary remnants of his candy, whipped the rod back, and threw.

**

Having conceded defeat, tired of Terrance's hectoring, his weary sighs and exhales, Nathan took the throttle. Clearing the bend, he gazed out at the blank darkness beyond the green and red inlet lights. A moonless night. Not bad for fishing. Easier to lure the snapper up off the bottom. But dangerous. Nathan struggled to discern where ocean gave way to sky beyond the bow, where sky yielded to ocean. He glanced rightward toward the jetty, where fishermen silhouettes usually offered parting salutes. They were invisible tonight (if they were present), as was the jetty itself of bulldozed boulders and dirt, just inside the green light. Not many boats out, apparently. A couple stern lights winked at them from the third reef, probably. Not a good sign, the winking, nor was the sea spray he lapped from his stubbly upper-lip just before the bow dipped below the crest of the first wave.

"WHOA," he uttered, immediately regretting it.

"You call this two feet or less!?" Terrance widened his stance, gripped the console's stainless steel frame. Nathan removed the clasp of the safety lanyard from the key-ring and clipped it to his belt-loop.

"Not me. NOAA."

"I don't know, Nate."

"Water's just confused here a bit. Won't be so bad out on the second reef. Offshore breeze'll die down. We'll stay at 60 feet or so. How's that?" This was what Nathan always promised, terms Terrance usually accepted.

"Drown just as easy in 60 feet as a hundred."

It was tough to argue with such logic, so Nathan didn't try. Not exactly.

"We're here," he countered, taciturn–a remark so nonsensically incontrovertible that it left Terrance dumbstruck.

Nathan motored the vessel to take the chop a bit sideward at the bow. As he couldn't see the waves, though, it was anyone's guess how to achieve this position. They took one wave over the bow before Nathan's eyes adjusted and he figured out what was what. Thankfully, it wasn't too bumpy once they cleared the sandbar beyond the inlet. Just rollers, it seemed, sufficiently spaced. Annoying, but tolerable.

They went about their business without words. Nathan scanned the coastline, spotted the telltale droopy Australian Pine silhouettes, the red beacon light in the background above Dixie Highway. He labored over 36 honey-holes between Pompano and Boynton along the shallow patch reefs and the inside and outside of the second and third reefs, recorded his spot, conditions (current, wave-height, moon phase, weather, water temp), date, and take in his journal. He adhered to a strict rotation, lest he deplete any one honey-hole. The yellowtail, the mangrove, the mutton, the king, the gag, the red and the black–these piscine morsels he gathered for Dixie Doc's to keep his charter business afloat–tended to bite with less trepidation under this sheet of darkness.

So here he was.

Nathan rose at nine or so most nights (he actually would have preferred to sleep until midnight, had it left him any chance of recruiting Terrance to their nocturne), then fished as close to sunup as his mate would allow. After dressing his catch, after dropping off his old friend, after sliding a cooler safely inside Doc's padlocked patio, he courted his insomnia until sunrise over weak tea with lemon served by Kati in coffee-stained ceramic at the ungentrified Caribbean Café. He'd wait there through the morning, along with his more successful cohorts, until summoned to his charge (with any luck) by the dockmaster, Marty. After a four-hour, six-hour, or full-day charter, or after waiting for one, after washing down the *Pray Fish*, after washing himself down less purposefully in the bleak stall of his rented apartment, Nathan would court a few precious hours of early evening sleep.

Terrance, seated at the stern now, sliced semi-thawed sardines for chunk. Nathan eased on the throttle as the slow-moving beacon neared the second notch in the tree line, just off the coast from sprawling San Remo, where the old Italians lived. Terrance, ripping off the cardboard top, slipped the first frozen menhaden block inside the mesh bag. Nathan, an eye on the sonar, motored eastward, slowly, the waves lapping the hull. Terrance slipped past to the bow and the anchor locker.

"Okay . . . now."

Terrance, a sneakered foot braced on the gunwale, threw the Danforth.

Nathan turned off the ignition and unclipped the safety lanyard from his belt loop.

The two stood there for a moment at the stern while they waited for the anchor to hold. Terrance, for whatever reason, always stood shoreside, while Nathan took the outside. The moon, a rusty smudge on the east horizon, struggled to rise as they waited. Stars salted the dark sky above. He could just make out the Seven Sisters, five or six of them anyway. Invisible whitecaps all about issued sporadic applause. Then, suddenly, the stern shifted to the north as if on a pendulum. The anchor had found its purchase below the brisk current.

Nathan set out the chum bag Terrance had prepared and tied it off to the cleat. Terrance tossed a handful of sardines off the stern, sliced thin as rose petals. They set about lowering their lines. Terrance flipped the bail of his reel, peeled off monofilament with his left hand, then flicked his rod upward with the right, enacting the exercise over and over, a conductor leading a symphony. Nathan offered his weighted line no such encouragement. He allowed the eighth-ounce split-shot to perform its own slow work while he gauged the strength, direction and depth of the currents, the monofilament slipping across the pads of his fingers at alternating tempos.

"Cold," Terrance observed, halting his symphony to throw the hood of his sweatshirt over his head.

"Little bit."

"How's the little gangster."

"Fine. I mean good. Big swim meet coming up. Regionals."

"Hair?"

"Same."

"And pop?"

"Not bad." Nathan exhaled. "Seems okay most of the time."

"God bless."

This wasn't Nathan's favorite kind of fishing. He considered it more like collecting, actually. Collecting a catch for Dixie Doc's. Paying the bills. But he relished the uncomplicated industry of fishing the reef late at night. While his drowsy town slept, here Nathan was, awake and alive and burning.

He savored this particular moment, especially, this brief spot of time between the bustle of setting up to fish and the actual fishing, the noisy, fragrant two-stroke shut off, the sound and smell of the sea returned to them, their lines just over the side, the bait slipping down the darkening column, negotiating the curious currents, speaking through his fingers, still a secret to the creatures below, the two of them settling in for the night, clearing their throats, a few quiet words exchanged, taking their essential human inventory before . . . before . . .

"Got one!" Terrance declared, flipping the bail. "Snapper," he predicted with confidence, reeling in the line. His drag *ziiipped,* then held. "Decent size." Nathan nodded, threw some more chunk bait over the transom as if to kosher the imminent catch, breathed in the ocean's restorative brine.

"Think you might need to step up from that split-shot, Nate. Gotta punch through that strong current about thirty feet down. Then bam!"

A good night. The offshore breeze calmed, the ocean lay down, while the current below remained brisk, spiriting the frozen chum along a productive trail. Nathan reached down to jostle the mesh bag every so often, as if to encourage a fresh pouch of tea steaming in a cup. When the bite slowed, he plopped ten "meatballs" or so into the sauce—fist-sized sand-spheres peppered with his proprietary recipe of oats, corn meal, hogmouth fry, and menhaden oil—the packed meatballs releasing their chum lower in the column than the frozen block, luring the bigger snapper and grouper from their grottoes.

The bull sharks and lemons weren't so bad. Only one mangrove snapper came up quivering, half-devoured—"gotta pay the tax collectors," Terrance noted—which they saved on deck for possible cut-bait later on. They worked efficiently, quietly, through the night, filling both coolers with mixed snappers, mostly mangrove (the water temp a bit cold for the yellowtail), a few blue runners Terrance insisted upon keeping, and one large cobia, shark impersonator, strange catch for dead winter, oddly lethargic during the brief battle before thrashing wild boatside, the still-green creature forcing Nathan to use the gaff, which he didn't much like. The deck a bloody mess. Every once in a while, they heard the distant celebrations from one of the other vessels out at the third reef, odd whoop and wail frequencies lingering in the mild southeast wind. Probably the Little Carlos, Nathan thought. An odd name for the loud boat, as Charlie was much smaller than his enormous center console. Plus, he wasn't Latino but an ethnic Indian of indeterminate Caribbean descent. A good night for Charlie too, apparently. He wondered if they were catching kings. Or cobia. Their own snappers weren't too big, not on this nearshore second reef, but they were all over fourteen inches, anyway, and fat.

"Call it a night, Nate?"

"Sure."

Nathan kneeled at the bow while Terrance took the wheel and fired the ignition. He always breathed easier upon hearing the engine's staccato growl. Nathan pointed toward where the anchor lay and Terrance negotiated the vessel, accordingly. "Got it," Nathan said, pulling up the rope.

"That as fast as you can pull, skinny-boy?" Terrance teased, expansive. It had been a good night.

Nathan was about to respond in kind when he heard a plashing portside followed by a lusty human breath. He turned instinctively toward the sound, his headlamp firing red eyes.

"Goodness gracious," Terrance uttered, giving voice to Nathan's thoughts.

"What's a turtle doing out here dead of winter?"

"Don't know, Nate. Never seen one so shallow in winter. You?"

"No. Don't think so."

This was something else that Nathan enjoyed about these nights collecting fish out over the reef. He never fished the same ocean. However much his state and city screwed with it (the nearby outfall, for example, spewing their vaguely "treated" sewage just eighty feet deep), the sea's inscrutable nonhuman order still obtained. Mostly. You never quite knew what you were in for just off the inlet: curious currents beneath the depths speaking through twelve pound test at his fingertips, a river of glowing photoplasm drifting atop the surface, a shadowy squawking flock of shearwater overhead, a lumbering manatee testing the nearshore waters, silver mullet charging the inlet during their fall run, muscular jack crevalle slicing through the underwater clouds, squadrons of shrimp charging the inlet weeks later on spontaneous winter nights, their eyes breathing fire beneath the incandescence of a lantern, ancient sea hares–gothic, winged creatures–relinquishing the fight, drifting inshore to expire, the heavens aglow in strange hues, a grouper sporting curious geometric patterns. Now, this small hawksbill turtle flopping around their waters in December chasing man-o-war and snappers. There was nothing second-hand or stale about his coastal life. An original relationship here to pursue along this spit of land and sea.

The way things were going, though, how long could he keep at it?

Divers admired these sea turtles for their gracefulness, but it didn't seem so graceful to Nathan. Rather, the hawksbill seemed out of its element, downright awkward, flopping around on the surface with clumsy flippers jutting from its clunky armor. "We still have that mangrove on deck?" Nathan inquired as he sealed the anchor into its locker. Terrance wordlessly retrieved the shark-mangled snapper and threw it over the side to the turtle, which seemed to have been expecting the morsel. Probably wasn't a good idea, Nathan contemplated too late. Making boats mean food to the creature. It negotiated the snapper down its gullet with its odd hawk's bill, bobbed its reptilian head. Shark food, Nathan thought, these turtles.

Terrance, smacking his lips, was thinking something else.

"Mmm-mmm. We'd *turn* that turtle back in the day, boy."

"What the heck you talking about, Terrance?"

"Pearl City back in the day, Nate. Turtle steak. Turtle burgers. Turtle soup. Turtle fritters. *That's* what I'm talkin' about."

"You never turned turtles at the beach, T. Your father, maybe. When he was twelve. Turtle burgers. For crying out loud, you ate subs from Grace's and Whoppers from Burger King with me."

"Didn't say *I* did. That's not what I said. Said *we* did."

Nathan, sitting on the bow seat now, taking a load off, didn't know what to say to this. He felt a curious pang of envy and groped to locate its source. The expansiveness of Terrance's we, one that spanned generations. It pierced Nathan, somehow. His partner was like one of those true-believer Jews taking over the place now, fringes streaming from their waistbands. "We were at Sinai together!" one of them had accosted Nathan outside Publix, shoving a pamphlet in his face. A nice thought, that, but too theoretical to offer him much ballast. The Florida Prays were ever few and fading fast.

"He looks okay, anyway," Nathan said, coming to and rising from his seat.

"Give him another one?" Terrance proposed. "Cooler's full."

"Probably not a good idea."

Terrance nodded.

"Keep fightin' the good fight big guy," Nathan said as he fired the ignition, causing the turtle to disappear beneath a patch of sargassum, lit now by the risen half-moon. He motored slowly to clear the turtle's possible sphere. Then, after removing his headlamp and securing it atop the console, he punched the throttle, exercising the Merc across the tranquil sea. As he piloted the boat, he pulled the frosty mentholated air into his bent-elbow nose and lungs. Within minutes, they reached the inlet, which Nathan took wide in outsized deference to the sandbar. Once inside the jetty, Nathan slowed the skiff off plane. He could see the jetty's jagged contours now beneath the risen moon. The fishermen, if they had ever been out tonight, had abandoned their rocky posts.

"Solid night," Terrance burst the sudden quiet.

"Yeah. Sure was." Nathan considered their coolers, performed a silent calculation in his head. The wind's echo still hummed in his skull.

"Fillet a few for the ladies?" Terrance asked after they pulled to the deserted dock, as Nathan knew he would ask. He noticed Charlie's parked trailer. And Nguyen's, the kingfish specialist. They fished Nathan's waters, more or less, fairly close to shore. Otherwise, hardly any hook-and-line guys left these parts. The few commercial fishermen anymore mostly stalked swordfish in larger, costlier boats, miles and miles off the coast in the northward flowing gulfstream. Snapper and grouper men worked the fishier Keys.

"Sure you want these blue runners, T? Got plenty of snapper."

"Now don't you be dissin' my runners," Terrance replied in his street voice. "Perfectly good eatin'. Good enough fish for anyone." Nathan smiled as he handed Terrance the keys to the truck.

While Terrance climbed up on the dock, Nathan opened the aft cooler and threw ten snappers and the blue runners into a five-gallon bucket. It used to have words on it, some kind of birdseed or something, but the salt air and water had long ago erased them. He set the bucket up on the dock and followed after it. Too suddenly. *"Ohhhh."* He stood still to gather his confused innards. Nausea sometimes gripped him shoreside, though never at sea, curiously enough. Gathering himself, he carried on toward the broad filleting tables while Terrance retrieved the trailer. There was talk lately of removing the stations, banning fish cleaning at this particular launch, which catered increasingly to an upscale pleasure-boater cohort, none too pleased in the morning by the sight and stench of stray, stripped carcasses about from sloppy nighttime fishermen. Terrific. Just one more imminent development sure to wound Nathan. And Charlie. And Nguyen.

He freed the fillets from their frames, then from skin and scale, quickly, skillfully, scoring practiced incisions at precise locales just behind the gill plates, close along the *bump bump bump* of the backbones (no meat to waste) and around the ribcages. Six healthy fillets for his ex-wife Sam and his boy, Miles—hell if his own son ate store-bought tilapia—four for Kati, two for himself, and eight for the larger Stillwater clan, plus the darker, oily blue runner slabs. He heard the *Pray Fish* rise from the ramp under Terrance's command, shedding its seawater onto the pavement like a canine shaking off its wet. He split open the fat belly of the next mangrove, throat to vent, and removed the viscera with a scoop of two fingers. He pierced its translucent intestinal sheath, its more solid stomach. Between the pads of his thumb and two fingers he inspected the semi-digested bounty: a few thawed sardine sheets, a gritty paste of pulverized menhanden. Skin and scale and bone and meat. The snapper had imbibed lustily in their chum slick. But what was this? Crab remains smaller than a thumbprint, a spindly exoskeleton leeched of its meat. Interesting.

Terrance joined Nathan at the steel table after running fresh water through the Merc and they scaled and dressed the remaining catch. Terrance scaled. Nathan gutted. There was a world, Nathan idly thought, that would have valued these gifted flicks of his wrist, the well-honed muscle memories of thumb and forefinger. A world of fishermen, butchers, bakers, carpenters, cobblers, coopers, drummers, plumbers, seamstresses and tailors. But this world didn't exist anymore. Instead, the world, at least the only world Nathan knew, had grown impatient with the familiar vocations, farmed them out on the cheap, along with the fish, themselves. Tilapia. This once-African species, genetically re-engineered to taste like mud–didn't anyone notice?!–farmed, flash-frozen, and freighted mostly from China, Vietnam, Costa Rica and who knew where else?! Befouling any number of third-world ecosystems in the bargain with the putrid runoff. Nathan had been born kicking and screaming into a world full of people prized for performing a ceaselessly expanding and subdividing list of arcane tasks. A world–or at least a country–where the teeming hordes didn't seem to *do* much of anything as far as he could tell. What would become of a nation whose citizens functioned two or three times removed from the actual realm of making and crafting and building and doing? Flimsy stuff upon which to build a civilization, or a town. The fisherman exhaled volubly through his deviated septum.

"What?"

"Nothing, T. . . . Crab on that second reef."

"Mm-hm."

**

They drove in silence across the deserted surface streets to Terrance's house, the timed lights blinking red and yellow now well after midnight, both of them mulling earlier words, knowing each other well enough to know that they were mulling those earlier words.

"It's not that I don't like fishing with you, Nate," Terrance finally confessed, exercising his fingers, flicking inward the pale undersides of his upraised digits, working out the kinks. "I'm still game for a while yet. Just we're not getting any younger is the thing."

"I know. It's okay, Terrance."

"Tournament stuff I'm all in. Sure enough. Just this late night thing . . . I don't know. Like I say, I'm still game for a while maybe. But if you want to fish with someone else, too. Or instead of me. One of those mates down at the marina, say. A younger guy like that would probably appreciate the money. Be more help to you too. Or maybe you can team up with Nguyen. Hasn't killed a mate in a while."

They shared a quiet laugh. Nguyen's last partner, fat Eddie, a drinker, had teetered over the transom dead in 120 feet of water. Potbellied Nguyen didn't have the strength to pull Eddie onto the deck over the high gunwales. So he tied his partner to a cleat and dragged his corpse home. Heart attack, the autopsy revealed a week later, which made everyone feel better. Everyone except for Eddie.

"I hear you, Terrance. No worries. I'll figure something out."

Camilla had left the driveway lights on for her husband. A family-room light burned, as well. She was probably still up, or had been woken up, anyway. There was a new baby, Michelle. Not much sleep to be had these days in the Stillwater house. There were four children, total, three boys older than Michelle. The Stillwater's fecundity mocked Nathan's quashed, erstwhile efforts. He couldn't deny a pang of envy.

It was a nice house. Not a gated community or new construction, an asphalt shingle roof rather than rolled tile, maybe a block too close to the Florida East Coast train tracks, but a solid house on the whole. South-facing. Plenty of natural light. 2,500 square feet or so. Split-plan. Large master bedroom and bath. Walk-in closets. Mexican tile floors. Remodeled kitchen with Corian countertops. A small kidney-shaped pool out on the screen-enclosed lanai. His mother had found the home for Terrance some ten years ago, waived her share of the commission. And Terrance, to his credit, had kept the property up. Freshly painted stucco, pressure-cleaned sidewalk and driveway, mulched garden beds of periwinkle, impatiens and petunias beside the stately mahogany. It evinced what his mother would call pride of ownership.

Terrance had only moved a few blocks west from Pearl City, but they were large blocks, miles and miles, it seemed to Nathan, from Terrance's grandfather's string bean and pepper picking days at the Raulerson Farm across the El Rio (supplanted by the Army Airfield, which, in turn, had yielded to the university), from his father's bus-boy days at the resort and his somewhat better paying stint as a leopard-skin clad tribal warrior at the long defunct Africa-USA theme park.

"Here, T. Your cut from last week. Almost forgot." Nathan, leaning over his partner, retrieved the small roll of bills from the glove compartment. Tens and fives tucked inside a Jackson double-layer. "It's yours, T. Go on."

Terrance contemplated the roll.

"Shucks, Nathan, we couldn't have caught more than thirty pounds or so last week with that mixed up current. You keep it. Least 'till the snook start biting again and things pick up at the dock. Can't be much there anyway."

"Terrance," Nathan uttered. His partner had never pulled this crap before. "Terrance," he repeated, brandishing the roll above the parking brake. "C'mon, T. Don't start this stuff."

Terrance, silent, opened the Tacoma door and groaned as he stretched a foot out onto the asphalt, though kept his butt on the cracked vinyl seat for the moment. "Always work for me at Carver, Nate. Like I said. Wouldn't be the end of the world, you know."

"I know, T."

"You'll go to school in the morning and leave in the afternoon. Livable wage. Benefits. Have dinner and go to sleep like a real person. Simple. Life's good when it's simple."

"Yeah," Nathan answered. "I know. I'll think about it," he said, wondering for the first time if he meant it.

"Anyway, hold up a sec,' 'milla made lasagna. Wanted me to give you a piece before you left." Nathan nodded. Terrance stepped out to retrieve the morsel. He shut the truck door behind him quiet as an apology, returning moments later with the leftovers wrapped like an aluminum brick.

**

Nathan parked the truck and trailer across a span of empty spaces near the fragrant dumpster and walked up the concrete steps to his door. Home. For now, anyway. He'd wash up a bit before heading to the café. The small building–two stories, only eight units–attracted itinerant immigrant bachelors almost exclusively, and fewer families. Upon landing here, Nathan anticipated a more stable, if hardscrabble, assortment of neighbors. An elderly lady, say, who sat outside her door on a folding chair to brook the heat during the wet season. (He would tithe her fish from time to time.) A bright-eyed child, maybe, exuding benign neglect to whom he might offer wise counsel. Nathan's folly, such fantasies. Instead, random dark men with patchy beards and V-neck undershirts advertising worrisome stains ignored him; fewer women fumbled with their keys upon spotting his presence along the corridor, then scurried into the safety of their unit; the occasional snot-nosed kid eyed him with utmost suspicion. These little stinging reproaches. He took up so little space, Nathan Pray. To have his meager portion questioned seemed especially cruel.

He entered the apartment, set the foil brick of lasagna and his snapper fillets in the refrigerator to keep company with the drooping bunch of parsley he should have sealed in plastic, the carton of OJ, the couple puckered limes, the lone lemon with a crescent carved into its side; Nathan had removed a wedge. He then repaired to the cramped bathroom and pulled the beaded chain–*click*–which fired a naked incandescent bulb. The bulb buzzed angrily while it burned, as if it resented its use and wished to be left alone. Bass notes of vague domestic rancor seeped through the porous wall. Strange hour for other humans to be awake. He didn't know the Latino couple next door, who'd surely be gone within weeks, like most others—the undocumented especially wary these days given the nation's hostile new regime. He stripped to his waist before the sink, his clavicles jutting like nascent, useless wings, and twisted open the hot water. It gurgled reluctantly from the faucet then ran, finally. He flicked a finger across the fizzy stream, testing the temperature.

While Nathan waited for the frigid water to grow a bit warmer, he surveyed the sea-battered visage staring back at him, a noisy clash of youthful and aged features. Without warning, it seemed, a complex network of intersecting lines and ridges—across his brow, beside his owlish eyes—had emerged, demarcating only his most unflattering expressions. Complementing the sudden topography, ginger stubble sprouted intermittently in prepubescent patches. Rising at the center of the blighted landscape was his proboscis bent like an elbow at the bridge, rendering it ill-fit for respiration. (There had been talk of rhinoplasty when he was a youngster, but his parents had decided against the procedure.) His teeth? Closer to gray than white. Soft too. Cavity-prone. Crowning the spectacle was an untamable thicket of confused red curls, which sprouted after being shorn with a vitality that only amplified Nathan's more prevalent contrastive qualities. The bleak bathroom lighting, casting shadows about, didn't help matters, but there was no denying it. Nathan looked a fright.

What had Kati asked him yesterday morning at the café?

"You sick, Nathaniel?" Nathaniel, she called him, which wasn't his name, but which he hadn't the heart to tell her. She had placed a hand upon his shoulder as she spoke, completing an electric circuit that took him by surprise, and set down a steaming tin carafe with the other.

How to answer such a question?

"No," he had confessed, causing Kati to lower dark, kohl-rimmed eyes. "I feel okay."

So, this was how he pretty much looked. Sick.

Nathan flicked his finger across the fizzy stream again, sufficiently tepid now. He twisted on the cold a bit to keep it from getting too hot, then bathed his face with a rigorous battery of splashes. He performed a brief exercise of coughs and hackings, mostly to muffle the persistent hectoring next door, partly to clear his lungs. He twisted off the hot spigot, splashed his face and neck a few more times with the invigorating cold, and then twisted off the cold spigot too. He reached for a towel and contemplated his circumstances anew as the faucet dribbled, emboldened by the baptism. He wasn't a young man, Nathan Pray. Not anymore, he knew. Yet if he was no longer a young man, he wasn't an old man, either. Not even quite middle aged, given current trends and expectations, his fortunate LDL/HDL ratio, his blessed blood pressure, his pristine prostate and polypless colon. So it was too soon by far to judge him an outright failure. True, his charter business and tournament record, after a promising start, foundered at the precipice of ruin, scarcely worth the trouble. Sam had divorced him (what was it now, two whole years?) and, worse, promptly replaced him with a more upright citizen of their race, whom even Nathan struggled to dislike. His precocious Miles–ah, to summon his boy's name was to reduce himself to mawkish tears–had less and less use for his father. Nathan's brother, gone. Nathan's father, going, going . . . Nathan's mother? Here. Very much here, in fact, but unwilling, or perhaps only unable, to cloak her disappointment with her underachieving son.

And yet, and yet . . . there was still time. He wasn't a young man and he wasn't an old man. Here he was, teetering at that great in-between, a fisherman who, for the moment, couldn't seem to catch any fish. No snook, anyway. But luck, as he'd been pointing out strenuously for some time to his main sponsor, had a way of turning itself around. And Chad at Swallow Artificials had yet to jettison him, despite

29

increasing gestures in said direction.

So up and at 'em, Nathan Herschel Pray!

Chapter Two

First-time buyers. Judy didn't have the patience. The ceaseless string
of asinine questions. The picayune protests. The top producer of the
Camino Real office for almost twenty-two years running (there had
been one or two anomalous years in the mix when a colleague's lucky
listing upset the apple cart, and it would be neck-and-neck this year
against a botoxed and collagened upstart), she didn't need to hassle with
these twenty-somethings, these lost puppies, treading warily toward a
starter house in the two's or three's, max. Somewhere in hardscrabble
Pompano or Lantana. Her clients were contemporaries, by and large,
some of them early retirees, who'd had the time to scale the upper
reaches of the tax bracket. They didn't waste her time, or anyone else's,
with quibbles. In truth, a good number of her buyers and sellers scarcely
needed a full-service agent to begin with, given the accumulating array
of discount brokerages and on-line operations, the plentiful crop of
FISBO's that had been sprouting up like garden weeds, threatening her
turf. Her clients might save for themselves the 3% commission. Yet they
continued to retain her services because that's how things were done in
the world they knew. You want to buy or sell a house? You hire a profes-
sional. A licensed realtor.

    Judy's only here with the Tates, she reminded herself, to babysit
Stefanie. With an f, the ebullient, newly-minted agent explained to her
mentor upon their introduction at the office. She had seemed impossibly

pretty, yet overdressed, to Judy, in her aqua pantsuit (Ann Taylor?), what with her bouncy dirty blonde bob and buoyant breasts (augmented?). A former cheerleader, Judy would wager, fairly dancing there on the floor in her smart pantsuit rather than in one of those aggressively pleated micro-skirts cheerleaders wore. She would be the one those beefy boys would toss twenty feet into the air.

"It's, like, a totally amazing honor that you're my mentor," caffeinated Stefanie with an f had exclaimed at the Premiere Properties office, offering Judy a tiny moist paw. It was really about time that Judy take on one of their new agents as a protégé–so her office manager, Chuck Levin, had pressured her. For a good while, she had been able to squirm her way out of participating in their mentorship program. There was no dearth of senior agents–French-manicured vultures–willing to take on the light duty in exchange for the 50-50 split of their protégé's first three transactions. But scrupulous Chuck, finally, was afraid that it just didn't look right for their top-producer to eschew her obligations and hoard her talents. And so here's Judy. Amid the dumpy old construction of ungated, unincorporated, if undervalued, Sabal Farms.

"Don't you just love these countertops?" Judy listened to Stefanie, scribbled mental notes. Good, she thought. Emphasize the remodeled kitchen. "This is real granite," Stefanie explained, rapping the marbled surface with her tiny knuckles for emphasis, "not that cheap Corian." She might have soft-pedaled on the Corian critique. She'd be sure to advise Stefanie accordingly during the post-mortem. The next house might have Corian countertops instead of granite, and *then* where would they be!? Plus, Stefanie was wrong. Corian was roughly the same price as granite.

"Yeah, I don't care much for Corian," the young husband concurred.

"Like *you* know what Corian is, Michael!" the wife snapped. It seemed to Judy that she'd been scolding him all morning, though it was difficult for her to gauge the tone, whether this was simply their way, whether poor Michael, a graduate student finishing up an Education degree at FAU, found it acceptable or even charming to be brow-beaten by his spouse over this and that. They're a black couple, the Tates. Judy's heard about how strong the women tend to be in the home. The way they run things. Camilla, Terrance's wife, ruled the home, to hear Nathan tell it. Well, they said the same thing about Jewish women. But this wasn't really true now was it?

"Mexican tile on the floor," Stefanie continued the catalog, leading the Tates out to the family room. "And take note of the vaulted ceiling, troop. That's a real perk in homes this age, these 1970-ish and 80s-ish homes we'll mostly be looking at given our price range."

Our price range. Good, Judy thought.

She could be saddled with a lot worse. Stefanie, in truth, was a natural saleswoman. Amiable and pretty. That much was clear from the get-go. But smart too. With instincts to boot.

"And what school district did you mention we were in here, again?" the husband benignly inquired.

"J. C. Mitchell!" the wife admonished. "Will you pay attention,

Michael? The girl only told us five times for Lord's sake." Poor Michael raised his hands in mock (or perhaps genuine) surrender, flashing surprisingly pale palms. "My bad," he allowed. "Shucks."

Judy couldn't remember the last time she heard a grown person say shucks. The expression struck her as so self-deprecating, so innocent, so downright wholesome, that the senior agent couldn't keep herself from rising to the young husband's defense.

"Don't worry so much, Michael. I think it was only three times that Stefanie mentioned J. C. Mitchell." Perhaps she could contribute some levity to the Tate's marital transactions. Her sudden voice surprised the others, who all looked over at her from across the family room. But Charlotte Tate was the only one who held Judy's eyes for longer than necessary. It seemed to Judy a challenge, of sorts. What business was it of Judy's to interfere with her necessary spousal discipline? And perhaps because Judy sensed the challenge, perhaps because she had never been one to truck youthful insolence, she stared placidly back and waited for the young wife to shift her gaze. She was an attorney, Charlotte. Judy couldn't recall what type, just that she had used that term, attorney, rather than lawyer, which struck Judy–perhaps unfairly– as affected. *I'm an attorney.* In any case, this wasn't her courtroom. Stare away young lady!

"So what kind of flooring did you say this was again, Stefanie?" the wife inquired, lowering her eyes toward the Mexican tile. Judy exhaled a burst of pent up air that surprised her. Spotting some paper towels and Clorox All-Purpose spray, she set about wiping down the counters, tattooed with oily fingerprints, as Stefanie retreated to the wing of undersized bedrooms with her clients. It's something that most visiting agents, the chazers, wouldn't think of doing, cleaning up the countertops for the next prospective buyers. Contemplating her above-board propriety only inspired Judy to put a bit more elbow grease into the exercise. There, she thought, sniffing at the bleach. Nice.

Standing there, Judy felt the gradual yielding of her initial impulses vis-à-vis Charlotte Tate. Buying a home was stressful. Especially for first-time buyers. So Charlotte was feeling a bit snappish. What was the crime?

Perhaps Judy shouldn't have stuck her nose in, but she only had the girl's best interests at heart. You couldn't treat a husband that way. They needed adoration, these . . . these . . . husbands. Coddling even. That special fragility of men. So she would counsel the young woman if it were remotely appropriate. If she were remotely qualified. If she were in any position, given her track record, to dispense advice on matters domestic. Still, Judy couldn't keep herself from taking the temperature of the younger couples she encountered on the job. *They'll last all of a year,* she'd find herself contemplating right in the middle of an appointment, while she was driving, say, listening to the backseat banter. *Better close on something quick!* All the while Judy knew that she didn't know anything. A most mysterious alchemy governed marriage. You couldn't tell which couples would endure. Judy wouldn't have bet against herself and Joseph. Nor would she have bet against Nathan and Samantha, for that matter. They had seemed so well-matched. Both Jews for starters. Both smart. Shared interests. They had met at some gathering for environmentalists, if she recalled. But her son and daughter-in-law didn't make it, just as she and Joseph didn't make it. So what did she know?

The Tates? They just might molder together for eternity in side-by-side graves.

**

He rehearsed his vital statistics. It's important to remember. To fire the synapses, nourish the neuron forest. Your name is Joseph. Joe. You come to the Rose Grunwald Center for Memory and Wellness every Monday, Wednesday, and Friday. Too young to be here, but you're here. Your Haitian girl, Louna, cares for you during the off hours. Long-term Disability. Worth every penny. Louna drives you for groceries. She drives you to the health club. She cooks for you. Poorly. Specializes in goulashes. Gassy cruciferous vegetables and gray meat. But that's okay. You ran the largest GI practice in Palm Beach County. GI Joe. King of the colonoscopy. You made a mistake. And now you're on Long-term Disability. And now you're here. Karen cut things off just after the case settled. Chickens coming home to roost, Judy'd say. A moronic expression, that. You left her years ago. Then she was not-your-wife. Sons too you left. But they're still your sons. Then they left you. Jacob, anyway. Nathan's still here, though. So's his boy, your grandson. Miles. Silly name, Miles. But named after your father. Morton. Which is nice. He swims. Like your father, Morton. Morton. Morton. Who didn't swim, really, so much as he floated as dark became light. Sunrise in the shallow sea. Mikveh mornings on Miami Beach.

36

"Ach, your turn," Sol finally announced, flipping the faces back down, a four and a Jack, jarring Joe from his mental calisthenics. "Let's see, where's that other Jack. . . . Here."

"Another pair," Sol observed, clucking his tongue. "Way to go, boychik. You should be playing pinochle with Herbie and the boys over there, not this pisher game with me."

"I don't like pinochle, Sol." Which was true.

Sol had known Joe's father in Miami Beach. He had stocked his slacks in the small clothing store he owned just off Collins before ceding it to the damn Cubans (as he put it) and retiring northward.

"Morty?" Sol had inquired upon spotting Joe his first morning at the Center. "No. Sorry. Morton was my father. He's dead."

"Small shtetl," Sol had replied, taking Joe in, lifting a handkerchief to stanch the flow of his sinuses. "I thought you looked too good. Small shtetl, though. Eh?"

Joe turned over Kings.

"A real card sharp, kiddo."

"It's just the memantine. Maybe the Vitamin E."

"Now don't be modest," Noma declared. She watched over the game from her vinyl chair, having grown tired, maybe, of arranging her scrapbook of familiar and not-so-familiar faces. Always dressed to the nines, Noma, her still-dark shock of hair pulled back, tight. Her nails ever polished in bold hues by those Asian ladies (Thai? Korean? Chinese?) at one of the local salons.

"Really, Joseph," Noma continued. "I've never seen someone

37

so good at Concentration. Ah, to be young."

"Well, thanks Noma," Joe replied, flipped over an eight and a ten. "See that, Sol?" he uttered, turning the faces back down, slowly.

People were kind here. Not just the nurses, doctors, and volunteers. But the clients too. The clients, primarily. That's what they called themselves. Not patients. It wasn't a hospital. Or a nursing home, where several of Joe's more unfortunate, glassy-eyed, farmisht cohorts spent their nights. It was more like a club. Best of all, Medicare covered their dues. They were lucky to spend their days here, in this new, airy, well-lighted Center, brimming with lithe young nursing students from the university and sorority sister volunteers, the solicitous older community volunteers–staving off their own decline, Joe suspected, through this immersion, or just cultivating some good karma–a well-stocked commissary, a wood and mirror exercise studio, a treasure-trove of board games, large-print books, art supplies, and other constructive diversions. And so a generosity of spirit permeated the place. They were all in it together, it seemed. Life, that is, stripped of extraneous confusions, its essentials laid bare. A pleasant conversation. A good lunch. A comradely game of chess or cards. Positive reinforcement all around. *Nice move. Well played. Handsome shirt.* Such was the repartee. And Joe, the young one (what a laugh!), the boychik, had come around to these essential terms. Mostly. For there seemed something cowardly too, retreating into these fatty embraces. He was lucid. Mostly. Just unpredictable. Rarely. He wasn't so far gone as to merit this suddenly soft existence. There was still business to transact. His former patient, Ida Weingarten. Poor girl.

And family business too.

"No one stitched the double-pleat like your pop," Sol noted, apropos of nothing, as he often noted, as if it were important to reinforce the record.

"Yes, I know Sol. You've told me. A great pleat. Solid stitching. Your turn. Remember?"

"Young men these days don't even know from pleats. Flat-fronts they wear. Like shlumps. No cuffs, even. As if the government was still rationing fabric. As if they never knew from tailors."

"Nope, not that one, Sollie. You don't want to turn that one over."

"Oh?"

"Trust me."

"Your father. Morty. You know I swam with him every once in a while. Sunup at South Beach. Before the damn Cubans took over. Lots of us did."

"Yes, you've told me, Sol. Maybe you should ease up on the Cubans. Some of them are Jews you know."

Sol shrugged, twisted his face to flash a skeptical mask.

"So I don't want to turn over this card?"

"I'm pretty sure it's a four." What Joe might have added was that it was a four the last time Sol turned it over, and the time before that, and the time before that.

"Here I got one," Sol declared, stalling. "A man doesn't feel so well so goes in to see the doctor, who examines him. Takes some blood.

Urine. The whole shmeer. 'Well,' the doctor tells him the next day, 'I've got some good news and some bad news. Good news is you have cancer,' he says. 'Cancer?' the man says. 'What can be worse than that?' 'Well, the bad news is you have Alzheimer's.' 'Alzheimer's?' the man takes in the news. 'Well, it could be worse. At least I don't have cancer.'"

"Good one," Herb Lutz said from the pinochle station two tables down. Herb was lucky. So was Ben, seated next to Herb, his pinochle hand quivering in his grip. Their wives were still alive and so they lived at home. The ladies just dropped them off a few mornings a week to enjoy a break, do some shopping, have lunch with the girls.

"Very funny, Solomon," Noma offered her mild disapproval.

"Jokes, jokes, jokes. What is it with you folk and the jokes?" Rose asked, working across from Noma on her own scrapbook. She was one of the few black clients at the Center. Most preferred the older place a scant mile away east of Dixie, near Rutherford Park. But the food was better here, she had mentioned. The books, newer, the corners unsmudged by oily thumbs. The chair-yoga instructor, clearer with her instructions. The mah-jongg competition, stiffer.

"I'm with you, Rose," Noma agreed.

"You told that one yesterday," Joe reminded Sol.

"Okay."

"Anyway, it's still your turn, Sol."

"Damnit! I don't want to play!" Sol snapped, suddenly furious. "Can't you see I don't want to play goddamnit!?"

"Okay, Sol. Not a big deal. We're done." Joe gathered up the cards, removing the source of Sol's anxiety. It wasn't unusual for Sol to explode in anger, having grown frustrated by difficulties to which he hadn't adjusted. He wasn't the only one. Many of them, most of them, were on newfangled antidepressants to smooth their rough edges. Ativan, too, or some other benzodiazepine.

"Now now, Solomon," Rose cooed.

"You're all right, Sol," Noma added. Rather than look toward him, however, she shifted some photos around before her, sparing Sol a measure of unwanted attention.

Herb and his companions looked over, silently. Reggie, one of the female volunteers, older than Joe, walked over and patted Sol on the back. "Can I get you something, Solomon?"

Sol declined.

"Just talk, boychik. Let's just talk. Okay?"

Joe talked.

"Your name is Solomon Podolsky. You knew my father, Morty, from Miami Beach. You sold his double-pleated slacks in the clothing store you owned with your brother, Louis. He died. So did your wife, Faye. You spend a few days a week here, at the Center. The bus takes you back to the Jewish Home at night. You're at the Center now. You were playing Concentration with me, Joe Pray. You knew my father, Morty, from Miami Beach. Morty. Morty. You sold his double-pleated slacks in the clothing store you owned with your brother, Louis. Louis. Louis. Louis."

**

41

Miles kept his eyes trained on the book, his field of view conveniently narrowed by his curtain of ginger dreads. Dr. Epstein. Mr. Epstein. Leon. Stepdad. Whatever. If his mother liked him that was chill–the guy wasn't a jerk or anything–but he preferred to keep his distance from Dr. Epstein, or Mr. Epstein, or Leon, or Stepdad, any of which was fine with the guy, as Dr. Epstein, or Mr. Epstein, or Leon, or Stepdad, insisted, but none of which sounded quite right to Miles, who could only really think of him as . . . *him.*

He lingered there beneath the doorframe, awaiting attention, which only steeled Miles' resolve.

"Mom wanted me to talk to you," Miles finally heard. *Mom.* Not *Your mom,* which would have been chill for some reason, but *Mom,* which, for some other reason, wasn't chill. Where'd he get off?

"Word?" Miles replied. Not turning, though. Leaning still on his elbows in bed, facing away from the threshold, pretending still to read on about this boy in Florida, which didn't seem like Florida, who was all wacked out over some stupid deer.

"Miles, I'd appreciate your attention."

Miles sighed. Even the way Dr. Epstein, or Mr. Epstein, or Leon, or Stepdad said this irritated him. Like he was so cool or smart or something. His real dad didn't talk like this. He didn't really talk too much at all, which was okay. He was too busy fishing at night–probably fishing now, it occurred to Miles, nauseated by the very thought, the sardine stink rising to his nostrils–and had usually been asleep still, or was just going to sleep, by the time his mother drove him the few blocks to school. Maybe his father was a screw-up, a hopeless child, irresponsible, immature, out to lunch, lacking all ambition, pigheaded, unwilling to face facts, like his mother used to complain when they thought he was already asleep, or maybe just out of earshot behind the hallway pocket door and bedroom door fortification.

But at least his dad never said things like *I'd appreciate your attention*. All hot-shit like, Miles thought as he turned to face . . . him. He leaned back against the headboard, dog-eared his page. Dr. Epstein, or Mr. Epstein, or Leon, or Stepdad, took a seat right on the bed all up in his grill, Miles thought, right on top of his old Miami Heat comforter, his skinny butt covering Dwyane Wade. He looked stupid, sitting there dressed in his work clothes, wearing that out-of-place rubber Ironman wristwatch. His cologne, orangey, invaded Miles' nostrils. Couldn't he have pulled out the wooden desk chair for crying out loud?

"Okay, Mr. Epstein. What? This isn't about piano, is it? Mom already said that if I was going to Hebrew School, since I have Bar Mitzvah practice now, I didn't have–"

"No, it's not about piano, Miles. It's about swimming."

"What about swimming?" The Mark Spitz poster against the wall, between his Dwyane Wade and Mos Def, captured Miles' attention. Those seven gold medals were cool, but the mustache made him look like a friggin' doofus–gross even–Miles thought. He would have taken the grainy poster down by now, but he didn't have the heart. His dad had bought it for him at the sports memorabilia store on Federal and always seemed to scan the room for it at their old house, saying something like *Great butterfly*, or *Jewish, you know*, or *Munich*, sounding all somber and stuff. If his dad had this thing for Jewish swimmers, word, but he could at least buy him a Lenny Krayzelburg. Cleaned up in Sydney, boy. Or Jason Lezak, fastest relay split ever in Beijing. There were lots of fast Jewish swimmers.

"It's just that she'd like you to breathe, Miles."

"I do breathe."

"During *all* your races, I think she means."

"But I don't have to breathe for the 50 free."

"Listen, kiddo, I get it. I run marathons, you know. I'm an athlete too. I'm hip to the scene." Miles winced. What a dork. "But I'm also a physician—"

"A psychiatrist, right? You just talk to people." His face fell here, Miles noticed.

"Yeah, sure. But I still, you know, went to medical school. Like everyone else. Went through all the . . . uh . . . rotations." Miles suppressed a smile as Dr. Epstein, or Mr. Epstein, or Leon, or Stepdad, fumbled over his words. "Anyway, the point is, your brain and your muscles need oxygen on a pretty consistent basis."

"I know. Jeez." Miles turned his head, pursed his lips to contain prospective curses.

"You say that, Miles, but I've seen you come out of the water. Gasping for breath. Blue-faced. It's not a pretty sight. You're putting yourself into pretty serious oxygen debt. Happens to me too kiddo when I push it." He tapped Miles' calf here. Miles reflexively withdrew, secured his upraised knees within the halo of his arms. The new phrase piqued his interest, though–oxygen debt–which Dr. Epstein, or Mr. Epstein, or Leon, or Stepdad, seemed to sense. "You're going anaerobic, forcing your muscles to break down glucose, building up all this lactic acid in your arms and legs. That's why you're so sore the day after your meets."

"I'm not *that* sore the next day."

"Come on."

"And I don't slice as smooth when I breathe. It's a speed thing."

"Seems to me you'd cut your hair if fast meant that much to you."

They fit under his cap, the dreads, which he was just about to explain. But he remained silent, instead, as Dr. Epstein, or Mr. Epstein, or Leon, or Stepdad, had crossed a line. All up in his business.

"Well just put yourself in your mother's shoes," he regrouped. "The other parents are starting to give her a hard time. It upsets them."

"That I always win?"

"That too, maybe. But mostly that you don't breathe. They're concerned. They think your mother pushes you too hard. It doesn't look good."

"So?"

"So . . . what?"

"So what that it doesn't look good. That people think stupid stuff about mom. Like, who cares?"

And here, before Dr. Epstein, or Mr. Epstein, or Leon, or St dad, lowered his eyes,

45

before he cleared his throat and leaned back away from Miles, as if

feinting from a blow, before he said, *Well, why don't you just think about it*

for now, lifting his skinny butt off Wade's face, retreating to the doorway,

Miles breathed in slowly through his mouth and discharged the last of

Dr. Epstein's, or Mr. Epstein's, or Leon's, or Stepdad's cologne to the

atmosphere through his nostrils, quite audibly, luxuriating in the knowl-

edge that he had managed to say exactly what he should have said,

and that Dr. Epstein, or Mr. Epstein, or Leon, or Stepdad, by contrast,

didn't.

Nathan, working the needles, considered his hands. Old man hands. His secret palms a confusion of crags, fissures, and fault lines, callous plateaus rising here and there. The backs flecked with brown spots. His knuckles, swollen. Scant swatches of unspotted flesh seemed oddly pale now, the melanin having long ago abandoned its fruitless protective efforts. Exposed flesh elsewhere—his proboscis, his forearms (incongruously hirsute), his feet tops, his neck—alternated between this odd alabaster and Hollywood-Indian red.

Kati's hands. Lovely, by contrast. He supplied her with fresh fish at least partly to glimpse her hands reaching toward him. Smooth olive flesh, the fingers unadorned by jewelry, tantalizingly bare, punctuated by bright quarter-moon nails. Here they were now, these olive hands, the fingers, just inches away across the Formica bar, patting cheap diaphanous paper napkins into the spring-loaded dispenser while the industrial espresso machine behind her whined, spitting its scalding water into the tin carafe. Nathan, absently working his needles, watched as Kati flipped the dispenser onto its other side, as she patted another small stack of napkins beneath the rectangular metal edges, silently, unhurried, like . . . Nathan groped to locate a comparable activity, then abandoned the mental effort. Here she was, performing this singular exercise with utmost care.

"Que bonita, Nathaniel," she appraised Nathan's efforts with his needles, setting the full napkin dispenser upright down the bar.

"Muchas gracias, Kati. Aprendi . . . desde . . . desde?"—Kati offered her qualified assent with a sideward nod—"mi abuelo. From Miami Beach," Nathan shifted to English. "It's for Miles."

Kati nodded, smiling somewhat vacantly as she cleared his plate, smeared with remnants of eggs and congris. It was a nice arrangement they had. Nathan pretended to speak Spanish when the mood struck and Kati pretended to understand what he said.

The whining from the giant machine having ceased, she retrieved Nathan's second carafe on the way back and deposited the steaming water before him, two Badia tea pillows steeping within. She lingered there across the bar for a moment before striding off toward her next chore, smiling shyly toward him to say goodbye for the moment. Kati was close to his own age, he suspected, but retained a youthful twinkle about her eyes that seemed often to accompany the plump.

The counter before him unobstructed now, Nathan worked the yarn quickly, efficiently, between the metal needles. Another blanket for Miles, which the lad didn't need, and which he probably wouldn't use.

The Caribbean Café was a Cuban establishment, or a Nicaraguan establishment, or a Columbian establishment, or a Spanish establishment. It was tough for Nathan to determine, exactly. The waitstaff all spoke Spanish, but seemed, along with several scraggly male regulars, to hail from any number of Latin American and Caribbean locales. Certain menu items were identifiably Cuban–lechon asada, ropa vieja, the medianoche sandwich–but the diner, hoping perhaps to court a broad clientele, also served Nicaraguan steak, Mexican enchiladas, conch fritters from Bermuda, and tamales nestled within corn husks from . . . somewhere. Gathered amicably behind the glass-doors of a behemoth refrigerator were green, brown, and clear bottles of Dominican, Mexican, Jamaican, and Brazilian beer. Cuban Hatuey beer too, brewed in Baltimore, along with multicolor cans of Inca Kola from Peru, Puerto Rican Maltas (made in Wilkes Barre, Pa), Cuban Materva soda (made in Miami) and Brazilian Antarctica Guarana (PepsiCo produced). An enormous batch of tres leches quivered in its aluminum casserole on the shelf below the soft drinks, the very sight of which inflamed Nathan's mild lactose intolerance.

Curious what else garnered valuable square footage on the Formica counter behind the bar. That enormous metal espresso machine, nozzles and handles extending helter-skelter like dislocated limbs. A pyramid of Café Bustelo tins, which seemed orange and gray to Nathan's colorblind eyes. Beside it stood an even larger stainless steel appliance, which angrily devoured whole stalks of sugarcane fed at the top by Kati or her cohorts, spitting out doses of liquid nectar below. Meat empanadas, plump purses that looked not unlike the potato knishes from Beth Shalom, sat on wax-paper lined trays inside a glass encasement along with chicharrón—fried pork bellies and rinds (which didn't look like anything from Nathan's Hebrew School days), the fat glinting beneath the heat lamps. Latino men drifted in and out, retrieving their bulging brown bags of fried pig flesh, oil-stains erupting instantaneously against the paper in complex island chains. Upon Kati's suggestion, Nathan tried one of the fat curls once, but spit out the gristle bolus into his napkin after only three or four tiresome chews, gaining newfound respect for the rules of Kashruth. Every once in a while, the old owner of the restaurant burst from the kitchen double-doors in his V-neck undershirt wheeling out a whole pig corpse on a gurney and deposited it swiftly in the back of an oversized van out front, as if the porcine creature were the victim of a mob hit.

"For crying out loud, Nate," Manny whined, tossing his keys and Camels up on the Formica bar next to Nathan's yarn. "You have to carry on with that in public?" The young captain scanned the empty dining area behind them as he descended onto the padded stool. "People'll be coming in soon."

Most patrons of the café occupied the line of tables at the far end of the dining room bordering the broad windows, to savor the unobstructed vista of the fishing pier and the Atlantic. It was a glimpse less precious to the captains, who favored the bar, preferring to stay within hectoring distance of the congenial, but sluggish, wait-staff.

"It's good practice for knot-tying," Nathan claimed. Truth was, though, knitting simply kept his hands and mind properly distracted. Plus, it reminded him of his grandfather, Morton, a tailor without hang-ups over his masculinity. Morton—not his grandmother, Essie, whom he couldn't remember—had taught Nathan to knit before he was old enough to know that it was for girls. He had stopped for years upon learning as much, but had always kept the needles and was surprised after Sam left him, or, rather, compelled him to leave (nice trick that!), while he sat around his rented apartment flipping desultorily through inane network programming, deprived suddenly of the incessant buzz of domesticity, that he remembered the requisite loops and wraps.

Who was Manny, anyhow, this twenty-something upstart, to give him the business? He must have used some sort of hairspray or gel to lacquer his dirty blond locks in those tiny waves that lapped behind the bill of his carefully curved visor. His legs were shaved bare (shaved!) to reveal muscled calves and tattoos on the sides of both shins, Oriental lettering that Nathan couldn't decipher. One eyebrow, too, seemed intentionally barbered in vertical bare patches. Young women (or "pussy," in Manny's whittled down frame of reference), apparently went in for this sort of thing these days, if even a fraction of the young captain's boasts were to be credited. And still, Nathan marveled, here Manny was, this clown, embarrassed by *him*!

What a strange thing it was to be a man these days, a man in search of women. At a time in history when the entire enterprise of heterosexual coupling had been called into serious question, thanks to the breathtakingly predatory exploits from the male side: comedians, singers, actors, directors, U.S. Presidents (current and former), senators (state and U.S.), TV hosts, news reporters and anchors, university professors, chefs and restaurateurs, book and magazine editors, bankers, CEO's, ballet masters . . . What was Nathan to do? At present, ever since Sam had left him, nothing. Dazed by the daily scandals and the new terms of bachelorhood—which seemed to involve a dizzying array of dubious online resources—he found himself hopelessly impassive, waiting for his romantic life to begin again as if it might magically happen without effort or risk on his own part.

The other captains, one by one–Del, Frank, Hollis–shuffled in from the still-darkness for their pre-charter caffeination, filling in the stools between Nathan and Manny. A couple sandy-haired mates entered as well, descending wordlessly into chairs in the adjacent dining area.

"Waters, doll. All around. Coffees too," Del declared, grabbing the final stool beside Nathan, its vinyl generously cracked to form a network of complex tributaries.

Kati nodded as she turned her back on the row of captains to work on their coffee, the more vital of the liquid supplements.

"Blanket?" Del inquired, glancing Nathan's way.

"Yeah."

Del nodded. "Herringbone?"

"Son of a gun, Del."

It never ceased to surprise Nathan. What people knew. What people didn't know.

He was fat, Del, unusually so for a charter captain, bearded and jowled, and tended to speak only intermittently and tersely, deploying the fewest possible words to convey his meaning, as if words exacted a great physical toll. His laconic girth somehow imbued Del with a gravitas Nathan wasn't certain he deserved. That he piloted a tricked-out Sportfisher and "placed" in most of the big billfish tournaments up and down the Florida coast bolstered his stature too. Plus, he frequented

Monday morning mass and a late Sunday service at St. Joan of Arc, an activity which the other captains wouldn't emulate but seemed to admire and even appreciate, as if Del were their spiritual proxy. They looked to him for counsel and took his lead.

And so here they all were. The bouillabaisse. Nathan sighed, the closing bell to his brief and pleasant shared solitude with Kati. There was something different about the group portrait. Nathan, pausing to sip and blanch at his tea (he had added too much lemon), couldn't quite place the change.

"Son'bitch, if that Kati lost twenty pounds and ten years, I'd give 'er a whirl," Manny proposed, Kati having retreated to the kitchen to retrieve their waters.

"Gee, I'm sure she'd really appreciate that." Nathan said. The bouillabaisse bubbled.

"Don't get all Jew-sensitive on me, Nate. I don't mean nothin.' I'm just talkin' here."

Jew-sensitive. He uttered the words with a sheepish grin, Manny, which somehow made it okay. His fellow captains could bust Nathan's chops, vis-à-vis his stiff-necked affiliation, and he wouldn't take offense. All in good fun. At some point a while back, it seemed, he had acceded to these terms. He couldn't afford to befoul the bouillabaisse. It wouldn't be too hard for his fellow captains to run him clear out of the water. Now Jake, his brother, would have found a different way. But where the hell was he? So Nathan let things slide. Still . . .

"Jew-sensitive. Brilliant." Nathan paused, sipped his tea to affect nonchalance. "You're a real poet, Emanuel." Nathan knew it peeved the young captain to be called by his proper name.

Maybe Nathan was bit touchy when it came to Kati, if not his Jewishness. For his own thoughts lately regarding the waitress were scarcely more honorable than Manny's. Thoughts, say, on that ass of hers, which he had just admired, unable to avert his gaze, well-rounded and curiously flared at the lower cheeks, testing the elasticity of her black pants. He had never been with an ample woman, hadn't previously been drawn that way, perhaps on account of his own diminutive stature. Sam, addicted to the Stairmaster, a cardio queen, was lean and muscled, her abdominals discrete and discernible, even after her pregnancy. One of those efficient human specimens, his former wife. Kati was something else altogether, a curvy dish of soft subcutaneous flesh. And so Nathan's recent impulses caught him wholly unawares. He found himself conjuring versions of Kati's nude form at random, sometimes inopportune, moments. The ass, yes, and her breasts too, unfettered by brassiere, heavy before him. Her swollen aureoles. Her dark gumdrop nipples. Her sex below. Such abundant flesh issued certain unspoken demands. Nathan wondered if he could negotiate such riches. It had been some time.

He doubted that Kati would take Manny seriously enough to fall for any of his puerile advances, this punk who thought it was the absolute zenith of comedy to exclaim *oh, shit!* When he sneezed rather than *achoo!* But Manny posed a more significant threat, business-wise. The randy upstart piloted a mid-sized panga with a folding tower, a crossover vessel which the young fisherman touted for its deep-water capabilities and its shallow draft, hoping, not without some shrewdness, to court inshore, nearshore, and offshore charters. Ever since he earned his captain's license, he'd been horning in on Nathan's waters, his fish, his client base of serious snook, tarpon, and ladyfish anglers and (increasingly) those fathers with small children, or weak stomachs, or both, who thought it a waste not to get out on the water during their vacation, but who didn't care to brave the open ocean. Chad at Swallow Artificials now sponsored Manny for Flatsmaster's competitions, and Manny had earned a surprising second-place finish at last year's SnookeRed challenge. (Nathan and Terrance landed, photographed, and released several redfish and fewer snook, but nothing with shoulders.) After the tourney, Chad had put Nathan on notice, dockside. "The economy," Chad uttered. Entrance fees had skyrocketed. Times were tough all around. Swallow Artificials could only front a limited number of successful anglers. Chad had emphasized this word "successful." Cruelly, Nathan thought.

"You gotta watch those Cuban girls anyway," Frank declared now from the middle of their line, hoping perhaps to defuse the tension. Particularly susceptible to the enticements of manifold bait and tackle purveyors, Frank, just a few years older than Manny, was festooned with a dizzying array of advertisements: Shimano cap, Yamaha T-shirt, Berkley bait sun-scarf dangling loose around his neck, brand new Costa Del Mar frames mysteriously secured from around his neck at the collarbone, Yo-Zuri wrist-bands, and, the pièce de résistance, ridiculous rubber shoes that made him look like some sort of disposable Dutch-man. Frank, Nathan thought, should have been on the bass circuit.

"You do 'em wrong, they'll slice you up ten ways to Sunday while you sleep," Frank continued. "Else pour boiling water over you."

"I think Kati's Columbian," Nathan said.

"Columbians!" Hollis interjected as if clearing his throat, the growl emerging from somewhere within the mysterious reaches of his thick goatee. "Shee-it, they're even worse." Hollis piloted the large drift boat at the marina, the *Ellen S.,* and earned the steadiest income, Nathan figured. As if responding to an afterthought, the drift boat captain lifted a hand to check the small adhesive disk at the back of his leathery neck, where a carcinogenic mole had sprouted.

"Word to the wise, Nathan. Frank and I just looking out for you here. No secret you've taken a shine."

Nathan exhaled, then traded his needles for a section of Del's paper.

Kati returned after several inexplicable minutes brandishing a tray of drip-stained glasses filled with tap water at haphazard levels.

"Doll," Del slid his glass away from him. "S' dirty. See?" He pointed with a stubby, nicotine-stained finger. He'd be elbow-deep in Menhaden chum in an hour and here he was, squeamish over what must have been a stray spec in his water, an oily thumbprint or lipstick smear on the glass. Kati nodded as she scooped up the offending object, smiling nervously, winking a dogtooth, singular and fetching somehow to Nathan amid the increasingly veneered and otherwise augmented female homogeneity about these days.

"Sorry, Del. I get you new one."

"Mmm-mmm. Made for comfort, an ass like that." Manny smacked his lips as Kati disappeared behind the swinging door.

"Please, Manny. Enough already. She has a daughter."

"So. What's *that* got to do with anything?"

Nathan wasn't sure. "Well," he pursued another tack, "we have to eat here."

The bouillabaisse simmered.

Nathan watched as his cohorts retrieved their medications from their plastic vials, ochre cylinders in various diametric proportions. The pills tumbled onto the tabletop, making light *clicks*, like so many Pez candies. White pills, blue pills, orange pills, green pills. Small pills, medium-sized pills, horse-pill sized. Round pills, oval pills, octagonal, hexagonal, and pentagonal pills, a pharmacological ode to geometry.

The captains sorted their medications into small clusters, even young Manny, who had surprised Nathan a while back by broadcasting the efficacy of his new antidepressant. The others were plagued, apparently, by high blood pressure, unfortunate cholesterol ratios, chronic muscle pain, allergies, arthritis, eczema, psoriasis, overactive bladder, enlarged prostates, acid reflux, GERD, diarrhea, constipation, nicotine addiction. All of them, save for Nathan–who'd never enjoyed the cigarette sublime–migrated through stages of smoking, nonsmoking, and renewed smoking. It wasn't the healthiest line of work, fishing. Stressful. Day-to-day. Hand-to-mouth. And hard.

Terrance, it seemed, had had enough.

Some days, even Nathan would rather not be fishing.

He couldn't help but feel somewhat inadequate, sitting there without a medicinal stash of his own. Where were his prescriptions? The opioid crisis notwithstanding, perhaps he truly needed certain medicines, preventative and/or palliative, but had failed to recognize the symptoms or pose the proper questions to Dr. Krauss.

"I'm telling you, Del, you should try Celebrex," Hollis suggested, then gulped down the rock-pile of pills in his palm, his Adam's Apple bobbing beneath his goatee. "Here, take one. Works like a charm. Wish it came out years ago. I'm tying Biminis now, no problem. Didn't even realize what a pain in the A-hole it had been till after I been on the juice for a week or so."

"Don't know," Del replied. "Doc already got me on Diclomax. Two pills already for cholesterol too. Some kind of satin thing—"

"Statin, you mean," Frank said.

"Yeah, that's it. Statin. And this other thingamajig—" he culled a two-tone capsule from the pile with a pudgy forefinger. "Also told me to grind flax seed in my cereal. Believe that? Flax seed."

For fishermen, they didn't talk much about fish, or fishing. Instead, they tended to catalog their physical maladies. Or they vented over their unreasonable alimony or child support payments, their insultingly brief visitation rights. Marriage and children were the unchallenged default prerogatives of his fellow captains, along with divorce. Nathan had proven no more prescient or impervious (if it were a matter of prescience or imperviousness) in this regard. Only Manny, young Manny, remained unattached and unscathed. The bastard.

"You had your prostate checked yet, Del?" Hollis inquired. "Ain't no picnic, but you're over fifty now. You don't need no prostate cancer."

"Better get that done," Del allowed, lifting his thimble of thick coffee to his mouth.

Kati returned with Del's water and three steaming plates stacked up her arm, setting them noisily on the counter before Frank, Hollis, and Del. "Be right back with yours," she told Manny. She didn't need to take their orders. Round steak and eggs. Or ham and eggs. Or bacon and eggs. Or pork roll and eggs. Black beans and rice on the side. Baskets of crisp Cuban bread, slathered with buttery oil. It was all they ate and Kati knew their individual preferences.

Nathan read the paper to the cacophony of silverware clinking against plates. He was the only one who forswore meat with his breakfast. Although he occasionally imbibed for the sake of expediency, he felt vaguely compromised afterward, diminished, for reasons not altogether clear to him. By contrast, he had no trouble at all eating heady quantities of snapper, cobia, mahi mahi, and kingfish, pulled from the depths and lathered in butter, lime, and spice.

"The old girl ain't gonna clean her own deck, Bobby," Frank called out through a full mouth toward his mate, still finishing his own breakfast behind them.

Bobby cleared his throat. "I'll get on it, cap."

"You too," Hollis called back to his blonde mate, casting an avuncular gaze over his eyeglasses.

"You heard, Nate?" Frank asked. "They're splittin' up the Southeast region on the Fishing Report. People been complaining about the focus mostly on Jupiter and Fort Pierce. Chip Holiday's looking for another captain to report southside. Could be here any minute."

That was it! The change in the tableau, which Nathan couldn't quite put his finger on! They were all freshly shorn and showered. Even Hollis's goatee was trimmed some, its outside borders clearly defined.

"Ever met him?" Hollis asked no one in particular. "Runt of the litter that guy. No more than five-two I'd say."

The captains gazed toward Nathan. Diminutive Nathan.

"A shock, kinda, when you see him in person," Hollis continued. "Livin' large and in charge, though. Wife's a real honey too."

"Been droppin' by the bait stores, the piers, other captain hangouts from Lake Worth all the way down to Pompano," Frank picked up the thread. "Acts like he's just shootin' the breeze, like real casual, but too casual you know. He lives down in Homestead or something. Shoots the report out of Orlando. Casting call's what it is. Doesn't make no sense, otherwise, him hanging around up and down our water. Mr. King of Sting," Frank joked. "He ain't fooling no one, that's all I'm sayin'."

This was purely a figurative expression for Frank–*that's all I'm sayin'*–and a misleading one at that as the utterance invariably presaged further sayings. Like now: "You imagine? Those damn fuckers have it made. 'Scuse the French, Kati," Frank called down the bar. Kati, her clear fingernails dancing across cash register keys, ignored Frank's apology or simply didn't hear. "Bettys all over 'em. Charters stacked up a whole season in advance. Not this day-to-day bullshit. Pretty sure they get those Chevy Suburbans and Pathfinders for free too, or close to free. No joke."

"Nah, free?" Manny inquired, glancing up Nathan's way toward Del. They all glanced toward Del, awaiting his word. The Boddhisatva, unhurried, downed the rest of his Cuban coffee, the small upraised mug nearly hidden within his thick furry mitt. He turned a broad leaf of his *Sun-Sentinel* and cleared his throat.

"Mm-hm."

"He's an inshore guy," Hollis remarked, then rubbed with a swollen knuckle errant yolk into his goatee, where it disappeared. "Might be the break you been looking for, Nate. Never know."

"Plus you use all those fancy words," Manny prodded.

"More than one syllable, Manny, doesn't make a word fancy."

Del's shoulders bobbed, a silent chuckle.

"Might as well talk about your precious snookies on TV," Frank declared. "There ain't no more to catch 'round here."

"They're here," Nathan protested. "It's just been a rough winter. They're layin' low. Headed further inshore maybe."

The bouillabaisse simmered. Manny, Nathan noticed, nodded down the bar, noncommittal—oddly contemplative for Manny, or apparently so.

Nathan's treasured snook. A.k.a. the robalo, the ravillia, the sergeant fish, the saltwater pike, the soapfish (poor cleaning practices back in the day left soapy skin on the fillets), the linesider, the bucketmouth . . . its aliases multiplied in inverse proportion to its presence. He was still searching for scattered, skinny remnants of the unfortunate colony. His snook working group–a volunteer outfit of anglers and conservationists, most hailing from the gulf coast–estimated a total state loss at around 200,000. After the last recent cold snap, Nathan had surveyed and reported the damage between the Lake Worth and Hillsboro Inlets. Thousands of snook, mostly small males but plenty of over-slot females too, drifted inshore with the tide, belly-up like so many logs. Nathan had secured a bandana over his nose, the air redolent with their sharp decay. His eyes had pooled with water. Black fly legions welcomed the bounty in whirly-gig patterns above the surface, a heady growling chorus. Nathan had leaned over his deck upon spotting a large female quivering atop the surface. He plunged his hands and arms into the frigid drink to revive the doomed creature. But it was no use. Since then, his survey of the warmer lee shores, stained water, and dark bottoms in nearby channels hadn't yet turned up a single survivor.

Cold snap aside, there wasn't much to keep the snook along his particular stretch of coastline. Bridges, docks, and spillways they still favored. The inlet, too, offered the current, depth, and salinity that fired their gametes during spawn. But their prized sulfurous mangroves inshore were barely holding on, leaning over the intracoastal in isolated patches as if in preparation for that final shove over the bank and beneath the depths. Acoustical bands of cordgrass, needle rush, spartina, and saltwort had been dredged years ago now, along with other vital underwater flora. (Long gone, the redfish and seatrout.) Hasty "renourishment" projects dumped tons of alien sand along the beaches to shield residents in their high-rise condos from the rising ocean, choking off more longstanding coastal residents in the bargain. The dredged-and-filled sediment scarcely resembled the crushed rock-and-shell granules that constituted the beach, proper. The too-fine coastal earth suddenly rebuffed the burrowing efforts of sand fleas and polluted the once gin-clear water with dusty plumes unfit for prey or predator. Waterfront real estate and yacht-friendly channels took precedence, creatures up and down the biota, snook included, Nathan included, having deferred unwittingly to those loftier principles bandied about by politicos and developers alike. Progress. Growth. Access. The American Way of Life!

"You know your problem, Nate?" Frank proposed now. "You're playing this whole Jewish thing wrong. Dock's crawling with Goldbergs. Half our charters, ain't that right, fellas? Del? It's not just my imagination, is it?"

"Nope," Del allowed, an unlit Parliament bobbing between his lips.

"You should be cleaning up," Frank continued. "But you go and name your boat *Pray Fish*, like you were Christian like us or somethin'."

"Should name your boat Jewfish," Manny suggested, revived by this turn in the conversation. "Perfect name what that is."

Frank pounded the counter with a palm, punctuating Manny's

suggestion. "There you go, Nate. Right there. Jewfish. Charters'll triple. Should pay Manny a commission for that one. Friggin' brilliant. Jewfish. Better than that Repeat word on those shampoo bottles."

"Yeah, well, thanks guys," Nathan replied. "You don't think it's a problem, though, that we barely have any Jewfish up here anymore? That I don't fish for them, anyway?"

"That a courtesy?"

The bouillabaisse boiled. Frank, too, howled at his own joke.

The Jewfish was a grouper that grew to gargantuan proportions and provided such succulent fillets that it was nearly extirpated while Nathan was still a youngster, causing the FWC to impose an absolute ban on its harvest. A niche catch-and-release fishery continued for these boring, dead-weight adversaries, mostly among boorish, over-weight sportsmen. The behemoth survivors, thriving mostly deep in the Glades and Keys, had been busily breeding since the ban, fat and snug in their underwater grottoes, emerging only to devour smaller grou-pers, snappers, and spiny lobsters (a.k.a "bugs") with heady abandon, inspiring the ire of less successful fishermen above. So it was probably a good thing, Nathan thought, that its name had formally been changed several years ago from Jewfish to Goliath Grouper, the powers-that-be having determined that its frowning, fleshy mouth had, in fact, inspired their derogatory moniker (even Nathan couldn't deny their uncanny resemblance to certain deceased elders), and that, besides which, those occasional online threads in fishing forums titled "Slayin' the Jews," "Jew-Hunting," and "Outsmarting the Jews," evading editorial restraint, didn't sound so good, anyway.

And so with a stroke of the pen David had become Goliath.

"Okay, then," Frank continued, wiping the mist from his eyes, regaining his sobriety. "You make it two words. Jew Fish? Like a question. Get it? Jew fish? Like, do you fish? Then it's not about the fish no more, but you still get the Jew thing in there."

Here was the new dispensation, bolstered by the predilections of their nation's current President. Few hesitated these days to broadcast the most asinine, if not outright churlish, views regarding race, religion, sexual orientation, what have you. Something about the way Frank reflexively uttered Goldbergs a moment ago, as if it weren't the first time he had uttered the surname, as if it were the new catch-all pejorative on the dock for Jews, generally. Nathan longed for the good old days when the comparatively entitled people in the country (whatever hysterical fears and prejudices they might have nursed) at least exercised a modicum of awkward discretion over such matters.

His fellow captains likely saw him as the exception that proved the rule about his insufferable brethren. Nathan wasn't rich. He was hardly scraping by. He certainly wasn't controlling the levers of power, as a shocking number of people apparently still believed. Nathan was only an inshore and nearshore guy. No competition. And he could take a ribbing. But how often did Frank and the boys bemoan these other monied Goldbergs taking over the place when Nathan wasn't around? These Davids-turned-Goliaths in this new Florida, this new nation and world?

"You really oughta ditch that last name for a real Jewish name too," Frank continued, "like . . . uh . . ."

"Schwartz," Manny suggested.

Kati's fingers paused here above the keys, Nathan noticed. Her eyes rose to reveal a mild frown. Then, she headed back to the kitchen. Nathan tracked her departure until she disappeared behind the swinging door. The ribbing bothered her, maybe. Or maybe not. Her plate was full, Nathan knew, without worrying over him. She had a daughter.

"Where'd you get a name like that, anyhow, Nate?" Manny inquired. "I ain't never met a Pray. You, Del? Hollis? Frank?"

Del shook his head, inspiring a chain reaction among his cohorts.

There was a story here, one that Nathan had shared with Terrance, but that he hadn't shared with his fellow captains. It wasn't a Jewish name, Pray. His great-grandfather, Chaim Schuss, had changed the name upon debarking in Galveston. It had been almost a month-long voyage in steerage, triple the time it would have taken to reach New York. European representatives of Jacob Schiff had warned Chaim about the difficult voyage all the way to Texas, via Bremen. But they also reaffirmed his suspicions about the gritty mean streets of New York. Too many Jews there already. And Italians. And Irish. And Poles.

Chaim was from Mezolaboricz, a czarist backwater in Hungary, Czechoslovakia, or Rumania (no one seemed to know the country associated with the town). He couldn't imagine clawing and scraping among these hordes. The American west, Schiff's pamphlet suggested, was the true golden land, ripe with opportunity for young and robust Jewish pioneers. Immigrants were still welcome across the wide open spaces west of the Mississippi River. Texas! Mexicans, indeed, weren't the only ones who sought new lives through the Lone Star State. In any case, Nathan's great-grandfather had been Chaim Schuss before reaching the Port of Galveston, but was Chaim Pray thereafter.

There was a lesson in the story. Something to extract. But what this lesson was, exactly, depended upon parts of the story that remained a mystery. Like what his great-grandfather was truly thinking at the time. *My name is Chaim Schuss,* Nathan mused. *Chaim Schuss. Not Charles. Not Pray. Chaim. Schuss. You want I spell?* Perhaps Nathan's great-grandfather hadn't shed his name, willingly; perhaps he had tried desperately to hold onto it. No one seemed to know the whole truth. So maybe the trick was coming up with your own useful version of the story. Nathan wondered if there was anything that Chaim's story of seizing opportunity in Texas might tell him regarding news of Chip Holiday shaking the local trees, looking for a new captain to report on their waters for the Sunshine Network's Fishing Report. Perhaps Hollis was right and this could be Nathan's big break. He inhaled deeply through his narrow sinuses to keep these thoughts inside.

"Okay," Del cleared his throat, a preamble to business, the divvying up of the water, the organized fish hunt. "Let's stay on 73 today, keep the weekend warriors from hornin' in. I got a full day charter. Regulars from Michigan. Can't disappoint. I'll take the outside edge of the Alley, 350 or so, work my way up to Delray. Start with green and yellow and black and red jellybeans. See if I can scare up a sail. Anyone got time to work their way up from the inside?"

"I got it," Frank offered. "Mahi's slammin' better in a buck-fifty, anyway. I'll give my pink skirts a whirl."

"Hollis, you got . . ."

The voices faded instantly for Nathan upon Kati's emergence. *Brrring.* Kati reached for the phone behind the bar as Nathan and the other captains watched on, expectant. Good news, Nathan knew as soon as she glanced his way, her dogtooth smile dawning on her face. The dockmaster's gravelly summons.

"Yes, Marty, he right here. Nathaniel," Kati announced, handing him the cordless across the bar. "For you."

Chapter Four

Judy glanced down at her Cartier. Where were they, already? Why was Stefanie dawdling about the cramped bedrooms? The most hideous grass wallpaper still festooned the walls in the entire wing! You didn't do your stop-and-chat in the most unflattering quarter of the property. You charged on to a more pleasing spot. Perhaps she had given her protégé too much credit. Didn't the cheerleader know a gosh darned thing? The senior agent glanced down again at her watch. It had been nearly five minutes.

> *Get out of the fucking bedrooms!*

"It's definitely high up there on the list," Judy heard the husband declare as the party finally crossed the threshold into the common room. They've seen eight homes today. Ten last weekend. Not many, all and all, but Judy could tell that Michael was beginning to feel badly that he and his wife couldn't seem to corral sufficient enthusiasm for any particular property. "We're really putting you through the paces," he had commented earlier in the day, after the fourth or fifth house. Such deference was unusual for clients of his generation, most of whom treated Judy, and other agents, with lazily concealed hostility.

"Pity the rooms are so small," the wife added flatly, tempering her husband's enthusiasm.

"You can't have everything," Stefanie answered the challenge. "Right, Judy?"

"Absolutely," she answered from the kitchen, though she wished Stefanie hadn't deferred to her. It sent a poor message.

"It's all about tradeoffs," the young agent declared. Yes, Judy thought. Continue. "Now I'm not trying to sell you on anything, specifically. I'm not talking about *this* house. No pressure. I'm not that kind of agent . . ."

Judy couldn't keep herself from smiling at this phrase. It was one of Stefanie's favorites, she'd come to realize. *I'm not that kind of agent.* This from a girl who'd only been *any* kind of agent for three weeks.

". . . You have to figure out what's really important to you. The non-negotiables. The rest you just have to let go."

Stefanie waited for her speech to take anodyne effect. And it did, Judy could tell. The Tates both loomed before their young agent, nodding their heads slowly. It was a good speech. Good because it was true. You couldn't have everything, not at most price ranges, certainly not at the Tate's, who had only been pre-approved for three-twenty-five. This was the house, Judy knew. An "A" rated school district. A fully remodeled kitchen. Mexican tile floors, which had just come back into style. A dipping pool, even, just beyond the covered lanai. So the rooms were a bit small. Rooms were for sleeping. Who cared? The outdated grass wallpaper they could remove themselves with DIF in a single weekend. The Tates wouldn't find a nicer property. But you couldn't just say that to your buyers. You could lead them to water, but they had to drink.

"Let's talk strategy in the car," Stefanie proposed, leading the way out. "They're motivated sellers. I can totally talk them down." Judy, bringing up the rear, took heart upon glimpsing the young couple grasp hands in the foyer. Stefanie's first sale, and after only a few weeks. She considered what she'd buy her young protégé for a congratulatory gift as she bent over the lock-box. A spa treatment, maybe. Or perhaps a gift certificate for dinner at Addison's with the girl's husband, a general contractor. Gentile, Judy had gathered, though she couldn't recall exactly how she knew this—was it simply because he was a general contractor? Yet before Judy even had the chance to rise and join the party waiting for her on the front lawn under the mottled shade of the winter-stripped royal poinciana, she heard Stefanie, irrepressible Stefanie, blurt out, "Now I'm not sure how you feel about those power-lines up there," whereupon Judy groaned, audibly she was afraid. "What d'ya think, Judy?" her protégé called back at her. "About those power lines?"

Judy rose and gazed over at the lines across the street above her Lexus. Not so close to the house, really. And not so large. They weren't talking mega-amperes. But it didn't matter now. The mere suggestion of the silent menace had scotched the deal. She could tell by the way the Tates stared silently into each other's eyes, as if to say, *run*.

**

"I know I've told you this already, Stefanie, but let me repeat. Don't be so quick to foist your own concerns onto your clients. They have their own peccadilloes, believe me."

These were the first words Judy uttered to her protégé in the car after they dropped the Tates off for the day at their apartment in Boynton.

"I don't know, it just didn't seem right to—"

"It's not like you were hiding anything from them, Stefanie! The lines are right out there in plain view!" Judy raised the blade of her hand toward the windshield to gesture toward imaginary power lines. She felt her heat rise, despite herself. Going into this arrangement, she had promised herself that she wouldn't grow too exercised. She'd suffer her protégé in good faith. Dispense what wisdom she could, then be on her way. What else was required? She wouldn't let Stefanie drag her into her vortex of need.

"Well, sorry I messed things up," Stefanie declared as she fiddled with her rear view mirror, more to check her lipstick, Judy suspected, than to adjust her rear view. Something about the way her coltish protégé said sorry made it clear to Judy that she wasn't truly sorry, that she wasn't sorry at all!

"I just noticed the power lines, and I was about to say something about them, but then I stopped myself, thinking exactly what you were saying about making a big deal about something that's not a big deal, but then I felt bad, you know, that I was about to say something, but then didn't because, let's face it, I figured they were just about to go for it, and then I thought that if *I* were them and thinking about having kids, and you know in a way I kinda *am* in their shoes, you know we're trying (Judy glanced out her window, envious of the outside) I'd want my agent to mention it at least, so I guess . . . it . . . just, you know, came out."

For god's sake! The poor girl would never sell a house if she kept this up. These obsessive ruminations. *That* was her problem. She thought too much. Not unlike someone else Judy knew. Nathan. Judy was about to continue her lesson, but was interrupted by Stefanie's ringtone, a popular music melody that Judy couldn't quite place. "I should answer this," Stefanie declared, having retrieved the phone from the center console.

It seemed to Judy, from Stefanie's monotonous string of *uh-huhs* and *yeahs,* that the person on the other end of the line called to convey the details of some report, perhaps a car repair estimate or a quote for some home improvement project–

"So then why would my vagina hurt?" Stefanie suddenly blurted out without apparent qualm.

. . . . or a doctor's diagnosis, Judy deduced. She considered turning the radio on, but then Stefanie wouldn't be able to hear. The cellular connection must have been poor, as the girl fairly shouted into the small device.

"Not a sharp pain, no . . . It's definitely there. Like just inside my vagina. . . . Are the ovaries *that* close. . . .Uh-huh. . . . So is sex with my husband okay? . . . We *should* be doing it now?"

Judy couldn't help but smile at this last bit, answering Stefanie's query silently for her own amusement. *Sex with your husband? No. You should only engage in sexual intercourse with strangers for the next six weeks.*

Was nothing sacred, anymore? Were there no boundaries? Had the private sphere dissolved, utterly? It appeared so, judging by the intimate smartphone conversations people insisted upon conducting within earshot of unfortunate bystanders. Maybe this was a good thing, Judy contemplated. She entertained the thought just long enough to dismiss it.

"Brad and I fight about this, but, as long as I have you on the phone, are we supposed to do it, like, every day if we can, or should we save his sperm up for, like, every other day–"

Here, Stefanie at least had the decency to glance over at Judy, sheepishly, as if to acknowledge the earful she'd administered.

This would all be awkward enough. Judy knew, however, still several blocks from the office on Camino Real, that Stefanie would feel compelled to offer her a full debriefing after the conversation, out of courtesy. So the vibration of Judy's own device against her hip came as something of a relief. Hugh? She wondered. Her friend? (She loathed that infantilizing term, "boyfriend.") Hugh checked in on her a bit too often for her liking, crowded her, as men her age tended to do, but otherwise . . . . She shimmied her slender hips, reached for the device.

NATHAN, she read her son's name on the digital screen, whereupon her innards blanched. The reflexive response gave Judy pause. What sort of mother was she, her innards blanching at the sight of her poor son's name? It was only because Stefanie was here, she assured herself, letting the phone vibrate in her dry palm. She only cringed at the prospect of speaking with her son in front of Stefanie. Did he need something? Probably not. Heaven forbid he accept any money from her, let his mother help him out so he could move into a presentable apartment. No, he was probably just between cockamamie charters, she figured, calling to hector her about his father. Her thoughts drifted to Joseph. Poor, stupid Joseph. If he would just apologize, Judy thought. Then she could visit him. She wouldn't withhold her solace. If he would only do that one simple thing. Was it too much to ask?

Or perhaps Nathan only wanted to tell her about one of Miles' swim meets coming up, or maybe he needed to use her garage to work on his lures. After Sam put him out on his ear (as Judy sized up matters) Nathan had moved all of his tools and various other fishing-related supplies to her garage, accepting this miniscule measure of motherly assistance, anyway. How on earth did he get by? Judy wondered. A brain like his. What a waste. Judy glanced over at Stefanie, jabbering on still about her conjugal rites. She wouldn't be able to hear Nathan, anyway, she rationalized, even if she tried. She clipped the phone back onto her belt, felt the vibrations cease, finally, which made her a little sad.

Stefanie finally clicked off her phone, deposited it by feel into the cup holder on the center console. "Sorry about that, Judy, but I figured you have an adult son who lives around here, right?" Stefanie said this as if adult sons broached such intimate matters with their parents as a matter of course.

"Yes, I have a son," she said. Admitting to "sons," after all, would only prompt questions she didn't care to answer.

"No daughters, right?" Stefanie asked, too brightly, as if she might audition for the role.

"No. No daughters."

Nathan glanced down at the name he had scribbled on the Post-it note Kati had handed to him. Stephen Wolf. A full day, he had booked. Called the dock directly, it seemed. Not through one of the hotels. "On his own," Marty had specified. "Asked a bunch of questions about you and your vessel. If you were *the* Nathan Pray." (Nathan couldn't tell if the dockmaster had meant this seriously.) "Sounds like he knows what he's doing."

A single fisherman usually signaled as much. Expertise. Nathan hoped so. Ineptitude usually came in twos or threes.

He parked and walked the gauntlet of larger vessels en route to his skiff, which he had launched and tied up at the marina just before his breakfast at the café. The briny east wind struggled to subdue the olfactory insult of pulverized baitfish. Larry, Moe, and Curly parted lazily for him on the battered wooden walk. "I don't have anything for you this morning, guys. Sorry." They lowered their heads and waddled off, disappointed, indignant even. Larry, Moe, and Curly were the dock's aged pelicans–the only birds all the captains tolerated on account of some vague sense of kinship with the scrofulous creatures. Frank's mate was elbow-deep in what looked to be his third five-gallon bucket of menhaden, whitebait, oats, shells, and sand. Additional miscellaneous ingredients–garlic powder, vinegar, soy sauce, moldy cheese, bacon–rounded out each captain's proprietary recipe. They chummed like crazy, his offshore peers. More than Nathan, even, with his loaded "meatballs."

"Hey Bobby," Nathan greeted the mop-headed mate, just a few years out of high school. He hadn't yet fully shed that gangly quality of adolescence, a natural complement to his overgrown curtain of sandy hair and the mild trace of acne that flared from either side of his mouth like a frown.

"Hey, Nate." The young man returned to his labors for just a moment before a thought struck him. "Yo, Nate!" he called down the dock, "what's it y'all have such a hard-on about, anyway? Frank's got me mixing five buckets here, Hollis havin' Dex and Greg do twenty on the *Ellen*. Both want us to wax the vessels again later on, Armoral the vinyl, polish the friggin' chrome. . . . I mean, what the fuck!?"

Nathan heard a truck door slam shut and glanced over at Manny, hopping down from his F350 and glancing nervously about as if he were in the witness protection program.

"The Chip Holiday business, I guess," Nathan answered. "You've heard the rumors, right?"

"Shee-it," the mate replied. "You serious? How long y'all gonna have your panties in a twist over that? Only so much we can take."

Panties in a twist. The mate must have picked up the cranky expression from Frank, his captain. Nathan shrugged his shoulders to affect nonchalance. Here he was, just a simple fisherman, cultivating poverty like some precious herb, above the fray, strolling off past Hollis' vessel now, past Del's. Was it so shameful to own up to a modicum of ambition? Nathan indulged in a reverie at last: The Sunshine Network's Fishing Report. Chip Holiday. *Let's take it on over to the Snookmaster,*

Nathan Pray. What's the good word, my brother, southside of the Southeast? He glanced about reflexively, foolishly, worried that an observer might read his thoughts. Gathering his wits, Nathan contemplated the possibilities anew. Frank was right about one thing. Those charter captains on the show had it made. Sponsorships, Nathan suspected, far exceeding the mere tournament entrance fees and the trivial swag–baits, rods, reels and such. Endorsements. Actual money. Nathan could buy a new boat and, more importantly, a new home fit for Miles. He wouldn't have to scrap for charters, but would have them slated days and even weeks (maybe seasons, for all Nathan knew) in advance. He'd enter tourneys with Terrance only if the mood struck. The money. The fame. The women. Nathan couldn't deny the pull of such enticements. Beyond such heady pleasures, the Fishing Report would offer him the chance to exert a positive influence, maybe, a forum to counter the grasping, conquering, gear-headed, environmentally unsound model of angling that crowded Nathan's waters.

Chip Holiday could do worse than select Nathan. He wasn't particularly telegenic, but neither were most of the good ol' boys on the show. He could focus on the inshore bite and get the offshore 411 from Del and the others, work in environmentally sensitive advice on fish-handling, releasing, and harvesting. "Don't catch your limit," he liked to tell his charters, "limit your catch." Why not offer such encouragements to a broader audience? Make an actual impact? He'd dole out some cash to his fellow captains to keep the wheels greased and display their photos judiciously, careful not to play favorites, offer them the requisite props (as Miles would say) on the air . . .

The sight of his charter standing expectantly on the dock above the skiff jolted Nathan to, specifically his eight-hundred dollar, 9-foot Orvis–no missing *that*!–which jutted at a phallic angle from the fellow's grip.

"9-weight okay?" Apparently, the charter had noticed Nathan's noticing.

"Fine. Perfect."

Besides the rod, the fellow looked like a walking Stone River catalog, what with his khaki vest pin-pricked with innumerable, multicolored flies—Nathan glimpsed a Dahlberg diver, a badger buddy, a D.C. wiggler, a marabou muddler, several sea-ducers and clousers—the breathable long-sleeve guide shirt beneath, the plastic stripping basket belted just below his waist, the polycarbonate Action Optics frames taming a wavy blonde dollop above his forehead.

"Must be Captain Pray," the man extended his free hand in greeting, a hand the size of a frying pan, which engulfed Nathan's modest, mottled appendage.

"Nate," the fisherman clarified. "No need to stand on ceremony."

"Stand on ceremony," the man repeated. "Curious expression." The charter gazed at him through squinted pale blue eyes for a moment, rather too obviously taking his measure, it seemed to Nathan. His broad face looked like an unblemished apple.

"You're Stephen Wolf then."

"Sure am. Nice old vessel you've got here. Classic."

An insult seemed hidden beneath the baggy clothes of the remark. "It's a quality skiff," Nathan declared. "May need to replace the Merc soon. I'm thinking of going four-stroke. Quieter. Better on the environment."

"The environment?"

"Mm-hm." Nathan stepped down over the gunwale into the skiff–right foot first, always the right foot first–groaning, a mere rhetorical gesture, formerly. Less so of late.

"The environment. Interesting."

Fumbling about the deck, taking a silent pre-charter inventory (keys, check; water, check; sunscreen, check; fuel, check; lures, check; ice, check), Nathan decided that he didn't much like this fellow, the way he unabashedly weighed his every utterance. Enough already. Perhaps Terrance was right. Maybe he just didn't like people very much, period. Nathan didn't like to think that this could be so.

"Permission to come aboard, captain?"

"Long as you don't have any bananas on your person." Nathan didn't ascribe too much validity to this particular superstition, but it was something to say and the charters expected such saying.

"You don't need that stripping basket," Nathan lifted his nose toward the basket at Wolf's waist. "I jerry-rigged that cylinder up on the casting deck for fly fishing."

"Nice." Wolf gazed toward the cylinder at the bow, nodded his apple face.

The Merc exhaled upon Nathan's command, then growled, spitting and sputtering as it idled as if it resented being woken. The burning oil and gasoline overtook the fishy brine in the atmosphere. The throaty growl of the engine, its spitting and sputtering, hindered casual conversation. Good. There was time to think as Nathan reached up to unfasten the bowline knot wrapped around the dock pylon amidships, the cleat knots from stern and bow, time to think as this Wolf fellow stepped and stumbled about the deck to give way. What kind of an asshole am I, Nathan wondered, that he took the mildest pleasure in Wolf's clumsy choreography?

So they'd be fishing the fly today. There were those who viewed the endeavor as the angling sine qua non, the purest mode of communion with the watery realm. Nathan wasn't one of these people. There were ample elements to appreciate. The focus on technique and sport rather than yield, per se. The pure geometry of the cast, its arcs and parabolas. Reading the water was imperative. Not optional. Fly fishing made sense in Montana, to be sure. The Keys, Flamingo, or Ten Thousand Islands closer to home. But there just weren't any true flats hereabouts anymore (Nathan kept a push-pole at the hull, but it was mostly for tournament time elsewhere in the state, where skinnier water abounded), or even the simple space to perform the requisite backcasts, given boat traffic. What's more, there was something downright masturbatory in the boutique apparel, the cavalcade of gear that accompanied the sport these days: innumerable rods, reels, fly and backing lines, and terminal tackle, ultra-specialized and overdetermined. This fly orgy, say, affixed to Wolf's vest.

Nathan was in agreement with Terrance about one thing. Sport, like life, was good when it was simple. That's why he was a spinfisher.

"Okay, here we go," Nathan shouted above the din.

"Push us off?"

"No need."

Wolf stood beside the console, Terrance's spot, his frying pan hand gripping the stainless frame. The Merc quieted some, now gainfully employed.

"Head up to the lagoon?"

"You sure, Stephen?"

"Wolf," his charter corrected him, then raised his big hand as if to apologize. "It's not a formality thing. Don't get me wrong. Just what everyone calls me. Wolf."

"Well Wolf it's a far piece up there, my friend." Nathan, without looking, twisted the left dial on the VHF, the radio's chirpy salutation pleasing to his ears. He glanced skyward at the cumulus clouds, reading their fast westward march. "Too rough for the skiff on the ocean," he added, "so we'll have to shoot the whole way up on the ICW. Factor in all the no wakes we're talking an hour plus each way." He looked down at the radio now, turned the right dial up one channel to 73.

"But better snook spots up there. Right?"

Nathan, north of the inlet now, nodded.

"And you're the snookmaster from what I hear." Wolf set

down his Orvis, gingerly, in one of the cylindrical rod holders at the console. The reel, an Abel wrapped with lime green fly line, was quality too.

"Sounds like someone's been lying."

"Well, yeah, heard you haven't been catching much lately. That's the word."

Nathan stiffened.

"But that freeze wasn't your fault. Can't catch what isn't there. Between the red tides lately on the gulf side and the freezes both coasts . . . shit."

They traveled for a time in silence. A kingfisher dove toward the rippled surface of Lake Boca, then abandoned the effort just above, chattering its complaint as it flitted off. Nathan considered pointing the bird out to Wolf, then reconsidered.

"Kingfisher," Wolf uttered.

Nathan nodded. "Good eye."

He heard the prefatory static over the radio, then the voice of his fellow captain: "Hollis here. Radio check, radio check, please."

Nathan waited a moment. No response. His fellow captains were screwing with Hollis. Nathan smiled as he picked up his mic.

"Loud and clear, Hollis. Nathan here. I'm in the ICW, just north of Silver Palm. Good luck on the drift. Over."

"Thanks, Nate. Rip 'em up today. Over."

"Couldn't leave him hanging one more second, Nate?" Manny prodded him over the line between the salty static.

Nathan shook his head and slid the radio mic back on its track.

"Might be that we should shoot for ladyfish or juvenile tarpon on the way," Nathan declared. "Lake Wyman's been decent. Maybe jack crevalles too just off the inlet once we get up to Boynton. You know, in addition to chasing snook. Question is, do you want to catch fish today or are you dead set on a linesider?"

"Linesider. They're still here, I think. Don't you, Nate?"

The fisherman nodded. "Yes. I do, Wolf. Yes I do. You got thirty pound shock leader on that ax of yours?" Wolf did. "Well let's do it to it!" They had reached the boundary marker for the no-wake. "You might want to remove that hat, Wolf. Bad things are gonna happen. If she *can* fly, she will. . . ."

The ICW broadened past Boynton as they made their way past Manalapan mansions and underused yachts up toward Peanut Island, a once decent fishing ground that had lately been overrun by noisy pleasure-boaters, inebriated overnight campers, and collegiate bacchanals. Before too long, they reached one of Nathan's favorite snook spots, the bridge and jetty at the Lake Worth Inlet. A light chop, nothing the skiff couldn't handle, dimpled this stretch of unsheltered water. East wind still. Not bad for fishing. The captain inhaled what he could through his labyrinthine nasal passages, enjoyed the pleasant brine off the ocean. The timing would be good too–a falling barometer, a strong incoming tide to push the finger mullet and pilchards to the ambush site beside the jetty rocks and bridge pilings–but he wouldn't broadcast this to his charter. Things probably wouldn't work out. The snook in all likelihood wouldn't be here. The creatures that survived the freeze had probably done so by seeking out protective inshore channels, Nathan suspected, where even his skiff couldn't reach. Still, the deep, warmer waters of this particular inlet, plus scattered deep-dredged channels up and down the ICW, would offer safe haven for a few. A few surely remained here. But he had begun to doubt his luck. Maybe it wasn't only a matter of scarcity. Maybe he was snakebit.

"Why don't you tie on that big Dahlberg diver," Nathan suggested once he slowed the *Pray Fish* off plane.

He heard the radio static again, then Hollis' voice. "Hollis here. Drifting in 250 off San Remo. Just a peanut so far. Couple undersized muttons. East wind pushing us in hard. Anyone hook into any sails? Come back."

"Del here. In 370. Off the Highland Beach water tower. Couple Bonita. No sails yet. Over."

"Sale at Macy's," Nathan recognized Manny's voice.

"Funny," Wolf uttered, but didn't laugh.

Nathan nodded, smiling.

"Hardee-har-har," Frank declared through the static. "Some frigate birds working a school about five bucks out or so, pretty much straight off the pier. I'm setting up now. Pretty frickin' sporty out here, eh? Anyway, I'll keep you posted," Frank sighed. "Over."

Nathan was glad that the bite wasn't too hot offshore. It eased the pressure on him to produce. He banked eastward toward the inlet bridge, the saline wind stiff now in his face.

"Mullet's been running up here still."

"Gotta match the hatch, right?" Wolf stepped to, padding his vest for the fly as if locating a book of matches.

"That's right, Wolf."

"Nonslip knot good?"

"Perfect."

Nathan, generally, kept his words to a minimum out on the water. The outsized remonstrations, gesticulations, verbalizations of his brethren . . . the garrulous Jewish everything, would only pierce the placid atmosphere. Even the Jewish charters, Nathan suspected, appreciated his laconic Florida cracker style. Frank and Manny were wrong, dead wrong, about what the "Goldbergs" wanted. They craved that crusty goyische fisherman more than anyone. The tips from his Jewish charters increased in direct proportion to Nathan's vaguely illiterate syntax, his malapropisms on the water–once deliberate performances that had grown frighteningly reflexive over the years. (*It's a far piece up there,* he had said to Wolf. What the fuck was that?) Most of his Jewish charters probably didn't even ponder how strange it was that their cracker captain looked every bit the nebbisheh red-haired Jew. Who would suspect him in these strange environs?

My name is Charles Pray, Nathan conjured his great-grandfather Chaim now, also small, also ginger-haired, just off the boat in Galveston, unfurling his American name like a flag before the porcine agent. His great-grandfather had had plenty of time on the ship to fashion his

Texas bona fides. Schuss made no sense here; Chaim made no sense here. But Charles Pray! *You don't look like no Charles to me? How about you just give me your real name, partner, and we'll take it from there . . .* Was this how Chaim's true story began? Maybe. Maybe not.

"So you're a member of the tribe, Nate, right?" Wolf's voice jolted Nathan to. What did this apple-faced Wolf know from tribes?

"Tribe?"

"You know, tribe of Israel. From the original 12. Jacob's sons. Asher, Benjamin, Levi, Naphtali. So on and so on. You're Jewish is what I'm asking."

"Yeah, Wolf. Just on my mother's and father's side, though." Nathan hoped a bit of levity might cap the irksome conversation. Was Wolf some nutso evangelical? Besides the black hats infiltrating the area of late, it was only these true believer Christians who seemed to know such arcane Judaica.

"Okay, why don't you hop on up the casting deck with that diver. I'm gonna shut her down, control the trolling from the remote, let the current take us to the strike zone."

"It's just that you look Jewish, Nathan." All of a sudden he was Nathan. "Sure you've heard."

For whatever reason, this Wolf character wouldn't drop it.

"Okay, ten o'clock, Wolf. Now. Just short of the piling with all those barnacles. Upcurrent." Nathan could see the tide ripping past the barnacled bridge piling. The ocean's exhale, offering its cleansing breath to the shore. High tide. There was a view, gaining currency, that nature was dead. Finished. Our unchecked hydrocarbon effluvia too much for the old girl. Even when we felt most inside its embrace, like now, it wasn't truly nature, but only our bastardized, counterfeit version, the chemical components of the very molecules above and below the ocean's skin irrevocably altered, the flora and fauna adhering to human-wrought patterns of flow (or expiring), the water and air temps nudged higher than true nature. So the logic goes, Nathan thought. He couldn't wholly dismiss the theory. His densely populated coastal ridge increasingly rebuffed these very tides, after all. No getting around that. Only isolated swatches of sand and seagrass, seagrape and mangrove received these tides now, tides greeted mostly these parts by concrete seawall.

Yet still–still!–the ocean continued to breathe, offered its determined inhalations and exhalations, the earth's edge slipping beneath the liquid crest now. High tide. There was some fight left in the old girl, it seemed to Nathan. Time still to salvage things. The pelicans had come back, anyway. He had grown up practically without the likes of Larry, Moe, and Curly, the DDT having rendered their eggshells too fragile for these clumsy foot-incubators. Given a reprieve, they had returned. Ospreys and eagles too. So, yes, nature was marked, violable, even fragile. But in equal measure dynamic, persistent, and resilient. Nathan felt nature's power most profoundly here on the water. More specifically, on this edge, this ecotone, this land and sea merge. Vigorous tides like this singular tide still moved him. He felt most human during these moments when he was here to greet the ocean's determined breath—inside, not outside, the game. He had to remind himself now to release the clutch of salt air he'd gathered into his lungs. Yes. Here I am, he thought.

Wolf threw his fly in expert fashion. Nice. It wasn't just the cast that Nathan appreciated. Lots of novice fly fishermen could set down a fly in the right place. But Wolf could mend too without being told. An expert flick of lime green line up current.

"Fine mend."

Wolf stripped. Then stripped again. "You look so Jewish, tell you the truth, it hurts my eyes," Wolf persisted. Nathan laughed, despite the Jew-hating implications. He couldn't help himself.

"Give it a couple more slow strips. Then reel and we'll just give it another shot."

They had drifted a bit too close to the strike zone. Nathan powered the trolling hard in reverse. Not good, he knew. Sound traveled far and fast in the thick liquid medium. Not much chance of a snook now. "Just wait a sec. Okay, now. Give it a cast. Let's see that mend again. Might want to put the hinge a bit farther up. Current's ripping."

"I'm a Hebe too, in case you're wondering."

"Huh?"

"A Jew."

"You don't say." Nathan didn't believe him, which Wolf detected. He cast back crisply and reaffirmed to Nathan that he was, indeed, Jewish.

"No offense, Wolf, but you don't look Jewish. I mean, not at all. You couldn't look less Jewish, matter of fact."

"Maybe this is what Jewish looks like too," Wolf proposed as he mended.

Nathan made a listening noise as he contemplated the implications of the remark. If Wolf was what Jewish looked like, what was the point?

"Shit, I have something. Didn't even feel it at first."

"Don't get excited," Nathan warned. "Sheepshead, I think. Their M.O. Odd on the Dahlberg. They usually just take live crustaceans. You don't have the wiggler on, do you? Or some crab imitation?" Wolf didn't. "Just bring her in nice and easy. There, see it?" Nathan's colorblind eyes were perfectly adapted for glimpsing the chunky monochromatic creature beneath the depths. Sheepshead, or prisonfish, they were called.

"You see it already?" Wolf halted his retrieve, lifted his Action Optics above his eyes, and then lowered them back in place. A semi roared across the bascule bridge overhead. Wolf continued his retrieve faster now. "Jesus, Nathan. You have eyes like a friggin' hawk."

Nathan kneeled on the deck and reached over the gunwale to retrieve the fat creature, taking care to elude its angry dorsal barbs.

"Well *now* I see it," Wolf said.

The specimen, true to form, had only nibbled on the fly with its eerie collection of old-man incisors. Nathan, feeling oddly the dentist, managed to extricate the hook from behind its set of lowers, using only his mottled hands. The degorger would have been easier, but the charters appreciated such barehanded expertise.

Sheepshead made for good eating on account of their finicky crustacean predilections. Nathan, however, couldn't bear to consume the creatures. Those tiny human teeth! Plus they were a bitch to fillet, their scale armor difficult to pierce. But eating this little fellow, or not, wasn't his call. He held the prisonfish up for Wolf's inspection.

"What's your pleasure, Wolf? Put him in the cooler?"

"You got that hook out pretty easy. He in good shape?" Nathan told his charter that he was.

"Just let him go then. We'll do catch and release. I'm in a steak mood tonight, anyway."

"Nothing wrong with steak."

Nathan lowered the prisonfish beneath the dimpled surface. A sharp, anal fin caught him on the release. Son of a bitch, the fisherman thought, but didn't say, lifting hand to mouth, tasting the iron of his blood and the tidewater's salt.

"Nice to get the skunk out, anyway," Wolf said. Nathan agreed, warming some to the fellow.

**

"Sorry we couldn't find you a snook," Nathan apologized some hours later once Wolf had conceded defeat, wearily depositing his Orvis into the holder. Not enough snook in the world, Nathan thought, but didn't say. After they caught the sheepshead, they had worked their way southward as the day progressed, taking inshore jaunts as far west as the canals and spillways allowed. They'd caught a juvenile tarpon, a toothy barracuda, and an undersized but feisty crevalle. All things

91

considered, it had been a decent day for inshore. Nathan had earned his fee. It was something of a humble-brag, Nathan's apology for their MIA snook.

"No worries," Wolf declared. "That's why it's called fishing, not catching, right?" Nathan smiled at the familiar refrain. The sun had nearly abandoned its efforts to the southwest as the *Pray Fish* broke out into the unsheltered ICW. The offshore breeze bit cold now, piercing their modest layers of clothing. Reaching beneath the console, the captain retrieved a windbreaker and wordlessly handed it to his charter for the ride back. They chugged southward along the minimum wake, slower than the boats that passed them port and starboard side, violating the simple guidelines.

Nathan wondered what Manny was up to today. Inshore or offshore. The bastard was awfully quiet about his luck lately. Was he catching linesiders somewhere? Manny had refused to join the snook working group. Too far a commute to the meetings, he claimed. Didn't see what was in it for him. Manny couldn't be bothered with those passive integrated transponder tags. Fine. But if the punk upstart had any news to share on these ever-dying creatures it was criminal to withhold it. Criminal.

"Here, let me give you my card," Wolf announced after throwing the windbreaker over his neck, presenting the rectangle from between his index and middle finger, a somewhat theatrical flourish. It occurred to Nathan that Wolf, oddly for a charter, hadn't mentioned what he did for a living all day. He peered down at the offering. ULEE'S

BAITS it read in simple typeface. Nice old Florida name. He'd give him that. Wolf's name and phone number, an area code unfamiliar to Nathan, were printed just below. No logo. No specialized font. No internet website. Nathan would have doubted the authenticity of this crude card were it not so easy to fabricate a more impressive offering, and were it not for Wolf's accomplished angling.

"Haven't heard of you guys."

"We're just starting out. Plant's out near Immokalee. Dirt cheap real estate. Privacy." Nathan nodded, noncommittal.

"We're on to something big is the thing. Real big. I myself like fishing the fly but that's not where the money is. It's still pretty much a boutique industry. Real money's in spinning baits, my brother. Your specialty."

So now they were brothers.

"That's where we come in, you see. You know Berkley baits, DOA, the stuff they been up to?" Nathan knew. The latest generation of scented baits had taken the industry by storm. Soft plastics impregnated with fishstuffs, then bathed in secret, putrid juice formulae, sixty times the olfactory strength of live bait, purportedly. A controversy, it seemed to Nathan, in search of a populace who cared enough to recognize the scandal. This unconscionable blurring of the live-bait/artificial boundary. It was one of the reasons Nathan stuck with Swallow. That neither Berkley nor DOA had expressed any interest in sponsoring Nathan was the other reason.

"We're gonna Harvard up on Berkley, my brother. Give the KO

to DOA."

All of a sudden, Wolf sounded like Miles.

"Those scented baits are weak sauce compared to what we got going on over at the facility. See, I'd like to give you a tour out there. You could use a new sponsor, from what I hear. Screw Swallow. Be nice to have a member of the tribe on board."

Nathan nodded, slow. A tricked-out Boston Whaler bobbed in its mooring as they passed. "It's gonna change everything, Nathan. I'm telling you. Change everything."

So this whole day had been something of a tryout, Nathan gathered. It didn't sit well. He was tempted to rebuff the offer out of hand. But something was there—curiosity, desperation, ambition perhaps—that gave Nathan pause. A pelican squadron veered eastward across the waterway. He sighed above the chugging two-stroke, inhaled through his labyrinthine nostrils, seeking knowledge from the salt air spiced vaguely with sulfur from the Merc's exhaust.

**

"So we'll train in the ocean Saturday?" Nathan proposed to Miles over the crackling cell phone reception. He had just entered the cab of his truck after parting from Wolf at the dock.

"Chill."

"Big meet coming up."

"Word."

"Your Grandma Judy's coming I'm pretty sure. Left her a message today."

The phone seemed to cut out.

"Wait. I'm losing you. Hear me, Miles?"

"*Yes*," his son insisted sharply, somewhat petulantly, it seemed to Nathan.

"Listen, you sure you want to swim in the ocean? We don't have to if you don't want." Nathan hated swimming in the ocean, and hated swimming, period. He spent most his time, after all, trying *not* to fall into the drink. What's more, his skinny body tended naturally toward submersion rather than buoyancy. His stroke was awkward. His breathing, labored. He only braved the ocean with Miles because his son liked the challenge of the waves and current, and because neither Sam nor he would allow Miles to swim alone out there, and because he was glad that Miles—bombarded with electronic media enticements—had found his own way to connect with the Florida outdoors. And because he'd be damned if he'd let that fucker Leon perform these fatherly rituals in his stead. But if Miles weren't truly excited about their ocean plans, he'd just as soon not subject themselves to the sharks.

"Yeah. I'm sure, dads. That'd be tight."

Dads. Miles had been such a normal son, until recently. He had liked to tell jokes when he was seven, eight. Nice, innocent jokes. Knock-knock jokes, especially.

Knock-knock. Who's there? Yodela-hee. Yodela-hee who? Wow, you're a good yodeler.

Knock-knock. Who's there? Pea. Pea who? Pea you! You smell.

Knock-knock. Who's there? I'm a pile-up. I'm a pile-up who? Oh, don't be so hard on yourself.

Knock-knock. Who's there? Boo. Boo who? Don't cry. You'll feel better soon.

Now Miles seemed to speak to him mostly in grunts, peppered with Ebonic flourishes, as if he were determined to keep pace with Terrance's son, Devon, who didn't talk anything like this, far as Nathan could tell. Nathan didn't know how much of Miles' laconic sullenness, or his ghetto cool–oh those red dreads–to attribute to the divorce, how much to attribute to adolescence, or how much to attribute to Miles just being Miles. So Nathan just tried to ride things out the best he could. All the same, he'd have to talk to him about the Torah speech draft he had just written, his Bar Mitzvah *drash*. Miles' black Moses meshugass. That'd go over great at Beth Shalom!

"Pick you up Friday, then? Normal time?"

"Okay, dad." *Okay, dad.* Not dads. The simple, familiar phrase (perhaps Miles had neglected to check himself) pierced Nathan. Still his son, Miles. As far away as Miles seemed, there was still time to contribute some measure of his own character, some Pray-ness, to his boy. But what must Miles think of him, living alone as a stone in a cramped apartment? His odd hours? While his mother had remarried a fancy doctor. While the three of them lived in an enormous stucco and Spanish tile property out west. A fierce competitor such as Miles would likely view his parents' divorce through the lens of competition, resulting in a winner and a loser. There could be little doubt what role Nathan currently occupied in Miles' imagination. It was high time Nathan challenged this tidy script.

"Mom got the fish you dropped off. Wanted me to thank you. Or whatever."

"Good, Miles. That's good."

**

The Efficiency. An illustrative name for his domicile, his current circumstances. This was life stripped to its core, after all. Efficient. Simple, one might say, but not altogether good. What did he say to Miles each time they entered the apartment? *This is only temporary.*

He would have to change his life, he knew, flicking Wolf's card onto the Formica bar in the kitchenette, contemplating Terrance's teaching offer, the baggier prospect of the Sunshine Network's Fishing Report.

In moments he would try to sleep. He would shut the blinds, although it was already dark. Wolf was a later and longer charter than usual. He would try to catch a few hours before setting out for more snapper. He would lay atop the sheets, naked, and think of Kati. *Que bonita, Nathaniel.* His hands might drift toward his groin. Briefly. Depleted by the day, he would surrender to sleep, instead.

But now he had to eat. No getting around that. He retrieved the wounded lemon from the fridge, rolled the bulb on the counter beneath his palm, freeing its juice from the membranes within. He then sliced the lemon in half and bathed his hands in the juices over the steel sink. The acid stung where Wolf's sheepshead had pierced him. He returned to the fridge and retrieved a snapper fillet and one of the limes from the bottom shelf, shoving aside the withered parsley and carton of OJ. The top shelf he kept bare, as if reserving the space for a nonexistent roommate. He rinsed the fillet under the steel tap after freeing it from its cellophane. The flesh was firm to the touch. Good. He lay the slab on the plastic cutting board, then lathered it in proprietary proportions of spice—onion and garlic powder, paprika, white pepper, cayenne, coriander. He fried the fillet in olive oil and less butter in a cast iron pan, spritzing it along the way with all the juice he could extract from the puckered lime.

He savored the delectable white flesh at the bar, clearing his throat from time to time to remind himself that he was there.

Book Two

Chapter One

His grandfather taught him. Nathan, partly to escape Jake's dominion, partly to escape his parent's perplexing acrimony, and partly because he liked his grandfather, spent as many weekends in Miami Beach with Morton as his parents would condone. They'd deposit him on the train in Deerfield with a small duffle. His grandfather would retrieve him from the station west of the causeway in his Pontiac convertible so that Nathan wouldn't have to brave the bus connection. Sometimes they'd walk to King Solomon on Lincoln, the shul long defunct now–the building housing a restaurant of indeterminate ethnic origin last he'd seen– so his grandfather could show him off. That's how he put it, Nathan remembered. "Let me show you off to the bubbehs." To Aunt Noma. Or Aunt Mildred. Or Aunt Nattie. Or Uncle Zip. Then to Wolfie's for tongue, or pastrami, or corned beef (the complex cross-section of meat layers between the rye recalling a geology lesson at J.C. Mitchell), for flanken bathed in its pot juices, for kishka smothered with brown gravy, the moist fatty filling bursting its intestinal sheath, for half-sours and Dr. Brown's Black Cherry Soda. He liked sitting at the bar, where waitresses barked at the customers, where his grandfather and he weren't forced to stare each other down and make conversation across a table, but gazed over the bar mostly, thinking about their thoughts. Without words, his grandfather would show him his trick, stripping the paper wrapper off one of the plastic straws, placing the crinkled paper worm between them. He'd dip the straw into the Dr. Brown's Black Cherry Soda can, extracting a medicinal dose by stoppering the top with his finger. A nifty trick that, all by itself. But more. Holding the dropper just above the crinkled paper worm, he'd summon the tiny beast to life, releasing one soda drop, two drops, three drops. Wriggle-wriggle-wriggle.

On the walk home, Nathan would enjoy the sweet punchy odor of his grandfather's green Hav-a-Tampa cigar, leavening the putrid sewer juices along the blighted streets. Morton, without Nathan asking, would peel off the red paper ring and place it on Nathan's forefinger. He liked wearing the ring for a few blocks, then bursting the paper with a flex of his finger.

Nathan would wake in the still-dark the next morning to Morton's violent, productive hacking in the small bathroom. For reasons still not altogether clear to him, he'd feign sleep on the fold-out sofa in the living room until his grandfather leaned over him, nudging him mildly at the shoulder. After a silent breakfast of cereal or oatmeal they'd walk the few dim blocks to the ocean. Nathan would carry the bucket with the frozen shrimp and the surf rod his grandfather kept for him on the small balcony. Nathan didn't like to swim, even as a youngster. The ocean water hurt his ears and stung his eyes, so his grandfather set him up with his rod a little ways down the beach, lathered him with a haphazard Coppertone coat, and impaled the first still-unthawed shrimp on the bronze hook below the pyramid sinker. Then his grandfather shed his outer layer of clothes to reveal underwear that he called bathing briefs, preparing for his immersion up the beach with the other old people. His skin was richly wrinkled and creased in curious locales, brown as a nut (no Coppertone for him), and looked even darker on account of the frosty hair on his chest. Amid the fur, a smooth droplet of skin–"my bypass souvenir," he explained–traveled toward the rise of his belly. Brandishing a metal tube from out of nowhere, he painted zinc oxide on his nose, only the nose, the final ritual before his immersion. "Now catch us a gefilte fish," he'd joke, dashing up the sand, elbows akimbo.

Nathan usually didn't catch much. Catfish and whiting, mostly, whiskered and foul-mouthed. He threw them back. The small sharks and snook, patrolling the skinny water like bandits, usually snapped his line with their teeth and gill plates, respectively, forcing Nathan to re-rig. He never got bored. He liked the sound of the not-quite-waves tickling the fine pale sand at his feet, could gaze all day at the cruise ships and freighters meandering to and from Government Cut, the lazy schools of rolling dolphin and prehistoric tarpon, gleaming silver kings.

"Hold out your hands," his grandfather would instruct after the sun had climbed high and it was time to leave. "Palms up," he'd command, rifling through his canvas bag for the lemon. "Your great-grandfather, Chaim. Too bad he never lived to meet you. Loved to fish for snook, my papa. Ah, Galveston," he uttered.

"Snook? Really?"

There weren't enough snook in the world, Nathan thought even then.

His grandfather pierced the fruit's fleshy middle with the

pincers of both hands, and then sheared the yellow bulb in half. Brandishing both rough halves high above Nathan's palms, his grandfather squeezed. Generous warm rivulets splashed down in Nathan's palms. He scrubbed his palms together, and then interlocked his fingers to coat every crease of fishy flesh. He bathed his arms with the citrus all the way up to his elbows, the sting rising from mild cuts and abrasions. "Only thing to cut the smell," his grandfather would say, as if every iteration of their ritual demanded this explanation. The ablution complete, he'd offer Nathan one of the spent halves. "Just a taste," he'd warn. "Bad for your teeth. The enamel."

On the way back to the apartment, the sun scalding and bright now, they'd pass old ladies sitting on flimsy chairs outside their weary tenements, clutching sea grape leaves between their dentures. The broad disks shielded their lips from the sun, his grandfather claimed, shrugging to betray his own doubts.

Next morning they'd visit the factory. It was open Sundays for a skeleton crew of frum seamstresses, who didn't work Fridays or Saturdays. Mostly women, but a few men too. "Men—like your great-grandfather from Galveston," Morton declared, "could be seamstresses too." His grandfather liked to stop in. Not stay, he'd promise, but stop in, just to make sure there wasn't any funny business going on. It was a long walk all the way to Lenox, but they always walked. "Good for the circulation," Morton claimed. This circulation business, whatever it was, seemed terrifically important; innumerable activities and potables seemed good for it. The factory didn't boast much frontage to speak of, not that Nathan could remember, just a single metal door in front that opened to a stairway leading to the second and third floors. He liked taking the freight elevator from the back alley instead, which wasn't like a regular elevator, but opened up-and-down, an unsmiling mouth. The second floor was where all the people were. They greeted him with extravagant cheer. Hard candies (the sugarless diabetic varieties stuck to his fingers before he could even dispatch them onto his tongue) and caramel swirls materialized out of thin air, the novelty of his presence offering a welcome distraction from their tedious labors. Or else they were simply kind. Natural light filtered into the room from windows facing the alley. The windows were smoky from the steam irons. Fifteen Singer sewing machines, maybe twenty, stood in formation like an insect army across the wide tables, dripping with multicolored cloth, solids and various patterns too: plaids, houndstooths, herringbones, stripes. Broad bins on metal wheels scuttled noisily across the concrete floor.

"What's this?!" his grandfather hollered at a worker one morning, a woman Nathan didn't recognize who was somewhat younger than the others. Morton clutched a fistful of fabric, lifted the offending article from the table. "This isn't Havana! We don't do shlub-work here, Marta!" A spittle spec escaped his mouth and rested on a small stubble island, which his grandfather had neglected to shave from his chin that morning. The poor woman's head–partly hidden anyway beneath a curious duck's bill looking glass–nearly disappeared between her shoulder-blades.

"Now take her easy, Morty," a male voice interjected from

somewhere. "No use getting worked up." His grandfather didn't seem to hear the man.

"It's Ready-to-Wear not Ready-to-Toss! You don't see this loose thread at the cuff!?"

"Yes, Mr. Pray, I do. I mean, no," she retreated, her voice quavering, "I didn't see before."

"Acch. Rip it out. Start over."

He wasn't all sweetness and light, his grandfather. Prone, rather, to protracted moments of distraction, of not-all-thereness (which didn't bother Nathan), punctuated by unexpected outbursts (which did bother him). His grandfather usually held his irascible side in check in his presence, which Nathan's mother seemed ever so much to resent. "He's mellowed since his operation, believe me, Nathan. These Jewish princes. So spoiled. Everything just so. Impossible. Drove your grandmother to an early grave."

And so Nathan remembered this particular morning at the factory, because his grandfather hollered at someone, and because a spittle spec escaped his mouth and rested on a small stubble island, which his grandfather had neglected to shave from his chin, and because he, like the seamstress, shrank from his grandfather, and because his grandfather saw what he had wrought and sought to make amends. Not with the seamstress, Marta. But with Nathan.

"Ah, come, my little luftmensch. My little dreamer. Let's go upstairs." The upstairs room was empty, and dark, and ungodly hot. Fabric piles lay in heaps on broad metal shelves against every wall. His grandfather grasped a broad beige swatch baring triangle teeth at the borders and brought it to the center of the room to the long, scarred wooden table. "It's not a bad thing to know your way around a shmat-teh. To use your hands for something. In case you don't want to be a big k'nocker doctor like your father. In my gesheft you come work." Nathan shuddered at the thought. Morton laid the fabric on the wood, then laid a cardboard cut-out on top, a giant's pantaloons.

"A template this is called," Morton said, replacing his dark-framed spectacles with the pair he used to read the *Herald* in the morning, which sat low on his nose. "First you trace your pattern." Brandishing chalk from thin air, he marked the borders. "Here, you try. Good. But firmer. It won't get shmutzig. Don't worry. We brush it off. Now stand back while I cut the pattern." He lifted a wooly arm above the table, reached for the tool hanging from a bowed arm attached to a track. It looked not unlike the mixer his mother used when she made brownies, but with a long metal tooth hanging down instead of beaters. His grandfather must have flicked a switch, because the machine sud-denly roared as if it were a much larger machine. Nathan covered his ears with both palms. His grandfather worked his way around the fabric quickly, efficiently, moving the fabric rather than his body with practiced pivots of his hand's heel. "Stand back I said!" he roared above the saw's whir. Nathan retreated.

"See?" he held up the behemoth pantaloons for Nathan's inspection after cutting the motor. Sweat moons rose full under his grandfather's underarms. The air was stifling. But it didn't seem to bother Morton. "Pants don't just grow on trees. First, the pattern you cut. Usually we do whole stacks at a time. Not me anymore. Too old. Point is, there's a way with the cutter. And with your body. Your hands. A procedure to master and to repeat. Every time. A right way and a wrong way, what I'm trying to say. You do the wrong way, you lose a finger. Kapeesh?" He handed Nathan the behemoth pantaloons. Nathan nodded as he licked the salty sweat from his lip. "Genug," Morton declared. "Enough."

They rode the funny elevator back down to the second floor. "Sorry I yelled," Morton uttered above the elevator's groan. "It's okay," Nathan replied, unsure of the episode to which his grandfather referred, his hollering at Marta or his hollering at him just now over the cutter. Nathan liked to hop out of the elevator early, before its lower jaw fully opened. He waited for his grandfather, who opened a palm toward an insect soldier, an empty station. "Sit down, Nathan. We're not done yet. Right here next to Mitzie. Mitzie's no blockhead, right Mitzie? Best girl in the shop." Nathan descended into the chair with no arms before the idle Singer next to Mitzie, this old woman his grandfather called a girl. She glanced over at him and smiled, the needles flashing between her lips. "Take these Suntans we just cut." Morton groaned onto a stool beside Nathan. The word confused Nathan, which his grandfather must have discerned. "Khakis, okay, they're called now. I call them suntans. Show you how to stitch a pleat. The basics." His grandfather looked at him intently while he offered instruction, his owl eyes peering above the low frames of his glasses. "A right way and a wrong way. You walk.

Then you run. We do a double-pleat here at Pray Clothiers. Not a triple. Not a single. A double. Makes a nice line on a young man no matter his size. A double-pleat won't ever go out of style.

"Now it's only a measured fold, a pleat. Held fast with stitching." Morton pumped the stool higher as he spoke, clasping some invisible lever below. "Partial pleats for slacks"–Morton folded over a pinch of beige fabric–"because they give way at a release point down the leg, you see? Deeper the seam"–Morton pinched more fabric–"the lower the release point. Kapeesh?" Nathan nodded. "We stitch a deep seam here at my gesheft. No cutting corners. A right way and a wrong way. Hardly need an iron, hang our slacks correct. With a proper hanger. Not that cheap wire and cardboard."

Nathan nodded.

"First, boychik, you need to know how to stitch." Morton grasped a needle from a cushion and slipped a protective rubber cap over his thumb. He handed a needle to Nathan too, a length of beige thread, a silver thimble. "That you put on your thumb. No, the other thumb. It's a volume business now, for better or worse, so we use a pleater. But anyone worth his salt can baste an even pleat by hand. No machine. No template. The basting threads, after we finish on the Singer, we pull out.

"Only a few basic stitches you need to know in this world. A basting stitch. A backstitch. A running stitch. A slipstitch. No need for fancy-shmancy. But you need to know what you know. A right way and a wrong way. Take this thread, your needle. First, we lick." Morton lifted the needle with his liver-spotted left hand, put the thread in his mouth with his right, inviting Nathan to do the same. "Then we thread the needle like so." Nathan, to his surprise, slipped the thread through the eye with ease and smiled at his accomplishment. His grandfather struggled ever so slightly. "Before Tish B'av, Zadie," Nathan mimicked one of Morton's favorite expressions. "Now, now," his elder murmured. "Old eyes. Old hands . . . there!" He finally threaded his needle.

"Okay, make sure you have three, four inches or so so you don't lose the thread and have to start all over. Yes, fine. Now take the long end like so. See? And let's wrap around the needle twice. Again? Watch. Pay attention this time. Like so. Good. Perfect. Now the tricky part. We pull this wrapped part down toward the eye of the needle. Yes, like that. Now over the eye"–Morton's voice lilted here, as if he were performing a magic trick–"like so. Maybe just watch me, boychik, before you try. Then we tighten. See? It makes a knot. Presto. Not hard. You try."

Nathan tried.

"Yes, YES!"

Nathan, upon tightening his knot, offered the needle and thread to his grandfather. "You're a natural. Careful, to work I put you."

Morton ripped out the knot with his mouth, then handed it back to Nathan and cut him a new measure of thread. "Now again do it," he commanded. Nathan did it again.

"A simple basting stitch we do now. A right way and a wrong way. We walk. Then we run. For nice even basting, we go right to left, long stitches"–Morton poked his needle beneath the suntan swatch, then popped it back to the surface–"same amount of space above and below the fabric, see?" Morton kept his eyes trained on his project as he spoke. Nathan watched, mesmerized, as his grandfather guided the shiny needle with knowing fingers, dexterous and nimble now. Then Nathan didn't notice the fingers anymore, the liver-spotted hand, but only the needle, gleaming beneath the hot lamp, diving and emerging like a dolphin from the fabric waves.

"Now you try, Nathan."

Nathan tried. "OWWW!" He promptly pricked his forefinger. Morton reached down, grasped the wounded digit and throttled it tight to draw a speck of blood. "OWWW!" A heck of a thing to do, Nathan thought, just before his grandfather put the finger in his mouth. An even weirder thing to do. Morton removed the finger, bloodless now, and blew on it, which felt good.

"There. All better."

Seamstresses loomed over them, plied Nathan with fresh dietetic candies. "I'm okay," he assured the ladies, wiping a tear that he had involuntarily shed. "I'm okay."

"Sorry, boychikele," Morton apologized, rubbing Nathan's back in clockwise swirls. "Truth comes in blows sometimes. Sorry, kiddo."

"It's okay."

"Backstitch we do, maybe, next weekend."

Nathan nodded.

"Point is, there's a right way to do things and a wrong way. Sometimes it's hard, maybe. The right way."

And so Nathan learned how to fish.

Chapter Two

This is what you do.

You commute westward across congested six-lane surface streets to the new construction where your former wife lives with her newer, better husband in a newer, better gated neighborhood of ghastly homogenous stucco. You brandish your photo identification at the gate to the guard, who checks the guest list on his computer screen and allows you passage. You pull up quietly in your old truck, careful not to park on the grass (but how do you avoid the grass on these ridiculous streets, miniaturized so as to maximize the square footage available in these two-story monstrosities). You shut the door of the Tacoma quietly, oh-so-quietly, on instinct, because you don't belong here. Overnight, the essential architecture of your life, the lives of the other people in the picture, reinforce the sheer inconvenience of your stubborn existence. These "on" weekends, which can only smack of compulsory sessions to your child. But he's still your child. Your son. Miles. And you love him. And so you submit to the new dispensation. And would submit to humiliation far worse. And so you're here . . .

"Snapper was tasty, Nathan." Leon looked small, framed by the oversized doorway. He balanced a coffee mug in his hand. Nervously, it seemed. "Come on in."

Nathan lingered at the threshold, his eyes fixed on the too-or-nate mezuzah, the nervous coffee mug. "Yep, it's a nice fish, Leon. Miles ready?"

Why couldn't Sam answer the fucking door? He wondered. She knew he was coming. Was it too much to ask?

"Miles is getting changed, I think. Jeez, Nathan, come in, come in. Samantha wants to talk with you, anyway."

Nathan complied.

Leon pranced on ahead toward the kitchen, sporting his fancy running tee and shorts, cut from the most advanced, moisture-wicking fabric available, no doubt. A matched set. Fancy side-piping bled from short to shirt. The shorts were cut high at the sides. Dolphin shorts, they called them when Nathan was a youngster. Something vaguely effeminate about them. Athletic socks stretched barely above Leon's spotless running shoes. Also girly, it seemed to Nathan. An irksome display, on the whole, this running get-up reinforcing—oddly enough—Leon's countervailing and unignorable maleness.

Nathan took a seat at the granite bar while Leon remained upright in the kitchen proper, affecting awkward proprietorship.

"It's so healthy for you. Fish. Can't eat enough of it, really. We had it last night. On the grill. Just a little olive oil and salt. Much appreciated. Really."

Nathan nodded. He seemed a bit more solicitous than usual, Leon. There were moments when Nathan felt that he could actually be friendly, if not friends, with the fellow. But then he would catch himself thinking, despite himself, that Leon, this affable guy, smart, soft spoken—if somewhat clinically so, psychiatrist that he was—nonetheless had a penis between his legs, a naked tumescent member, of modest size

Nathan would bet, but a penis all the same, a penis which surely entered Sam to her disciplined delight with yeomanlike regularity. He was a marathon runner. Trim and fit. His countenance, the most handsome incarnation of Levantine, the type easily mistaken for Italian, Greek, or some other swarthy Mediterranean type. Nathan took some solace in Leon's retreating hairline (dark wisps conscientiously combed forward where a side-part otherwise would have been visible), yet hadn't he read something about baldness and escalated testosterone? Plus, as a doctor, Leon enjoyed easy access to those medications, which purported to furnish powerful long-lasting erections on demand. Manny, a surfeit of nubile women to please, made no bones about Viagra's recreational benefits. Nathan wouldn't put it past Leon to self-medicate for recreational purposes. He was vain, Leon. His weakness.

Sam's a middle-aged woman! Nathan felt like exclaiming right there in the kitchen, courting the absurd chivalry that clothed his envy. Don't get any ideas, buster!

Leon cleared his throat, as if preparing to say something significant. "Well, I was just leaving," he uttered, instead. He downed the last of his coffee and set his mug on the granite bar with a *clink*. "Have a good swim. Better you than me." Leon snatched up his keys, his fancy smartphone. "Do me a favor and tell Samantha I went to the gym?"

Nathan nodded. "Sure."

At least Leon didn't call her Sam. Nathan liked to think that there was something deferential about this. Mensch-like. Still, it was an odd, abrupt exit.

He sat there alone at the granite bar, waiting for Sam, or Miles, to make an appearance. The home seemed lifeless. All high space and hard surface. The original artwork all about–canvases set at perfect right angles framing abstract brushstrokes in subdued hues–scarcely warmed up the place. Miles should have a dog by now, Nathan thought. Or some other pet. His son had loved his hamster, Honey-mustard. The rodent had died after only a year or so, stupidly obstructing its innards by swallowing its bedding material, and hadn't been replaced. Were Nathan still the paterfamilias, he'd have gotten Miles a dog by now. A beagle. Or lab, maybe. But it was tough to imagine a nonhuman animal puttering about these hard, antiseptic halls.

He heard Sam's efficient steps descending the stair. He could tell by the very cadence of stiff sole on wood stair that she was dressed for the office, even on a Saturday. Freshly showered, no doubt. A light dusting of makeup. A bit of color, not much, gracing her lips. She took advantage of these free Saturdays to bill a few more hours at the firm. Please the partners.

"Well don't you look nice for a Saturday."

"I wish you wouldn't say that."

"Okay, you don't look nice."

"That's not any better."

"Sorry, Sam. I'm doing the best I can here."

"No. No you're not."

He didn't have a response for this.

She was right. It was petty of him, pathetic even, to carry on like this—to cultivate and (worse) broadcast his injury at this late date. Her Saturdays at the firm. She had changed. *That* was the extent of her crime. "You win!" she had answered his charge before their prim marriage counselor. "I changed. Get over it, Nathan. *Life* is change!" Rather than continue working for pennies ad infinitum at the Department of Environmental Protection, she had accepted a job at Kirkpatrick & Rose after Miles was born. A—*gasp!*—corporate litigation firm. Rather than enforce the law, vis-á-vis the environment, she now proffered environmental "consultation" for developers, mining industry executives, citrus farmers, and sugarcane growers. You couldn't always do exactly what you wanted, she claimed. You had to face facts. Heaven forbid she consider their child's future.

This argument wasn't quite fair, it seemed to Nathan now, taking in the high space and hard surface, the abstract brushstrokes in subdued hues, glancing nervously at the bit of color, not much, gracing Sam's lips. For these changes weren't sacrifices at all for her, were they? Rather, this was who Sam truly was; it only took her some time to figure it out. Were he a bigger man, he'd be downright happy for her. Only he wasn't a bigger man.

Maybe he should have made the larger sacrifice, if it were a question of sacrifice–change along with her, as Sam had implored. Take that job with Terrance and get on with things. Fisherman's hours weren't fathering hours. He wasn't nineteen anymore. Why couldn't he accept the terms everyone else seemed to accept? What made him so special? He might eventually have complied had he ever suspected that she'd actually give him the boot. She showed him. Talk about change! And this was what still rankled. It had been such an outsized move. Wholly disproportionate. Were things really so terrible? Did he beat her? Did he cheat on her? Did he utter so much as a cruel word? It was as if she had set their house ablaze upon spotting a single mouse in the cupboard. Did you give up on a home so easily? Try as he might, it was still difficult for him to accept the notion that they didn't live together anymore simply because she didn't care to live with him anymore and no earthly law required her to do so.

He had never quite grasped the severity of the circumstances. This had been his failing. The whole thing had seemed unreal to him, like theater. *Okay, here's the part when we pretend to argue. When we pretend to see a marriage counselor, who takes great pains to emphasize that marriage is a choice, that slavery is dead. When you pretend to hire a lawyer. When you pretend to ask me to leave. When I pretend to comply.* The truth came slowly, and only settled in after his first solitary meal at his Efficiency. They had argued. They had visited a marriage counselor, who took great pains to emphasize that marriage was a choice, that slavery was dead. Sam had hired an attorney. She had asked him to leave. He left.

"So where's Miles?" Nathan asked now. "Up in his room?"

"I told him I'd call him down in a minute."

Nathan stopped breathing.

"Listen, there's no good way to say this so I'm just going to say it."

She said it.

Nathan nodded his head. He started breathing again. But he didn't say anything. What was there to say?

"I knew you'd be upset."

"I'm not upset."

"Okay. That's good." Sam looked at him, worriedly, as if he were a hastily constructed Lego tower that might topple over at any moment.

"I'm not surprised." She nodded now, slowly, wondering, Nathan knew, whether not-surprised replaced not-upset.

"We would have waited, Nathan. I wanted to wait. It's soon, I know. But I'm not getting any younger. And the risks. . . . You can't always do what you want."

"I know, Sam. I know." *You can't always do what you want.* Did she mean to bruise him with this remark? Was she aware that she had retrieved her familiar scold? Probably not. She wasn't cruel, Sam. Things would be easier if she were. The only vitriol she ever ventured was to call him emotionally abusive during one of their therapy sessions while their counselor nodded, pensively. Refusing to accede to your wife's essential wishes and not shouting about it, Nathan gathered, now qualified as emotional abuse. He wanted to be over Sam, completely, yet he feared that he just wasn't the type of person who got over things. Even now, hearing this news, he knew that over was probably beside the point.

"Congratulations, Sam. Really."

**

It wasn't that Miles smelled bad. Not exactly. Nathan wouldn't describe the odor permeating the truck's interior as bad. Musty was more like it. *That hair!* Miles washed his dreads regularly, he claimed. So maybe puberty was the culprit, these hormones run amok, broadcasting Miles' sudden maleness through every pore. Nathan, in any case, knew enough to keep his mouth shut about the ripe odors emanating from his child. There was a more pressing matter to pursue. Not Sam's pregnancy. He wasn't even certain whether Sam had told Miles yet. He had forgotten to inquire. In any case, he couldn't imagine raising this issue with Miles. Not yet. There was that other matter, though, one that he wouldn't broach head on. There was something feline about kids, especially adolescents. You had to come in at an angle.

"So school's fine?" Nathan asked once they were headed eastward on Palmetto. Miles' grades, Nathan knew, were strong, and would always be strong. Effortlessly so, which should have pleased Nathan, but didn't. It left him with so little leverage. *School's fine?* was just something to say. A harmless prologue.

Miles didn't answer. Not exactly. Rather, he turned in the truck to face his father, tilted his head and exhaled audibly through his mouth, a gesture more dramatic on account of his red hair ropes slithering behind the seat-back. The wordless response told Nathan that his son knew that his father knew that there was something feline about children, that you couldn't approach them head-on, that you had to come in at an angle, and that he wished his father would just cut to the chase.

"There is, actually, something we should talk about, Miles."

The road was the best place for raising such matters with his son. No pressure on either one of them to make eye contact–the traffic, the roadside strip-malls and advertisements, the occasional pedestrian or swooping bird. Welcome distractions, all. Nathan even left the radio on low, the bass vibrations (Miles had selected his pre-set hip-hop station before putting on his seatbelt) thrumming through the upholstery.

Miles fiddled now with the air-conditioning vent at the dash, his pouty mouth agape, flicked the plastic screen up and down, up and down, up and down, up and down. The careless flicking annoyed Nathan. *If he breaks that vent, goddamnit!* Annoyed him too much, he feared. There was bit of Morton, a bit of his father and his brother, Jake, in Nathan. He felt their influence during these small angry moments and recoiled. Checked himself.

"F'it's about swimming, dads," Miles finally uttered, "the breathing thing, I wish you'd all just step back. You don't have–"

"Huh . . . what? It's not about that, Miles." Nathan didn't know about the "breathing thing." That it was a topic of concern, anyway. This stung, but Nathan put it out of his mind for the moment.

"It's about your Torah speech. I read your draft. Mom gave it to me. I mean, it's well written, of course. But what you want to say about the Passover story. The Egyptians. Moses."

"Yeah. So."

"I don't know, Miles. You might want to think about your audience a bit. Moses, an original gangster?"

"Gangster?" Miles constricted his voice, overemphasized the

"r" to mimic his father. "You sound like a dweeb, dads."

"Dweeb?" Nathan turned to his son and smiled. Miles laughed.

"Yeah. A dweeb. It's gangsta', not"–again, Miles affected dweebishness–"gangster." They both laughed now, which emboldened Nathan.

"Okay. Gangsta'. But you don't really believe all that stuff, do you? Moses being black."

"Sure 'nough. Think about it dads. The Egyptians came from Ham, who was black, so they're black too, word? Moses passes as Egyptian for forty years or something, so how's he *not* black?"

"Seems kind of sketchy to me, Miles. In terms of evidence."

Why couldn't his son's Bar Mitzvah coincide with a less controversial Torah portion. A story that didn't resonate so strongly in black churches, reinforcing Miles' predilections. A harmless story. The binding of Isaac, maybe. Noah's flood. David and Goliath. Sodom and Gomorrah.

"I don't see why you gotta make a huge thing out of it. It's not like we don't talk about blacks during Passover all the time anyway. It's right in the haggadah, all that civil rights stuff. I'm just puttin' it out there a bit more. I bet Terrance and them'll like it."

"You know, Miles, I think Mr. Stillwater's okay with Moses just being plain-old Jewish."

This silenced Miles, who glanced out his side window at the sterile strip-mall scenery, banishing Nathan from his field of view, making Nathan feel shitty.

"Listen, kiddo, I want you to say what you want to say. Really. So does your mother. It's your speech."

He had struck just the right chord here. Supportive. Generous. Conciliatory. Miles, as if to reward his father, turned his liquid eyes back to look out the windshield.

**

The two red-headed Prays stood before the swells while they gathered their goggles and wet-suits from the mesh scuba bag. Their twin shadows rippled northwesterly across the sand. Miles' shadow stretched nearly as far as Nathan's. He wouldn't be short, thankfully. Nathan, glancing upward from their shadows, stole sideward glances at his son while they suited up. Nathan had been a late bloomer–his ego suffering some from this lateness–so he was pleased to notice the hardier follicles of ginger hair now dappling his son's legs, the mossy trail southward from Miles' navel. The muscle squares just above betrayed some complex combination of strength and skinniness. Miles was lean, except for his broad, freckled shoulders and those strange muscles jutting from his back like wings. Lats, Nathan thought they were called. Swimming had marked his body. Productively so. Fishing, by contrast, had only imbued Nathan with mottled hands and peculiar, outsized calves.

"What!?" Miles had noticed his father's noticing. Heaven forbid he look at his son's body.

"Nothing. Sorry." He turned toward the sea. The water was winter-rough. Nathan glanced back toward the wooden lifeguard station, thankful to see a muscled attendant leaning over his watch. When he turned again toward the ocean, Miles had already tied his dreads behind his head with what looked like a broad, dingy rubber band.

"You should wear flippers," Miles declared, as if he had read Nathan's thoughts about the rough ocean. He crouched, reached into the bag, then tossed them toward his father.

"Steady?"

"Huh?"

"That okay?" Miles clarified.

"Yeah. Sure. So you're not wearing flippers too?"

"Nah. Don't need 'em. I'm just working on form today. Breath control." Miles brandished a snorkel to emphasize his point. Nathan wondered whether his son was being easy on him, not wearing his flippers. He decided that he was.

"You fit'na use a snorkel too, dads?"

"No way. I can't breathe through that thing."

Miles nodded.

"Shall we get this over with?" Nathan, scanning the sand for beached man-o'-war, took a few cautious steps toward the water and reached the ridge above the damp tideline.

"Le's just sit up here for a sec. Chill." Miles sat, lifting bony knees to hold up his elbows. "Waves rippin' some. Best study the swells." Nathan joined his son. The south wind from Miami shouted in his ear.

"You know your great-grandfather, Morton, he died before you were born, he used to swim in the ocean down in Miami Beach. Pretty much every morning, I think. It was usually calmer down there."

"Word?" Miles seemed impressed.

"He'd take me with him when I stayed over weekends." Morton's fierce love. His outsized everything, Nathan thought. "It wasn't really swimming, I guess. More like floating."

Miles nodded, less impressed. A weary exhale escaped his nostrils. Sadly, Miles showed little interest in these ancient days of the Prays, which must have seemed impossibly remote to him. Morton might as well have been Moses, Miami Beach ("*Your*-ami," Miles intoned, when he was just learning to speak) a distant Mediterranean shore. There was something forgivably or unforgivably American, maybe, in all this. It was a nation of the here and now. Who had time for there and then? An amnesiac nation, America. Or maybe it was just adolescence. Maybe Nathan only had to wait Miles out a few years.

It was tough to be patient, though, when he felt his son slipping . . . slipping . . . somewhere. An overarching anxiety defined his most recent feelings when it came to Miles. Urgency. Like now. Nathan wanted to tell his son more about his great-grandfather. That Morton stitched a double-pleat at Pray Clothiers, that he smoked fat green cigars and placed the red paper ring on Nathan's finger on their Miami Beach walks, that he bathed Nathan's fishy hands in astringent lemon juice torrents, that Morton was the one who taught him that crinkly paper worm trick (*remember Miles?*) with the straw wrapper and soda droplet. But he wanted Miles to tease out these stories. Otherwise, it would just be another lecture, another provocation for one of Miles' insufferable exhales. Morton deserved better. So did Miles. Oh well.

"Here we go," Miles finally uttered, striding ahead toward the water. Nathan, wearing his flippers, shuffled backward toward the water's edge. Miles, unencumbered by flippers, stomped right in and performed an arcing dive beneath the depths, his hands interlocked before him, the whole display a bit show-offy, which Nathan found endearing. He remembered what it was like to be an adolescent among grownups, that urge to perform the dramatic gesture. Miles' head emerged from the chop like a curious seal, waiting for his father ("One second, Miles!"), his dreads impervious to the submersion. The water was cold against Nathan's exposed calves. He gritted his teeth. Some of the captains enjoyed swimming in the ocean. Manny sometimes snorkeled to locate snook. Well, bully for him! Once he reached thigh-high ocean, Nathan half-assedly collapsed backward into the chill. The wetsuit would be helpful once they got started, Nathan knew, but he hated these first moments of immersion, the cold water slowly seeping through the neoprene.

"Graceful," Miles teased.

"Listen, boychik. Just go on ahead. I'll follow." Old, too, he tended to sound with his son. Old and white and Jewish.

Nathan righted himself, chest down now, and lowered his own face and curls beneath the water. The cold that had seeped through the wetsuit had started to warm. A relief. He felt his mood improve. Fluttering his flippers (quite an advantage!), Nathan reached his son's side, holding his breath to observe Miles' first few strokes through the cloudy current. There was something Miles did with his arms, something mysterious, a curious S design beside his torso. Real swimmers knew things about swimming that normal people didn't know, as if these real swimmers were part of some secret guild. Like the Masons. The freestyle stroke was so curious that Nathan neglected to breathe for too long while he watched Miles underneath. He lurched his head from the water, finally, gasping for air, lowered his flippers (which he probably shouldn't have done) to tread water while he caught his breath. He struggled some to figure out the coordination with his flipper-feet, and to keep his head above the chop. A glance shoreward revealed that they were farther at sea than Nathan thought, and Miles was suddenly five or six lengths ahead. He seemed to be taking careful, deliberate strokes, his elbows above the water arcing toward high, practiced angles, his small feet gurgling at the surface. Nathan, with no such grace, tore through the rippled surface to catch up. It shouldn't be so hard with flippers, he thought, laboring to breathe upon each stroke, swinging his head to the right, to the left, to the right, to the left. He wondered whether the snorkel offered Miles an advantage that rivaled his flippers. He didn't think so. There was so little air to be had through the tiny pipe. Breath control, Miles had said. The snorkel trained his lungs to work on less, not more, oxygen.

He finally caught up with his son, swam past him to the outside with the help of the flippers. They swam on, northward, mostly side by side for several minutes, until Miles tapped Nathan's side.

"Can I show you a few things?"

"Yeah. Sure, Miles." This was strange. Miles had never offered to show Nathan a few things.

"You don't get a prize for taking the most strokes, dads. Idea is to make every stroke count. Go slower. You gotta go slow to go fast."

"Okay," Nathan spat above the chop. He struggled more than Miles to keep afloat. Why was it so effortless for Miles to tread water? He didn't even seem to use his hands, gesturing freely with them above the chop during his instruction.

"And you gotta control your breathing, dads. You're just wastin' energy swinging your head back and forth like a spaz. Put your head all the way down and try breathing every third stroke, steady? Once you get in shape, you extend to every four strokes, then five, then six. That's the only reason I win. Breath control."

"Okay."

"Go ahead. Before you tank. I'll watch."

Nathan swam on ahead. Now what was he supposed to do? It was such a struggle just to keep his head above the chop while they treaded water. It was hard to pay attention. Slow to go fast. Fewer strokes. Head down. A breath every . . . third stroke? What stroke was he on? Disoriented, he turned his head to breathe and swallowed a mouthful of salty chop, but managed somehow to expel the water, keeping his head to the side while his flippers kept him horizontal. Okay, again. Head down. Slow stroke. Third stroke. Breathe. He felt weariness setting in, the first hint of a cramp, too, tugging at the arch of his right foot. He should have stretched. Stupid! He couldn't seem to inhale enough oxygen every third stroke, so began breathing every second stroke and labored to draw air. He was about to stop, call it quits (*sorry, Miles*), when he felt a light tap at his ribs. He lowered his legs and lifted his head from the water.

"Head in?" Miles suggested.

"Sure. If *you* want to."

Reaching shore, Miles strode out onto the sand, seamlessly shifting from stroke to stride like some instantaneously-evolving creature, while Nathan, encumbered by flippers, fairly beached himself in the foam. He reached down to remove the sudden impediments and rose on impossibly heavy legs to collapse beside Miles. He rolled and lay prostrate on his back, his chest heaving. Was it possible he was so depleted?

"Sorry, dads."

Nathan rolled away from Miles and hacked up a curious admixture of phlegm, saliva, and saltwater, a shameful thread dripping from his mouth to the sand. He wiped it away. "It's okay. It's okay. I'm fine," he assured his son, lifting a hand to reinforce his point, gasping for air, still coughing between his inhalations.

Nathan sat up and coughed once more, less violently, while Miles hid a smile against his shoulder. Nathan supposed it was funny, this brave face while he coughed up a lung.

"Okay, dads, if I swim back?"

"Uh, sure. I guess. Stay shallow."

And so Miles slipped back beneath the foamy chop while

Nathan, shivering some in his wetsuit, walked alongside on shore, just yards away. He sure was fast, Miles, without seeming fast, somehow. Slow to go fast. It made odd sense. A gannet skimmed the surface a hundred yards or so beyond Miles, looking even slower, going even faster.

"You sure clear a lot of water," he greeted his son back at their starting point, wrapping a towel around his oversized shoulders. Miles lifted an index finger to stopper a single nostril, expelling the contents of his open sinus onto the wet sand, then completed the identical exercise with the other nostril, the other index finger. This seemed theatrical too, like his son's earlier arcing dive. Was that all we were, a collection of performances and imitative gestures, this whole life business one big show? It was tough to know what was real anymore. When it came to people.

"You don't want to clear water, dads," Miles uttered, crouching to shove his goggles and snorkel into the scuba bag. Miles' tone wasn't petulant, but instructive. Patient. "You wanna be smooth."

"Oh. Well then, you're smooth. I just meant that you were fast, really. Efficient."

"No worries."

**

"So Whale's Rib?" Nathan inquired back in the truck, meandering southward on the A1A.

"Sure."

It killed Nathan to pay money for a fish sandwich, but his son had always liked this restaurant by the pier, preferred its pricey lobster roll and fried clam bellies to the medio pollo grill and ropa vieja at the Caribbean Café.

Miles twisted the volume up higher on the radio dial. Instead of rap music, a commercial–something related to credit-card debt–blessedly resounded.

Nathan cleared his throat before his next utterance.

"You'll stay tonight, Miles?"

Silence. He was old enough, Miles, that roughing it on his father's foldout didn't seem like an adventure to him, but just sort of stupid. His bedroom just minutes away at his new house was practically as large as Nathan's apartment. Plus there was cable. And his music. And his manifold electronic devices. So much stuff, these days!

"What if I don't stay, dads? You'd have something to do?" Miles finally uttered.

"Well, sure. I'd probably head out, scout the ICW for snook."

Miles nodded.

"You could come too you know. If you want to. Shrimp might be running. I can take you home later."

Netting shrimp during their sporadic runs had always entertained Miles, but Nathan probably shouldn't have said anything about it. He couldn't guarantee the shrimp run tonight.

"I don't know, dads." Miles sighed.

"Or we can forget the boat. Go to a movie or something, instead. Fine by me."

"Together?"

Silence.

"What would you do, Miles, if I took you home? And you sure it's okay with mom?"

"Might go to the movies with Devon and the crew. Mom'd drop me off. Pick me up. It's chill with her."

Nathan nodded. He supposed it wasn't so unusual that his twelve-year-old didn't want to be seen in public at a movie with his father. It was normal, maybe. Since the divorce, Nathan found himself laboring to locate normal. It was just so difficult to navigate his son's adolescence, regardless of complicating variables, that he often didn't know which way was up. So maybe this was okay, that they both knew that the other had something to do tonight, even if they wouldn't be doing this something together. Like most nights. And most days.

Or maybe it wasn't okay.

Will you remember me in a year? Miles' strangest knock-knock joke began. Nathan remembered the precise moment his son told it to him, tugging his palm on their short walk from J. C. Mitchell, stirring his ocean-weary father toward greater wakefulness.

Yes, Miles. I'll remember you in a year.

Will you remember me in 5 years?

Of course.

Will you remember me in 20 years?

Mmm-hmm.

100 years?

Absolutely, Miles.

Knock, knock.

Who's there?

You forgot me already?!

**

Joe watched the boats from his balcony. It was Saturday, because there were so many of them, bobbing over the chop, leaving a white fizz wake. And because the puzzle was so difficult. The bitch-mother crossword, Saturday. They all seemed to head north for some reason. What was so great up north? He'd have to ask Nathan. ____ *legomenon (word or phrase used only once in a document or corpus)* What the fuck?! His former daughter-in-law would probably know. Was Nathan out today? Too big, that boat. That one too. Probably not. If he knew the least bit about his son–pretty much the case–Nathan would avoid crowded weekend waters. Why did he pilot such a small ship? It wasn't money. There was another reason, something Nathan had explained, but he couldn't recall. This wasn't the illness. This not recalling. You couldn't remember everything. And thank goodness for that! Baruch Hashem, as his father would say. Still sharp as a goddamn tack. Mostly. *Mathematician _____ Henrik Abel?* Niels. N-I-E-L-S. Take that! Just distracted. Distracted sometimes. Was that any reason for Alan to throw him under the bus during the depo? What could you expect from an anesthesiologist? Prima donnas, the lot of them. Worse than ophthalmologists. A red hull. The *Pray Fish* had a red hull. Nathan was probably with Miles today. Too bad his grandson didn't like to fish. Too bad for Nathan. The boychik couldn't catch a break.

Chapter Three

A vacated feel to the ramp so close to midnight. The rattle of Nathan's trailer against the weathered asphalt shattered the silence. He pulled the *Pray Fish* around in a great ear-shaped arc along the one-way. Only Charlie and Nguyen were here, Nguyen aboard his Dusky with a hose, washing off the ocean, talking with Charlie who stood below on the ground, getting the skinny on the current, most likely. An archipelago of murky puddles from hoses at the wash-down betrayed the recent human traffic along with the fetid trash about, the rubber garbage bin having over-brimmed hours ago, apparently. The detritus of the weekend warrior crowd fanned out from its vortex: quivering bladders of melted ice sacks, ripped cardboard shreds from chum and bait boxes, dented beer cans, mostly cheap American light varieties.

Feral cats and street-people now poked their heads out here and there. They skulked around mostly invisible, both human and nonhuman persons making a go of it beneath the bascule bridge and picnic tables, along the crusty stand of sabal palms, and aside the dimly lit restrooms. During winter nights when Nathan was on the water, a veritable cat pride slept under his vehicle, savoring the engine warmth, their acrid piss stench wafting up to infiltrate the vinyl interior.

He pulled up in the on-deck lane next to the Little Carlos and hopped out of his too-small truck.

"What's the good word, gentlemen?"

"Mutto'," Charlie declared. "Mutto' bitin' goo', mah'."

Charlie's native language was English. It was the only language he spoke. Yet his dialect was so strongly inflected that it was difficult for Nathan to understand him. He tended to accent the most unlikely syllables and dropped altogether the last beat of pretty much every word. He uttered hard "t's" in places where Nathan expected a proper "th" sound. Nathan wondered how much of Charlie's speech to chalk up to his particular origins in some former British colony backwater (Trinidad? Guyana?), and how much was simply unique to Charlie.

"Mutton, eh? How deep?"

"Hun'red twent-, t'irty fee-. Live pilcha- o' t'e botto'. Brough 'em righ' up."

"Kingfish too," Nguyen called down more intelligibly from atop the Dusky, wearing a once-white V-neck undershirt, his exposed flesh fatty and impervious to the cold.

It was a tough game for small-boat captains, hook-and-line guys, the commercial harvest. Most relied on something else on the side to scrape together a living. Or they had a working spouse. Charlie lined swimming pools with whatever newfangled epoxies they lined swimming pools with these days. Nguyen had the working spouse. Fishing was hard. And so it had taken several years to merit such daily catch disclosures from Charlie and Nguyen. But the pair–both about fifteen years older than Nathan–had long ago let their guard down with their junior captain, divulged honey holes here and there. They had known him for near eighteen years now and also knew that he was mostly an inshore charter captain, that he only got out two or three times a week (and hardly at all during daylight hours), that he chummed lightly and tended to stay on the second reef, around 75 feet or so, and that he pretty much left their prized kings, muttons, mahi, and wahoo alone, favoring the nighttime yellowtail and mangrove harvest.

"One smokah. Heah. Look." Nguyen thrust his hose nozzle in a rod-holder in the gunwale and reached toward the deck, disappearing for a moment. He reemerged cradling a monster kingfish just above his paunch. Fifty pounds or so, Nathan figured.

"Forty-five pound," Nguyen declared. "Twelve more small ones too. All ovah place." Nguyen looked down about his feet. "No fit in coolahs."

At two fifty a pound, not a bad take, Nathan thought. He congratulated Nguyen on his catch.

"Little bit too rough your boat. Three to five. Inlet okay. Wheah you pa'tner?"

"Home. I guess. But it don't matter." Nathan heard his conjugations shift to the current frequency. "I think I'm just staying inside tonight. Scout for snook."

"T'ey go' fro- hea', mah'," Charlie declared, stroking his wispy black mustache.

"You need new boat, my friend," Nguyen said. "Cheapah boat maybe. But bigga boat. Then you be big man. Like me. Like Charlie. King of sea." Nguyen flexed both biceps, jutting his lower teeth. Clearly he was pleased with his kingfish. "No make no money on only snappa', my friend."

Nathan considered his rent, his dwindling savings, his manifold insurance premiums and licensing fees, his taxes, his child support.

"I know," he said.

Nathan left Charlie and Nguyen to throw his cast net under the bridge for a few pilchards, greenies, glass minnows . . . whatever. He wasn't above using live bait for scouting purposes. Commercial catch purposes, too, odd days anymore when there were livies to be had in the inlet. Throwing a wrap of his ten-footer over his shoulder as if it were a tallit and he were in synagogue, he crept stealthily toward the seawall edge under the ochre bridge lights. He made a conscious decision not to ponder the feline or human origins of the piss stench as he dodged crumpled beer cans, faded foil wrappers of god knew what, and plastic grocery bags, which lay about like leaf litter. The net's maw opened upon his command, the leadline pelting the waterway in rhythmic *tat-tat-tat-tat's*, mimicking the sudden onset of a downpour. He let the net sink toward the bottom, under the bridge light's beam, then pulled sharply to secure his catch. *Ahhh.* A productive take. The mixed whitebait quivered and gleamed beneath the bridge light as he retrieved the bounty and dropped the leadlines into his bucket. He wouldn't need a second throw.

His livewell full, Nathan lowered the *Pray Fish* into the drink while Charlie lowered the Little Carlos, while victorious Nguyen drove off in his dripping vessel. Charlie rushed off the ramp fast after parking his truck, offering Nathan a dark palm. Charlie and Nguyen often fished solo clear out in the gulf stream. No life jackets. Rough seas to boot. Nathan pulled the skiff out into the ICW more deliberately, sighing. He'd been sighing a lot lately. Probably not a good thing. He was too young a man for these long sighs. He reached into his front dungaree pocket and fingered the rectangular card, Wolf's card, making sure of its presence. ULEE'S BAITS. And when might Chip Holiday make his appearance at the café or at the dock? Nathan wondered.

The water was high and thick and still as he made his way southward. Slack tide. Not a prized time for inshore fisherman, the baitfish inert wherever they happened to be, their predators–jack crevalle and tarpon schools, sole barracudas, Nathan's snook–laying low too, preserving precious calories. But there was magic in these slack tides each day, Nathan's accustomed earth stock still for the briefest moment, holding its breath, figuring out what it wanted to do, *if* it wanted to do. Then, finally, breathing once again, stirring from its slumber, taking small steps, then larger steps, then stomping like a giant out toward the sea or in toward land, ushering great life to and fro in its wake. Nathan felt his own pulse slow in his throat as he puttered along the no-wake, hugging the shore. He reminded himself to breathe, pulled in a mentho-lated dose of winter air. Setting a slow course, he divided his attention between his bearing and his preparations. He popped a Lemonhead into his mouth, then geared up two of his inshore rods with leader and his wooden plugs–marking the wood type and cellulose dye pattern, the date and the time in his log; he checked his tagging device, the batteries in its transponder. His timing was perfect. The tide would be gathering

itself, exhaling once again by the time he reached the skinny water locales he had in mind. The snook were somewhere. Survivors. Holed up
in some mocha grotto, the dark-stained brew holding more heat. There
were just so many canals to survey. So many mysterious bottoms.

New moon tonight. Dark. Only two sailboats moored in the
lake, their tiny mast lights impersonating the stars beyond. Approaching
the old pink hotel and resort, he could see Charlie's high stern light to
the east, clearing the lake, heading under the high bridge out the inlet toward his mutton and kings. "Tear 'em up, Charlie," Nathan muttered beneath the growl of the Merc. Facing ahead, he saw another stern light,
lower, about two hundred yards off under the small Camino bridge,
which he recognized instantly as Manny's. Or not the light so much as
its distinct spray against the boat's stern and wake, the angle of the mod-
ified panga, *Chasin' Tail* (typical Manny prurience), as it chugged along.
Manny for sure. And then Nathan surprised himself as his mottled hand
lunged toward the console, flicking off his own lights. He knew before
he knew, somehow, that he'd stalk his quarry.

"Now what's Manny doing out here this hour?" He spoke
beneath the Merc now for his own ears. Manny claimed not to scout inshore waters in the wee hours. Waste of fuel and time. "The snookies,"
Manny argued, were either out here at the inlets, bridges and spillways,
or they weren't. No point in chasing after them inside. Nathan would
keep his stealthy distance. What was the kid up to? Something not-quite-
right, he suspected. Was he setting seine nets for mullet and pilchards?
Harvesting and selling baitfish on the down-low? There was something

off about his rival. Sneaky. Not normal fisherman's coyness. But sneaky. Nathan was only too anxious to catch Manny red-handed, not that he had any idea what he'd do if and when he caught him.

He wasn't used to running the skiff at night without lights. It was illegal for one thing. Dangerous for another, especially on such a black night. But it was strange and thrilling too, slipping across the water, invisible. It felt quieter, somehow, even with the Merc running. The air smelled sweeter. The hair on the back of Nathan's neck tingled against the stiff offshore breeze. Nervous, suddenly, Nathan popped three more Lemonheads into his mouth and felt the crunch in his ears as he inched closer to his quarry. He soon found himself drawing too close so pulled the throttle back to neutral and waited. Manny's stern light started to bob some on the mild chop. He had stopped too. What was he doing out there in the middle of the ICW? Taking a piss? Nathan cut the engine so he could hear better. The chop licked his bow. Chimney swifts giggled abovehead, invisible. What the hell were swifts doing here still in December? A hawksbill turtle . . . Now swifts?

Nathan knew Manny was moving again once the stern light stopped bobbing. He nudged the Merc into gear and inched ahead. After a few moments, Manny's starboard light (looking like the color his parents had always assured him was green, the color at the bottom of all stoplights) emerged low and just as quickly disappeared. A second later, the whiter, higher stern light winked and disappeared. Blackness. Manny had turned westward off the ICW, the Chasin' Tail hidden now behind seawall. Nathan tapped the throttle to catch up. He was pretty certain about the canal Manny had taken up ahead, but one more turn before Nathan got there and he'd be gone.

Thankfully, Nathan spotted Manny's stern light just as he arrived at the T. He was going fast now, Manny, too fast for the no-wake. Ghostly yachts beside marbled mansions undulated in their slips, bucked mildly against their restraints. He followed Manny westward toward the El Rio. His rival made detours along the way, in and out of various labyrinthine developments, but, strangely, didn't pause again. This is crazy, he thought, after following Manny for an hour or so, after slipping under the low bridge on 18th, where he and Terrance used to catch small mangroves and snook from the bank with cut shrimp and squid, where mostly black men still caught blue crabs by dipping wire traps baited with raw chicken. He didn't like going this fast inshore, especially as the canals narrowed, as concrete seawall and dredged channels gave way to jutting mangrove, seagrape, and capricious natural bottom. The underused marble estates and yachts yielded to mildewed ranch-style properties and aluminum Jon boats in makeshift slips past the mild rise of Camino Gardens, where the old Africa USA theme park used to be. Nathan inhaled deeply, mustering some patience. Instead of mentholated salt air, he now drew the thicker, sulfurous breath of the mangroves into his lungs and the carbon aromas of someone's backyard fire-pit. He couldn't lose Manny. Not after this hassle.

Only he did lose him. He had taken his eyes off the panga for an instant, only an instant, but it was suddenly gone. Vanished. Like before. Must have turned again. Well, he'd find him. There was a web of canals up ahead to the left, Nathan knew. Manny had certainly entered that neighborhood. He was so sure that he'd see Manny's lights that he gulped a fistful of astonished air upon reaching the blackness. He punched the throttle harder, peering across the blank waterways to the left and right. The red light atop the hospital where Miles was born glowered at him–the hospital built only after the Drummond kids on Camino drank poisoned milk in '62 and expired before they could get them all the way up to Boynton. Nathan took one of the turns at random, looped back around in vain to the main canal, then backtracked to a separate turnoff, which also yielded nothing. Desperate now, Nathan punched out to the El Rio and headed further inshore, closer to the hospital. There was a shallow westward bend up ahead. Perhaps Manny hadn't turned off into a neighborhood, after all, but only disappeared around the bend.

He motored fast, too fast, along the narrow waterway, nearly flying forward over the console as he ran the skiff aground with a *cruuu-unch*. Instinctively, he cut the engine. The tide, apparently, had already receded this far inside. He considered motoring out, but decided against it. Bad for the river bottom. Plus he might damage his prop. Time to get wet. *Fucking perfect!* So much for his surveillance.

He put on a headlamp, took off his dungarees and jumped over the gunwale, making a splash. Deeper than he had thought. He must have run up on a narrow shoal. Just his luck. Here he was, a sneakered and boxered buffoon! A creature stirred in the mangrove and frightened the piss out of him (one of the iguanas infiltrating the area of late? A night heron? A raccoon?). He could only hope there wasn't a water moccasin slithering about in the drink. So distracted was he with his own incompetence as he made his way toward the bow, uttering wicked oaths beneath his breath, thigh-deep in the frigid black canal, that it occurred to him only after he shoved the hull loose, only after he scrambled back atop, panting on his back, gazing up at the stars, that Manny might have been closer all the while than he had realized, that his fellow captain might have simply cut his lights, like he had done, that Manny might have done so having glimpsed and recognized his rival on his tail. As dark a night as it was, the upstart might have been mere yards away. Yes, it was suddenly clear. Manny had known that he was there, perhaps from that first pause in the ICW. Perfect. Just perfect.

He was too addled to settle in and scout for snook now, and had pretty much missed the productive currents of the outgoing, anyway. Lifting the livewell hatch, he dipped his hand-net and set about retrieving and releasing the pilchards, greenies, and minnows into the brackish water. A few dead ones drifted seaward atop the surface, but most darted spastically down toward cover. No fun being a baitfish. Nathan was surprised to notice under his headlamp a small pinfish in his net, its patch behind the gill-covers an inky smudge. Not too many of them left down here along the mostly grassless estuary. Sailor's Choice, the big ones were called. Nathan didn't touch the spiny creature, but lowered the hand-net into the murky water. "Your lucky day, little guy." The pinfish hesitated at the net's lip, distrustful of the gesture. Then, it was gone.

Kati set about filling the napkin dispensers. She had waited for as long as she could. It occurred to her only then, while she told herself that she had waited for as long as she could, that she set aside this task until last each morning so that she might linger at the bar and speak with the redheaded fisherman once he arrived, the fisherman who usually arrived first and looked sort of funny, but not bad funny, and smelled like lemons. He knitted horrible blankets, hats, and scarves. Like a woman. But he wasn't otherwise marica. He sometimes used fancy words she looked up in the English-Spanish dictionary behind the bar after he left. He also used words that the old Jews used, which weren't in the dictionary. But he didn't seem fancy to her. Or Jewish. She thought about this for a moment as she patted the paper napkins into the first dispenser. What did Jewish seem? Old, mostly. And they used those different words for lots of things, too, words that must not have been American words, like nosh and oy and gezuntheit and enoughalready. Different American words they used, too, like Arnold Palmer, which meant they wanted her to mix half a lemonade and half an ice tea. ¡¿Quien putas es Arnold Palmer!? Whoever he was, his drink tasted pretty good. Even Alicia liked it, and she couldn't get Alicia to drink anything, which was why her mierda was sometimes too hard.

Kati wondered what she'd do if Nathaniel asked her out on a date. She hadn't gone out on a date with an American. Not since Hernando left. It still wasn't clear to Kati whether he meant to escape

America, mostly, or escape them—Kati, and her mother, and Alicia. She had slept with two men since Hernando, both Columbians, which wasn't really the same thing as dating, or sleeping either, cogiendo and then not seeing them again, except in the restaurant. It felt good after so long, coger, especially with the first one, Gustavo. He tried very hard to make her happy before giving up and asking her if it was okay if he come, to which she said okay—squished beneath his weight—only after feeling the throb and pulse of his pinga inside, his stronger and pleasing motions. And then it was over. Why was it that it only felt good for those few seconds at the end?

Nathaniel would need lotion for those nasty hands (Crema de Rosas, she would give him), but the rest of him was nice. Even his bump-nose, which made him look like a sad puppy dog. He liked her, she thought. Unlike the other fishermen, he put his napkin and fork back on the plate to make it easy for her to clear, which usually only meant that the man was married, but Nathaniel wasn't married anymore. It would be easy to have his light body on top. Nathaniel wasn't a big man, like Gustavo or Hernando. Smiling vacantly at the metal napkin dispenser, she imagined him between her thighs. She would reach down—was the hair curly and red down there, too?—and grasp his pinga. She felt the perspiration beading atop her lip, her nipples straining against her fortified work bra.

"¡Que puta que sos!" she chastised herself. "Dejá de pensar así." Her English wasn't good enough for an American, even if it must have been better than Nathaniel's Spanish. After three years here, her

English should be better. She should try to find a job at an American restaurant. Denny's, maybe. Where they wouldn't make you pay if you forgot just once to add the Presidente to a customer's bill. There were two Denny's on Federal. One on Palmetto. One on Hillsboro. Ademas, estoy mas comoda aquí. She liked the food here and she could watch her novelas when it was slow. No Univision at Denny's. And the food there? Wacala!

She wondered if the fishermen would come in today. It was already raining and windy. The sea churned beneath the spotlight in cotton waves. So maybe they'd sleep, instead. Kati might be sleeping herself, but she liked the four AM to two shift on weekdays. This way, her mother could walk Alicia to school and Kati was able to meet her at release, spend the afternoon and evening with her niña. And she liked these dark quiet hours, before Maria la gorda arrived and loomed over her. She liked to be alone. And she liked it too when Nathaniel walked in and de repente eramos solo nosotros. Somehow it still seemed they were both alone. Only together.

Kati wiped down the Formica bar with a damp rag. It was something to do. Alicia would love to fish, she thought. Just like Kati had enjoyed fishing when she was a girl and her abuelo took her to catch peacock bass and cichlids and tilapia in the lago. Alicia would love to fish, she thought again. And then she stopped thinking about that, because it was silly. Life was strange. Alicia chattered in English now and was doing good in school. Her daughter had less and less patience with Spanish, had taken to barking at her mid-sentence on their walks home from J. C. Mitchell, "English, mama! English!" Kati never thought she'd be able to live in Florida so long without speaking better English. But here she was.

This was one thing she learned here in America: how little you actually had to speak with other people.

Maybe they weren't sleeping today, after all. Because here was the young one now, coming in out of the dark. Not Nathaniel. But the one called Manny. Behind him, gracias a Dios, was the one called Frank. She didn't like to be alone with that young one no more with the tattoos and sharp white teeth and funny-striped eyebrows, even if Lupe was back there, cooking. ¡Bicho raro! How did they say in English? She didn't trust him as far as she could throw. A couple months ago, he had reached over the bar and patted her bottom (which she barely felt through her constricting support hosiery) when she turned to retrieve his café con leche, and then four choices: murder the baboso—her first impulse—scold him more mildly and see what he do, smile or laugh and see what he do, or pretend she didn't felt the pat and hope he would pretend he never patted. She decided on this last choice and, gracias a Dios, the young fisherman with the tattoos and sharp white teeth and funny-striped eyebrows hadn't patted her bottom again.

She nodded wordlessly at the two fishermen, who nodded back. Frank said, "Morning." She set about preparing their café con leche.

"Usual," Frank said to her back.

"You know what I like," the young one called Manny said, smiling like a baboso she could tell even though her back was still turned. Yes, she knew what he liked. She uttered the orders to Lupe through the pass-through. She was busy slicing open green plantains. Within moments, the others arrived, groaning into their seats, tossing heavy keys and cigarette packages onto the bar. Nathaniel came in last, which was strange. She told him, "Buenos dias," then reddened upon realizing that she hadn't offered the same greeting to the others.

After placing Nathaniel's order with Lupe she tamped out the depleted Café Bustelo grinds in the sink basin from the Rancilio, sliced fresh oranges for the juicer, and ran three stalks of sugarcane through the loud machine. "Well, well, Captain Pray, out past your bedtime last night?" she heard the young one ask. Strange, somehow.

Nathaniel didn't seem to say anything behind her. Maybe he nodded or shook his head. Or said something quiet. It was okay for her to listen, because it was good for her English. And from listening she also learned a lot of interesting things, not just about the sea and fish, not even mostly about that, but about other things, like which politicians should be locked up, where you could buy cheap rental buildings for Mexicans in Lake Worth, the hospital in Pompano you didn't get caught dead in, fucking China, the best medicine for sore hands, the gun rights that could be taken away any day now after the school shooting just a few miles west, the taxes only a tonto paid, and the goddamned federal government. They talked about all sorts of things. Like now, once she returned from taking the order from table 4. She thought they'd talk about the weather, but they weren't talking about the rain pelting the roof now and stopping the sunrise. They were talking about something else, maybe so they wouldn't have to talk about the weather.

"Give you some advice. Forget the shape. Shape's overrated. Weight's the key. Troy and I won that thing five times. You get yourself an iron ladle, a Bunsen burner, then melt down a bunch of old split-shots or egg sinkers. Carve out a circle in the bottom, then pour in the lead."

"Shit no," she heard Manny say. He used bad words a lot, like Frank, the one who wore crisp clothes and baseball hats that said Shimano and Berkley and Costa Del Mar. "No way you pour the lead in the bottom. Hollis, you're just talking out your ass. My dad and me got to states when I was in Webelos. Weight has to be in the back. Far back as you can get it. You drill a hole, Frank, straight through at a cross-section behind the rear axle. Then melt the lead, put it on its side with a nickel at the bottom to stopper it, then pour."

"Won't it shimmy with the lead so far back?"

"Not if you make only one pour. Keep the air bubbles out."

"They're talking about a race called the Pinewood Derby," Nathaniel explained to her. She must have failed to disguise her blank expression. "Para . . . uh . . . coches pequenos," he added in Spanish, holding his mottled hands before his chest about eight inches apart. This was what none of the other captains would think to do. Translate for her.

"Didn't know Jews were in the Boy Scouts, Nate."

"Yeah, Emmanuel. They've been letting us in for the past few years now."

This was what was called sarcasm, Kati thought. In America, everyone could join everything. As long as you had money. This was another thing about the Jews. The money. And the sarcasm. It was funny sometimes. Sarcasm. But not now. Nathaniel didn't usually say sarcasm. She didn't like it from him. And he didn't seem to have much money. His truck was old and small.

"What d'ya say, Del?" Frank asked. "Any pointers? Me and Brian got the derby comin' up next week now."

"Yeah, Del," said Hollis. "You did the derby with your boys back in the day, right?"

Lupe rang the bell and Kati retrieved Nathaniel's plate from the pass through. By the time she returned, Del still hadn't answered. He was nodding his head, instead, sipping his thimble-full of café Cubano.

"Nails," the fat captain finally uttered through his beard. "Nails the secret. Gotta grind down and polish the axle-nails."

**

Kati saw the strange man come in before the captains noticed him. She had just turned from the Rancilio with Nathaniel's fresh tin of scalding water. He seemed like an important man to her right away. Maybe because he was so small (smaller than Nathaniel, she thought) but walked in ahead of the tall man, who seemed to be with him and who looked around the restaurant like he was nervous about something, while the small man didn't look nervous at all.

"Can anyone tell me where I might catch me a sailfish 'round heah!?"

And then they all noticed him. Yes, he was definitely an important person. Because he put one hand on Del's back and one hand

147

on Hollis's back, and no one ever touched them, and they didn't seem to mind, and Manny set his visor down on the bar and touched his crisp hair, and Frank shifted on his stool all the way to face the small man, and Nathaniel took a sip of his tea, even though there wasn't anything left in his taza. "Here, Nathaniel." She stepped to and filled his cup with steaming water from the tin pitcher. He was definitely a fisherman, Kati knew, because his hands were more rough and cracked than Nathaniel's hands, and he had that ugly beard that they all had, except for Nathaniel. Goatee.

"Welcome to our small slice of paradise, my friend," she heard Frank say, opening his arms to show off his Shimano chest. "It may be a bit soggy, but we call it home." He sounded funny, Frank. More loud and like a song. Sort of like Don Francisco from Sabado Gigante, only in English.

"My oh my, as I live and breathe," Hollis said. "What brings you to these parts, Chip? Slumming?"

"Sure did pick a shit day," Manny said. The tall man laughed a little at this.

"Chip," Del said. Then the fat captain cleared his throat, as if he wanted to say something else, but couldn't think of anything so decided to just make a sound.

Nathaniel didn't say anything from the end of the bar. He sipped his weak tea, stabbed the whites of his eggs with his fork. Kati wasn't sure if this was smart or not. She wondered who this small man was. His blue hat said Yamaha. Did he own all the boats?

"That the east coast snookmaster layin' low down theah!?" the small man cried, peering toward Nathaniel.

"Mm-hm," Del said.

"Snookmaster my ass," Manny said.

"Now Manny." Hollis.

"That's our boy Nate!" Frank.

"Hey, Chip." Nathaniel finally said something. Bueno.

"We squeeze in here, cap'ns?"

The small man with the Yamaha hat wanted to sit near Nathaniel. Kati didn't know if this was a good thing. There was a great *clacking* of silverware and ceramic against the Formica as the captains shifted down in their seats, as the small man and the tall man parted Frank and the others from Nathaniel. Del groaned as he rose, and then groaned again as he descended two stools down. Kati handed laminated menus to the two men. They both thanked her, which was nice.

"Now, Nate, you ain't still sore at those boys at Parabola are ya'?"

Nathaniel shrugged, then summoned a stiff smile.

There was something different about the way the small man spoke. He talked funny the way the others did–his cap'ns and ain'ts–but something about the way he used these words told Kati that he knew better words, like Nathaniel.

The restaurant picked up now that it was after six so she couldn't stand behind the bar and listen. The boy at table eight spilled his whole mango shake. The parents gave her the evil eye as she wiped up the mess, as if it was her fault. If they wanted a paper cup and lid they could have said something, yes? Nathaniel seemed to be talking good, though. The important man nodded a lot beneath his Yamaha cap and made listening noises. Sometimes he lifted a short finger and stroked his bristly beard. The other captains said things from time to time, and the small man said things back to them, but he didn't make listening noises for them or lift a short finger to stroke his bristly beard.

"What you got here that we don't have so much south and west is size," she heard the small man say when she set down his plate of huevos and bistec de palomilla. "*If* they're still here."

". . . I've seen at the SnookeRed tourney how you hold 'em by the belly, not the lip, for the photo before release," she heard as she refilled the tall man's café Cubano. "So *that's* why? I'll be a monkey's uncle."

". . . for an artificial man you sex 'em up like no one's business," the small man said as she cleared their plates. This sounded like a compliment, even if she had no idea what sexo had to do with fishing.

And so maybe it was because the small important man talked to Nathaniel more than he talked to the others that Nathaniel lingered at the bar after the small man left, *clinking* his sewing needles . . . *clink, clink, clink* . . . lingered there long after the others left, too, with an absent smile on his face, that he said to her . . . "Nathan."

"Ay, perdón. You don't like Nathaniel?"

"No, Nathaniel's fine."

"So?"

"It's not my name is the thing."

"Oh."

"Maybe, Kati, you and me . . . you know . . . could see each other, sometime, uh . . ."

Her eyes narrowed on their own accord. What did he mean, see each other? They were seeing each other now, weren't they?"

"I'm not talking any funny business." He raised his rough palms, having read her expression. "Honest."

"I have a daughter, Nathaniel. Nathan."

"I know, Kati. I have a son."

"It's not the same thing."

"I know."

"Pues. . . as long as you know."

Next day, the fisherman made his way west, as if he were heading toward a gulf coast tourney with Terrance, trailer and skiff in tow. But he was alone now, unhitched, headed toward Immokalee and the Ulee Baits facility to meet Stephen Wolf, against his better judgment. Chip at the café had offered him a screen test up in Orlando for the Fishing Report. So there was that. But Nathan was curious about Wolf and what he was up to with the baits he'd bragged on the other day out on the water. So here he was on the highway.

Ersatz communities crowded his shoulders well west of Fort Lauderdale. Weston, this newish stuccoed outpost was called. It seemed to take longer and longer to reach the bristling sedge cords on Alligator Alley. By the time he reached the sawgrass–impostor cattails poking up here and there–the undulating expanse seemed tall and pea green under the gunmetal sky. Another rainy day. Shouldn't the high sedge be matted down, brown and brittle this time of year? It wasn't Everglades proper, Nathan reminded himself, but a Water Conservation Area now south of the subsidized cane fields. The Everglades Agricultural Area, they called those cane fields, closer to Lake Okeechobee.

The Water Management District fiercely regulated the flow whatever the season, "wet" or "dry," hewing to certain inscrutable calculations vis-à-vis drinking water supply and suburban flood control. He hoped they knew what they were doing, but it seemed that they usually did the opposite of what the land and sea required, hoarding the water supply in the Lake O when the swamp was parched, precipitating hypersalinity in the Florida Bay, and releasing torrents of water from the lake into the gulf, the Atlantic, and the Glades when the Glades were already waterlogged. The red algal blooms menacing the gulf coast were intensified by these releases of polluted freshwater via the Caloosahatchee River. The outbreaks transformed Florida's sugar-sand beaches into fetid stretches of fishkill, decimated the manatees, dolphins and sea turtles, stung human eyes and seized human throats. A toxic blue-green variant had recently blanketed the canals on the east coast just north of Nathan's fishing zone. Even these innocent-looking cattails along the roadside, Nathan knew, were byproducts of the nitrogen and phosphorus runoff from the livestock industry and Big Sugar, which paid lobbyists, lawyers, and television advertisers millions of dollars annually to deny culpability. Any number of forces threatened the singular splendor of the state and seemed intent upon squeezing Nathan.

Clusters of willow and bay leaned over the roadside canal now. Nathan could see a few isolated hammock stands of mahogany, cypress, and sabal palm in the murky distance. But mostly it was sawgrass, cattail, sawgrass, and more sawgrass as he puttered along too slow in his too small truck. He could see why Napoleon Broward didn't hold much reverence for what must have appeared a vast, soggy, mosquito-ridden landscape, why Broward and his band of white pioneers probably would have dredged the whole woolly middle of the state off the eastern coastal ridge had they the wherewithal, and why Henry Flagler too would have devoured a broad swath of Everglades for his railroad had it been remotely feasible to lay track along the more direct route to Key West through the muck to Cape Sable, then across the Florida Bay to Key West's north shore. Flagler had settled for plan-B when he blazed the more circuitous, island-hopping path.

The traffic was light, as usual, as he neared the Miccosukee and Seminole reservations, where the Indians offered their Billie Swamp safari, Everglades porn for pasty German tourists. Newer cars and trucks occasionally zipped past Nathan on the left as they made haste toward Naples or Fort Meyers. To his right, Nathan noticed the red-shouldered hawks and turkey vultures on fenceposts, their feathers fluffed up to brook this weird winter cold and the spitting sky. No bass boats out today. Kingfishers stood higher than the raptors along the electrical line, peering downward toward the blank canvas of the dark canal. Flocks of boat-tailed grackles, big as crows, skittered about here and there, unperturbed by the gloom.

Sawgrass gradually gave way to dense stands of cypress, swamp apple, royal and sabal palm and isolated thickets of paper-barked melaluca invaders—their seeds sprinkled like pepper from small prop-planes decades ago to help "redeem" the swamp for agriculture—as Nathan approached the Big Cypress National Preserve. Intermittent alligators slithered lazy S's along the managed waterway just over the fencing. They seemed to have it too easy, these alligators. Hardly the case, he knew. Herons and egrets flashed pale along the shoreline and within the canopy, deeper. He spotted a great blue heron perched precariously atop a sloppy cypress, festooned with bromeliad. It seemed odd to him, this enormous gray creature acting like a bird.

Nathan reached the turnoff at last. Left to Everglades City and Chokoloskee, to Ted Smallwood's old trading post, the stomping ground of Edgar "Bloody" Watson back in the day, who built his two-story frame house on an old Indian shell mound halfway up the Chatham River. Nathan felt a mild affinity for the mysterious plume-hunter, alligator-skinner, and erstwhile sugarcane grower. Watson, fair-skinned, blue-eyed, and red-haired, like Nathan, spoke rarely, only softly when the mood struck–again, like Nathan–but was a Scotsman. Snook fishing was still solid out around Watson's Ten Thousand Islands, between the red tides, anyway. This was where Terrance thought he might guide. But this was Blanton's, and Hueston's, and Holiday's home turf. The land of the buzz cut and goatee, generally. The good ol' boys and their confederate flags. A Florida constituency—though not Blanton, Hueston, and Holiday, far as he knew—who decried the "hoax" of global warming during these isolated episodes of cold winter weather. Nathan had no people here.

In any case, he wasn't heading down toward the Ten Thousand Islands today, but northward, toward the interior, toward Ulee Baits and whatever else was up this way. Nathan's inner giant wasn't terrestrial, but ever veered toward the edges–coastline, estuary, reef. He had never ventured up this particular road. He read a yellow warning sign to his left.

DANGER

PANTHER CROSSING

ONLY 30 REMAINING

The 30 was crossed out with dark spray paint, a 29 painted crudely in its place. It was an old sign. The panthers were actually doing somewhat better now hereabouts, thanks to a rewilding effort that involved the release of several female panthers from Texas. Over 100 of them now, last he'd heard. It was nice that one Florida creature was doing better these days, not worse, even if there still weren't enough panthers, or snook, left in the world. He turned left about ten miles up the way at the blighted gas station bearing Spanish advertisements, following Wolf's directions that he'd scribbled on his palm.

The scruffy land turned more managed, agricultural. Orderly orange grove aisles flashed kaleidoscopically by. A black and white bird, all angles and edges, soared abovehead, shifting sharply on its keel. Swallow-tailed kite, Nathan knew. The orange groves abruptly gave way to tomato fields. The fruit must have been ripe, or whatever passed as ripe, as Nathan spotted muddy human packs crouched between the canebrakes, plucking morsels from the vines for Florida and the nation's fast food burritos and burgers, wintertime. Backbreaking labor. These were the people the nation ought to fear? Dilapidated school buses stood nearby each human cluster, looking out of place to Nathan. Reading the directions he scribbled on his palm, he followed what seemed an improbable right-hand turn and drove for miles and miles northward, or roughly northward. Tomato and pepper fields yielded to drier, scruffier land, squat cabbage palm, palmetto and scrub oak. Incongruous herds of skinny cattle stood ass to ass in warming clusters blinking lazy eyes against the drizzle beneath hairy slash pines, which stretched their feathered heads high above the scrub. Nathan never felt frightened out on the Atlantic. Even at night. Even alone. But this patch of interior Florida loomed alien and forbidding. How far out in the hinterland was this Ulee's Baits outfit? He should've stopped for gasoline at the dilapidated station an hour or so back.

Some miles and minutes later, Nathan peered dubiously toward the curious structures 200 yards or so off the main road. Then toward his palm. Then toward the structures again. Could this be it? There was no frontage to speak of, as Wolf had warned. Only two random, pale buildings interrupting the scrubland, end-to-end like railcars. Weeds burst from cracks in the sunbleached macadam off the main road as he drove unimpeded toward the long, low-lying buildings. He had expected some sort of security system, perhaps a stationed guard or the gesture of fencing at the very least. The buildings, as he crept closer, seemed built mostly of rust-stained fiberglass siding hinged by a spindly architecture of metal framing topped by shallow corrugated roofing. Something about the structures suggested poultry to Nathan, but what did he know of poultry?

He parked the truck beside the first of the buildings, relieved to see a few other vehicles on the premises. A silver-bullet semi, the kind used to transport combustible liquids, or maybe milk, hid between the buildings. Otherwise, the place seemed deserted. He had to look about to find a door worth knocking on. It was a short door with a new metal lever handle and lock. Just above the door, he noticed the small video camera, trained on him, much newer than the building itself. He knocked, quietly. After a pause, louder. The rain picked up again, as if in response to his raps on the door. What the hell was he doing out here? He was about to knock again when the door flew open. The blonde dollop. The apple face. Big Wolf, wearing a long white coat and prescription spectacles now, filled the entire frame. All Nathan could see was blackness over Wolf's shoulder. He could tell that his host's squinting eyes hadn't adjusted to the outside light, that he hadn't yet fully recognized his visitor.

"You made it," Wolf finally uttered, as if he were surprised. He offered his frying pan hand for Nathan to shake.

"Here I am." Nathan shook.

"Come in. Come in." The fisherman obeyed. Wolf reached behind Nathan to shut the thin door and suddenly it was pitch black.

"Uhh, Wolf?"

"Don't worry. Here we go." Wolf opened a second door and they were inside a less-dark, but still-dark chamber. The air was hotter and wetter. "Your eyes will adjust!" Wolf shouted above the roar of the filtration motors. Nathan, struggling to see, heard the whir of the motors, the splashing of water nearby. And that ammoniac smell . . .

"Those goddamn chickens!" Wolf cried above the noise. He must have read Nathan's thoughts. "Gone for months! Staying power, eh!? You thought fish smelled bad!"

Nathan nodded. "What is this!?" The noise edited both their utterances to the most essential words.

"What do you think!? Research facility!"

Nathan had expected to see a lure factory, a fluorescent space outfitted with heavy machinery: metal molds, balsa extruders, foil and eye stampers, enclosed paint sprayer stations, conveyer belts, test tanks and the like. Parabola had sent him to their factory in Estonia, which was probably cheaper than sending him all the way to their main plant in China. They had put him on a modest retainer after his back-to-back SnookeRed victories and just as quickly jettisoned him when his silver mullet prototype purportedly failed to perform to expectations. Two years later and *voila*, Nathan noticed his stickbait, overpriced, giving him the fisheye from the rack at 7-Seas Bait and Tackle on Second. It was his silver mullet, for sure, right down to the red bucktail dripping from the rear treble hook, the faux blood trail. Bastards!

Nathan's eyes slowly adjusted. A far corner of the ceiling issued forth bands of filtered illumination (had they hung some sort of cloth?). He saw four circular ponds now, like the ones at the Mote laboratory. They progressed in size down the line. But the last one at the far end was enormous, bigger than the Mote tank, and deeper. He heard a splash in the second pond above the whir of the motors.

"You don't have snook in here!" Nathan stated more than asked.

"We don't!?"

These splashing creatures couldn't be snook. They were fairly hopeless candidates for aquaculture. Even Mote hadn't yet tried to induce spawning in their tanks. They had thus far deployed their aquaculture energies foremost upon the less finicky redfish and seatrout. Stock enhancement research on the snook had just gotten started, and their nascent efforts were proving troublesome, as everyone in the snook working group pretty much expected. Things worked okay up to a point. Using seine nets at spawning passes and inlets along the gulf coast, the researchers managed to collect the frothy milt from the males, the globular eggs from the females, and then released the frisky adults back into the tannic waters. Back at the lab, they brewed the heady milt-egg concoction in seawater and then hatched the eggs in larval tanks. The next stage went smoothly too, as the fingerlings readily enough thrived on zooplankton. The juvenile tanks were a bust, though, as the upstart snook promptly set about cannibalizing each other to oblivion in their confined quarters, forgoing processed pellets. The scientists had considered hormone induction, but once you went down that road . . . What's more, a disproportionate number of survivors suffered from Lordosis, bent-back syndrome. So much for aquaculture. But it was illegal for Wolf's outfit to use seine nets. Nathan tried to keep the heat from rising in his face.

"Seine nets are illegal, Wolf! You know that!"

"Whoa, whoa! Who said seine nets!?"

"How else can–!?"

"How else you think!?"

Nathan considered the darkened room, the curious bands of light, the hot, moist air. "Can't be spawning adults in here!"

"Photothermal manipulation, Nathan! Water temps! Day

length! Lunar cycle! Lunar cycle's key! You know they only spawn couple days before and after new and full–!"

"Yeah, I know! Of course I–"

"Plus depth! Snook like it deep!"

Nathan couldn't tell if Wolf meant to sound like a lewd bumper-sticker.

"Dumbasses at Mote been dragging heels! Got our Israelis on it! We're already there!"

"Israelis!?" Nathan shouted, bemused.

"You know what they say! Bomb! Computer! Tomato! Get Israel on it!"

"People say that!? Who says that!?"

Wolf shrugged, leading Nathan to the large tank. There was no floor to speak of. Just dirt. "Filtration system set to simulate tides!" Wolf shouted over the motor, which grew even more deafening as they neared the tank. "Really whirring now, eh!? High tide in Sweetwater!"

"Sweetwater!?"

"Closest town! We're not too far from Sarasota! Truck in fresh saltwater from outside any red tide zone every few months! Treat it in the spartina tank! Other than that, totally self-contained!"

They climbed four metal stairs to stand on the small platform over the tank. Through the dark skin of the surface, Nathan could see the even darker silhouettes of ten or so creatures, undulating at the bottom to remain in place. Snook. No doubt about. Every fish had its distinct silhouette, the sleek but thick-shouldered snook, included. It's why their fillets held such ample, succulent meat. The shoulders.

"See them in there, don't you!?"

Nathan nodded. He didn't quite know what to think. Or say.

"Damn, those eyes! Would've been great fighter pilot! Or baseball player!"

"Seems like lot of trouble!" he cried, ignoring Wolf's comment. "For a bait outfit!"

"Let's go outside!" Wolf pointed to his ear, half-hidden by his blonde shell. They headed outdoors. It had stopped raining and was impossibly bright. "I'll take you to the next building!" Wolf shouted, before realizing that he needn't shout any longer.

"You know, Nathan," Wolf located the proper volume as they walked, "we run a seven billion dollar trade deficit in fish and seafood every year."

"Who's we?"

"America. Who do you think, Nathan? See, bait's only part of the story here. We'll take that over, easy enough, but the big prize is full-scale commercial aquaculture. Not that redfish crap, either." Wolf paused and spread his arms, showcasing the scrub. "Right here where we stand after a few years. Just working on investors. Permits'll come easy enough once we grease the wheels."

Nathan agreed with Wolf on the redfish, anyway. Red drum was horribly bland as far as fish went. Had the crusty Cajuns not come up with their proprietary blends, the bull-headed creatures would be doing a heck of a lot better in the wild.

"Now snook. Mmm-mmm!" Wolf smacked his lips, salaciously. "Imagine it, Nathan. Fresh farm-raised snook available at the grocery year-round. Like salmon. Just ten bucks a pound."

Nathan thought about it and didn't like it as they reached the door of the identical second building. He'd wrapped his head around the necessity for restocking the fishery at some point down the line. Maybe. But he hadn't connected the dots toward this likely endgame.

Part of him, he realized, was glad that the snook stocks had plummeted in the 50s, which forced the government to shut down the commercial fishery. Most people would never taste a snook and this was a good thing. There weren't enough wild things in the world. What was the salmon now but a poor emasculated creature. Even half of the so-called "wild" stock in the Pacific was hatchery-born, escapees. Salmon was something you picked up at the grocery, nestled on the shopping list between the butter and bananas. As for the farmed salmon, it was unsustainable, pounds upon pounds of pulverized menhaden, sardines, and anchovies necessary to fatten one salmon. Plus, those coddled creatures tasted like crap.

Would Nathan's snook suffer a similar fate? Once you farmed a creature, it lost more than just its flavor. It lost its very . . . creatureliness. You just couldn't segregate farmed from wild. Surely not from the imagination. There was something grand about the undomesticated, wild snook. Untamed, because untamable! He admired their recalcitrance, their unfathomable snookness. Had Wolf's scientists figured them out? Nathan hoped not. He felt the heat rise in his face.

"You know, Wolf, maybe you and your scientists should just stick with the fake tilapia and leave the snook alone."

Wolf was about to open the door to the second building, but removed his large hand from the handle. "You act like we're some sort of interlopers or something, Nathan."

By *we're*, Wolf meant Jews, Nathan realized, even though this wasn't what irked Nathan about Wolf or his scientists. At least he didn't think so.

"It's our state as much as anyone's," Wolf continued. "Where do you think the name Ulee comes from?"

"Good Florida name. I'll give you that."

"So the name Ulee Levy means nothing to you. That it?"

Nathan shrugged.

"And Moses Elias Levy? Nothing?"

Nathan shrugged again.

"You think Meyer Lansky was our original Florida Hebe? Moses Levy was here first, before most anyone. Fled Jew-hating Europe and settled the sticks in Gainesville in the early 1800s, before it even was Gainesville. Before it was even Florida! Set up Pilgrimage Plantation, a farming village for other European Jewish refugees." Wolf's apple face shined red. "His son, Ulee–yes, a Jew named Ulee–fought the blue-bloods up north to make Florida a state. That fucker John Quincy Adams called him an alien Jew delegate–don't read about that in the history books do you?–but that didn't stop our Ulee. State's first senator, Nathan. First goddamned senator a member of the tribe. Name like

Ulee. What do you think of that?"

Nathan thought . . .

Chuck. Short for Charles. A good Texas name, Chaim thought on deck, squinting against the sun. The heat. No mountains or clouds to impede its broiling efforts. He could see the impossibly flat, scruffy Texas coast now. Word traveled fast below deck. Shipmates soon crowded him at the elbows. Jews. But not only Jews. Many prayed to strange Gods, elbows on the rail, heads buried in the blades of reverent hands. Chaim wouldn't pray. He prayed in Mezolaboricz. He needn't pray in America. He needed a last name. A good American name. Schuss wouldn't do. He glanced at his reverent shipmates. He grinned a devilish grin.

Maybe, Nathan thought.

"Look around, Nathan," Wolf jolted him from his reverie. Nathan followed his gaze across the combs of palmetto, the dusty oaks crusted with bromeliads, the alien bramble. "This has been our desert to claim well before Flagler and his cronies colonized the place. You can stop skulking around."

"I don't skulk around."

"Sure you do. And you don't even know it. That's the problem, Nathan. Our disease. Tread lightly." Wolf strode softly in place on the rubber mat. "Don't step on anyone's toes. Can't have anyone calling you a moneygrubbing Jew, a loudmouth Jew, a sarcastic Jew, an obnoxious Jew. Keep quiet. Defer. Heaven forbid, defer."

"Just cut it out, Wolf. You're acting like a fool."

"Am I?"

In lieu of a response, Nathan exhaled through his deviated septum. It was so hard to know these days how to go about being a Jew in Florida, how to go about being a man, or even a person for that matter.

They entered the second building and walked directly into a fluorescent space with dingy linoleum flooring. It wasn't a large space. He wondered what other chambers lay beyond. Two whitecoats bent over their stations, oblivious to their presence. Wolf led him toward the nearest scientist, leaning over a microscope. White thickets above both ears accentuated the fellow's bald pate.

"Avi," Wolf declared, jolting the man to. The scientist pivoted on his wheeled stool and put his hand on his heart as if to keep it from leaping out of his chest.

"Sorry, Avi. Here, meet Nathan. Fisherman. Might join the crew." Avi rose and shook Nathan's hand in a single vigorous pump complemented by a nod of similar intensity. He seemed a man irritated by obligatory gestures. He was short. Shorter than Nathan. And stout, betraying frivolity–misleadingly perhaps. He had missed a patch of salt and pepper bristle when he had last shaved, a day or so ago from the look of things. "Pleasure to meet you," the scientist said, his English thickly inflected by Europe more so than the Middle East, it seemed to Nathan.

"Nice to meet you too, Avi."

Avi and Daniel over there invented the lotion that prevents sea lice. Avi shrugged his shoulders and lifted wooly eyebrows under the strain of the compliment, an old world gesture that fairly evoked his grandfather Morton.

"Israel produces more patents yearly than the US, you know that?" Nathan shook his head. "Anyway, Avi and Dan made it to Israel after the Soviet Union collapsed. Should see what they were up to with the sturgeon, Nate. Now they're all but gone, those sturgeon. Russian Mafia controls the waters. They're poaching the hell out of them in the Caspian Sea, the Volga spawning grounds. So much for democracy. Frigging A-rabs in Iran not helping much, either."

"Persians," Nathan said. Wolf screwed up his blond face. "The Iranians are Persians, right? Not Arabs."

"Sure, Nate. Whatever. Anyway, the sturgeon aren't too different from snook, the freshwater-saltwater thing they both got going. Sort of a natural transition for Avi and Dan, even if the snook are a tougher nut to crack. Heck, Avi needed a challenge, right?" Avi, seated again now, peering once again into his microscope, ignored the mild provocation.

Nathan glanced over toward Daniel at the other end of the room, dark-haired, younger, and slimmer. He presided over a whirring centrifuge. The whole room, the harsh lighting, the centrifuges and microscopes, the glass beakers and petri dishes about, the heavy tables with innumerable narrow drawers, the cloying formaldehyde smell–mostly the smell–reminded Nathan of his undergraduate bio major days in the lab at the U of M.

"Show him the distillate?" Wolf proposed.

Avi wordlessly pointed his free thumb left, toward a small beaker filled with black liquid, or what appeared black to Nathan. Wolf grasped the beaker and led Nathan back out to the harsh white light of Florida.

"The science is complicated," Wolf declared as they made their way back to the first building. "Would've had Avi explain it, but he'd just throw a bunch of fancy words at you. I can tell you the principle. It's the scent. And the taste."

"So, big deal Wolf. Scented baits have been around for a while. Berkley's been juicing their baits for years now." Nathan didn't elaborate to express his concerns on this front. Scented baits had come a long way from stinky cheese for catfish. The particular juices were growing fearfully potent, scientifically honed, the terms of engagement skewed more and more against the piscine creatures. The snook, however, had proved more impervious to the concoctions than their cousins. They were capricious eaters, the snook. You never quite knew when they'd be biting, or what they'd be biting. The match-the-hatch theory didn't always obtain for these particular creatures, who sometimes seemed to appreciate novelty. Other times, not.

"We're not talking just scented bait here, Nathan. We're not lathering plastics with shrimp-sauce, stuffing it with shrimp-bits. That's rookie crap. Jesus Christ!" Wolf halted in his tracks, smacked the back of his tanned neck with a frying pan hand. "Fucking mosquitos." He resumed his stride. "We're talking science. Pheromones. Amino acids. DNA." Wolf's pace quickened under his enthusiasm, the tail of his white coat flapping behind in the breeze. Nathan hustled to keep up as Wolf spoke over his shoulder, ushering his words into the atmosphere behind. "Now what have all the scented bait companies done so far? They know snook prey on shrimp, so what do they do? They make a chemical derived from shrimp that smells like a shrimp. Sounds pretty smart, right? It's the logical thing to do. Fine. But what if it's not so much the whole smell that the fish craves, but something *in* that smell? Something *in* that taste that makes them hold on rather than spit? Some particular component they register through their nervous system? Their lateral lines and olfactory system? And what if you could isolate that component, splice it, intensify it? Create a distillate?"

"You got me, Wolf? What?"

Wolf paused at the door to the first building rather than enter the noisy tank-room.

"See, it might not even smell to you and me anything like a real shrimp, any more. It might not even smell that way to the snook. Smells *more* than that way, is the thing. You've amped up mother nature. Amped up the real. Left live bait in the dust. Here, smell the distillate. Go ahead." Wolf lifted the black contents toward Nathan's nose. Nathan breathed in, cautiously, through his deviated septum.

"Come on, Nathan. Be a man. Smell!"

He took a deeper whiff and winced against the rancid stench.

"I know. Like a real bad yeast infection, right?"

"Jesus, Wolf! I don't know."

"That's what Avi's still working on. Trying to figure out if we can extract from the distillate that salient smell *we* smell without removing the chemical components that trigger the snook response. Color too.

No one likes black. Black's a bitch. Especially on boat decks and clothes. Stains. Only so much the recreational angler will suffer, even if the sauce works."

"How'd they figure out the components?"

"Lot of it's just hit-or-miss. Catch-as-catch-can. Break the genes down to the aminos. Test out the combinations. Like how they discovered DEET. No one really knows why that stuff works, you know. Just that it does."

"Listen, Wolf. No offense, but this all sounds pretty hocus-pocus to me." He doubted the science, or perhaps he simply wanted to doubt it. Over millions of years, the snook had developed a yen for particular creatures that couldn't be sliced and diced, broken down into better-than-shrimp chemical components. Scent helped some, no doubt, but only because the smell was like a shrimp, or a pilchard, or a greenie. A real live shrimp couldn't be improved upon, could it?

"Relax, Nathan. Follow me." The tank room was significantly brighter by the time they entered the space. Perhaps it was near sunup in Sweetwater. The space seemed less impressive, mostly visible as it was now, a barren swatch of sheltered dirt except for the tanks, filters, and motors. There was also a corrugated metal office-room with tinted windows at the far-end near the deepest tank, where the snook purportedly spawned. He still couldn't quite make out the ceiling, whether some sort of screen or drop-cloth constituted the faux sky. Wolf led him toward the large tank.

They scaled the platform. The snook were clustered–a few

groups of twos and one larger cluster–at the far, deep end of the tank. Wolf brandished an eye dropper from out of nowhere and squeezed a modest column of black distillate, holding the vial between them. "Now five drops is roughly one part per 5 billion in this tank. Got that?" Wolf raised the vial above the tank. Nathan nodded. He couldn't deny his curiosity. "Here goes." Wolf squeezed five black drops into the drink, slowly. *Drip . . . drip . . . drip . . . drip . . .drip.*

"Well?"

"Just wait."

They shifted. That's the first thing Nathan noticed. The whole school, to the last specimen, simultaneously shifted a hundred and eighty degrees like levers.

"Interesting."

"Wait a second." Wolf lifted a hand.

One darted toward them, causing Nathan to flinch. The fish smacked the shrimpless surface then descended. Another followed suit. Then another. A pattern of strikes emerged on the surface. The filter must have been swirling counterclockwise. And then there was no pattern, just a boil of stupidly snapping snook. A persistent boil. Nathan felt embarrassed for the duped creatures.

"My god, Wolf."

"Something, eh?"

The frenzy finally abated. Nathan glanced dazedly at the surface, which slowly settled.

Wolf led Nathan back outside, then extracted from his breast pocket a small zip-locked plastic bag. "Here." Inside the bag were a few plastic shrimp, eight or so, bathed in black juice.

"You make those here?" Nathan inquired in lieu of claiming the package. Wolf lowered the bag to his side.

"We contract out the plastic molds. Shape's basic. Distillate's the key. Try these. No strings." He extended the offering once again, which Nathan accepted. He could always toss them in the trash. "SnookeRed tourney's not too far off, Nathan. Nice to have a member of the tribe on board, like I said. But if not . . ." Wolf shrugged, alluding to nebulous alternatives. Nathan nodded, pensive, dumbfounded still from the irksome display inside.

"Listen, you all right getting home? . . . Nathan? . . . Nathan?"

"Yes," the fisherman answered. "Home. Yes. I'm fine."

Chapter Six

"You'll stay tonight?"

"So you want me to stay. Tonight."

"Don't start, Hubert. Please. You know how I feel about you."

Judy didn't see why Hugh had to be such a child. Wasn't he getting what every man supposedly wanted? No-strings companionship replete with frequent coupling? Turned out that men didn't appreciate these terms, after all. Not the men in her age bracket, anyway. It wasn't only Hugh. All of her companions over these past several years wanted more of Judy than she was willing to share. She wouldn't entangle herself now, at this late date–be someone's nurse or purse like half of the silly divorcees her age. Dogs returning to their vomit, it seemed to Judy. A harsh analogy. But that didn't make it any less true.

"I'll come in for coffee, I suppose."

Judy clasped Hugh's hand and led him inside.

"So much space," he observed in the foyer, as he always observed, gazing up at the vaulted ceiling. Judy absorbed the blow as she measured out the grinds into the filter.

"Now not so strong, Jude."

"Okay, dear-heart." She toppled the coffee ground precipice off her final spoonful. She would be as conciliatory as possible. It had been such a nice evening, after all. The chicken parmigiana at Runway 84, scrumptious. Her dirty vodka martinis, potent. The original plan was for them to take in the Boca Pops first, but they decided that dinner and the pops would be too much for one evening. Judy usually found the music jarring, in any case. Why did everything have to be so loud? Hugh was perfectly affable at dinner, prattled on about a trip to Naples he had taken (Italy, not Florida), the squalid charm of the place, if somewhat too decorously eliding reference to his former wife who had surely accompanied him. A younger diner seated next to them overheard Hugh's remarks and offered his comradely agreement. He must have been about Nathan's age, but seemed an entirely different species. His dark hair was lacquered straight back from his forehead in discrete combgrooves; a gold stud winked from one of his small earlobes. Hugh and the young man spoke for a short time while Judy exchanged smiles with the fellow's sequined companion and savored a vodka-drenched olive. It was especially nice, somehow, to see Hugh in pleasant conversation with a young man. She was feeling loose and expansive halfway into her second martini. Pecking at her ricotta cheesecake, while nursing that second drink, she had looked forward to sharing her bed with Hugh later on.

The coffee maker issued its final steamy exhale. Judy still hoped he wasn't dead set on spoiling things now. She poured their decafs and slid Hugh's porcelain cup and saucer across the granite bar. "Dinner was lovely, Hugh. Again, thank you. It wasn't necessary."

"Acch," he batted his hand as if to say that it was nothing. "No one does a bracciole like Runway 84."

"I was secretly hoping you'd order it so I could have a taste. Those peas. And the pine nuts."

"You think I don't know that, hon'?" She detected a mild smile as Hugh lifted his cup and slurped a decaf dose. They had merged onto smoother terrain. He was a handsome devil–a tennis body he assiduously maintained–but thankfully didn't seem hyper-aware of his charms. His modest tuft of salt and pepper hair on his torso accentuated his still-toned stomach and pectorals. He wasn't as beefy as Joseph. Hugh had been a chiropractor (Joseph would surely scoff at his dubious medical bona fides), so had taken especially good care of his spine and abdominals, what he called his core. She had to admit that he walked taller and sat straighter than most men in their thirties. Certainly taller and straighter than Nathan, who slouched, it seemed to Judy, out of sheer stubbornness. Feeling underutilized in his retirement, Hugh frequently plied Judy's neck and back with therapeutic strokes and kneads. He adjusted her vertebrae. She had never suffered back or neck problems and so hadn't realized that there were so many of those vital knobs, that their state of alignment, the soundness of those curious discs within, were so crucial. Judy took a sip or two of her own decaf (too weak for her taste), then deposited it into the sink.

"Join me in the boudoir, my dear." Somehow, the French seemed both more lurid and couth.

"In a minute, Jude."

His mild protest? No matter. Judy retreated to the bedroom to prepare herself for bed. She disrobed, hanging her silk blouse in the closet. Thankfully, she hadn't spattered any red sauce on it. She strode to the bathroom, nude, surveyed her figure briefly in the mirror. She wasn't exactly chopped liver, herself. She didn't log all those hours on the elliptical trainer for nothing. What did Hugh call her once? A tight little package. Most women her age, as he surely knew firsthand, suffered that unfortunate migration of flesh and fat from rear to stomach. But here was Judy. Still a perky little bottom, dimpled only modestly with cellulite. A mostly flat tummy too, the skin hardly stretched at all from carrying her two boys. Her small breasts a definite advantage at this point, adhering more or less to their essential geometry. She washed her face then turned a cheek to the mirror, taking in her profile. Sighing, she dabbed lotion onto her forehead, her cheekbones, her faint crow's feet, then set about rubbing in the emollient, stroking upward. Never down. She prided herself on not having any work done, not even Botox, all these years. On making do.

Judy emptied her bladder and washed her hands. She took care to scrub her teeth and tongue with the Colgate, then lathered the rough spots of her flesh–her elbows, her knees, those stubbornly calloused heels–with lotion, a less costly variety than the emollient she dabbed on her face. She retreated to the bed and flicked off the lights. Then she flicked the lights back on, repaired to her dresser drawer and surveyed the contents, extracting a lacy negligee. What the heck. She'd be a sport. All the same, she flicked the lights back off once she returned to the bed. No use getting carried away. He was a good lover, Hugh. He didn't try so gosh darned hard like the others, but actually seemed to enjoy himself, which she found pleasing. He knew how to interpret her subtle cues, knew when she was ready for him to bring things to a conclusion.

He was able to do so too, thank heavens—likely assisted by a prescription she didn't ask about—perspiring very little through his labors.

Hugh walked into the room and entered the bathroom. Perhaps he had simply been waiting for her to finish her business. He was a bit priggish that way. From the bed, she could hear him fiddling through the drawers for his toothbrush, the prophylactics he grudgingly wore. He would pout some in the morning, she knew. About the general state of their relations. What he liked to call her hardness. *You're a hard woman, Judy*, as if it were her duty to be soft. But he wouldn't complain tonight. She'd see to that.

"You sure you're there somewhere?" he called, coming out of the bathroom's light into the darkness.

"Yes, Hubert. Here I am."

**

Morning. Judy knew it was Nathan upon hearing the first peal of the telephone. She wasn't certain how she knew this. Just that she knew. "Today?" she greeted Nathan's query. "Now?" She gazed out the breakfast nook window toward the royal poincianas, pallid and spindly now, the sopping fairway beyond, worrying her gold hoop earring between the pads of her fingers. She had removed it so that she could hold the receiver, comfortably.

It wasn't kind of her to act put out. Yet she didn't fully approve of her son's way of being in the world, and, as he refused to accept any real assistance or advice from her quarter, acting vaguely put out by him was the only form of mild protest available. Which didn't mean she felt good about it. She often felt pangs of guilt that she wasn't quite there for her son as fully as she ought to be, especially during his childhood— when Jacob had somehow attracted the bulk of their attentions—during her divorce from his father when she was scrapping to fend for herself and get her business off the ground (how she had succeeded!), during Nathan's own difficult marriage, and now as he struggled to find his footing. But *he* was the one who resisted her attentions, it seemed to Judy. He kept her at arm's length and refused to confide in her.

She knew that he wasn't lazy, and that he expended a great deal of effort and time at cockamamie hours doing odd things related to his vocation–his craftsmanship of those pretty little wooden creatures in her garage, for example. It was *her* vision, she knew, that was probably too narrow. Unforgivably unforgiving. He was a good father to Miles, any-way. She ought to learn from his example, maybe. Put herself out there a bit more, and less grudgingly, for Stefanie with an f, who was keeping her plenty busy, carting the Tates around to listings Judy knew wouldn't pan out. That's one thing her little cheerleader needed to learn, how to marshal her efforts more efficiently.

CRACK! A bolt of lightning struck something, hopefully not someone, nearby.

"Yes, I see it's not exactly fishing weather. So come by then . . . Of course . . . Yes. Fine. You have a key in case I'm out . . . How's Miles? . . . Yes, Hugh's fine."

She would have liked to ask after Samantha, if only out of cu-riosity. But she supposed that Samantha was none of her business anymore, as she was none of Nathan's. And he didn't seem to like it when she brought up the topic of his ex-wife. Judy had run into her former daughter-in-law months ago at the Publix out west, where Judy usually didn't shop. She had just signed a listing at Symphony Bay. Samantha spotted her first, because Judy glimpsed her turning on her heels with the cart before realizing that it was too late, feigning surprise at having just noticed her former mother-in-law. Judy at first felt sorry for the poor girl. This was no way to live. Sneaking around. Strolling past the canned tomatoes, peas, and beans en route to greet her former daughter-in-law, she had intended to tell her that it was okay, that she needn't feel awkward, because she didn't blame her, entirely, that there was surely enough blame to go around. But then she remembered that Samantha had the audacity to remarry, already. A doctor of some sort. (Had the little tart been cuckolding poor Nathan all along?) That Samantha and this new husband of hers had purchased an opulent property in the eights in that chichi new development west of 441. Finally, she remembered feeling that a more supportive, nurturing wife would have found a way to steer a husband onto the proper path and that abandoning a perfectly kind man, especially when there was Miles to think about, was just plain selfish. You couldn't always do exactly what you wanted. Thinking these thoughts, feeling these feelings anew, had emboldened her. She shared clipped pleasantries with the mother of her grandson without feeling particularly good about it.

Judy hung up the phone now and sighed, glancing out still toward the skeletal royal poincianas, which offered priceless curb appeal

179

in bloom, blooms her son couldn't quite see on account of his color-blindness. It was how they belatedly discerned his ocular condition, that he couldn't see the brilliant orange and red blossoms bursting from the foliage all about town each May or so, that the trees still looked pretty much green to Nathan. For weeks, Judy had convinced herself that her son was just being stubborn, while Jake insisted that his brother was merely stupid. "There!" Judy had brayed in the Vista Cruiser, pointing toward a brilliant specimen on fire by the roadside. "You can't see *that*!? You mean to tell me you can't see *that*, Nathan!?"

"Well?" Hugh asked from the kitchen bar between oatmeal spoonfuls.

"It was my son. Nathan. He's coming over soon."

"Oh." Judy's lover lifted his morning coffee to his lips, gulped a generous dose. "Sure."

**

Judy should really get going, herself. She had floor duty in an hour. But she figured she'd wait for this odd winter storm to subside some. The world was overheating, the seas rising. (That the boat docks at the fancy waterfront estates she listed and showed often had to be raised to pass inspection was enough proof for her.) Yet what a strange winter they were having. Waiting out the storm, in any case, would allow her to see her son. She wanted to check that Nathan hadn't lost any more weight, that he was shaving his ginger stubble and keeping himself tidy. She didn't care if he was a fisherman, he'd never find a respectable woman looking like a shlump. She could only imagine what someone like

180

Stefanie would think of Nathan. In fairness, he wouldn't think much of her, either.

She'd get some work done at home while she waited. She'd printed out the most recent listings, preferred hard-copies to scrolling through her tablet. She flipped absently through the computer pages at the granite bar, cradling an indelible marker between her teeth. Lots of properties, which wouldn't last long. Had Stefanie spotted this new one in Pheasant's Walk for the Tates? She circled it. Plenty of building still going on out west, beyond 441. Plenty of people, thousands, moving to south Florida every week. The market, recovering. The last hurricane shifted west at the last moment and mostly spared their coast. It was a good time again to be an agent. Even the marginally literate could make a decent living as an agent these days if they hustled, as many did. It killed her that her protégé, perfectly likable Stefanie, would probably be flush with money in a few months, while her son could barely butter his parsnips. She'd encourage Nathan to study for his license if she thought there was a remote chance he'd take her up on it. She had vague notions that he ought to go back to school, earn his Master's degree in one of the sciences—he was so intelligent—but she wasn't so sure what he could do from there, career-wise. Something.

She heard Nathan working the lock with his key, for some strange reason held her breath above the sheaf of new listings while he did so, as if he were a prowler.

"Oh. Mother. Sorry. I didn't think you were still here."

"I waited for you."

"You didn't have to."

There! Did he have to push her away like that?

"I know I didn't have to."

She rose and presented a perfumed cheek to her son, who kissed it. He had her coloring. Her diminutive stature too, alas. He looked well. Showered and shaved now. Not pallid at all. He still hadn't taken her advice and bleached his teeth, but at least he had trimmed his ginger curls recently, which tended toward Afro. Perhaps there was a woman in the picture. She hoped so. Men needed women. All in all, objectively speaking, her son was not an unhandsome man. His nose added a measure of masculine charm at this point, whereas a woman would never be able to carry off such a proboscis. There was a young actor now with a similar nose. An Italian from New York who often played a Jew from New York, or a foreigner from some frigid Baltic outpost.

Judy followed her son out to the garage, his studio for all intents and purposes, where Nathan now kept his lathe and sander, his drill with the fancy bits, machined in Sweden, plus his various chemical compounds–epoxies, wood hardeners, paints–his treble hooks, phony eyes, and those metal tongues, the size, contours, and angle of which, he had explained in a moment of weakness, determined with absolute precision the swimming depth and jittery movements of the false, barbed creatures. He opened the garage door to offer himself some air and light. Rivulets of water cascaded from the clogged roof gutter onto the driveway pavers.

"Gutter must be clogged," Nathan announced, reading her thoughts as he negotiated the wooden rectangle onto the lathe, centering it between the prongs. "I'll clear them out after I'm done, once this storm lets up."

"Thank you, dear . . . Is that oak?"

"Dogwood, mom. I don't use oak, remember? Too knotty. Messes up the weight and its wave signature in the water. I get these scraps free from the Paraguayan furniture store on Glades, just give the owner a lure once in a while."

Yes, he had already told her. She watched from the door as he lowered his safety goggles into position, flicked on the whirring lathe, then shaped the form with gougers of various sizes, extracting them from a leather case which seemed quite fancy. He worked at an impossibly slow pace, which tested her patience. *Go!* she urged, silently. *Faster!*

Several wooden creatures at various stages of completion dangled from the peg-board, their glues and epoxies curing, their paints drying. They were lovely. So many beautiful shades, blues, greens, violets and reds bleeding into one another across the wavy grain. Silver and metallic flecks glinted from the lacquered undersides of several, like the mica in old sidewalks. They were too fine, too beautiful, it seemed to Judy, for mere fishing. Maybe that was the problem.

Nathan flicked off the lathe, which ceased its whirring. He rotated the dollop of wood manually, slowly, inspecting its contours. Brandishing a metal file from out of nowhere, he began to ply the wooden dollop with short strokes.

"They're so beautiful, Nathan. Really."

"Thanks, mom."

"How do you know what color paint to use? Your eyes."

"They're cellulose dyes. They're marked. Anyway, mom, I can see most colors. At least I think so."

"Do you have a favorite?"

Nathan turned on his stool to face her now, befuddled lines erupting on his flushed forehead. A strand of dark, not-red hair adhered to the perspiration just above his woolly brow. "Why are you so interested all of a sudden, mom?"

"I just am." Judy crossed her arms. "Is that a crime?"

He didn't answer. Instead, he looked up at his peg-board and pointed to a silver creature, which Judy would have taken to be his least favorite. Pretty plain compared to the other multi-hued dollops of wood, the only colorful feature its red string trailing behind.

"What do you call it?"

"It's just a simple silver mullet," he declared while he buffed a wooden plug with sandpaper, his back toward her. "The first plug I made when I was still in Miami. I added the red feather a bit later. But it's basically the same."

"So they catch fish? All of them?"

"That's the idea. But . . ."

"What?"

Nathan exhaled. "Hard plugs like these aren't so much in fashion anymore." He held up the plug he had been sanding over his shoulder for a moment. "They're using more and more soft plastics now, mass-produced in molds. They impregnate them with stuffed shrimp. Even bathe them in other chemicals. Fish attractants. Everything's changing."

There! Was it so hard for Nathan to spit out a few words about his business? Judy could tell that her son didn't approve of the recent trend. These soft plastics. It was just like him not to approve of the conventional wisdom, to find a way, somehow, to put himself on the outs. He would have been happier had he been born fifty years earlier, she thought, but knew that even then he'd find a way to prefer the goings on fifty years prior to that. For it was a personality trait, above all, a flaw, this fuddy-duddyness, this old-fartness. All the same, her son possessed special abilities. He was extraordinary, in his way. Objectively speaking. Judy wasn't the fawning Jewish mother type, but she wasn't blind, either. She wondered how different they truly were, she and Nathan. He had devoted himself to his craft and was unyielding about the terms of engagement. She was every bit as focused and unyielding in the practice of her own vocation, such as it was. She gazed up at the wall of finished and half-finished plugs. He was an artist. That was the difference. Such a pity that he couldn't quite translate his gifts into substantive remuneration, as she had, that he didn't try harder, or at all, to do so.

"They seem valuable, Nathan. You're absolutely sure you couldn't . . ." Judy swallowed her words just as Nathan turned his back to her, stretching his neck as if to relieve a kink. *She* was the kink, she knew. They had been through this before. People weren't willing to spend more than eight dollars or so on something they threw into the corrosive saltwater, often as not cut off by a barracuda, snagged on coral or tree stump, lost by a careless, weak knot or compromised monofilament. Nathan wasn't able, or perhaps he just wasn't willing, to work at a pace that would yield a decent profit.

"You see your father lately?"

"I'm going to see him today," her son uttered, his back to her still. A terse, lame response. Her son the literalist all of a sudden. What did Nathan want from her?

"Well?"

"He's . . . you know. You could . . . ." Nathan let his own words trail off now, as they had been over this terrain, as well. There weren't many safe topics between them anymore, Judy reflected. Even the topic of Miles had grown freighted of late. Neither Joseph nor she would have tolerated such a hairdo. You sit the child down in the barber's seat and that's that, it seemed to Judy. She could see Nathan letting things slide. But Samantha? What was her excuse? Was she going to let him keep that hair for his Bar Mitzvah? Judy just couldn't fathom this new parental dispensation. The laxity. What was it all about, those tangled tentacles? Her grandson only shrugged when she inquired. But it couldn't be anything good. Nothing Jewish she could see in that hair.

This wouldn't do. These stingy feelings. Poor Nathan. She really did hope there was some woman in the picture. Judy wanted to say something kind before leaving him to his labors. Something simple and uncomplicated and true.

"They're beautiful, Nathan. Those lures. Really. Beautiful."

**

The wet weather had exacerbated the cat-piss stench of his cab. His mother. Her barely restrained digs and tortured kindness. He cranked the window down. The wet pavement rippled beneath the tires, pleased his ears and calmed him, along with the more pleasant copper aroma of the rainsoaked outdoors. He had almost fallen off the roof clearing her gutters he had been so distracted, so irritated. He clutched another intake of restorative outside air into his lungs, dogwood-dusty still from his labors.

At least she was trying, in her way.

Something was going to happen, he knew. He had been asleep for some time, but was beginning to awaken. He had to be careful. For it wasn't just his mother who sought to stir him from his slumber. His world was suddenly full of people tugging at his shoulder, seeking to usher him into their particular world, their version of the real. Everyone had a stake to claim. Terrance hawking his nine to five bliss. Life's good when it's simple. Well, maybe. Frank and the boys with their Jewfish exhortations. His mother the top-producer at Premiere Properties wanting him to produce . . . something. Chip and the Fishing Report guest spot around the corner. And then there was Wolf, who had an entirely separate agenda. He glanced down at the black baits, still stewing in their juices on the cracked vinyl passenger seat. He doubted he would try them. Like using steroids, for all intents and purposes. Nathan fished artificial bait because it was hard. Not because it was easy. You had to be an angler to catch fish throwing hard plugs or skipping simple spoons under the mangroves. A seismic shift was afoot, though. In a matter of a few years—months, Nathan feared—live bait would seem a downright handicap. The bait-slingers, as Nathan derisively thought of them, would suddenly emerge as the more ethical cohort. Live bait, suddenly, the *hard* way to fish. The old-fashioned way. The fair way. And behind it all? Behind this cataclysmic shift? Behind the whole aquaculture scheme, to boot, out to tame, domesticate, and neuter Nathan's sublime snook? Wolf. So why hadn't he discarded the rancid-smelling plugs already? Wolf. Nathan couldn't deny a certain pull to his arguments. He wasn't the first person to accuse Nathan of skulking around, seeking sick comfort in his reticence, his implacable ethics, his refusal to enter the fray. His brother Jake, too, had given him a hard time this way.

**

Nathan pulled his truck onto the still tar-scented asphalt of the new center. The recent rain issued a pleasant eucalyptus and chaparral smell to the air on these dusty, neglected acres of the university campus, replacing the metallic aroma of the busy streets and outmuscling the asphalt smells. Beyond the stuccoed center lay several relocated burrowing owl nests, cordoned off here and there by wispy ribbon rectangles. The owls and the alter kockers, Nathan contemplated. And his father. The lot of them tucked out of the way near the few blighted Army Air Field shacks left over from the war. The El Rio barely trickled now just beyond the nests, choked by swamp lettuce and duckweed along this stagnant stretch above the spillway, byproduct of all those nutrients from the lake. Memory and Wellness, Nathan read the bronze words emblazoned on the stucco exterior. Sounded good, even if Adult Daycare probably hewed closer to the truth. Here was the real, anyway. These cold clear doors, the fluorescent lighting, the linoleum floor. Yet Nathan had to give the center props–as Miles would put it–for warming the place. Framed elementary school watercolors graced the halls, a compulsory exercise for the schoolchildren, but sweet all the same. Chipper music issued forth at an unignorable volume from speakers hidden somewhere . . . *I like to be in America! O.K. by me in America!*. . . music Nathan some-how recognized from *West Side Story*. The singing voices sounded only quasi-professional. Probably a recording from the university production, he guessed. The staff invariably played dated tunes, probably to spark memories, fire the synapses, but Nathan wondered whether such music didn't prove disorienting.

All in all, the center wasn't quite depressing. Bracing maybe. But not depressing. It wasn't a nursing home. There was lots of life here still. A palpable energy, if only verbal. *I like the shores of America! Comfort is yours in America!* Only a few sad sacks lay about, drugged and dazed, or just dazed, sloppily concluding their earth business. Nathan preferred visiting his father here at the center rather than at his oceanfront condo-minium. Neutral territory. There were others about with their attendant human goings on, a wide range of genuine feeling about to buffer his correspondence with his father, which had actually grown more easygo-ing of late, his father's debility sanding away a calloused layer between them.

Joseph's boy again, Rose gathered, glancing over her tiles. That thicket of brick-red curls. Gracious. Shorts, he wore, with big pockets and a threadbare, long-sleeved tee shirt. He seemed to have shaved this morning, at least, but she couldn't truck shorts on a grown man, not while visiting your people. It was a matter of simple respect. Young people these days. The things they wore. Even those nice white girls from the sorority who did the dishes now and again, the strings from their unmentionables in plain sight clear above their low-slung dungarees.

> *I've just met a girl named Maria,*
> *And suddenly that name*
> *Will never be the same*
> *To me. . . .*

"Pong," she declared, turning over her red dragon pair.

"Well done, Rose."

They kissed a lot, these Jews, grasping for cheeks between their meaty palms. Even the men. She had lost her breath when Ben's brother–brother? Yes she thought so–had kissed him full on the lips outside the center at pick-up. For all the world to see. It didn't stop at kissing. They were after all sorts of monkey business, these Jewish men, at least judging by all the jokes and carrying on. What had gotten into them? Which was why she took notice that Joseph's boy, she couldn't remember his name (Sidney? Daniel? Samuel?), didn't kiss or even hug his father, but just pinched his shoulder, stood over his back.

"Hi Pop." She watched as he lay another hand on Joseph's

other shoulder–that was more like it–and rubbed. Rose, somehow, could feel the massage.

Joseph didn't rise to greet his boy, looming over him still, but maintained his focus on his cards. "Nathan," he said. *Nathan. Yes, that was it.* There was something prideful about the display, it seemed to her. *My son. Here he is.*

"Your turn again, Rose," Noma prodded.

Maria!

"Hold on, sugar."

So impatient. The main weakness of these Jewish ladies. Smart enough. Especially Noma, who for some reason pulled back her darkened hair in a severe pony tail. But no patience. As if the sun rose and set over their druthers. Sylvia, Jewish but from Charleston, was the exception. Forced once again to draw from the wall, Noma fidgeted there worrying her lip between her teeth, tapping her tiles with her ridiculously manicured nails. Couldn't she just listen to the music for a spell? Rose would let her stew some in her juices. Something about this impossibly young Joseph (handsome too, in truth) and his disheveled son (not quite so handsome, poor child) interested her. Perhaps only the novelty. People didn't do visiting here. Didn't Joseph and his boy know that? The center was where they all went to offer their people some space. Like her own daughter, Horacene. She had her hands full enough with her wild boys, her phlebotomist's job on the bloodmobile. She couldn't look in after her mother during the day. And Rose wasn't quite ready to give up the tranquility of her single bedroom apartment on 20th, even after flooding the washroom by accident last month; she had forgotten to shut off the sink where she was bleaching her whites. It was enough, at least for now, that Horacene checked in on her in the evening, drove her to the center in the morning.

I've just kissed a girl named Maria . . .

"The fish maven," Solomon belatedly greeted Joseph's son, as if it had just occurred to him.

"Sit down already," Herbert said, that protuberant lower lip of his fairly flapping. "You're making us nervous." Rose watched out the corner of her eye as Nathan sat just outside the circle. Couldn't Herbert do something about that loose, wet lip of his? Hold it up better?

"Before Tish B'Av, Rose," Noma declared, making Rose smile. What was Tish B'Av?

Rose knew that Noma was gathering winds and circles. She wouldn't give those up. Better to discard a character tile to Janet, who was a little out of it today. What did the ladies say? Far-blond-jet. She'd rather lose to Janet, in any case.

"Chow!"

"Mm-hmm. Good for you, Janet," Rose uttered.

"Son of a bitch," Noma murmured. Rose shuddered. She had a mouth like the devil, that Noma. Was she raised by wolves?

"How nice, Janet," Sylvia declared in her southern falsetto, scanning her tiles. It was unusual to hear a southern accent this far south. Despite certain unsavory associations, the lilting southern cadence and restrained timbre seemed classier than the extravagant glottals of Sylvia's peers.

Maria,

I'll never stop saying Maria!

"Gin rummy," Rose overheard Joseph declare, snapping his cards face up on the table. He'd bend them showing off like that.

"And it's such a shame they're having such troubles conceiving," she picked up the thread of a sentence from her own table as Sylvia plucked a tile from the wall. "She's just adorable, my niece. Stefanie. With an f," she clarified, as if they might be called upon to spell the name at some point. "Just started out in real estate. She'll make a killing." Sylvia was the prettiest of the ladies, boasted a healthy shock of her own hair still, straight and colored like honey. Her blue eyes weren't so rheumy yet above her delicate cheekbones. All the same, she must have had that plastic surgery on her face, Rose deduced, as the skin from her neck below sagged like overlong drapes, revealing her age. Well into her 80s, certainly.

"That Natalie Wood was one pretty girl," Janet said, as if she had just recognized the song emanating from the speakers.

The most beautiful sound I ever heard.

Maria . . .

"Tragedy what happened to her," Noma said, then sucked at her teeth to make a pity sound.

Rose reached silently for the wall.

"They go too far, trying these days," said Janet, returning to the subject of Sylvia's niece, the real estate agent named Stefanie. With an f.

193

"If it wasn't meant to be it wasn't meant to be."

"Well that's a stupid thing to say," Noma declared. She was reckless with sharp words, Noma, severe as her hairstyle. Words like stupid and liar and various profanities she tossed haphazardly around the room, not caring where they might fall or whom they might strike.

"They're thinking about adopting a baby from China," Sylvia said. "That's what the kids do now." She stroked her fair cheek, worriedly. "She married a Christian boy," Sylvia added, as if to explain something.

"Still your turn Janet," Rose interjected, somewhat uncomfortable with this turn in the conversation. "No hurry now."

Maria, Maria, Maria, Maria . . .

Janet finally discarded a tile, snatched one from the wall.

"Kong!" Noma declared, flipping over her east winds. Noma was going to beat Rose today if she wasn't careful. The wall was shrinking and Rose was behind. Maybe it wasn't such a wise idea to accumulate bamboos. But it was difficult for her to maintain her focus with the men carrying on beside them. Ben and Herbert had excused themselves to take their medication. Joseph excused himself, as well, to "see a man about a horse." A ridiculous, crass expression, but it must have reminded Mr. Solomon about a joke.

"What did the bartender say to the horse, kiddo?"

Joseph's son chuckled in anticipation of the punch line. "I don't know, Mr. Podolsky. What?"

"Why the long face?"

"Good one," Nathan said, but he didn't laugh again.

"So? Why?"

"Huh?"

"The long face? You're too young for such a punim." Rose didn't know this word, but guessed that it meant face or expression.

"Fishing every day is such a chore?"

"No. Who's complaining?"

"You make things too complicated. That's your problem. You young people. You know what matters in this world?"

"Family?"

"Screw family! Lay off the platitudes, kiddo. My wife was swell but she's dead twenty years now. Look at me." Solomon scooted his chair back, the legs whining against the hard floor, then lifted his short-sleeve button-down shirt from the waist of his trousers. Rose couldn't help but peek over at the intersecting keloid scars across his protuberant, furry trunk, a long scar straight down from his chest, the other straight across the belly. X marks the spot, the phrase flashed across her mental screen.

"Mr. Solomon!" Reggie, the volunteer, called over. "Rules, Mr. Solomon." He lowered his shirt.

"I've had my chest cracked open like a nut. Twice! Twice with the bypass operations. My appendix, gone. Gall bladder, gone. My liver they chopped up piece by piece from the cancer ten years ago. Kidneys'll be the next to go, mark my words. Brain's mostly kaput."

"Come on now, Mr. Podolsky–"

"So you know what I believe in, boychik? This." Rose watched

195

as Solomon patted his torso down, as if searching for spare change. "The kishkas. Your parts. Shtupping and dying, boychik. That's all there is. Shtupping and dying. Might as well live a little."

"Enough already, Sol!" Noma shouted, smacking her thigh with a palm. "*This* he needs to hear!?"

Noma's outburst jolted Rose. She had thought that she was the only one eavesdropping, watching.

> *I feel pretty,*
>
> *Oh, so pretty . . .*

Sol batted a hand toward Noma as if shooing a pesky airborne insect. Then he looked back at Nathan, paused, his mouth agape. Rose knew that look from Sol.

"Who are you, again?"

"I'm Nathan, Mr. Podolsky. Joe's son. You knew my grandfather, Morty, from Miami Beach. Remember?"

"Morty?"

"Yes."

"From Miami Beach?"

"Yes."

"You don't look anything like him."

"I know. I look like my mother."

"Could really stitch a double pleat, Morton."

"Yeah. I know. I used to visit him. I've told you this before, Mr. Podolsky. Sollie."

Here the child did something strange, leaned silently across the table, touched Solomon's bare arm with his hand, as if to complete an electric circuit. The young man's hand was strangely mottled, Rose noticed. Bovine.

The circuit complete, the child tried again now.

"Joseph Pray, your friend now, is Morty's *son*. I'm Nathan Pray. *Joseph's* son. Remember me now, Solomon? Remember?"

Presented with such a question, most of Rose's peers here at the center nodded, either out of courtesy or embarrassment, or some combination of the two impulses. But Solomon didn't nod.

"No. Afraid not. Don't take it personal."

It's alarming how charming I feel!

"And she could have married anyone," Rose homed in again on Sylvia's pleasant southern frequency, her unpleasant words. Their conversation had apparently returned to Sylvia's niece while Rose eavesdropped, while Janet labored over her tiles, volubly sucking her sugarless hard candy. "She's just gorgeous, Stefanie. Doesn't look Jewish at all. Dirty blonde hair in a bob. Perky little nose. The cutest little tushy. She could have married anyone."

Sylvia's niece, it seemed to Rose, had become even more beautiful over the past twenty minutes. And less Jewish looking, whatever that meant.

For I'm loved

By a pretty wonderful boy!

"He does make a good living," Sylvia allowed. "A general contractor, and you know they make a killing down here, the gonifs.

Stefanie's husband's honest, though, I'm sure."

"Listen, things could work out with the husband," Noma said. "Maybe they won't have to adopt a Chinese baby. They can do amazing things these days. The doctors. It's a new world."

"Sure I can drive you someplace next week, Pop," Rose overheard the boy's words, this small young man with the shorts and brick-red curls, who could drive his father somewhere next week. "No problem. Just let me know when, exactly." The two of them were alone now at the table beside them, Joseph and his son. Lord, she had already forgotten his name. She could spit she was so angry with herself. *Sidney? Daniel? Samuel?*

"Heard from your brother?"

Joseph's son didn't seem to hear his father at first. He didn't say anything. It was Rose's turn. She could hear Noma tapping her sneaker beneath the table.

Somewhere a place for us . . .

"Have you been using your moisturizer, Pop? You have some dry skin flaking off your ears."

"Nathan," Joseph declared, but his son didn't reply. *Yes,* Rose thought. *Nathan. Nathan. Nathan. Nathan.* "Jacob's birthday was just last week. You call him?"

Hold my hand and we're halfway there . . .

The child must have heard Joseph's question, because he leaned back in his chair and exhaled, loud, as if to expel the words from his insides. Rose finally discarded a tile, pulled a separate one from the wall.

Another circle. Now what was she supposed to do with that?

"You hungry, dad? Feel like a nosh? They have turkey from Flakowitz's up there–"

"Nathan!" said Joseph again.

"Yeah, Pop. I called him. We always talk on our birthdays." The sentences were clipped sharp, like fingernails.

"Well?"

"He's fine. Kids are fine, seems like."

"That's it?"

"He never has much to say, dad. You can try calling him your-self if you're so interested."

He was testy about his brother, or, rather, testy about his father's interest in his brother.

"I tried," Joseph said. Rose wondered at the when of the remark. *When* did Joseph try? Last week? Last month? Last year? Five years ago? Ten?

"I guess he's just decided to live his own life, Pop. We'll just have to live with it."

"I know that. I know."

We'll just have to live with it. It seemed like a harsh thing to say. Why couldn't Joseph's son offer his father a wider berth, she wondered, like he had offered Solomon just moments ago. His father–didn't this Nathan know?–was sicker than he appeared. Joseph's mostly dark hair and the meat on his bones had tricked even Rose, before she found the young man stumbling over the word for fork the other day. Why was it so hard, Rose wondered, to offer kindness to your own, to be sweet?

"I still talk to *you*," Joseph was saying now, slowly, "and your mother still talks to you and your brother, at least I think she talks to your brother, and your brother still talks to the two of you . . ." He was working this all out as if it was an arithmetic equation, it seemed to Rose, studying his hands on the tabletop " . . . so that just leaves you, the only one of us who talks to everyone."

"Yeah, I guess, Pop. I haven't thought about it that way."

"It's not nothing. You're the only thing holding us all together, Nathan. The only thing."

There was a long pause.

"Maybe he'll come to Miles' Bar Mitzvah," Joseph's boy finally said, which made his father open his eyes wide. "I invited Jake, of course."

"Mah-jongg!" Sylvia cried closer by, and louder.

Rose tightened her lips around her teeth, suppressed an audible groan. Served her right. Her comeuppance for eavesdropping.

Chapter Seven

Nathan grinned chimp-like before the tattered bathroom mirror, knowing that there were all sorts of things a fellow in his position was supposed to have done that he hadn't done. These teeth, for example. They were straight enough, yet marred by a grayish pallor that had suddenly been deemed unacceptable. His teeth should be whiter, given current standards and expectations. He drew a copious dose of medicinal mouthwash, and winced from the sting as he gargled. You either felt one way or the other about mouthwash. Most believed that you could gargle and there would be no pain. Nathan didn't understand such people. He spat into the basin and gazed again at his teeth, a mossy cast now to the gray. There were procedures at the dentist's office, plus countless over-the-counter gels, pastes, and potions designed to make everyone's teeth the whitest white white could be. Manny smoked, yet his teeth gleamed within his goatee, the canines unusually long and sharp for a human, it seemed to Nathan. Even fat Del's teeth gleamed. Divorced Del, pushing sixty, but still very much in the sex game. Maybe sick Solomon too, given all his bluster. Shtupping was important. Nathan didn't wholly disagree with his elder. Everything was in it. Or could be. Life whittled down to its concentrated fury. But who'd share a bed with Nathan looking the way he looked? He had visited the barber for his Jewfro, anyway, shaved the ginger bristle from his face, but his skinny ass, his bent-elbow nose, the crevasses across his brow, his copious thatch of dark-red hair about his groin, and these hands. What could be done about Nathan's mottled paws, impervious to sunscreen or the lanolin-rich Bag Balm ointment his fellow captains swore by? In fairness, the brash mid-day light streaming into his bathroom wasn't doing him any favors. It made sense that most people courted their lovers at night, under the kind cover of darkness.

We can take a walk. It seemed harmless enough for a first date. Hardly a date at all. Denuded, thankfully, from the specter of sex. *We can take a walk*, Kati had suggested. He liked that Kati had offered the suggestion rather than leave it for him to determine their plans. And that it was such a humble plan. That she didn't expect anything from him. No fancy meal or entertainment. Just his company. They decided to walk the pier near the restaurant. Just after her shift. It was a good plan. Yet he found himself worrying about matters on the short drive down A1A. What would they talk about outside the realm of coffee, congris, napkins, forks, and como se dice?

He drove slowly, as if en route to an unpleasant medical procedure, one of his father's colonoscopies, say. Nonetheless, he arrived early at the pier's entrance. You didn't keep a woman waiting. He shuffled his feet against the concrete floor and gazed up at the crude tackle festooned against the corkboard inside the pier's open office. Thick wire leaders. Heavy pyramid sinkers. J-hooks. Styrofoam floats.

"Fishing or sightseeing?" a thick old man finally asked behind the desk, gazing up from his Sun-Sentinel, opened wide like a scroll. A cauliflower ear somehow held a pen.

"Just sightseeing. But I'm waiting for someone." The old man nodded, gazed back down at his broad sheaf of newspaper.

It took Nathan a moment to spot Kati's approach. Only after she smiled toward him, flashing her fetching dog tooth, was he certain that it was her. He had expected her to be wearing her work clothes. Black stretch pants and a simple white top, her jet black hair tamed in its pony. But she must have brought a change of clothes to the restaurant, because she wore blue jeans that hugged her ample hips and a sheer blouse in a rich color Nathan couldn't quite determine, scoop-necked to accentuate her décolleté, sprayed by a tantalizing constellation of chest-freckles. Her hair was down now, tickling her tender neck and clavicles. She surprised Nathan once she reached him by leaning in and planting a chaste kiss beside his mouth, a quick jab that left no time for Nathan to respond in kind, which might have been a good thing. As she withdrew, he smelled the pleasant foodsmoke clinging to her beneath the cloying floral notes of freshly applied perfume.

"You made it. Great."

"Of course I make it." She crinkled up her nose, rabbit-like, amused or perhaps only confused by his apparent surprise.

Her lips were full and red, the top one slightly plumper than its partner below. He wasn't used to seeing her lips painted. The faint kohl outlines demarcating the borders of her brown eyes seemed to be the only makeup she wore at the restaurant. She was especially lovely, Nathan thought. More lovely than he had known, as if her beauty was a secret she had only now decided to share. This new Kati affected Nathan, powerfully. Not so much her scrubbed appearance, but that she had brought a change of clothes, had applied a coat of lipstick, shpritzed a deodorizing dose of cloying floral perfume he didn't much like to mask the foodsmells from her job. For him.

"Shall we head out?" he suggested, gathering his wits. Kati nodded. He brandished two single dollar bills for the old man, who nodded and cleared his throat and lifted a hand to his cauliflower ear to grasp the pen, then jotted something down in a ledger. Nathan placed the bills beneath the heavy lead sinker, stationed there on the counter, apparently, so that the old man need not rise unless absolutely necessary, but could just nod and clear his throat and jot something down in a ledger. Nathan was glad that Kati allowed him to pay, that she lingered silently behind him, yet felt somewhat embarrassed by the nominal charge. Big spender, Nathan Pray.

"So Alicia's with her grandmother?" he inquired once they walked through the low gate, passing the dingy dog kennels, where nobody left their dog.

"Mm-hm," Kati answered. He considered reaching for her hand but decided against the gesture. He could scarcely imagine groping for her elegant fingers with his leather mitt. Perhaps to relieve them both of the pressure, she crossed her arms beneath her bosom as they walked. It was a blessedly warm wintertime day, but a stiff south wind buffeted them now that they were on the pier.

"Are you cold?" he inquired, not knowing what he'd do, exactly, if she were.

"No. This is no cold. You cold, Nathaniel? . . . Nathan?" she corrected herself. She leaned a shoulder into his shoulder, just slightly higher up, bumping him off his line, playful.

The true pier rats, exuding vague homelessness, fished the deepest end, where it widened into a rectangle. There weren't many people along this shallow end of the pier: a preternaturally short Latino couple, the small mother pushing their oversize toddler in a flimsy umbrella stroller; a few youngish white girls with stringy hair, facing northward to release the vapors of their e-cigarettes to the atmosphere; an overdressed middle-aged black couple gazing over the side, looking baffled to have stumbled across the Atlantic. There were any number of things that he and Kati ought to discuss, probably. Their backstories. The most salient, digestible nuggets first. Details to follow, depending upon how things proceeded. Yet Nathan didn't feel like making these clumsy inquiries or responding in kind. He only wanted to be there with her.

"Such pretty clouds. It's nice here," she observed, clutching an audible dose of salt air into her lungs.

Nathan gazed out toward the collection of smokestack cumulus clouds offshore. "I used to fish here once in a while with my friend when I was a boy. Terrance. Miles, my son, used to like walking the pier with me too. Before he was embarrassed to be seen with me."

He meant this as a mild joke, but it must not have come off that way, because Kati looked up at him with a furrowed brow.

"He only twelve, yes?"

Nathan nodded.

"Children can't act like that in Colombia. Not nice."

"He's a good kid, really."

"I know."

Halfway down the pier they encountered a few fishermen, scrawny bare-chested teenage boys with boxers hanging up over the waistband of their shorts, pubic hair trailing above toward their navels. When Nathan was that age, his peers wore overlong boxers that streamed below the short legs and their corduroy OP shorts, never these sagging shorts that exposed their underwear at their waists. Perhaps when you got right down to it this was the only difference between generations: each finding its own way to look, and be, ridiculous.

"Oh, he catch something!" Kati stopped in her tracks and pointed toward one of the boys pulling up a small flat fish over the rail. It gleamed like a silver dollar. She grasped Nathan's arm with both hands, as if to protect herself from the piscine creature. "What it is? You know?"

"It's called a lookdown," he explained, pleased that he could explain something to Kati. "Decent panfish. A challenge to fillet, though." For whatever reason, it hadn't occurred to him that the fishing pier might offer him this opportunity to sound intelligent.

They remained at a slight distance as the boy landed the fish directly into the steel sink at the center of the walkway. After doing so, the kid returned to the rail, carved another flap of soggy defrosted squid-flesh and baited his hook.

They walked to the sink and gazed inside. Dozens of gleaming lookdowns, stacked like silver coins, quivered in the deep basin.

"Oh my," Kati said.

"Stupid." Nathan shook his head. "They should let some of those small ones go."

Kati nodded. "Let's go," she suggested, grasping his hand now, which surprised Nathan. Her flesh, the warmth finally seeping through his hardened palms and digits, felt impossibly soft.

"I'm sorry about my hand. I know it's rough."

"It's not rough," she lied, gripping his hand tighter. "I like your hands. They smell like lemon always."

The air grew saltier to the nose as they walked and the wind gusted stronger. Kati, a few times, lifted her hand to tuck a lock of hair behind a tiny ear. "I should walk like this more," she said, "so I don't get more fat."

"You're not fat, Kati."

They reached the veranda at the far end just before the end of the pier, where it flared into its rectangle. Thankfully, Nathan had remembered to bring change, so he bought two colas at the vending machine. He liked that Kati didn't ask for diet.

It was still early for the dock rats, but a few had already arrived to claim their patch of real estate along the rail at the end of the structure, mostly twenty and thirty-something men—white, black, Asian and Latino–wearing stained undershirts, grungy fish towels streaming from the sides of their baggy shorts. A woman fished there too, her soft white belly protruding from beneath her too-short tank top. Nathan and Kati weaved around the coolers, bait-buckets, and heavy rods to survey the goings-on. The rods had to be stout to horse kingfish and cobia the forty feet or so from water to the pier deck, even with the benefit of their hoop nets.

Releasing Nathan's hand, Kati leaned over the railing to gaze down at the sea. Her shirt rode up at the waist and Nathan couldn't help but notice the caramel flesh at her hip, dappled by three paler fingers where her skin had stretched. He joined Kati's side and peered down at the ocean bobbing like bathwater. The water was clear and blue. Too clear and blue for productive fishing. He could see a behemoth puffer fish scooting along at the bottom and the silver dollar flash of lookdowns that had thus far escaped the carnage at the shallow end of the dock.

"What's that big fish?" Kati asked, tugging at Nathan's arm, pointing to the toothy torpedo on the ground at a fisherman's feet. Nathan turned from the water to take in the large barracuda, which he hadn't noticed.

"'Cuda," the fisherman beside the barracuda declared, having overheard the question. The fisherman was tall and black. A rainbow rasta cap sagged like a scrotum, holding his dreads.

"They taste good?" Kati asked Nathan.

"No. They don't eat them." He led Kati away from the fisherman, back toward the veranda. "Too bony. And some big ones like that have ciguatera, a deadly toxin. They bring them up and kill them to keep them from scaring off or eating all the snapper and grouper they're hoping to catch for themselves."

"But you don't like that."

"How'd you know?"

They reached the bench under the veranda and sat. It wasn't cold under the shelter, but she sat near, gripped his closest biceps with both hands. He could feel the warmth of her thigh against his own leg. He appreciated the contact, which felt more intimate to Nathan than it might have felt to Kati. This human touch.

"I can tell what you think. You don't say much, but your face, Nathan. Your face always say what you think."

Nathan nodded. He knew this about himself, his inability, or maybe only unwillingness, to disguise his feelings. "It's not the biggest deal in the world that they kill the barracudas," he explained. "They fish for food, these people. Which makes a difference. Most people don't, even those who eat their catch. So you have to take that into account. But it's never seemed right to me to kill barracuda for being barracuda." Kati nodded, made a listening noise. "He probably caught that one over there right under the dock, where they prowl. But they cast their lines way out there." Nathan batted a hand out toward the Bahamas. "That barracuda wasn't eating anything they're after. It's mostly just superstition, killing them. Or hedging bets. People should treat them better." He took a deep inhale through his nostrils, savoring the tang of the sea brine and bait.

"You're good at should," Kati declared brightly, making a joke. He looked toward her, returned her smile to let her know that he didn't take offense.

"The way you think about fish. Those silver ones. And this big one with teeth. You're different than Manny and the other morning men. It's because you're Jewish, maybe. Yes?" The question, its bluntness, surprised Nathan. It took him a moment to gather his wits.

"No. I mean, I don't think so. Technically, anyway, fish don't rate so high on the Jewish scale. Jews can't hunt birds or mammals. It's not kosher. You can't control the pain when you hunt. Probably other reasons too. Birds and mammals must be slaughtered under very specific conditions. Sharp blades. Trained slaughterer. But fish don't fall under the meat category. They don't have to be domesticated and slaughtered. They can be gathered, kind of like wheat. At least the ones with fins and scales."

"So it's *not* Jewish, the way you think?" Kati joked again, flashing her dog tooth.

She wasn't just sweet and pretty. There was something wise about Kati. That "good at should" quip. Now this kernel she had gleaned from within the layers of Nathan's words. His Talmudic acumen didn't extend much beyond the watery realm. He had only researched the Jewish rules, vis-à-vis fish, to counter Miles' claims as a seven-year-old that fishing was cruel. "They're God's creatures too," his son had argued. Nathan conceded the point, but a few days later offered Miles the full Jewish picture, which did little in the end to bring Miles around.

"And the snook fish? Why you like the snook fish so much?"

A laughing gull, treading the northward currents over the railing, stared straight at Nathan, mocking him with a staccato series of *ha-ha's*; the drag of a nearby fishing line *zipped* upon a strike; a fisherman farther away cried, "Son of a fucking bitch!" in response to some frustration. Shark, maybe.

"Is it okay I ask?"

"Yeah-yeah, it's fine. It's just tough to answer, I guess. There's lots of reasons. They're both familiar and strange, the snook. Right under our feet, haunting our canals and estuaries blocks from our homes. A fish for everyone, really, unlike the swords, mahi and grouper miles offshore. Yet they're more mysterious than those deepwater fish. The more we find out about them, the more it seems that we don't know anything."

"Anything?"

"Well, I'm exaggerating a little. We've figured out their spawning sites, their lunar preferences. We know that they start off as males, then become females after a few years if they're lucky enough to live that long–"

"No."

"Yes. Honest. Nice trick, huh? Protandric hermaphrodites, they're called. But there's still a lot we don't know. Where, exactly, individual snook migrate inshore, and why, and when. They're unpredictable. I've kept a log of every single snook I've caught since I was seventeen–location, date and time, the moon phase, the weather, depth, the lure–and I'm only beginning to patch together a meaningful pattern. Probably never will. They like freshwater. We know that. They need it for the larvae to survive, but you'll find them in the backcountry at the strangest times, and then glimpse one cruising the surf dead of winter. Fish we've tagged up in Stuart have shown up in the Middle Keys, which doesn't seem to make much sense as a migratory pattern. And their feeding patterns? Forget about it. On neap tides–when the water doesn't move quite as much—you don't expect them to be biting, but then *bam,* they'll surprise you. And then they'll get lockjaw for no apparent reason. Spring tide, neap tide, warm weather, cool weather. Whenever. Can dangle a live shrimp right in front of their nose and they won't so much as look at it."

"Sounds like a smart fish."

"Yes. Smart. But they're vulnerable too. Almost seine netted to oblivion in the forties before the first net bans and bag limits were imposed. Only helped so much, those first regulations. People still overharvested them during the summer spawn. Using live bait, it's like shooting fish in a barrel at their staging areas during spawn."

"In a barrel?"

"Just an expression. Sorry. All I mean is that as wily and intelligent as they are, they're also incredibly sensitive. See, they have one major weakness. Temperature. They can handle water close to 52, 53 degrees if the drop is gradual, but never as cold as 50. And a quick snap down to 60, 55 . . . gone. That cold snap from the polar vortex we had last month may have wiped out our whole southeast population. It was more devastating for the snook than the red tides on the gulf coast over the summer and fall. I'm not sure if they're still here. Where they might be if they are. Or if they'll return if they're not. I've looked. I'm still looking."

Nathan looked over at Kati who nodded her head and stared over the railing. It was tough to read her thoughts.

"There aren't enough snook in the world," he uttered. "I guess I just like to know where they are."

He waited for Kati to say something, but she remained silent.

"I know this all sounds sort of weird," he said. "Or silly, in the grand scheme of things. It's not like I don't know that."

"No. Not weird, Nathan. Or silly." She still gazed out over the railing. Nathan followed her eyes toward the brown pelican now staring straight at them, stationary in the air beyond the railing. It seemed to have taken over on shift work from the laughing gull. "I think it's good to care so much about something. Maybe it doesn't matter what. Most people, Nathan, I don't think care about nothing."

He nodded. They sat for a while without talking, which didn't feel awkward to him and didn't feel awkward to Kati either, he somehow knew. Perhaps because she remained so close, her thigh touching his thigh, because she lifted one of her hands from his biceps to pet the red fur on his forearm in slow, unhurried strokes.

"That man," she finally said, "who came into the café, called you Snookmaster. Kip—"

"Chip, you mean. Chip Holiday."

"With the bad hands, yes?" she rubbed her hands together and scrunched up her nose to make a funny face, which made Nathan show his teeth, then she clutched his arm again as if seeking ballast.

"Yes, that's him."

"He's an important person. Yes?"

Nathan admitted that he was. He explained what the Fishing Report was all about on the Sunshine Network, the audience of anglers it reached, the chance it afforded him to make his mark, finally, if things worked out the way Nathan hoped. Chip Holiday had already scheduled him for a guest appearance up at the studio in Orlando. Artificial spoons and plugs, Nathan would endorse, rather than live bait, which was practically cheating. Simple light tackle. Catch and release. A conservationist ethic, above all. *Don't catch your limit, limit your catch!* Kati liked the slogan.

"It could change everything for me. In a good way," he said. "If it works out." She nodded, slowly. A salt breeze buffeted them and felt good in his nose and lungs. It seemed to Nathan that she was mulling over her next words, choosing them with care.

"And if not. If it not work out. That's okay." Her words detonated a response in Nathan's belly that felt not unlike nausea. It was something large and generous that she had offered him, something that only those who most cared for you thought to offer. Permission to fail.

Now is when we kiss, he thought. He vaguely remembered how this was done. You turned to face your partner, who offered you her parted mouth. But could he perform this hackneyed ritual still without feeling ridiculous, surrender to the moment? It had been some time.

"Are you sure this is okay?" he asked. "I'm not . . ." he couldn't quite locate his next words. *I'm not Latino? Columbian? Catholic? Christian? Young? Handsome? Gainfully employed?*

There were so many things that Nathan wasn't.

"Yes. It's okay," Kati uttered, turning toward Nathan, pulling at his arm ever so slightly, pulling him into the moment.

Chapter Eight

Nathan should have consulted his journal entries over the past several years on the inshore and offshore goings on circa tonight's date. Parked at the washdown now, he should be thinking about the incoming and the outgoing, the barometric pressure and moon phase, his go-to baits and honey-holes. He should be thinking about what to do with Wolf's damn baits stewing still in their putrid juices on the Tacoma's passenger seat. It was a big night, the crew on its way from the Sunshine Network to take some preliminary film of Nathan in action.

But here he was, gearing up his inshore rods beside the *Pray Fish*, absently wrapping Albrights to secure ten-pound braid to his thirty-pound fluoro leader (popping corks on two rods), tying his gleaming spoons and dogwood lures with loop knots he neglected to wet between his lips before tightening, waiting on the film crew for the Sunshine Network's Fishing Report and thinking of Kati. Thinking of sex with Kati, specifically. They would go to bed with one another soon, he contemplated. His blood stirred, but an odd wistfulness descended upon him too. Everything would change.

It was something everyone negotiated, one way or another, it seemed to Nathan, the tyranny of sex. He had lived outside of sex for several months and there were certain advantages, he'd discovered. It left you with so much blessed time, for one thing. He had tapped the celibate sublime. Yet it was no way for Nathan to live long-term, this monastic version of the real. He didn't need old Sol to tell him as much.

And so here he was, thinking about sex once again, losing time, giving over his now.

**

"You're Captain Pray, mate?" Nathan detected what he thought was a British accent. But wasn't "mate" an Aussie flourish?

"Umm, yeah. Nate's fine."

"Simon," he said, extending a fleshy hand. Nathan shook. The blonde fellow carried a square canvas bag that somehow betrayed photography (the padded strap?) over his left shoulder. Tied somewhere beneath his pregnant belly were the sleeves of a black windbreaker. "I'm from Sunshine," the cameraman abbreviated the network's name. Nathan chuckled. A person couldn't seem less like coming from sunshine. Fat like Del, but pasty, plagued by razor burn about his jowls, the fellow seemed hopelessly out of his element here. The accent might have had something to do with it. He wore oversized khaki shorts (odd for a cold night), sneakers and tube socks, pulled high up his chubby, hairless calves. The Fishing Report was probably a minor part of his duties for the Sunshine Network, which likely sent him mostly to nonpiscatorial goings on throughout the state: Hemingway lookalike contests in Key West, the Strawberry Queen Pageant in Plant City, the Watermelon Festival in Newberry, the live mermaid show in Weeki Wachi, the Davie Rodeo, boiled peanut festivals and county fairs here and there.

"You're alone, then?" Nathan asked, glancing over Simon's shoulder.

"Yes, just me I'm afraid. We only need a few frames. Hopefully

216

a fish or two. We'd like to run less file footage. People are getting a mite weary of seeing the same tarpon and redfish film."

Yes, Nathan had noticed the monotonous footage on the Fishing Report Thursday nights.

"I probably won't be able to help you with the redfish and tarpon. Ladyfish, maybe. Mangrove snappers. Jacks. Snook only if we're lucky."

"Snook would be brilliant. They're still knocking about this way? After the frosty spells?"

"If we're lucky. Like I said."

The cameraman nodded, acceding to the terms. "Small vessel," he declared, glancing toward the *Pray Fish*. "We're only fishing the intra-coastal tonight, yes mate?"

Nathan bridled at the insult to his vessel, but tried not to show it. "Yeah, we'll stay inside. It's a bit sporty out there past the inlet. East winds fifteen to twenty. Seas three to five. Anyway, I'll launch her. You can wait up there on the dock over beside the ramp." The cameraman wordlessly obeyed, leaving Nathan to think ill of him (unfairly) for not offering to help unclip the winch hook from the eye, hold a bow line . . . something. Nathan exhaled wearily inside the Tacoma, backing the trailer down the mossy concrete ramp. It was pretty strenuous, disapproving of people all the time.

Low tide. The prow bobbed in the drink several feet below the dock. Nathan, after loading the surprisingly heavy camera bag, helped Simon negotiate his way safely on board. "Maybe you should sit down on the dock first. Yes. Now don't step on the gunwale. Put your foot here, directly on deck. . . . Right foot first if you don't mind. . . . Well, whatever. Fine. Take my hand now. Good."

"The boat always drains like this?" Simon asked as soon as he straightened himself, clutching his lower back with two meaty paws. Nathan glanced back toward bilge, pissing a robust stream into the murky ramp water.

"Umm, no." Nathan, preoccupied by thoughts of Kati, had forgotten to screw in the plug at the transom. The automatic bilge had kept them afloat, but he could see the aft sitting lower than usual in the water. Affecting nonchalance, he stepped slowly toward the stern, reached down beneath the skeg and plugged the boat. The bilge continued to drain. "We're good now," he assured his companion, returning to the console, placing his wallet and mobile phone in the glove box. He lowered the Merc from the switch at the throttle and fired the engine, which spit and coughed but found its idle. He backed the *Pray Fish* slowly off the trailer and then pulled the skiff fast to the dock with his hand. He needn't clear the ramp as it was a typically vacant night. He didn't even see Charlie's or Nguyen's trailers in the lot. Maybe they weren't starting out until late. The reef bite over the past weeks had been coming on ridiculously late, or early, depending upon how you looked at 3 AM. No point in even trying to get Terrance to join him.

"Stay here a sec'," Nathan said after tying off the bow and two spring lines to the dock cleats. He'd normally only tie off the bow, but after his shaky start . . .

"Stay here? On the boat? You certain now?" Simon looked

about warily while he zipped up his windbreaker. Nathan heard the bilge sputter behind them as it squirted a few more water ropes, then cease. Good. He hopped up on the dock. "Yeah. No worries my friend. I'll be right back."

He parked, relinquishing the truck to the feral cats, lurking on their haunches beneath the palmetto fans near the picnic bench. He spotted the glowing eyes of two or three of the ammoniac creatures in his headlight beams. They'd scurry underneath the warm engine as soon as he cleared out. He glanced over at the vinyl passenger seat after setting the brake, snatched the plastic bag of Wolf's baits stewing in their juices while gritting his soft teeth. Simon seemed especially relieved to see him again, as if he doubted he'd return. Nathan backed out the *Pray Fish*, flicked on his white stern light, his green and red bow lights, and headed north up the ICW, kept it at 14 rpm's, minimum-wake. He savored the brackish aromas that quickly displaced the catpiss and beery smells at the boat ramp. The moon was more than half-full and bright above the Atlantic beyond the barrier island, the sleepy Australian pines and stray high-rises. On the wane, Nathan knew, because the moon was a liar, its illumined portion forming the "C" as if it were coming, not the "D," as if it was decreasing. Not so good for the bite, this bright night, but the mild chop would help. The tide, too, should be fairly strong. If he chanced onto a decent pulse, who knew? The lapping water beyond the bow was pretty, bathed in the moon's silver. Probably good for filming, he imagined. He'd head up to Lake Wyman first for ladyfish and jack, then head back down and try the crusty bridge pilings around Pioneer Park for sheepshead, the lighted docks up the El Rio and Hillsboro for snook, maybe head clear up to the spillway well inshore if Simon was game.

"Shall I wear a lifejacket?" the cameraman half-asked and half-said, crouching with his bag on the cushioned seat in front of the console.

"Do you *want* to wear a lifejacket, Simon?"

The cameraman shrugged. Nathan pointed to the hatch at the bow. "Help yourself." Few of Nathan's inshore charters wore lifejackets. The only nice ones he kept were the youth-sized, as children were required to don the PFD's. Simon gazed into the hatch, lifted a mildewed Mae West between two pincers of his meaty paws for inspection, and then lowered it back into its compartment.

"Very well, then. Let's get a pic or two of you at the helm there."

"Sure."

Simon bent down and unzipped his canvas bag, a *zippp* Nathan barely heard on account of the two-stroke chugging behind him. When he warily rose, facing Nathan, he was peering through a miniature camera, smaller than the camera with the disposable flashes that Nathan's mother had used when he was a child. Things used to be big to be impressive, Nathan reflected. Now they were small. Smaller the better.

"You're going to wear that hat, mate?" Simon asked, as if he had only noticed the hat through the lens.

Nathan reached up to feel his baseball cap and headlamp, which he had forgotten were up there on his head. "Umm, do you *not* want me to wear it?" He wondered what his shell of ginger curls must look like by now, pressed under the cap, then chastised himself for worrying about his hair.

"It's just we won't be able to see much of you underneath the bill."

"So you want me to take it off is what you're saying. . . ."

". . . . Perhaps take it off. For now." Nathan obeyed. "We just need one shot. You've seen our show, yes?"

Nathan nodded.

"They'll post the image on the screen toward the end of your segment while you're reviewing the inshore and offshore highlights. They'll advertise your website at the bottom. Be good for your . . . uhh . . . business." The fellow uttered business as if he had already gleaned that it was probably an overblown word for whatever operation Nathan was running.

"I don't have a website."

"Your telephone number, then." Simon raised the tiny silver camera. "Don't worry about smiling, Nate."

"Okay." Nathan didn't quite know what to do with his face. He tried to affect a toothless gaze of affable neutrality. A tiny bulb flashed. Simon lowered the camera, gazed down toward its back at the tiny screen; he didn't seem pleased with the image.

"You didn't come out, quite. Let's try again." They tried again. Simon looked down into the screen and looked scarcely more pleased. Nathan, for the first time this evening, felt sorry for the poor fellow, stuck with this crappy assignment, foundering in his chosen profession, perhaps, just as Nathan struggled in his own.

"One more time, then. . . . Okay, that'll have to do."

"One of those fancy digitals, eh?"

"Not fancy. Good enough for this kind of thing. We don't subject the quality to the saltwater."

Nathan glanced at his Timex. Still early. Plenty of fishing they could do. After failing to cast net up a single pilchard or sardine earlier, he had shelled out fifteen bucks at 7-Seas for some lethargic shrimp, only arguably "live." Three or four good snappers he'd have to catch later to compensate for the outlay. Remembering the shrimp, he flicked the livewell on to give the critters some oxygen. He heard the intermittent piss-stream of water as the sloshing thirty-five gallon well dipped below the valve. It was contra his inshore principles, these live shrimp, but he needed to scare up a fish or two for the cameras. Principles were one thing. But he wasn't a fool. You couldn't do exactly what you wanted. He wouldn't be a total fool, he had promised himself. Nathan nudged the throttle to 16 rpm's. He glanced to the west shore at the low dock with the blue underwater lights. A regular snook spot. He glimpsed their phantoms tearing through the wrinkled sheet of the surface, their buff yellow dorsal fins, slamming finger mullet and juvenile ladyfish. But they weren't there now, he knew, motoring past. The snook were farther inside if they were anywhere. Within moments they reached the gaudy mansion with the faux Michelangelo sculptures, then the Wyman's mouth, which opened to receive them.

"Son of a bitch," Nathan uttered loud enough for Simon to hear. He had spotted the *Chasin' Tail*, anchored up just inside the red channel marker and bobbing mildly in the light winter chop. Any other night he'd want to spy Manny's deck, check it for a seine net or some other evidence of poaching (mullet flopping about, inordinate sand or debris about the gunwale and transom), but not tonight with the Fishing Report cameraman on his skiff. His fellow captains would know about the broadcast soon enough, but he didn't care to be hazed at the Caribbean Café ahead of time.

Manny had someone on board with him, Nathan could tell. Two headlamps on the panga flashed toward the *Pray Fish* in unison. Manny and his buddy had spotted him. Perfect. No avoiding them now. It would be bad form to chug off without stopping a moment. You didn't just leave a fellow captain bobbing in your wake without checking in, the charter captain's code that even Manny abided. Thankfully, Simon's gear was safely sealed now. He looked enough like a green nighttime charter, even though nighttime inshore charters were usually the more seasoned anglers, and were more a late spring through fall thing too, the mangrove snappers migrating inshore with the bait pods, catch-and-release tarpon and snook fattening up for spawn, less wary of line and leader during the October mullet run.

Manny and his buddy lifted their hands to turn off their headlamps as Nathan pulled alongside, sitting the *Pray Fish* at the *Chasin' Tail's* knee.

"Fancy seeing you here, Bruce," Simon greeted Manny's companion before Nathan even had the chance to greet Manny. "Nifty torch, mate. You look like a spelunker."

"You two know each other?" Nathan asked, switching off the growling two-stroke (which he hadn't planned on doing). Manny looked equally perplexed, his jaw fixed behind the helm.

"Bruce . . . umm . . . shoots for the Sunshine Network, as well," Simon confessed, just now gleaning the awkwardness, it seemed.

"Haven't gotten seasick yet, have you, Simon?" Bruce was tall and seemed fit, even beneath his windbreaker, which brandished the network's solar logo. Had Manny been assigned the better cameraman?

"Well, how's the bite?" Nathan asked his fellow captain as casually as he could muster. He had to say something, anyway.

"Just started out. Tryin' to chum up some pilchards. Cold as a witch's tit out here." Nathan could detect the lie beneath Manny's evasiveness, partly because Bruce gave him a double-take.

"Yeah. It's pretty cold," Nathan uttered. "Well, best be on our way." He fired the Merc. Simon lifted his hand toward his colleague, who did the same.

"Tight lines," Manny declared above the two-stroke, smirking beneath his goatee to flash his sharp canines.

Nathan headed toward the west shore as far from Manny's panga as possible. Why couldn't Manny stick to Broward waters? He had to horn in on Nathan's honey-holes? He turned off the ignition and used the trolling once they got two hundred yards or so from where he intended to fish. Slack tide now so he wouldn't have to bother with the anchor. They could just drift with the chop alongside the mangroves, scare up some ladyfish and jacks. Crouching over the trolling motor,

Nathan heard a *whoop* from Manny resound across the silver water. He glanced over his shoulder and saw the bright camera light flashing on the Chasin' Tail. Simon must have heard the *whoop* too. But he didn't seem to look back at the panga. And he didn't say anything. Nathan appreciated that. They wouldn't speak about the rival footage being shot across the way.

"Want a Lemonhead?" Nathan asked, rattling the cardboard container.

"Lemon head?" Simon asked, confused.

"It's a candy. Like a lemon drop."

"Sure."

"Take the box."

"Cheers."

"You're from England, I guess?"

"Liverpool."

Nathan worked the shoreline for the next hour or so without much success. Simon held his video camera at the ready on his shoulder, which addled Nathan, somewhat. But he was patient, Simon. He'd give him that. And he didn't talk much, which Nathan liked.

"How do you know what they are before you see them?" the cameraman asked between modest blue runner catches, which he insisted on filming.

"Herky-jerky," Nathan explained. "Every species bites and fights a bit different."

Another hour passed.

"Shall we try a different spot, mate?" Simon finally inquired. Nathan had exhausted his arsenal of rigged lures, had thrown a few live shrimp, which was how he got the blue runners.

"Thing is, this is our best shot at ladyfish." Stretching his back, his deviated septum to the sky, Nathan inhaled, seeking insight from the atmosphere. The east wind carried a skunk's perfume from Red Reef Park. He really wanted a ladyfish. Or a friskier jack crevalle. He glanced down at his Timex. He didn't like the idea of moving on without one or the other. Manny was on some fish. No doubt about that. The tide was just coming in. Ladyfish or jack, Nathan figured. Barracuda maybe. He wasn't whooping and wailing over piddly blue runners.

"Just give me a sec'." Nathan stepped off the casting deck and sat beside Simon before the console, withdrew the nail-clippers dangling beneath his shirt from its shoestring and set about re-rigging. The cameraman's thick middle pressed against his side.

"Cozy boat."

"My girl."

Simon, no doubt, had taken note of Manny's larger vessel, its custom T-top with the rocket launchers, the fancy hull treatment, Chasin' Tail, emblazoned in bubbly, Day-Glo cursive. Perhaps he expected Nathan to justify his more modest boat. But you didn't make apologies for your vessel. You didn't even think unflattering thoughts if you could help it. Even if you had foolishly sacrificed a decent V hull for a skinny draft; even if a more aggressive bow and more narrow beam would make a heck of a lot more sense given the dicey inlet; even if it were high time Nathan stepped up to a true center console–maybe a panga, like Manny's; even if the spitting and sputtering long-in-the-tooth two-stroke would force matters to a crisis before too long. Somehow, he'd have to scrape together the funds to buy a new boat. But he wouldn't think ill of his skiff while she was bearing their weight.

"My girl," Nathan repeated, frisking himself for the plastic baits, marinating in their black juices. What would it hurt to try just one of Wolf's stewed baits?

"*Whew,* that sure smells frightful."

Nathan nodded.

"What is it?"

"Just something new. Soft plastic in a fish attractant soup. They're all doing it. All the artificial bait outfits."

Simon nodded.

"Well *that* didn't take long!" the cameraman declared moments later, rising to the occasion. His movie camera was rolling, Nathan knew, because it bathed the entire mangrove shoreline just twenty yards before them in its ochre light. As he labored silently over his bent rod, Nathan caught a glimpse of glowing red eyes in the shoreline foliage. A night heron. Or maybe a small raccoon.

"Act like it's giving you a tussle, mate."

"It *is* giving me a tussle."

"But *act* like it."

Nathan didn't go in for the outsized gestures when he was on a fish. He didn't grit his teeth or horse it in. He didn't hoot and holler. He didn't boast over its fight or its size, even when he was certain he had a lunker on the line. He kept his cool, even once he landed a trophy catch. An artist acted like he'd done it before and would do it again. An artist made it look easy, not hard.

But this wasn't what Simon wanted him to do. So Nathan leaned his shoulders back and bent his rod. He reached down and loosened his drag, extending the fight, letting the poor ladyfish tire itself. The ladyfish, emboldened, leapt at ten o'clock, then splashed down in the drink.

"Brilliant!" Simon exclaimed. "I got it! Snook!?"

"Afraid not. Ladyfish, though." Nathan wouldn't have treated a snook the way he treated this ladyfish. Here Nathan was, tossing one of Wolf's stewed baits, yukking it up for the camera, worrying over what he did and what he said, and how he did and how he said. Worrying about how everything looked. Yet he wouldn't sabotage himself tonight. If things worked out with the Fishing Report, he'd have plenty of opportunity to broadcast his loftier fishing ethics.

"Okay, here she comes." The depleted silver fish listed beside the boat, offering Simon, looming above, a perfect shot. It was larger than Nathan had anticipated. Two pounds, easy. Closer to three, maybe. Nathan lowered his hands over the gunwale to dehook the weary creature in the water.

"No-no," Simon said. "Lift him up onto the boat. I'll get a nice shot of him hanging from the line."

"You sure? It's sort of tough on their organs to hang them vertical. And they're sort of known for–"

"Yes, definitely. Please."

Nathan complied, whereupon the flopping ladyfish, mustering its reserve, spackled its rusty shit all over the deck, and all over Simon. Nathan tried not to feel good about that.

"Oh, dear," Simon said, flicking off his camera light, glancing down at the coffee goo spattered across his shorts, tube socks, and sneakers.

"So much for these trainers."

"Trainers?"

"Sneakers, I mean."

Nathan nodded. "Sorry about that, Simon. I tried to warn you. Their name is something of a misnomer you might say. It's no lady."

"Ah, no worries, mate."

Nathan labored to extricate Wolf's bait from the poor creature's gullet, brandishing the dehooker he usually used for barbed catfish. He should have been happy to catch a decent fish for Simon, but it bothered him how quickly the juiced soft bait produced, how hungrily it was devoured.

"Bugger really swallowed it, eh?"

Nathan nodded. "Gut-hooked, I'm afraid. But I might . . . there. Got it. She might be okay."

He lowered the silver creature back beneath the crumpled skin of the water. Dead weight in his hands, too weary to flinch. The fish gleamed silver beneath the moon.

"You don't eat them?"

"No. Most of us don't, anyway. But I've seen some Vietnamese fishermen spoon the meat off the bones at the dock to make fishballs out of them. People call them baby tarpon 'cause they're so scrappy and sort of fight the same. You saw how it jumped."

The ladyfish quivered, finally, bucked. Nathan removed a hand from its belly but grasped it still by the tail, forcing it to gather its legs before swimming off.

"But they're not as prized as tarpon."

"No, but they're a good fish."

"But not as good as tarpon."

"No. Afraid not."

"Or snook."

"No."

Nathan opened his hand, released the revived creature. "But a good fish, still. A good enough fish for anyone." It's something Terrance would have said, and the few Vietnamese men he'd seen scraping ladyfish meat from the spine with a spoon to make fish balls. Something Nathan believed too. He kept his eyes on the ladyfish beneath the twin beams of moon and headlamp before it disappeared five feet down or so into the brackish water. "She just might make it, Simon."

**

They never quite made it up the Hillsboro River to scout for snook in greater earnest. Switching back to his homemade silver mullet, Nathan patrolled the canals just south of the inlet and landed a frisky barracuda and a smaller ladyfish. Using every last live shrimp, he also pulled up a solid sheepshead beside a bridge piling at Pioneer Park. He had to negotiate around a few wire crab traps.

"Well mate," Simon uttered after filming the sheepshead, "I have a bit of a drive ahead of me back to Orlando. Need to stop for petrol. We're in fine shape for the segment. No worries about the snook, captain." And so Nathan headed back to the dock, his thoughts returning to Kati as he motored along the minimum wake canals, the two-stroke spitting and sputtering rather contentedly. Then his thoughts veered from Kati toward his earlier business with women, toward Sam, despite himself.

**

He met Samantha at a Snook Working Group meeting at the Lake Worth Civic Center. Drawing, no doubt, the short end of the stick at the DEP's West Palm Beach regional office, she had been "volunteered" to review the agency's planning and management response to the Coastal Zone Management Act of '72. She was by far the most attractive state or federal employee to address their group, most of whom, men and women, set the dowdy and disheveled bar high, sheathed loosely in polyester blends. Samantha, by contrast, wore a fastidiously pleated pastel suit, cotton or maybe even silk, with oyster-shell buttons, surely above her pay-grade, which accentuated her disciplined waist, her modest bustline. Her ample shock of brunette hair–she wore her hair longer just out of law school–she tamed with a decorative brass comb toward the back.

Henry "Skip" Foster, who fished out of the Sebastian Inlet,

had introduced her, listed her credentials. U of F law. Summa cum laude. Managing Editor of Law Review. But she was nervous, Nathan could tell, because she didn't speak extemporaneously after rising to the Formica lectern, even for a few seconds, not so much as a quip about the traffic or the lackluster civic center appointments, but launched right into her presentation after thanking her host. They didn't constitute a large group, only fifteen of them or so. Seated close in his fold-out metal chair, Nathan could see the perspiration beads on her top lip as she read her speech, worded carefully to underscore the DEP's yeomanlike efforts to balance the competing interests of environmental protection and economic development. Every once in a while she lifted her head from her notes to make brief eye contact with her audience. It seemed to Nathan that she gazed his way with disproportionate frequency.

She transitioned to an overhead projector about halfway into her presentation, Skip flicking off the lights upon her manicured cue. The silhouette of her pointer trembled across the expanse of Florida as she highlighted the locale of a few newly acquired estuarine reserves. When she resumed her speech proper, the fluorescents blinking back on upon Skip's command, Nathan noticed tiny cotton beads at both corners of her mouth. He rose as quietly as he could (Samantha lost her place in her text for a moment, but quickly rebounded), retrieved a small paper cup of water from the gurgling cooler at the back of the room, and set it beside her notes on the lectern. She nodded and took a short sip, cleared her throat. Nathan liked the way she tasted her lips before continuing. Her speech was over within a few minutes, however, leaving him to wonder whether his effort to be helpful was worth the disruption.

There was a brief, respectful Q&A, toward which Nathan didn't contribute, an equally respectful round of applause.

He approached the lectern as she gathered her notes, the quivering transparency from the overhead projector. She slid the sheets into a soft leather satchel that bespoke lawyerhood.

"Thanks for the water," she declared before Nathan could thank her for her presentation. She extended a moist hand.

"No problem. You're welcome. Thanks for coming." He might have ventured an innocuous query. *A Florida Gator, eh? . . . What's it like working for the DEP?* Instead: "You realize that your bosses are making a royal mess of things."

"Really?" Finely manicured eyebrows punctuated her question.

"Estuarine reserves as field laboratories to estimate long-range human impact? It's just a bureaucratic smokescreen. I'm sure the Fanjuls are thrilled. You want to know why the inshore fish stocks are depleted, why the snail kites are disappearing along with the apple snails? Big Sugar's been poisoning the Glades with nitrogen and phosphorous ever since Castro shooed them out of Cuba; the cattle industry above the lake isn't much better. The Water Management District's pumping stations have basically been channeling cow crap directly into the Kissimmee Canal–once an actual river by the way–and into Lake O for the past twenty years. Ask the bass brotherhood of guides along the lake what's happened to their fishery. It doesn't take a PhD. I mean, how many longitudinal studies do you need to perform to tell you why it stinks in the bathroom?"

He had grown more exercised than he had intended. But it was tough to keep himself in check once he got started. After all, there had been so many fish for Terrance and him, and the waters had already gone to pot by the 70s. They had missed the truly fishy south Florida years, to hear the salts tell it. Samantha, at any rate, didn't seem to take offense. Rather, she seemed vaguely amused taking in his ardor, her mouth, free now of the cotton saliva specs, parting to reveal moist teeth, fetchingly rounded.

"Your name, again?"

"Nathan. Nathan Pray."

"Nathan," she tasted his name in her mouth. "Pray."

"Yes."

"Interesting name Nathan Pray."

**

Sam had already remarried, which was tough enough. But Sam's latest news: growing a perfect little Epstein sprout in her womb.

At least she wouldn't have a child with the shmuck, he had rationalized almost immediately after Sam told him that she was seeing someone, and that it was serious. She didn't want him to hear about it elsewhere and be shocked. She had met someone else. Of course she had. People, Nathan knew, should be with people. A wisdom as old as the commandments. But at least she wouldn't have another kid, he had taken petty solace. At least she was through with all that, surely. Well, she sure showed him. Good for her, he thinks now.

Was Nathan, too, up for a new start?

**

The cameraman was full of chipper praise as they said their goodbyes at the washdown, but Nathan wasn't so sure. It was tough to discriminate between Simon's enthusiasm for the footage and his thankfulness simply to have made it back ashore. "Good luck to you, captain," were the closing words from the pleasant fellow before he slapped Nathan's shoulder and trotted off to his car.

Nathan would have brooded longer over their excursion. He would have fretted over the goings on on Manny's panga (was he still out there?) as the Merc completed its freshwater, rabbit-eared rinse, were it not for the roar of Nguyen's truck and trailer swinging around the one-way bend. He took a step back to clear out of the way and raised a calloused hand to greet the kingfish specialist. Nguyen, upon spotting him, stopped short of the ramp, bringing his trailer and boat to a groaning halt. He hopped out of his truck, left the door open.

"You done' fish tonight, my friend?"

There was something about the way Nguyen held his pot-belly before him, something prideful, as if it were a muscle. He was the only person from Vietnam who Nathan knew as an individual, which made it sort of ironic that he went by the most anonymous of Vietnamese surnames, Nguyen.

Nathan told him yes, that he was done.

"Early for you. Yes?"

Nathan admitted that it was, that he was planning on going out for snapper but that it was too rough on the outside for his skiff.

"Want'go more fishing with real fish'aman?"

Silver from Nguyen's fillings and more elaborate dental work gleamed from his mouth. Nathan peered over Nguyen's shoulder toward the truck's passenger seat. No one was inside.

"You serious?"

"Yeah-yeah. Serious. Make big money tonight. Kingfish. Need 'notha fisha'man. Neighba' say no. Pay fifty cent' pound we catch. What you say?"

Nathan did the math. He looked up at the eight Penn conventional rods on the Dusky, the stout wire tackle, the creaky Cannon downriggers at the port and starboard corners of the stern.

"Dollar let's say." Nathan smiled to leaven his counteroffer. "Dollar fifty for snapper and grouper."

Nguyen smiled too, showing even more silver. Then his smile disappeared. "Seventy cent' pound only kingfish. My boat. My gear. My gas. Rough sea. You no get out inlet in *Pray Fish*, yes?"

Nathan let the proposal marinate. He didn't smell any alcohol on Nguyen's breath, or from his pores, which was good. Knowing firsthand about the offshore bite would help him for his segment on the Fishing Report. Plus, he was curious about how Nguyen fished, precisely, and where Nguyen fished. And there was the money. But these weren't the main reasons he'd go. After poking around with Simon and aping for the camera, tossing Wolf's juiced baits, he was itching to lose himself in some actual fishing, to put his hands to good use.

"Dolla' f'snappa'," Nguyen sweetened the deal, misinterpreting Nathan's brooding silence for reluctance.

"Deal, captain!"

Chapter Nine

After parking the *Pray Fish*, after reorganizing some gear and locking the hatches, after rejecting his better instincts vis-à-vis a lifejacket (there was the offshore pitch and roll and fat Eddie's unfortunate fate to consider, but he didn't want to insult his skipper), Nathan hustled to the ramp dock and waved Nguyen back. One of the trailer's brake lights was out, but he wouldn't mention it. He inspected the lines of the twenty-four foot Dusky as Nguyen lowered it into the lapping water. Nothing subtle about the vessel. Aggressive bow. Hard chine giving way to a deep V. Not a pleasure cruiser. The sharply angled chine would invite plenty of hull slap. It would spank down more than slice through the waves and list some in the swell on account of the heavy T-top. It wouldn't plane easily with that single Evinrude 250. Fully loaded, it would top out at only twenty-five, thirty knots, max. But it would get you where you needed to go–clear out to the islands if you wanted–and get you home safe, providing you didn't do anything outright stupid. Or you didn't lose power. He hoped his skipper carried a spare battery.

Nguyen finessed the boat off the bunks and into the drink and Nathan held it to with a bow rope. It was near high tide now, so the boat sat especially proud. Nathan considered the high freeboard amidships to aft. The wide gunwales hardly dipped at all toward the stern. It wouldn't be easy hauling anything with size over top onto the deck. No wonder Nguyen couldn't haul in Eddie when he had teetered over from his heart attack, but had to tie him off to a stern cleat as if he were a chum-bag. A tuna door at the transom would have been nice. Oh well.

Nguyen returned after parking his Chevy and they headed out.

Nathan stood beside the captain at the console. He was pleased to see the captain abide the channel the long way around the lake even though the tide was high. It boded well, such deference. "Heah, take wheel," Nguyen said, glancing down at Nathan's canvas sneakers. He walked to the bow and leaned over a hatch as if he were looking into a deep well, then returned with a pair of high rubber boots. Nathan accepted the offering. He sat down on one of the two hard plastic chairs at the console to slide them on. They were a size too big, but that was okay.

The inlet wasn't quite so bad as Nathan feared, but breakers from a north swell shone blue beneath the still-bright moon. Negotiating the inlet would have been near treacherous during the outgoing. Nathan wondered whether Nguyen would have braved it then, whether he had consciously waited for the kinder incoming tide, or whether they had just gotten lucky.

"Not too bad, I guess."

"Nah. No problem, my boat. This good girl." Nguyen patted the console with his thick hand, offering canine comfort to his vessel. Nathan gripped the stainless T-top rail as Nguyen slipped out the south jetty inlet between two breakers. A single fisherman on the rocks lifted a hand. He liked that Nguyen timed the swell and that he didn't try to motor over the breakers like most people with decent sized boats tended to do. The wind beyond the jetty seemed to come from the southeast now, which might be good for drifting along the reef edges. The salt air

239

drenched with wet felt good in Nathan's lungs.

Nguyen kept his bearing to the southeast, against the wind, which surprised him. He thought Nguyen would head north after clearing the sandbar to the well-defined third reef off Spanish River Park or Jap Rock (the outcropping crudely named still after the defunct Japanese agricultural settlement), up around Highland Beach or Delray or Boynton, where he'd spotted his Dusky trolling plenty of times. Maybe Nguyen was heading for one of the wrecks off Broward. Or maybe he just didn't want to divulge his honey-holes. But that didn't make any sense, Nathan thought. He wasn't out here *not* to catch fish.

It wasn't a true three to five beyond the inlet, thankfully. Only a well-organized two to four. Stiff, nonetheless. So Nathan was surprised when Nguyen punched the throttle, bringing the reluctant vessel on plane. The Evinrude labored noisily, but steadily, behind them. Nathan took care to bend his knees as the Dusky's hull slapped each wave. Good thing he stood on the dry side of Nguyen. If it were his boat, he probably would have plowed slowly wherever he was going rather than motor through the whitecaps. But it wasn't his boat. He didn't know what the vessel could handle. He only hoped that Nguyen wasn't trying to impress him. He didn't peg him as the kind of captain who would pull something like that.

Nathan's eyes lingered on the lighthouse winking toward them from the point, nearby. Nguyen motored down after a few minutes and eased them off plane. Nathan looked down toward the console as the captain flicked on his broad split-screen Lowrance.

"I don't have GPS," Nathan uttered, their hearing restored.

"Naah," Nguyen growled. "No GPS?"

"Don't really need it, I figure. I know where I'm going. I never go too far."

He didn't need GPS. Although the inshore bite was a challenge hereabouts–the surviving mangrove and spartina patches near relics of a bygone age–Nathan knew he was lucky to have such fishy nearshore waters. Productive reefs flexed their long muscular legs clear down the coast just outside the inlets. The rippling northward current of the gulfstream banked westward here too, as if to take a peek at this southeast patch of Florida real estate, depositing peripatetic wahoo, mahi, cobia, kingfish, and blackfin tuna for the taking. Decent structure in the gulf was harder to come by. Commercial grouper and snapper fishermen burned gallons and gallons of fuel to ferry themselves miles offshore to productive wrecks and reefs—dodging the red tides, too, these days. They needed satellite navigation. But who needed GPS here when he could glimpse with his own eyes the high-rises in the foreground and background, slipping languidly away as he motored northward or southward, the ocher lights of the San Remo, the flashing red beacon high above Dixie, the tell-tale contours of seagrape clusters and notches along Australian pine stands, the positions of all these markers relative to one another betraying Nathan's latitude, the sonar completing the equation?

Nguyen shook his head. "You old time fish'aman, my friend. Old time fish'aman."

"I *do* have sonar, anyway. I'm not *that* old time."

Nguyen nodded, smiling, then banked to the east, offshore, gripping the suicide nob at the wheel. Nathan glanced at the sonar side of the split-screen. 40 feet. They were in the flats between the shallow patch reefs and the better-defined second reef. Nguyen was probably heading out to scout the second reef. "We see where they are," Nguyen said, jabbing a stubby finger toward the Lowrance, "what depth they at. Then go back. Cut through trail." The skipper made a slashing motion with the blade of his hand. "GPS save trail. Tell us where to go, exact. Exact."

"That's pretty good. I don't really troll much is the thing. I usually just anchor up." Nguyen nodded.

"Did you fish back in Vietnam?"

"Yeah-yeah."

"Good fishery?"

"Good fish. Uh-huh. Reef ev'ywheah. Shrimp. Crayfish. But too many fish'aman. All catch anchovy for nuoc-mam."

"Nuoc-mam?"

"Fish sauce."

Nathan nodded, bent his knees into the ditch of a stiff incoming. Nguyen, he noticed, broadened his stance, but kept his knees practically locked.

"Fishing betta heah I think," Nguyen declared. "Ev'thing betta heah. America."

Nathan glanced toward the captain. Silver winked again from Nguyen's mouth. Everything was better here, Nguyen felt. Did Nathan's great grandfather, Chaim, feel the same way? Probably. He had adopted a new "American" surname, something Nguyen hadn't done.

"So, Nguyen's a really common last name in Vietnam, right?" Nathan asked. "Like Smith?"

"Yeah, yeah. Right. Most common. You have mobafone?" Nguyen changed the subject.

"Huh?" Nathan leaned an ear toward the captain.

"Mobafone," the captain repeated over the chugging Evinrude.

"Oh . . . mobile phone." Nathan patted down his chest, as if fumbling for loose change. It seemed a queer time to ask such a question. "Yeah, I got one."

"Good. Mine no work."

They reached the outside edge of the reef, 60 feet giving gradual way to 80. Nguyen banked north. They plowed along without dipping any lines for several minutes. This was why Nathan didn't troll. It just seemed like such a waste of time and fuel. He breathed deeply and looked about. Fast moving cumulus clouds intermittently blocked the moon, which threw discernible shafts of light onto faraway patches of boiling sea. Nathan admired the rising columns of light, but Nguyen was growing impatient. He could tell, because he started humming a discordant melody at a jarring timbre. Nathan hoped his captain wasn't agitated on his account.

"I don't know Nguyen. This seems like a fishing expedition," he joked to lighten the mood.

"Huh? What you say?"

243

"Umm . . . nothing . . ."

"*Haaa,*" Nguyen burst out laughing. "Fishing expedition! I get now. Good one."

They passed the next several minutes in more comfortable silence.

"*Theah!*" Nguyen pointed at the sonar. "Theah fish." He lifted a finger and touched a button on the GPS monitor, marking the spot.

Nathan studied the screen. Numbers flashed beside each fish arc, revealing the precise depth.

"Big school," Nguyen said. He motored fast well clear of the prize, then made a slow 180 degree turn and put the throttle in neutral. The Dusky, adrift now, bobbed like a cork, listing this way and that, its port bowing to the incoming waves. The southeast wind strummed a low flat chord against the monofilament of the rods on the rocket launchers. "They be deep heah all season," Nguyen said as he made his way to the stern, feeling his way along the gunwale for ballast like a blind man. "Betta when shallow. Mo' easy. You use downrigga'?"

"Of course," Nathan replied. This was a tad false.

"Heah, I do first. You watch." Nguyen might have detected Nathan's counterfeit expertise. He reached into his bait cooler and pulled out two semi-thawed Spanish sardines.

"For crying out loud, Nguyen. I'll bait 'em, at least." Nathan reached for the silver fish, which his captain relinquished.

"I got froze' blue runner and goggle eye for lata', cigah minnow too, but we try sardine first."

"Should we butterfly them?" Nathan grasped for the knife at his waist. Nguyen's face contorted as if he had bitten into a sour fruit.

"Waste time. No need."

Nathan nodded. Leaning his knees into the Dusky's inside wall to maintain his balance, he impaled the sardines on the double J-hooks of two stout rods, one hook below the dorsal and the second through the eyes. Bigger hooks than Nathan used for snapper–six-aughts, he'd guess–tied to wire. Standard haywire twist. Albright to the mono.

"We using twenty-five pound test?"

"Thirty."

Nathan nodded. Heavier fishing than Nathan preferred, but a no-frills honest rig, not unlike Nguyen's boat, itself. He appreciated its simplicity. Once he baited his two lines, Nathan stood back, deferring to Nguyen. They'd each be working two rods on their downriggers, clipped to the cable at separate depths. He had figured out that much.

"Now watch heah." Nguyen stepped to and threw Nathan's first bait behind the boat, then let it drift out with the north current. He lowered the heavy lead of the downrigger a few revolutions to the first clip, then attached the mono to the cable. He gripped the downrigger handle again and sent it twirling a few more revolutions to the next clip, then attached the second line.

"We take to sixty click. See?" Nguyen pointed to the meter. Nathan nodded. "Mine to forty. Maybe fifty. Then we into fish, man." Nguyen leaned his meaty shoulder into his labors this time and started spinning the baits down with a practiced coordination.

"Whoa, captain. I can take it from here. Relax."

"Good." Nguyen straightened his back, thrust out his belly-muscle, then repaired to his starboard side to see to his own preparations. Nathan was glad that Nguyen had given him the outside of the stern, which he preferred. The rolling deck hummed with the throaty breath of the idling two-stroke, the pleasant buzz of winding cables, the single chord from the rod strings rising and fading with the ocean's breath. The winter gusts bit some through his shabby windbreaker and long-sleeve layers. He clutched great fistfuls of the salt air through his deviated septum, the fifteen knot gusts ushering the Evinrude smoke ashore and away. Nathan's cable stretched northward some beyond the stern, even with its heavy lead weight, even with the boat adrift, unanchored. Brisk current. He paused to glance ashore toward the blinking eye of the lighthouse, the building silhouettes over its shoulder, marking their spot for his own future use, perhaps, which Nguyen probably wouldn't have appreciated. Spooling out the cable wasn't hard, but the precise coordination eluded Nathan. His spool whirred loud, then soft, loud, then soft. Nguyen's buzz was smoother, faster. Nathan, once he completed his own drop—having started much sooner—noticed Nguyen's sweeter solo music.

"I almost beat you. And you have head start!" Nguyen's silver mouth flashed in the moonlight. He was feeling expansive, it seemed, hopeful, having located their first school and wetting their lines.

"You the man," Nathan conceded, using another one of Miles' favorite phrases.

Nguyen, checking the Lowrance, tapped the throttle a few times with the back of his hand to coax the engine to seven knots, eight. The pitch and roll abated as they motored now between the waves. Nathan remained at his post, his eyes darting between the four rod-tips and the all-seeing eye of the lighthouse. Nguyen manned the helm, focusing mostly on the Lowrance, stealing glances out the stern from time to time to check the lines. The southeast wind had blown them in a bit from the kill zone he had marked, so he headed mostly east first, then banked southward in an arc, wide so as not to foul the lines, toward the waypoint. It seemed a brisk pace for nighttime trolling, but maybe this was what the downriggers allowed.

"*Whoa!* Fish on!" Nathan cried as the reel sizzled. First pass. The monofilament rose from his bent rod, having broken free of its underwater clip. The shallower clip. They hadn't even reached the waypoint. Nathan yanked the rod out of the holder and started winding the conventional reel with his right hand, clumsily. Nathan preferred spinning gear, which entailed winding with his left hand below the rod.

"Jesus!"

"*Haaa!*" Nguyen bellowed, throttling down almost to neutral, feeling for the gaff at the console. "Big fish you think!? Smokah!?" The boat listed violently again, adrift now. The rocket launcher rods resumed their low, flat chord. Nathan ceased his reeling, gripped the gunwale to regain his balance and then returned to his labors.

"Not sure," he answered, although he figured it was at least a decent size. He wouldn't boast and then bring up a schoolie. The fish made a blistering run eastward, the mono screaming out of the reel, spraying Nathan's face with salt he licked off his lips. "Definitely king, anyway," he said. "This ain't no bluefish." He reached down and tightened the star drag some. Not much. "*Whoa,* Nguyen. Looks like you got one on too, skipper." Nathan lifted his ginger chin toward a bent rod at the starboard side. The drag wasn't zipping out so Nguyen's fish couldn't be very large.

"Ah! We on fish, my frien'." Nguyen dropped the gaff on the deck and lunged for the rod. "Just small one," he said, horsing it in fast. "No need net even." Nguyen flicked the stiff creature over the gunwale, leaving it there to flop about, and returned to Nathan's side with the gaff.

Enough already, Nathan thought. He'd farted around with this king for too long, forgetting the stout gear, which facilitated more efficient landings, more productive nights. No need for this knock-down drag-out.

"Must be big fish, eh?" Nguyen asked, leaning over the bobbing gunwale with the gaff.

Nathan was embarrassed by the production he was making out of all this, especially after Nguyen had made such short work of his catch. "Almost have it, skipper. One more run, maybe. Nope, here it is." The silver torpedo gleamed at the surface.

"Ah, good fish!"

Nathan nodded, relieved more than excited. It was larger than he had expected. Fifty pounds if it were ten. Such fight on strong gear. Of course. But they still needed to land the smoker.

Nguyen wrapped a stretch of the mono around a gloved hand, then flicked the gaff with the other hand behind the king's gill plates. He tried hoisting the impaled creature over the gunwale in one motion, but it was too heavy for the potbellied captain. The beast bridled against the gaff, revived by the barbed insult, smacked the listing freeboard as Nguyen stood there, panting, gathering his strength. Nathan dropped the rod and lunged almost clear over the gunwale. Avoiding the king's business end, he grasped the creature below the anal fin–"*Okay, now!*"–and the two fishermen hauled the king over the gunwale onto the deck. Rich red blood streamed from its gaff wound as it flopped madly about. Nguyen put a boot on the beast, unsheathed the knife at his waist and sliced into its brain—its writhing ceased—then carved deep, nearly decapitating, gashes below its armored gill plates to bleed out the fish. Nathan liked that he put the king out of its misery, quickly. Nathan, too, routinely dispatched the snapper he caught with surgical precision rather than leave them to asphyxiate in the cooler.

"Some fish," Nguyen finally uttered, gaining his breath.

Nathan shook his bleeding hand, just now feeling the wound as his adrenaline dissipated. "Shoot, it got me." The bony finlets near the tail must have pierced his calloused palm. But it wasn't a big deal. Just a small laceration, which stung on account of the salt.

"No bad," Nguyen said, leaning over Nathan's hand. "I give tape." He stood up again, pounded Nathan's back with three hearty blows. "You real fisha'man, Nate. I thought you go over boat! I thought I lost 'notha one! *Haa!*"

Nathan smiled, shaking his head and inhaling the briny air perfumed with fishblood and his own human smells, rising. He popped a Lemonhead into his mouth and crunched down hard, summoning the invigorating power of the tart morsel. He knew that he had done well by Nguyen's lights in spite of (or, rather, because of) his recklessness. He had lunged headlong over the side after their prize (what was it worth to them, $100 max?), foolishly hoping to impress Nguyen.

Nguyen, chuckling still, dragged the dead king by its tail with his gloved hand to his largest cooler, built into the fore deck. He dispatched the smaller kingfish on deck with his knife and slid it into the cooler, as well. He handed Nathan some fishing tape, then set about mopping down the deck with ocean-drenched towels beneath his boots. The slippery blood on the gel-coat rendered the deck unfishable. It needed to be cleaned up before they could continue.

"Now we do again," he announced.

"Right on, captain."

They did it again . . . and again, taking several passes through the large school and taking several kings. They afforded themselves only short breaks in between to gather their breath and gulp scalding doses of coffee from Nguyen's metal thermos. The caffeine and sour candies (Nguyen sampled a Lemonhead, but frowned) kept Nathan alert. You didn't fuck around when the fishing was good. And it was good. It wasn't like fishing with Terrance, exactly. Their choreography about the deck wasn't nearly so smooth. Nathan didn't know exactly what Nguyen would do, and when and how he would do it. He didn't know when he could expect Nguyen to hand him a fresh bait, and when Nguyen expected the same; he didn't know how Nguyen would negotiate around him to assist with the gaff. And so they were forced to exchange too many words. They bumped clumsily against each other from time to time, laughing it off, though. The fishing was good, after all. Nguyen was a good fisherman, better than Nathan had expected. Artful, in his own way. He knew exactly what he was about. Nguyen might prove a good resource for Nathan on the offshore bite if Nathan managed to secure himself a spot on the Fishing Report. Perhaps he might be able to do something for Nguyen too, set him up with some newer gear from the show's various sponsors. He considered mentioning the prospect to his captain, his upcoming guest appearance on the Sunshine Network, yet bit his tongue. He had only shared this confidence with Kati and treasured their small secret. Plus, he didn't want to jinx himself.

Yes, fishing with Nguyen wasn't like fishing with Terrance, but Nathan nonetheless managed to lose himself in real time by the third pass or so. In real time, he didn't hear the throaty breath of the idling two-stroke, the pleasant buzz of the winding cables, the low, flat chord from the rod strings rising and falling with the wind. He didn't feel the sting of his small wound or the winter bite through his core. He didn't smell the fistfuls of salt and iron fishblood through his sinuses. He didn't feel the pitch and roll of the deck or see the lighthouse winking upon them, shoreside. He didn't feel the minutes marching past, for time scarcely existed in real time. Nathan scarcely existed in real time. He was wholly in and of the game. Not the least bit outside its borders. He would savor the sweet erasure had he any sense of himself at all.

The vibration at his chest brought him to. *Fuck,* Nathan thought. He padded down his windbreaker for the device. *Fuck Fuck Fuck.* He should ignore it, but feared it was an emergency. His father. Miles. His mother. Kati, even. Personal tragedies could still befall him. He was lucky this way. One way of looking at it.

Nathan unfolded the antiquated cell phone, losing some respect for himself as he raised it to his ear. Everyone nattered into their fancier smartphones these days, but Nathan couldn't help feeling ludicrous doing the same. They were in the middle of a run–Nguyen didn't halt their troll for Nathan and Nathan hadn't expected him to–so Nathan had to plug his ear with his salt and blood finger to hear his son's voice at the other end.

"You're *where!?* You're fucking *where!?*" Nathan couldn't contain his curses. "Tell me you're joking! . . . Well, you'll just have to sit tight, Miles. I'll be there as soon as I can." Nathan snapped the small phone shut, the very dimensions of which denied him a sufficient gesture for the occasion.

"Bad?" Nguyen inquired over the two-stroke.

"Yeah. Afraid so, captain. I guess I have to ask you to take me back to the dock."

Nguyen motored down, but didn't say anything.

Nathan considered their catch thus far, worked a rough calculation in his head. "I'll just take half-share. For putting you out like this. How about that?"

Nguyen nodded silently, throttled up. He knew a good deal when he heard it.

Book Three

Chapter One

It probably wasn't a good idea to set up directly across the canal from the bigger boys. Twenty yards up or so. That would have been fine. He might have known. Only he didn't.

"Yo! Poindexter! You think you're hot shit 'cause of that rod!"

"No," he answered. He had to raise his voice some to be heard above the current rushing over the dam between them. But he didn't want to yell. The black boy on the other side of the canal was older. His brother's age.

"What's that!?" the boy yelled. "Cat got your tongue? Speak up."

"It's just a Zebco."

"It's just a Zebco," the boy mocked him, constricting his voice. The other black boys, two of them, didn't say anything. They were younger. His age. Shirtless. They sat with their skinny legs dangling over the concrete while they fished the water below the El Rio spillway, keeping their eyes on their spools. The line was blue. That's how they fished. Right from the spool with blue line. Just then, the thin one pulled a black-striped fish out of the pool, grasped it with his bare hands while he fiddled with the hook over a white bucket. Probably lived in those apartments just a hundred yards behind them. Lucky, Nathan thought. To live so close to the canal.

"You some rich whiteboy, I bet," the older one continued.

"From over there." He stood on the grass up some from his companions, lifted his nose westward *over there* (where Nathan lived) while he twirled his bait in great circles beside his ear like it was a lasso. Then he threw the line upstream, above the spillway.

Nathan considered whether, and how, he should fend off the accusation. He didn't think he was rich. If he was rich, he'd be in the private school on St. Andrews, right? And they would fly to the mountains to go snow skiing during the winter. And they would belong to a beach club. The one up on Linton. Or maybe the one right next to the lighthouse in Deerfield. Or maybe they *were* rich, but didn't belong to a beach club because they were Jewish, which wasn't the same thing as being plain-old white.

"I'm not rich," he said, weakly.

"Don't that just beat all," the boy looked back down toward his companions. "Some rich whiteboy come to fish with us."

"Cut it out," he shouted louder now. "I'm not rich." He should leave, Nathan thought. Walk twenty yards up the bank to another opening through the willow. Yet his feet wouldn't budge.

"Well, might as well come across and fish over this side." The boy's voice grew friendly all of a sudden. "Fishin's better here. We got red worms for the bass up here." His hands occupied, he gestured with his head up above the spillway, toward fresh water. "Shrimp for the Prison Fish down there." He glanced downstream, past the waterfall, toward brackish.

"You mean it?"

The two younger boys looked up at their leader but didn't say anything.

"You can walk right across. Right top of the dam there. It's hardly under water none."

"Demetrius," one of the boys sighed, the one whose ribs showed through his flesh.

"Okay. Sure."

"Demetrius," the same skinny boy uttered, stronger. "What you doin'?"

"Hush up!"

A thin sheet of water flowed over the curve of concrete. Nathan took a step, holding his Zebco in one hand, his plastic tacklebox in the other, for balance. He took another step.

"There you go."

Nathan favored the left side some, as it must have been a six foot drop or so off to the right, over the dam. He lifted his foot for another step, thinking, this is easy, just before committing his weight to a patch of green concrete. His foot slipped from under him so quickly, so utterly, that he didn't even have a chance to struggle for his balance. He landed flat on his back on top of the dam.

"OWWWW!" he shrieked, rolling off the ledge into the shallows. He somehow gained his footing in two feet of water and clambered for the bank, crying hot tears, brushing aside the duckweed and algae. Blood streamed from his elbow in complex tributaries toward his palm as he retreated. He didn't know what happened to his Zebco. Or to his tacklebox.

And there were things he didn't hear.

"You okay!?" the skinny boy called.

"Shut yo' face, Terrance!"

"That's it richboy! Go cry to yo' momma!"

**

Nathan returned home, not crying anymore but hangdog and dripping, empty-handed, his hair a tangled ginger net flecked with green canal goo, his elbow smeared with dark blood.

Jacob, pitching tennis balls at a piece of plywood propped against the garage, greeted him on the sloped driveway. "Who did that to you!?" his brother asked, letting the tennis ball roll past his feet into the road. Not, *What happened?* Which would have been the more logical question, but, *Who did that to you?* A question that only made sense coming from an older brother accustomed to having a younger brother who let people do things to him.

A braver child would have lied. But Nathan wasn't a braver child.

"Get your bike! Show me!" his brother demanded, muscle cords bulging from his neck, his face rubicund with rage. Nathan was powerless to resist.

They were still there, the boys, fishing the canal. "Is that him?" Jacob asked, pointing across the water at the largest boy, taller than Jacob, Nathan thought. But not bigger.

"What are you gonna do?" Nathan asked.

"Is that him!?" Jacob demanded.

Nathan nodded.

"Whach'ya come back here fo'? Git y'own water, whiteboys."

Nathan watched, fearful as Jacob strode across the thigh-deep water, smart enough not to traverse the slippery dam. The black boy stood up a bit straighter, wary of the swift, silent approach. But not so wary as to drop his rod. Jacob swung at the boy without words as soon as he climbed the dusty bank. Nathan cringed at the *smack* of fist against cheek.

"What the . . ." the black boy muttered, feinting from the blow, dropping his rod now.

Summoned to the occasion, the boy lashed back at Nathan's brother with a series of windmill punches, to which Jacob responded in kind. The two were a blur of flailing arms and shuffling feet, performing some complicated dance. The smaller boys, rather than join the fray, stood back, mute like Nathan. It was difficult to tell who was winning. Few blows landed clean. Jacob seemed to throw fewer punches, especially after the initial flurry, but they were straighter, more disciplined strikes toward discernible targets—sternum, stomach, lip. He kept his fists high between punches, elbows in, protecting, or trying to protect, his face and frame. Blood painted the black boy's lip and seemed to spill on his chin, but it was difficult to tell against his dark skin.

"Stop it!" Nathan finally heard his thin voice carry across the canal. And then there were bigger black boys, men almost, breaking the two up, pulling at Jacob's shoulders and at the black boy's shoulders, and smiling. Smiling!

"You made your point, big man. Now git on home."

"I'll stomp your lily-ass!" The black boy spat blood, adding fury to his oath. His eyes were glassy.

Jacob, his anger spent, shrugged off his restraints and walked back, silent still, through the water. His lip was puffed up, Nathan noticed, but not bleeding. A raspberry ripened above his cheek.

"That your tacklebox?" Jacob asked at the bank. Nathan nodded. His brother didn't actually look down at the tacklebox (how did he see it?), but held his adversary's gaze across the canal.

"That your rod there in the water too? Pick that up." Nathan obeyed, glanced up at the skinny boy his age at the other side of the bank, watching him.

It might have been a nice moment, the bike ride home. Brotherly. Only it wasn't.

"You're such a fucking wuss," Jacob declared, hocking a thick blood-stained lougy down at the asphalt and riding off ahead. "Such a fucking wuss."

**

And now? How to describe his relationship with Jake now? Nathan pondered as he made his way across the vacated town streets to retrieve Miles from the police station, depleted and damp, stinking of fish and salt from his aborted excursion with Nguyen. Better, maybe, things with Jake. Less contentious, certainly, as they were adults and no longer shared such close quarters. But more remote, too, which wasn't better. They spoke over the long-distance wires pretty much only on their birthdays. Even then, they didn't have very much to say, despite the manifold happenings that accrue over a year in a life. Their correspondence was obligatory. Vaguely contractual. They shared the same blood. And so it was important enough to the both of them to verify certain facts about their brother on a regular basis. *He's alive. His mind and body, sound for the time being. He's not living on the street.* Yes, obligatory. Contractual. But not without an underlying current of genuine feeling, too, Nathan thought.

He recalled their most recent conversation. Jake had his hands full with his own son, Ephraim. He had broached a surgery that the boy needed to undergo for his eyes. Nathan's stomach had leapt to his throat and stayed there the whole time Jake summarized the details—inexpertly, haltingly—before it finally became clear over the long-distance static and Jake's exasperating pauses that it was only a minor surgery, after all, that his nephew's eyesight would be just fine. It was only after Nathan hung up the phone that he pondered his brief panic and marveled that he had been so worried, and worried foremost not over Ephraim, his nephew, whose eyesight might be in peril, but over Jake, his brother, who had a son whose eyesight might be in peril. And so, yes, his relationship with his brother was distant, obligatory, contractual. But tough enough to hold on account of that underlying current of genuine feeling, which might be tapped at any moment. It was something, anyway.

**

"But not a daughter?" Stefanie had asked, too brightly. So Judy might have foreseen this purple morning summons.

"I know it's late. Or early. Or whatever," Stefanie sniffled at the other end of the line. Judy recognized the timbre of her protégé's voice in an instant, her senses instinctively rising to the occasion.

"Where are you, dear!? What's the matter!?"

But she wasn't thinking of Stefanie now en route to Mercy. Instead, she found herself thinking of Jacob, unaware that Nathan too had been thinking of Jake, that he too had received a purple morning summons. That's what happened when you were jostled from your practiced routine, is what she now thought. When you received a purple morning summons and found yourself speeding along eerily vacant streets without the time even to put on your face. Your defenses down, you found yourself thinking about things. Little stinging things. Like helping Jacob with his math in second grade. Or maybe it was third. Simple subtraction. Not a chore for Jacob. But he worked through the equations out of order at the breakfast room table, going down the columns rather than across the rows. There was a ball he always squeezed in his hand. Rubber. Pale pink. He was futzing with it then. "Dearheart," she had said, "you're supposed to go across with the numbers. See?" She swept a painted finger across the top row. "One, two, three, four, five."

He had shot her that querulous look of his, the expression painted across his brow from infancy, which had surprised her in the maternity ward. No such determination would paint Nathan's ginger brow, who even greeted gas pains with an expression of bemused victimhood.

"What's it matter which way I do it?" Jacob had challenged her, curling a lip, squeezing his pale pink ball.

"It doesn't, really, but why not just do it the right way, the way it says?"

"Why? I don't get it. What's it matter?"

"It just does, Jacob!" Here she was stern. "Is it so difficult to follow directions!? And give me that ball."

"You giving your mother flak?" Joseph called out, absently from the kitchen, milling around more purposefully in the fridge.

Jacob surrendered the pale pink ball and returned to his equations, but still worked down the columns, silent, petulant, the yellow pencil bobbing in his still small hand. Judy gritted her teeth and exhaled as she shook her head.

Such an iron will.

Where had they gone wrong with Jacob? She could blame their domestic discord and divorce, which truly meant blaming Joseph and his wandering phallus; she could blame Beth Shalom's Hebrew School, which fairly amounted to Holocaust School, peppered with a Zionism chaser; she could blame the Jewish National Fund's plant-a-tree project that she had allowed Jacob to pursue for his Bar Mitzvah tzedakah requirement, those green conifer arrowheads filling up the posterboard like a Ponzi scheme.

He was such a good boy was the thing. He might have been one of those problem kids, instead. He might have played hooky and spent his days surfing at Spanish River, or smoking grass on one of the surviving Clint Moore pepper fields, hidden between the canebrakes. Like some of her friends' rotten kids. But he hadn't done drugs, and hadn't ever skipped school, at least to her knowledge. Rather, he graduated in the top 5%. He played catcher on the baseball team, greeting base runner assailants at the plate with terrific immovable ferocity. He scored high on his college boards–though not as high as Nathan–and had been accepted to practically every university to which he applied, but inveighed upon her to defer for a year his matriculation at Vanderbilt.

A year off between high school and college. *That's* what they had agreed to. Matt Levine was doing the same thing. (Judy checked with Roz; he was right.) A yearlong hiatus on a kibbutz before heading off to college. "If not now, when?" Jacob sang like a wiseacre, echoing that rabbinic nugget. Neither Judy nor Joseph dared be the one to deny their iron-willed son. Joseph had cultivated a self-serving, laissez-faire parental policy, anyway. A year in the godforsaken desert cleaning chicken pens. Fine. Where was the harm in it? Joseph had convinced her. She only vaguely feared that Jacob would refuse to return home.

But she couldn't claim utter surprise when he confessed over the phone some months later that he had decided not to return, and that he wouldn't be attending Vanderbilt in the fall, after all. He was moving to a settlement in the north, near Nahariya, wherever the hell that was. His letters by that time had grown infrequent, their twice-monthly phone conversations terse, labored, which Judy couldn't blame entirely on the salty static, the awkward long-distance delay between speaking and hearing. Frightful outrage came naturally, nonetheless.

"Have you lost your mind!? What do you mean you're staying!?"

"I've decided to stay here. That's what I mean."

"What do you mean stay!? You mean forever!?"

"I don't know."

Jacob's words traveled lazily across the ocean, underscoring his recalcitrance. Judy couldn't understand his adamantine calm. Was he drugged on hashish? Had he been brainwashed?

"So you're not coming home. Is that what you're saying? Ever?"

"This *is* my home now. I'm making aliyah."

"Don't lay those Hebrew platitudes on me, Jacob! I'm your mother!"

"Yes. I know."

Now what the hell did he mean by that?! At the very least he'd been prepped, Judy could tell. Trained by some chicken farmer or orange grower on how you broke the news to your parents in the states.

"You belong *here*, Jacob! In America! Israel doesn't need you!"

"It's not about Israel needing *me*. It's not that. This is just where I want to be. You wouldn't believe the solidarity here. The feeling. When soldiers want to go someplace, they just pick up and walk down the highway, stick an index finger down. Any car with a seat will stop and take them where they want to go. See, that's the difference. Everyone's in it together here."

Big fucking deal, Judy thought, but didn't say.

"You're speaking nonsense Jacob," she said instead. "I'm coming there right now. Do you hear me? Right now! I'm on a plane! I'm on a plane!"

"Wait, mother. Relax. Don't do anything right now."

"You've done enough for Israel, Jacob! You planted trees for your Bar Mitzvah! Don't you remember, Jacob?! You planted trees!"

Judy could blame the obvious things. Their domestic discord and divorce; Hebrew School; the Jewish National Fund's plant-a-tree project that Jacob completed for his Bar Mitzvah.

Yet she wondered now–speeding north on Jog to Stefanie at the hospital–whether it was any use ascribing blame, or whether it was even a matter of blame. Her elder son wasn't dead, anyway. He wasn't unhappy, either, as far as she could determine. He had simply built a life thousands of miles away that only marginally involved her. He didn't care to visit Florida and she could only manage the flight to Israel every few years or so. It wasn't how she would have scripted his life, but it was *his* life. She needn't feel as if it were a personal reproach. Not at this late date, anyway. It was pathetic, truly, to nurse such ancient resentments. What did it do for her, other than crowd out more troublesome feelings? Judy felt her stomach slip from its mooring, escaping her vigilance. She reminded herself to breathe. She missed Jacob. It was a simple feeling, really. A simple hurt. Why complicate it? Could Judy, finally, just miss her elder son? Nathan seemed better at this sort of thing—feeling, that is. Maybe it wasn't such a weakness, after all.

**

The fecal stench greeted Judy before she stepped across the threshold into her protégé's shared room, a stench so unignorable that her eyes only fleetingly registered Stefanie's shrunken presence on the overlong bent bed before scanning the room for the offending source. Two strides delivered her to the curtain, semi-drawn. An elderly woman laid flat, apparently unconscious, sparse tendrils of ashen hair spilled on a defeated pillow. Linens lapped over the lip of a garbage-bag hamper in the far corner. Judy advanced past the bed's foot toward the spindly hamper. Muddy smears shadowed the undersides of the crumpled linens. Soiled sheets.

"Jesus Christ!" Judy growled under her breath, grasping the spindly hamper, sliding it across the linoleum out into the hall.

"You okay?" she asked Stefanie, as if it were a secondary concern.

Stefanie nodded. "I know it's gross. But they're trying to find me anoth—"

Judy was gone. En route to the nurse's station, hamper in tow.

A mousy nurse rose to face the aural and olfactory onslaught. "You can't bring that here, ma'am. An orderly–"

"What's the meaning of this!? You have a young girl in recovery lying beside a cess pool! It stinks to high heaven in there!" These shiftless nurses in their scrubs—Judy sized them up in an instant—three of them ensconced behind the high fort walls of their station, the two still seated spearing plastic forks into their Tupperware and crinkling their noses against the hamper stench.

The mousy nurse had at least set her Tupperware down. "We can't transfer her yet, ma'am," she uttered with more practiced restraint now, flashing pallid palms. "We don't have any other beds available. Now an orderly's on the way to take the sheets–"

"No. No. That's not good enough. The woman's probably soiled the sheets she's lying on now, or her diaper, while you're all stuffing your faces. It smells god awful in there. It's unsanitary."

"Now ma'am!"

"You can't leave a woman in her filth!"

"We just changed her," a younger, pony-tailed nurse chimed in from her chair, slipping socks back into her ridiculous rubber shoes.

"It's not visiting hours," the one sitting beside her added. She was vaguely Hispanic, or Pakistani, or Lebanese, or something.

Judy paid them no heed.

"Just give *me* the sheets. Give *me* a washcloth. Where do you keep these things?" She bounded down the hall, leaving the hamper behind, jostling the metal handles of unmarked doors. "I'll see to the woman if you won't. *I'll* see to her." A squeaking cacophony of sensible shoes trailed after her.

"Okay, ma'am. It's okay. We'll take care of it. Leave it to us, ma'am. We have it from here."

The poor woman moaned as the nurses changed her gown and bedding from behind the curtain. It wasn't often that you heard an actual moan. The meekest protest. Something about this woman smacked too close and inspired a reflexive recoil. You steeled yourself was the thing. Or at least Judy steeled herself.

The nurses had closed the curtain behind them as they tended to their labors, whether for the sake of the old woman's dignity or to keep Judy from snooping over their shoulders, or simply for the sake of established routine, she wasn't certain. Despite the partial privacy, it was impossible to talk with Stefanie or even to focus on her with the

267

audible goings on behind the curtain: the old woman's feeble groaning, the whining bed frame, the loud, over-enunciated instructions from the mousy nurse. *Now I'm going to roll you to the right, Mrs. Milstein. Ready . . . here we go . . .*

So Judy just stood over the girl's bed for the moment, at Stefanie's elbow, affecting an expression and posture of simple immovable thereness. Stefanie's blue eyes seemed shrunken and gray behind her plastic eyeglass frames, the lids puffy, her sparse lashes bordered with pink from earlier weeping. Judy had never seen Stefanie in glasses before. They were unfashionable and clunky, the kind someone as well-scrubbed as Stefanie would only possess because she wore contact lenses, instead. Judy surprised herself by reaching for the girl's clammy hand, which she probably wouldn't have done had they been able to converse. This is what a girl's hand feels like, she thought, wondering what it would have been like to have a girl. Stefanie flashed a quick, awkward smile to answer Judy's touch, then gazed toward the wall beyond the foot of her long bed toward the generic pastel print of a floral bouquet. They had reached a silent agreement. They would wait until the nurses departed to speak.

"I wear contacts, usually," Stefanie uttered as soon as the nurses cleared the room, releasing Judy's hand now that they could communicate with words.

Judy nodded, smiling. "I gathered."

"I'm sorry I woke you."

"Don't be silly, dear. I wasn't doing anything."

"It's just that Brad's on a job in Tallahassee. And my parents aren't here. Mom's flying down tomorrow, or today, or whatever. And my Aunt Sylvia's too old. And, I haven't really made–"

"*Shhh.* It's fine dear." Judy reached again for Stefanie's hand. "Tell me what happened."

"That pain I was having. Remember?" Judy nodded. "It changed to my back earlier today, and then I had spotting, and then more pain earlier tonight. Like really bad. Stabbing like—"

"Are you in pain now?" Judy took a backward step, raised a hand toward the threshold. "Did they give you something?"

"Yes. They gave me something. Come back." The girl placed a hand on her mattress to inch herself higher on her inclined bed. It seemed to cause her mild discomfort.

"I called my mom and she told me to go to the emergency room–"

"You should have called me *then*, Stefanie. *I* would have taken you."

"I just didn't know it was such a big deal." She looked away, toward the curtain. Judy reached into her purse and handed the girl a fresh tissue. Stefanie dabbed her nose. The borders of her fine nostrils were inflamed, like her eyelids. A small pimple on her cheek seemed to fester beneath the harsh fluorescent lighting. Maybe it wasn't such a terrific idea for the poor girl to rehearse the details now.

"It's okay, Stefanie. You don't have to–"

"They gave me an ultrasound right away and could tell it was ectopic."

"*Shhh–*"

"But they couldn't just give me drugs. The emergency room doctor said . . he said that, ummm"—Stefanie struggled for the proper word— "it was too developed. My doctor came in around midnight, which kind of scared me more. He needed to go in right away and get it out."

"Yes."

"Just a little cut he made. Down here." Stefanie's tissue-holding hand swept across her diaphanous hospital gown to settle at a spot just below her waist. "He used lapara . . . lapara . . . what do they call it?"

"Laparascopic, sweetie. It's wonderful that they can do that now. It won't even leave a scar."

"I don't care about that." Stefanie's glasses darted away from Judy and toward the curtain again. The girl lifted the tissue to dab her nose.

"I know, dear. Of course. I'm sorry."

"I just don't know why this had to happen." Stefanie smacked both her hands, palms up, onto her small lap, as if preparing to receive a burden in her arms.

"Sometimes freak things happen, dear. There's nothing you can do. That's life."

"He said he thought I'd be fine, anyway. My doctor. That I'd heal up without any blockages. That I could still have kids, like, almost ninety percent. But I don't know Judy."

"What don't you know, dear?"

"Maybe it's a sign. It's been so hard. Maybe I'm just not cut out to have kids."

The words tattered Judy like crisp little blows. Here Judy was, summoned inexplicably, yet summoned nonetheless, to this place, to this moment, to this girl. Judy, who knew nothing of girls, who had bungled most of the moments that mattered with her boys. But it was her turn to say something. She wanted to say something comforting and hopeful. Yet true. Time was too precious to stand on ceremony. She offered Stefanie's tiny paw a reassuring pulse and smiled as her mouth gave voice to the words.

"It's all right dear. None of us are."

Nathan parked the Tacoma and walked beneath the coconut palm sentries into the fluorescent foyer of the police station. It occurred to him on the way to the elevated reception desk across the linoleum that despite passing the station hundreds of times over the years, thousands, he had never crossed its threshold. Lucky him. Not so lucky tonight, though.

A compact female officer wearing a disciplined pony-tail studied his driver's license from behind an impregnable glass window. A slit in her earlobe marked the absence of a gold stud, hoop, or diamond.

"It's an old photo," the fisherman stupidly explained. Dressed slovenly, reeking of fish and salt and blood, he probably seemed like a homeless drunkard now.

She glanced toward her computer screen and punched a few keys. It all seemed terribly high-tech to Nathan, who somehow would have preferred to see her consult a heavy wooden clipboard.

Finally she nodded, handed Nathan a Visitor sticker through the gap at the bottom of the window, then pressed a button high on the wall beside her, making a second door buzz open before Nathan. She lifted a rigid finger and pointed behind her ear.

"Officer Shelby. Down the hall to the left. Ask someone when you get down there." She was all business, this officer.

He saw Camilla and Terrance first in the small waiting alcove, their dressy attire calling attention to their presence. They sat placidly along a line of plastic chairs with both Devon and Miles, their initial upset or anger having been spent. Michelle lay swaddled and sleeping in the hammock of skirt fabric between Camilla's legs. Clearly, they had been waiting for him to arrive, not wanting to leave Miles alone.

"Thanks for waiting up, Terrance, Camilla. I appreciate it." Nathan struggled to locate the proper tone, and realized immediately that he hadn't found it. "Where were you two coming from at this hour?"

"Nowhere," Terrance answered, standing. "Home. 'Milla's mother came over so we didn't have to wake Logan and O."

Nathan nodded as he absorbed this knowledge. Camilla remained seated in her business suit, which she might have last worn before the children came; she had worked as an accountant. He sensed a definite chill coming from her quarter. This had all been Miles' fault, apparently. He scanned the boys, their faces and fists. Not so much as a mark.

"You okay, Miles," he declared more than asked, hoping to strike a tricky chord of concerned chastisement.

Miles nodded, silent, still unsure about what version of his father he would face tonight. Nathan appreciated his son's anxiety and wouldn't ease it.

"Devon?" he asked. Devon nodded too.

"You have to speak with Officer Shelby. Over there," Camilla said, lifting her chin toward a young blonde officer at a metal desk. Nathan nodded and made his way. A couple officers he passed jotted desultory notes at their desks. A stout black officer appeared to be taking a statement from an elderly white woman, worrying the wooden beads of a rosary.

"I'll wait for you," Terrance said, which sounded almost like a warning. Camilla rose and headed off to the car with hangdog Devon, steering his shoulder with the pincers of one hand, Michelle cradled inside her other arm.

"Officer Shelby?" Nathan inquired upon reaching the officer's desk, whereupon the young man lifted a freckled face from a spiral-bound notebook and stood.

"That's me," Shelby stated, too cheerily for the early morning hour and the occasion. "You're the father of Miles Pray, I take it? I see the hair." He lifted his nose toward Nathan's crop of confused curls.

"Yes. Sorry for your trouble." Nathan extended his hand, which the officer shook with one pump. Shelby's easy smile revealed braces on his teeth with visible rubber bands stretching between the uppers and lowers. He didn't know what to make of this child policeman. "I came as soon as I could, officer. I didn't have time to change my clothes."

"Fisherman, eh? That's what I hear."

Nathan nodded.

"How about that. Anyway, sit down." They both sat. "I won't keep you long. It's just like I explained to Devon's parents over there. We're really cracking down on this sort of thing."

"What sort of thing, officer?" Nathan didn't mean to sound so peremptory. "I'm sorry, but I didn't get too many details from Miles or the Stillwaters."

"Adolescent truancy. Loitering. Fighting." Shelby's tone had grown sharper, rising to the occasion of Nathan's mild challenge. "We're actively breaking up large groups of kids where they've been hanging out at night. The shopping centers. Movie theaters. It's no good. Recipe for disaster. The businesses are complaining too. Folks are staying away. We don't want any trouble is the thing."

"I see."

"So you understand," the officer declared. "Belle Glade. Pahokee. Riviera Beach. We just can't have that stuff going on down here. Fighting and whatnot. It's always been a peaceful community."

Always. Nathan's eyes settled on the pristine patch on the officer's uniformed chest, the Spanish ship, sails on mast, piercing the inlet, Ponce de Leon drunk with dreams of dark slaves and gold? What did this kid know about *always* in Nathan's town?

"You realize that none of this is going on your son's record. There isn't any record, far as I'm concerned. This is only a warning. But best practices dictate that I talk with you. In person. 'Cause next time . . ."

"Yes, I appreciate that, officer." Nathan softened. "Really."

Shelby crossed his arms and bobbed back in his chair. "You might think he's a bit young to get into real trouble, but trust me, sir. He's right at the age that stuff starts hitting the fan. Now's the time when you and the boy's mother have to give him the full-court press. Watch who he hangs out with."

Watch who he hangs out with. What was all that business about? On the whole, the lecture didn't sound natural coming out of the young officer's mouth. He had likely gleaned and regurgitated the whole thing from a senior officer, or some "best practices" training manual. But wasn't the whole to-do a bit over the top? Racist, to boot? It hadn't been much of a scrape outside the movie theater, unless Miles had flat-out lied over the phone. And Miles, not Devon, had likely been the instigator. Nathan gritted his teeth as he pondered the fishy waters wasted, the half-share he had relinquished.

"I'm sure your son's a good kid," Shelby rose, clearly ready to clear the episode from his desk. He extended a smooth hand, which Nathan shook.

**

Terrance had wanted a word with Nathan, alone. Somehow this had been clear to him even before Terrance told him he'd wait by the way Camilla trotted off with Devon and the baby. Nathan had asked Miles to go ahead to the truck. It didn't surprise him when Terrance told him outside that Camilla and he thought Miles and Devon ought to take "a break" for a while.

"So you're banishing Miles? That's basically what you're saying, right?"

"Don't be so dramatic, Nate. Don't make more of it than it is. You're always doing this, you know. Making too much of things. It's a weakness of yours."

"Jeez, Terrance. Come on. You know it pisses me off when you call me sensitive."

"There you go again, see?" Terrance removed a hand from his pocket to gesticulate. "I didn't call you sensitive."

"Still."

Terrance exhaled and looked up at one of the palm sentries as if seeking its mighty counsel. Nathan followed Terrance's gaze. The palm's coconuts drooped up there like testicles.

"Let's sit a sec', Nate." They sat on the wooden bench, down the walk a bit from the overhanging coconuts. Nathan felt the cold now in the air.

"Remember Chief Brownie."

"I guess. Not really, Terrance."

"You'd remember him probably as that skinny old cat with the funny white lid, that southern gentleman who told us stories at auditorium about the good old days, Pirates in the inlet, the barefoot mailman, all that malarkey."

"Yeah, sure. Now I remember."

"He found Jesus by then, I guess. But back in the day, Nate, back before we were born, he was the meanest son of a gun you'd ever want to know. Even if you were white, what I hear. But if you were black . . ." Terrance rattled his lips with his breath, as if no further words were necessary. But then he spoke again:

"You didn't get caught in white-town after dark. He'd beat the black out of you, ask questions later. Pop was lucky. Had only one run-in with Brownie. He was walking back from work late. If you worked at the resort, you could do that, be out in white-town after dark on the way home, 'long as you took Camino, then Federal. Straight back. Head down. Single-file if there was more than one of you. Couldn't cluster. But pop was alone when he ran into Brownie one night. Chief was standing there on the sidewalk by himself wearing that same white hat. It wasn't unusual to see Brownie out and about. Pop wasn't much fazed. He knew the drill."

Here Terrance ran his fingers down inside both lapels. "All yessirs and nosirs. But he still had on his headrag from the kitchen. He'd worked his way up to the kitchen by that point. Forgot he had it on or he would have taken it off, Nate. But Brownie didn't let him forget.

"You'll take that hat off when speaking to me, boy!'" Terrance mimicked Brownie's hick drawl, which Nathan couldn't remember, drawing chin to chest. "Then he smacked pop upside the head, smacking off the do-rag."

"Jesus, Terrance. You never told me that story before."

"Haven't thought about it in a long time, Nate. I haven't had much reason to think about police officers over the past thirty years. Don't really want to start thinking about them now, either, if you know what I mean."

"I know. I get it. I'll talk with Miles. I said I'd talk with him."

"I know you got your own stuff to deal with, Nate. I know that, but–"

"I get it, T." Nathan felt the heat rise in him some. He wasn't sure why.

"Miles can do the whole hip-hop thing. The dreads. The 'tude. He can even go saggin' for all anyone'll care–"

"Miles won't be going agging' Terrance. Come on."

"We just can't risk Devon getting into any of this. It's different for him. For us."

"All right. I get it, T. I'll talk to him."

"Like I said, I know you got your own row to hoe. I know the
good ol' boys haven't always been easy on you, either, horning in on the
fishing and all. I get it. You got your own stuff to deal with, but . . ."

Nathan nodded. Terrance was right. They did each have their
own row to hoe. Their own lives to live, the best they knew how. Miles too.

**

Nathan made his way home with his son past the blinking red and yellow lights. It was especially silent inside the truck, their windows closed
against the chill. Miles seemed small and cold in the silence, cowering
beneath his curtain of hair, his elbows crossed within his sweatshirt.
Nathan was pleased to remember the broth in his refrigerator that he
had prepared yesterday with stripped snapper carcasses, onions, carrots,
garlic, bay leaves and lime. Sam never much cared for it, but Miles had
always slurped down the scalding broth with relish. A great tenderness
for his son seized Nathan. That hair. Nathan remembered how he used
to dip splayed fingers into his son's thatch of softer curls at bedtime, how
he balanced Miles' whole skull in the palm of his hand, teasing his son's
scalp with his fingertips. Miles had appreciated the massage, bent into it
for a few years before he started leaning away. Nathan tried to stanch the
untimely rush of feeling.

Miles heard the silence and pounced: "You're not gonna tell
mom, are you?"

"No, Miles. I'm not. *You* are. Tomorrow. Soon as I drive you home." Sam thought that Miles was sleeping over at Devon's. There wasn't any need to wake her now.

"But she'll bug out, dad. You *know* that." This sounded almost like a threat, as if Nathan should be the one to worry about Sam bugging out. He felt those Pray hackles rise, but he wouldn't take the bait. At least Miles had said "dad" and not "dads."

"Don't underestimate her, Miles. She might surprise you."

That rush of feeling had left Nathan flat-footed. But it was time for him to seize control, to be the parent. He cleared his throat to steel himself. "What exactly did you think you were doing, anyway, Miles? Explain *that* to me."

"I dunno."

This wouldn't do.

"Well, how did it all start?"

"He was making fun of me, dad. My hair."

"And so you just hit him? Over something so stupid? Because he made fun of your hair? I mean, you have to expect that sort of thing, hair like that."

"I warned him, dad. He wouldn't cut it out."

Nathan nodded. He wasn't sure how to proceed.

"And it's not stupid," Miles added.

How could his son be so much like Jake, the uncle he had never met and might never meet? Part of him, he had to confess, admired Miles for his moxie, as he had admired his brother. Perhaps Nathan let too much slide, took things too much in stride, his unwavering saltwater principles, too, only a weak cover for his retreat, his failure to engage. Even tonight at the station, had he been too deferential before Officer Shelby? Perhaps Miles had made the wrong telephone call, entirely. Sam would have stormed in guns blazing in defense of their son. She would have deployed all her lawyerly acumen and maternal heat. What right did they have to detain her child!? Nathan's mother, too, would bring more grit to the occasion. But was this the way to navigate the terrain, fists flailing against every enemy and insult, real and imagined? Nathan wondered whether such strong feeling and action were only shapes sloppily deployed to fill an unrelated lack. There was an honorable battle to be waged, surely. But maybe it wasn't the battle that most took it to be. Maybe the true struggle lay beyond their field of view, awaiting their best efforts. . . .

Your last name, pray tell?

Yes. Good. Pray. My last name. What did it matter here? Pray was as good a name as any for a new land. Chaim Pray. He tasted the new name in his mouth. It tasted good.

Maybe, Nathan thought. Probably not.

It wasn't time now for reveries. Miles demanded focused counsel.

"You're going to have to learn to pick your battles in this world, Miles."

This cliché! Nathan would have to do better. He rolled down his window, sought knowledge from the brisk winter air, from the useless marquees along Palmetto: nail salons, day spas, art galleries, white table-cloth restaurants, financial brokerages, boutique real estate agencies specializing in unreal properties. Miles stared out his window too, but didn't lower it.

"I know it hasn't been easy for you, Miles. I know that."

Miles didn't respond, nor did he avert his gaze from the outside. Nathan wondered whether his son was crying, but doubted it.

"Listen, I wish I had my own shit together," Nathan declared, louder. Miles turned at this, offered Nathan his profile at least, the rare profanity from his father's lips having piqued his curiosity. They reached one of the town's bigger intersections, the light solid red, unblinking. Nathan stopped. Glancing sideward, he noticed Miles' hand grasping the shoulder-strap of his seatbelt, as if it were a lifeline. But he wasn't crying. "You think I don't blame myself, Miles? For this? There's lots of things I wish I could change. That I hadn't screwed things up with your mom for one. I wish I could be there for you. That I could be more . . . I don't know . . . present. But the truth is, and as I'm sure you know, I just *don't* have my act together. Not yet. I haven't figured things out as fast as Devon's dad. And your mom's got her own stuff to deal with."

"Yeah. I know."

The petulant tone told Nathan that Miles definitely knew about his mother's pregnancy, and that he resented the news. Of course. Nathan should have spoken with Miles about it. He should have eased him through the whole thing rather than nurse his own wounds. A better father would have done so.

"We all know it's not a picnic for you, Miles. No one said it was. But it could be a heck of a lot worse too. You're lucky in lots of ways. I'm sure you know."

"I do. I know." Miles' throat shredded his words, on account of emotion or the onset of puberty, or both, Nathan couldn't tell.

The light turned green. Nathan eased across the intersection, shifted softly from first to second gear.

"It's your life, is the thing. Sooner than it should be your life, maybe. But it's yours. You have to treat it with care, with respect. Because everything that you do matters. Like Rabbi Plotnick says all the time on the high holidays. Everything you do, even the small stuff, gets written down in the Book of Life."

Miles released a jet of dismissive air between his lips. "Come on, dad. You really believe that?"

"Maybe not literally," Nathan admitted, downshifted to slow his speed. "But as an idea, sure. The idea of it I do believe. So no more of this nonsense. You have to think. You!" Here Nathan lifted his mottled index finger from the stick shift and tapped his temple. "Make better decisions. Because it's your life now. You have to claim it. Sort of like your mom's doing, maybe. Don't blame her for wanting another kid, Miles. I know how it might seem to you, but you can't fight something like that. You never know, you might even like being a brother."

Nathan wasn't certain, but he thought that Miles chuckled at this last remark. He glanced over at his son, gazing out his window again at nothing in particular. The ocher streetlights danced over Miles face.

"I'm trying to get my act together too, Miles. I have an opportunity coming up I haven't told you about. It might change things for me. For us. Get me out of that crappy apartment."

"Chill," Miles said. And in the next breath, "But your crib's fine." It was a nice thing for his son to say.

"Thanks, Miles. Listen, though, does any of this make sense to you? Because I don't really know what else to tell you, kiddo. I wish I did."

Miles groaned. But it wasn't a bad groan. Not quite. It was the groan, rather, that Miles deployed from time to time to tell his father to relax, that he had already digested whatever morsel he was being fed.

"Yeah. It makes sense." Miles sat up suddenly, making the vinyl seat squeak, and faced him. "Word, does that mean I can say what I want for my Torah speech? You know, since it's my life and all?"

Nathan chewed his lip. A born litigator, this son of his. Wouldn't Sam be proud? But, yes, Miles could say whatever he wanted for his *drash.* At least Miles cared. Nathan's son would never be one of those people whom Kati bemoaned, the legions who didn't care about nothing.

"Yes," Nathan uttered, happy that Miles had offered him the opportunity to say at least one positive thing tonight. "Moses can be a Zulu prince for all I care. Say whatever you want. Absolutely."

"Zulu prince. Fuh'real?" Miles laughed. "That's messed up, dad."
Silence.

Miles yawned. A big long cat yawn. It was late.

Nathan turned into the parking lot of his small complex. Home sweet home. A putrid olfactory wave lapped inside his open window, but quickly passed as he motored beyond the dumpster.

"I have some broth in the fridge. Might warm you up."

Miles bobbed his dreads. Nathan would dice up some fresh car-rots and celery–was there a sprig of fresh thyme in the fridge?–drizzle in some more lime and maybe add a fresh snapper fillet too, up the protein a bit for his rangy son.

"Sorry about all this, dad. You were rockin' it out there on the water, word?"

A lazy laugh escaped Nathan's mouth. His son said "word" and Nathan heard "nu." Maybe there wasn't such an enormous difference. He parked in his assigned spot, set the parking brake, which croaked, toad-like. He'd pick up the skiff at the ramp later. "Yeah. I was doing okay out there, Miles. How did you know?"

Miles unbuckled his belt, threw open the thin truck door.

" 'Cause you smell sorta funky, dad."

Joe's errand. The cab of his son's truck smelled like his grandson, Miles. Like a wet dog. Those dread locks. Plus fishbait and ironblood smells, and the slightest ammoniac catpiss odor, but this might have been Joe's imagination. Nathan didn't own a cat far as Joe knew. His son had promised him the other day at the center that he would drive him and he hadn't forgotten. He was good that way, Nathan. Reliable. Joe navigated from the passenger's seat, glancing down toward his chicken-scratch directions on his lap. He didn't like plugging addresses into his phone and then relying blindly on the device. So he had scrawled the directions on one of the several pads of paper that Merck foisted on the office, back when he had an office. He struggled now to read his own writing. They missed their turn at Hypoluxo, headed back after figuring it out. Now here they were at the two-story condo.

"You sure this is the place, pop?"

"I'm not sure of anything anymore, boychik," Joe answered, honestly enough.

Nathan nodded, pensively. Joe didn't mean to sound so morose. He was just stating facts, increasingly slippery fish. His last PET scan wasn't so terrible. Plenty of neurotransmitters still doing the best they could. But in time, he knew (how much time was anyone's guess), his hippocampus would shrivel, his ventricles would bloat. Beta-amyloids would clump into plaques, wreak havoc with his synapses. Tau proteins and their tangles would do him in altogether. Cell death. A fucking bitch.

". . . .Yes," he added. "I'm pretty sure this is it."

His son wondered, of course, why he just sat there studying the small green door out the open truck window. Joe glanced toward his son. That bent shnoz of his. Perhaps they should have had it fixed, as Judy thought they should do. But the risks of general anesthesia, the sheer bone-crushing violence of rhinoplasty. Nathan's actual symptoms weren't so terrible. Some snoring. A sinus infection once in a while. Joseph couldn't see their way clear.

"Did you forget why we came here, dad? It's okay. Maybe I can help you figure it out. Or maybe they'll know. We can go up together." Nathan pulled up his parking brake hard with his right hand.

He was a good son, Nathan. Good in all the ways that mattered. Joe should have loved him more. All this time he should have loved him more. But love didn't always do what you wanted it to do. Love kept its own council. Or maybe this was only a sorry excuse.

"No, Nathan. I'm fine. I'll be right back. I remember."

He remembered. That was the thing. He remembered all sorts of things. Big things. It was only yesterday, only today, the hundreds upon thousands of crucial small things, which eluded his grasp, flitting off into the ether like so many dandelion balloons. He wasn't so far gone yet. He hadn't yet put away his apartment keys in the refrigerator; a spoon, thank God, was still a spoon; his windbreaker today (an Eli Lilly gift) was eminently appropriate for the brisk outside air. He threw open the flimsy truck door. What a strange winter! Time to face the music, he thought, or did he actually utter these words out loud?

"Huh?" Nathan inquired.

Yes, he must have spoken the words.

"Nothing. I'll be right back. Shouldn't be long kiddo." He threw a leg out the door, as if it were someone else's leg.

Jake had driven him to distraction while Ida Weingarten was under. While he handled the scope. The big things he remembered. Polyps all over the fucking place. What had happened to Jake? *Joe,* Alan, the anesthesiologist, had warned. *Careful there, Joe. Easy!*

He hadn't perforated a colon his whole goddamn career. His technique was legendary. He was GI Joe. King of the colonoscopy. Had almost singlehandedly consigned the flexible sigmoidoscopy to the dustbin. How many guest lectures had he been invited to deliver at Duke, at UF, at Miami, at Vanderbilt, at Texas Southwestern, at Alabama, at LSU? How many pisher students and residents had oohed and aahed over his shoulder? How many comely nurses batted their lashes over their surgical masks? How many colleagues had waited in line for him to perform his procedure on their own person, half of them forswearing general anesthesia, gritting through it just so they could watch on the screen in real-time their insides scoped by the master?

None of that seemed to matter now. Because he had failed his final patient. He had done her harm. Perforation. Sepsis. Organ failure. Not entirely his fault. Ten years tardy for her procedure. Her wasted colon, paper-thin. Her heart and lungs, tired. But enough his fault. Jake had driven him to distraction, as he distracted him now, making his way up the chattahoochee walk. The audacious blue blossoms of the plumbago shrubs on either side of the walkway mocked him with their incongruous cheer.

He had flown with Judy on El Al to retrieve their elder son. That was the idea, anyway. It was the last time they had joined in common purpose. She had insisted on paying her fare and he had allowed her to do so. Pure misery, the stretch from Kennedy to Ben Gurion. They sat toward the front of the fuselage. At sunup, seven or so black hats woke him from his fitful slumber, crowding the aisle beside him, davening toward Jerusalem. As if it mattered what end of this fucking metal cigar they prayed from, hurtling five hundred miles an hour through the atmosphere! Joe wanted to hate these bearded brethren, but the yeshiva bochers–younger than he had originally thought–weren't the ones responsible for Jake's lunacy. It wasn't so much a religious thing with Jake. He apparently saw himself more like a pioneer, like one of those old-time yishuv Jews. Pathetic. It was all so . . . derivative. Jake couldn't even flip out in an original manner.

Judy made their arrangements. Two rooms in Nahariya, a fairly straight shot to the coast from Jake's new kibbutz. The hotel was spartan on the whole, its stone front barely announcing itself amid its neighbors, but somewhat too quaint for their purpose, as was the town itself. Joe wasn't sure exactly what he expected Nahariya to look like, but certainly not the rough-hewn coastal beauty that greeted them. Jake would only grant them a precious few hours each day (he had responsibilities, he warned in advance) so what else could Joseph and Judy do but take in the city?

He didn't like it. He didn't like the outdoor cafes and restaurants and ice cream parlors along the main thoroughfare (what was it with Israelis and ice cream!?); he didn't like the dry air drenched with Hebrew glottals and amateurish chords from ubiquitous acoustic guitars; he didn't like the baby-faced soldiers in twos and threes, automatic weapons (uzis?) slung over their shoulders like purses; he didn't like the smell of sea salt and lamb and eucalyptus and fried chick peas; he didn't like the horse-drawn carriages and their canoodling passengers beneath the canopy of papery trees; he didn't like the lapping rush of the Ga'aton River in his ears–the name of the fucking river he remembered!–flowing toward the Mediterranean from smack dab in the middle of the street; he didn't like the broad promenade along the coast offering its vista of nubile sunbathers, sea and sky. He wasn't there to be charmed by this infuriatingly charming Israeli city along the coast.

Jake's kibbutz wasn't so charming. It struck Joe not unlike a cheerless version of the Pocono summer camp where they had sent Nathan and Jacob one year so that he and Judy might "work things out." A lot of good *that* did! Jake had given them the nickel tour when they arrived, pointing out the various realms of his adopted kingdom without pride or effacement. He had decided, it seemed to Joe, to withhold any ardor that might be interpreted as immature. Jake would project sobriety. First, the residential area. Dusty wood-paneled quarters in various sizes and configurations stood squat like army barracks around a larger A-frame dining hall and auditorium. Brown asphalt shingles, much newer than the structures themselves, topped all the quarters. Sparse gardens and listless playgrounds boasting only the most basic metal appoint-ments (swings, slides, seesaws) bordered a few of the homes. Just be-yond the residential area, up a modest rise of cement-hard dirt road, lay a cloudy greenhouse, where they had just begun to graft several apple tree varietals to (hopefully) cultivate finer fruit than the Druze farmers. Beyond the greenhouse were the chicken coops and two larger sheds, one for the cows, one for the horses. It was their newest enterprise, Jake insisted, showing the faintest trace of enthusiasm now. Horseback riding for tourists. There was a scenic path along the cucumber and corn fields, farther off into the distance. Everything about the place exuded dingy, utilitarian . . . what was the word? . . . existence. That's what it seemed to Joe that people must do here. Not live, quite. But exist. Still . . .

"It's greener than I expected," Joe had extended this peace offering their first day with Jake.

"It's the rainy season now."

"So when do they take the kids from their parents?" he asked the second day, passing a gaggle of boisterous boys and girls.

"We don't do that, dad. That's ancient history for Christ's sake. Kids live with their parents. For crying out loud."

"The women work the fields too?" he asked on the third day in the commissary, gazing toward a table of dusty girls.

"Sure." Jake looked over his shoulder to follow Joe's gaze. "Why not?"

"Just wondering."

They seemed happy, Joe had to admit on his third day there.

The women. The people, generally. Implausibly chipper. Quick to show their teeth as they laughed or carried on. They didn't seem too beaten down from the work, which must have been difficult. Or this plain food. How much baked chicken and overcooked broccoli could they eat? All in all, they exuded a robust healthfulness that belied the weary architecture and the dirtsmells tilting toward animal excrement.

They smoked like banshees, though. Even in the dining hall nicotine plumes cast a gray pall in the atmosphere, modestly lit to begin with. At one point, a coughing fit seized Judy, which Jake interpreted as a personal reproach.

"Mother!"

"Don't 'mother' her!" Joe cried, his first outright harsh words to his son. "She's allowed to cough."

"I'm okay!" Judy uttered between coughs, raising a hand to quash the bickering. "I'm okay, boys. Go, Joe. They're calling for ice-cream scoopers. Go help scoop ice-cream."

"They sure do like brown," Joe mentioned on the fourth day, lifting his nose to the quarters Jake shared with four other single men in their twenties.

"What would you suggest, dad? That we paint the roofs red? Make a target of ourselves for the Syrians?"

"No, of course not. I was just talking."

Things had begun to deteriorate by this point.

"The grounds look very nice, Jacob," Judy said. She was still hoping to mollify their son and win him over with kindness, a strategy

Joe didn't quite understand.

He visited Jake alone on the fifth day. "Let me go out by my-self," he suggested to Judy, who acquiesced. What did they have to lose?

"I know you don't think much of me anymore, Jake. But have you thought about what you're doing to your mother? Have you?"

Jake was busy cleaning the horse stalls, scraping a flat shovel against the concrete. The bothered dung released its tangy aroma. The smell Joe could take (he knew a thing or two about shit), but the sound of the metal shovel scraping against the gritty concrete hurt his ears. *Scraaape.* The whole display angered him, in any case. He knew that Jake had planned it. *Here dad. Look at me. Cleaning horseshit.*

"Do you really want to talk with me about that, Dad?" *Scraaape.* "That's rich. What *I'm* doing to Mom." Here Jake straightened his frame, leaned a wrist against the wood handle of the shovel and laughed a hearty belly-laugh. The whole tableau was ludicrous. His son leaning against a shit-stained shovel issuing a belly-laugh. Who did he think he was? Eddie Albert from *Green Acres*?

"Jesus, Jacob. Things happen. You're not a child anymore. How long do you want to hold all that against me, son?" Jake shrugged and returned to his labors. Joe wasn't sure why he had intoned his son's full name. "If all this has anything to do with that, with me–"

"It doesn't." *Scraaape.* "Not everything's about you, Dad. *You're the one who brought it up.*"

This wasn't technically true, but Joe let it pass.

"Or your brother. What about Nate? You've never been the best of friends, but he's still your brother. You really want to live so far away from your only brother? Have you really thought all this through?"

"Nate'll be fine." *Scraaape.* "He's got his own life to live." *Scraaape.* "He doesn't need me." *Scraaape.*

Joe pursued a different tack: "You know, Jacob, if you just want to spend more time in Israel I can understand. It's just the extremity of what you've been saying that has your mother worried. That has *me* worried. Take another year. Hell, why not? You've never looked better. I'll give you that."

This was true. He contemplated his son's form as he followed him to the next stall. He had lost some weight over the past year, weight that Joe didn't realize could be shed toward healthful effect. But he looked trim and fit now, his biceps and triceps working more discernibly beneath his flesh. He looked darker now too; his olive skin had deepened a shade. He maintained a well-trimmed beard and had let his dark hair grow out a bit, the way he had worn it as a young child in the 70s, which rocked Joe upon first glance a few days before.

"Enjoy the mountain air," Joe continued. "Work the land. Build your muscles. Eat your own tomatoes and oranges and chickens and eggs and milk. Fair enough . . . ."

Here's what Joe wanted to say next: *Enjoy nailing these tough promiscuous girls for a while longer.* Because he was convinced that these earthy Israeli women were part of the equation. How could they not be? He had eyes, after all. But Joe couldn't approach such a topic with Jacob.

". . . You'll spend another year. I'll even keep you in the shekels, and then you'll come home and start at Vanderbilt."

"Okay, right now . . ." Jacob stopped shoveling. . . "stop patron-
izing me, Dad."

This was all Joe could take. He felt the heat rise in his face.

"Snap out of it, Jake! You're acting like a spoiled fucking brat!"
Joe's voice boomed against the rafters and the slatted metal roof. A
horse whinnied.

"So fuck off already then! I didn't ask you to come! Just fuck
off and die!"

Joe's fist flew on its own accord, kissing the spot below Jake's
eye. Joe had never struck either of the boys with a closed fist. He
couldn't deny the rush. It felt impossibly good. For the past four days,
Judy and he had padded around Jake on cat-feet, the both of them nodding deferentially when Jake prattled on about this and that: the great
dignity of honest work, the deliciousness of simple homegrown food,
the breathtaking view of the Hula Valley from the Golan Heights, the
sweet eucalyptus air in the crisp morning, Arafat's latest meshugass. But
enough already!

His son, one hand braced against the shovel, lifted a hand to
check the heat on his cheek, seeking tactile confirmation of what had
just happened, as if he could hardly believe it. For the briefest moment,
Joe wondered whether his son would lash back with the shovel and take
his head clear off. But he didn't.

"I'll let that go," Jake offered with disconcerting calm. "Because
I cussed. But try it again Dad and I'll lay you out. You know I will."

Yes, Joe knew. Clearly there was no reasoning with the boy. Joe exhaled. He felt the ache rise in his knuckles. A gray horse in the next stall snorted and snuffed, clacked a hoof on the hard ground, as if hoping to intercede.

"We took you and Nate horseback riding when you were young. Remember? Out at that ranch in Wellington off 441. Remember?"

"No. Not really."

And so he let Jacob go. What else could he do? He was an adult, as the American Consulate in Tel Aviv reminded them. They had visited the impossibly average-looking hayseed (from Iowa, Joseph would have guessed) the afternoon before their flight. Joseph knew it would be a waste of time, but Judy had insisted. "As long as we're here, Joe."

"He'll get tired of the place," the hayseed assured them, as he'd probably assured dozens of other concerned Jewish-American parents. He wore a plain blue suit with a red tie, probably the only suit and tie the fellow owned here; likely kept it on a hook behind his office door. "You'll see," he continued. "He'll fly back on his own. Most do. Eventually."

And so Judy and Joe boarded the El Al jet alone.

Joe's anger with his son had made things easier those first few years. He tended that anger like a crop. He outright refused to return to Israel to visit Jake. If Judy wanted to be the sucker that was her business. But maybe it wasn't even anger, mostly, that he felt. Not even behind his fist in that fetid stable. Maybe it was something closer to envy, he thought now on the front walk, standing between these impossibly cheery plumbago shrubs bursting with blue. Envy that Jacob had found such purpose in his purposeful life, a life that truly didn't revolve around his shlong and those earthy Israeli women. When Jake's first child was born—a daughter, Hannah they named her, presumably after someone on his wife's side—Joe finally flew to Israel to see his first grandchild. They were living at a moshav, which struck Joe as more normal than the kibbutz. But it was a painful visit, punctuated by belabored courtesies, awkward silences, and impatient outbursts, partly attributable to the exhausting demands of the mewling infant. The new parents were too busy to deal with the likes of a self-absorbed parent. Joe felt like an intruder, which, in a way, he was. Jake didn't even try to hide the relief on his face when he dropped his father off at Ben Gurion. It would have taken an awful lot of effort to salvage his relations with his elder son. That's what it came down to, Joe realized. Effort. It was a pity. Neither he nor his son had it in them to expend such effort. Not toward each other, anyway. Now he feared that it was pretty much too late.

Some accounts you couldn't quite settle. Others you could.

**

His father paused there on the chattahoochee walkway between the plumbagos. Bright blue, colorblind Nathan thought. Or was that what people called purple? But what was his father doing just standing there? Those damn synapses just wouldn't fire. Plaque. Plaque and tangles. It had something to do with plaque and tangles, Nathan had learned, crowding the nerve cells in his brain. Should he get out of the truck? He didn't think so. Not yet. His father was well enough to resent any help he might offer. The disease would catch up to him eventually, though.

Nathan had read up on the signs and kept a watchful eye. His father's judgment would go–he'd bake a carton of milk in the oven or something–and it would fall upon Nathan to decide what to do. The Jewish Home, at some point. No getting around it, probably. In the meantime, he'd help his father tidy up his earth business.

This strange errand. Nathan looked out his open window opposite direction of his father. He thought he recognized the development, the cluster of white condos laid out like an oyster shell around the blue pearl of a pool, slash pines here and there, bursting illogically from the thick St. Augustine carpet. Was this where Aunt Noma had lived after moving up from Miami? Maybe. But it couldn't be Noma that his father was visiting, or any other relative. All his distant aunts and uncles, including Noma, had died off ten years ago, longer now, and hadn't been replaced. By other relatives. Or even by other Jews, most of whom had begun retiring elsewhere.

His father resumed his progress. Good. Nathan watched as he opened the screen and knocked on the door. Three decisive raps . . . *Tat-Tat-Tat* . . . as if he were ripping off a bandage. His father closed the screen again, took a step back. Still plenty solid, his father. Maybe no one was home. For some reason–Nathan didn't know why–he hoped that no one would answer, that his father would retreat back into the safety of the Tacoma so he could take him back home to Louna, his Haitian caregiver. But then someone did answer the door, an upright man roughly his father's age with tinted eyeglasses, square shoulders, a flaming shock of white hair. The man was surprised by his guest and none too happy about receiving him. Nathan could tell by the thrust of his square chin, the hand that still grasped the screen door, barring entry. Nathan knew who the man was now, feeling stupid for his slow knowledge. Of course. The husband. The widower.

The white-haired man uttered a few sharp words, words that Nathan couldn't quite make out. Only the bass notes made their way to the truck. His father must have been talking too, but quieter and he didn't use his hands. After a few moments, something seemed to change in the fellow. His square shoulders dropped. His lips stopped moving. So Nathan wasn't surprised when he backed away some from the threshold and held open the screen door with a woolly arm, when his father stepped into the home to conduct his business and shut the door quietly behind him.

Nathan scoured his skiff at the dock, wielding a bottle of Simple Green in one hand and a sponge in the other. Console. Deck. Trolling motor. Chrome. White light of day now so he could see the grime all about the *Pray Fish*. No charter for him today. Oh well. His fellow captains hadn't done much better. Hollis' *Ellen S.* was out on its morning drift (whether it carried enough paying customers to justify the fuel was another matter), but the other boats were still tied up, bucking impatiently in their slips. There were just so many variables vying against Nathan and his cohorts these days. On top of global warming, red tides, dying reefs, and depleted seas, they now had the manifold enticements of internet-based games and whatnot, which proved irresistible to kids and even grown men—the minutes his fellow Floridians spent outdoors whittled away by the latest media distraction.

Nathan spied Frank and Del loitering about their vessels, futzing with this and that. Manny leaned over his steel filleting table, carving a long bloodline from a kingfish, tossing the scarlet thread in the general direction of Larry, Moe, and Curly, the dock's aged pelicans. Nathan wasn't the only captain, or creature, struggling. Reminding himself of this made him feel better, for the split second before he felt bad that he felt better.

At least there was the Sunshine Network's Fishing Report taping in a few days. Plus, there was work to do now. You couldn't pilot a dirty vessel. He shifted from Simple Green to Soft Scrub as he tended to the vinyl. Bleach was tough on the deck's gel-coat so he only used the caustic cleanser on the vinyl cushions topping the coolers and casting seat. It took some elbow grease, nonetheless. He rinsed the soapy seats with torrents of hose water, ushering the runoff toward the bilge at the stern. He returned to the Simple Green and his sponge and labored with care over the last bits of dried detritus on deck–ladyfish excrement, fish scale, shrimp-shell–that had resisted his earlier efforts with soap and sponge. He noticed the blotch of gray on deck for the first time, perhaps on account of this new cloud overhead, which masked the cold sun. Nathan intuited the culprit in an instant. Wolf's juiced baits. Son of a bitch. How did he miss this spot two days ago? He doused the stain with a copious Simple Green dose. *Pump pump pump.* The blotch disappeared upon his first swipe with the lathered sponge.

"Yo, Nate, do me a solid and lend me some of that Simple Green?"

Nathan looked up from his labors. It was Frank's sandy-haired mate, Bobby.

"Yeah. Sure, Bobby. No problem." Nathan rose and handed the mate the bottle.

"Cool. We'll get you on the flip-side. Just don't have time to run out right now. Afternoon charter on the way."

Nathan nodded. Bobby spoke an awful lot like Miles, it seemed to Nathan. Perhaps everyone of a certain age spoke like Miles these days.

Arching his weary back, relieved of the Simple Green, Nathan glimpsed the blonde dollop, the apple-faced approach. He groaned in vague protest, then supped the pleasant marine funk through his nostrils to bolster himself. Not now. He was some ways off, Wolf, clear down by Manny's panga. Larry, Moe, and Curly parted to allow Wolf passage. Nathan wouldn't raise an arm to usher him over. Instead, he lowered his gaze toward the console, fiddled with the squelch of his radio, hoping lamely to discourage Wolf's inevitable approach. No dice.

"Thought I'd hear from you by now, Captain Pray."

Nathan looked up at Wolf and his immovable presence. A leather folder seemed shrunken within one of his frying pan hands. Nathan felt small, suddenly, cowering below in the skiff. Grasping the steel ladder, he climbed up on the dock and was immediately disappointed that Wolf still towered over him. Perhaps he should have remained on the *Pray Fish*.

"You come all this way to tell me that, Wolf?"

Wolf exhaled. "Don't be coy, Nate. Just cut the crap, okay. Have you tried the baits or not?"

"Yeah, I tried them," Nathan admitted, before it occurred to him that he might have lied.

"Well?"

"They work. I'm sure you know they work."

"So, can we count on you or what? Let's talk turkey here. We know you're on the short list for the Fishing Report–"

Nathan raised an open hand in reflexive protest.

"*Don't* try to deny it. You're a crappy liar, Nathan."

This was an insult, apparently. Nathan lowered his hand and

exhaled the saline and sardine odors out his labyrinthine septum.

"We want a commitment here. I've brought the paperwork." Wolf stepped beside Nathan and opened the leather folder before him to reveal the elongated pages, indented subcategories and lower-case Roman numerals of the wordy contract. "Here's what we're offering. Not a run of the mill deal." Wolf stabbed the document with a gleaming gold pen. "In exchange for our exclusive stake on you–Ulee's Baits is the only outfit you'll be hawking–we offer a signing bonus and fixed annual stipend. This ain't peanuts, Nathan. Look at these figures." Wolf stabbed the contract once again with his pen. Nathan looked. "Full tournament sponsorship . . . you're obligated to compete in all the Flatmaster's and FLW circuit tourneys . . . wardrobe approval . . . we'll put a kick-ass sponsorship wrap on your hull . . . rename this skiff . . . Ulee's Dream, something like that . . . you sound like a friggin' evangelical now, name like *Pray Fish* . . . we do tap a modest percentage of any winnings . . ." Wolf nattered on some more as Nathan's attention drifted toward his fellow captains, clearly looking on from their slips. Shame seized Nathan's innards, not unlike the inchoate shame he felt the other night when he degorged Wolf's juiced bait from the pierced innards of the ladyfish.

". . . so what do you say, Nate? I'm only trying to help you here." The rigid scaffolding holding up Wolf's face relaxed some; Nathan didn't trust this abrupt softening.

"Truth is, I'm just not interested, Wolf. The juiced baits. The aquaculture. The genetic implications and whatnot. I'd prefer not to get mixed up in any of it."

"You'd *prefer* not? You'd *prefer* not!?" Wolf's wide-eyed response betrayed some combination of anger and befuddlement. "Can't you read the writing on the wall!? How do you think you're going to feel two years from now when everyone and their mother's using Ulee's Baits, when you'll have no choice but to use them!? We'll be selling them by the bucket every bait store and sporting good shop Key West to Myrtle Beach, Galveston Bay to Homosassa. You can't stop it, Nathan! Haven't you figured that out!? You're like the guy who tried to stop the automobile for Christ's sake!?"

Nathan crossed his arms as if to protect his soft organs from the hard sell. "I guess I'll have to be okay with that," he said. His calm only angered Wolf further. The muscles in his jaw bulged clear back toward his ears. His pale eyeballs seemed to quiver in their sockets.

"Don't fuck with me, Nathan!" Wolf clamped the leather folder shut with one hand and gripped the shirt fabric beneath Nathan's crumpled collar with the other, yanking Nathan's ginger chest hair beneath. It was a gesture straight from elementary school, the nostalgia of which Nathan couldn't quite appreciate. Wolf's left hand still held the folder low, he noted.

"Lay off!" Nathan cried, smacking Wolf's grip, but not quite strong enough to free himself.

"You smart-ass bastard! You fucking pissant! You wonder why the good ol' boys here can't stand you?" Wolf shook Nathan off balance with his fist. "I'd *prefer* not to!" he aped Nathan's words, constricting his windipipe to affect effeminacy.

Nathan swung his right fist just as the wave of Frank, Manny, and Frank's mate, Bobby, crashed over them, clearing the target from Nathan's errant blow. Frank had gripped Wolf's shirt with both his fists and pushed him back on his feet. "*Whoa!*" Wolf uttered, throwing up his arms, knowing when he was outnumbered.

"This asshole messing with you, Nate?" Frank asked. He was shorter than Wolf. They all were. But Frank was solid.

"Should we fuck him up?" Manny asked without a trace of irony, which surprised Nathan. Manny?

"Just let him go," Nathan declared. "Let him go, for crying out loud." Frank let Wolf go but jutted his goateed chin at him still. Nathan reached down and picked up the leather folder, where Wolf had dropped it. He handed it to Wolf through the wall of Frank, Manny, and Bobby. Wolf snatched the offering with a frown.

"It's your fucking conscience these boys don't like! Your goody two-shoes, holier-than-thou conscience! They're fucking *fish*, Nate! Get over it! They're just a bunch of stupid fucking *fish!*"

"All right, partner, best be on your way," Del uttered from somewhere behind Nathan, having lumbered finally to the scene of the struggle. Marty, the dockmaster, had slipped out of his tiny office to take the measure of the goings on, deciding whether or not to call the police.

Wolf retreated. Marty headed back into his office, Nathan noticed, his cordless phone half-hidden in his fist.

"I really think I had that under control," Nathan said once

Wolf was beyond earshot.

"Sure you did," Frank replied. "All hundred pounds of you. Had him quaking' in his boots." A gull screeched over the hum of vehicular traffic on the A1A.

"Lame-ass punch you threw," Manny said, inspiring a chorus of belly-laughs.

"That was fun as shit," Bobby said.

"Anyway, thanks," said Nathan. "Thanks, I guess."

"You been bettin' on the ponies down in Pompano?" Del inquired through the crease in his beard that was his mouth.

"No, he's just a bait guy. You probably screwed up your own chances for a piece of what he's selling."

"Shee-it," Frank said. "Dime a dozen, those whores."

Nathan nodded, taking note of Frank's DOA cap, the Costa Del Mar sunglasses dangling like a necklace above the diagonal SHIMANO stitched across his Columbia captain's shirt. He inhaled through his nostrils another deep draught of saline air spiced with baitfish.

"Big dude," Bobby said. "Give him that."

"So," Del uttered, then paused while he snuffed out his nostrils, making it clear somehow that he was shifting the topic. "When were you planning on telling us?"

"Telling you what?"

"Fucking Nathan," Manny cried. "You're the worst fucking liar in the world." This was the second time in the last five minutes Nathan heard as much.

"Here, son." Del handed Nathan a thin sheaf of papers, then waddled away.

"Kick some ass for us," Frank said, then followed Del. Bobby trailed after his captain. "That's all I'm saying. Kick some ass up there in Orlando."

"You're giving *me* the 411 next week," Manny declared, flashing his canines, poking a finger at Nathan's chest before pivoting on his absurd rubber clogs.

"And stay away from those ponies," Del shouted from down the dock, initiating another round of laughter. Even Larry, Moe, and Curly cackled, bringing up the rear, drowning out the more distant cries of several gulls now, waddling away just like Del.

Nathan raised one hand to quell the sting that rose again on his ginger chest, his adrenalin spent. He glanced down at the crumpled sheaf of lined paper in the other. The sheaf trembled in his hand. The altercation with Wolf had rocked him. "Wuss," Nathan admonished himself under his breath, standing in for his brother, Jake.

Del had handed him their captain's reports for his segment on the Sunshine Network's fishing show. They knew! From Manny, no doubt. Even the date of the broadcast, somehow. Wolf seemed to know, too. He shuffled through the sloppy sheaf before returning to the report on top. *Captain Manny Lynch of Chasin' Tail Charters,* Manny had scribbled at the top along with his phone number and website. *I'm slamming ladyfish in the intracoastal between the Hillsboro and Boca inlets using sardine chunks on a chartreuse Bass Assassin jig head. Lighted docks and bridge pilings*

are producing sheepshead using live shrimp. You gotta hook them under the
horny ridge just in front of the dark spot with a 1/0 or 2/0 circle hook. You gotta
expect to lose plenty of shrimp, but you'll get more bites baited natural this way.
And you gotta use at least a split-shot to get the shrimp down to where the fish
are. Offshore, the kingfish bite has been wicked in 45 feet between the first and
second reefs. Plenty of smokers. Fish at night using whole sardines with a double
or triple 4/0 J-hook, wire leader or at least 80 pound fluoro. Butterfly the baits if
you get too many window-shoppers. You can slow-troll between 5 and 7 knots or
anchor up. Try bucktail jigs if you anchor up, skirt if you troll. Any color works
as long as it's chartreuse. Vary the weight from freelining to 2 ounce 'til you hit
the money-spot in the column.

"Any color works as long as it's chartreuse," Nathan tasted the words again. Fair dose of wit there, he had to admit. He shuffled through the rest of the reports. Del had offered some good info on the daytime mahi, blackfin, and wahoo bite well offshore. For targeting grouper on the wrecks, he had included complicated instructions on rigging his three-way swivel. Frank had ponied up on the midnight swordfish bite even farther offshore. Deep-dropping large squid, apparently, was the way to go. Hollis had scratched a few barely legible notes about the party-boat goings on fairly near shore, misspelling the word "column" as "collum" three times, which somehow moved Nathan.

He'd have to incorporate these useful nuggets into his script. He quartered the sheaf with two folds, then slid the square into his front khaki pocket. They seemed to have been written with the same blue ballpoint pen. Big Del had likely corralled the notes just a few hours earlier at the Caribbean Café bar while Kati served them their steak and eggs, while they nursed their steaming cups of bitter Cuban coffee. He pondered the spirit of the gift as he checked the mooring of the *Pray Fish* one last time. It wasn't simple generosity. His fellow captains stood to gain, should Nathan mention their names and contact information on the show. But it wasn't wholly mercenary, either. Something about the way Del had offered Nathan the reports. Some current of feeling there that Nathan couldn't deny, even if his inflexible saltwater ethics, as Wolf implied, mostly alienated his local brotherhood of fishing guides. His fellow captains, even Manny, had just taken care of Wolf on his behalf. No getting around that. Even Manny, whatever shady business he was up to late at night on that panga of his.

Orlando. Nathan hated Orlando. Mostly on account of its inland locale in a constant state of construction. He found it hard to breathe here, crowded on all sides by miles and miles of fresh odoriferous asphalt, stucco and strip mall. The studio building, apparently, was located along the weary outskirts of the new mirrored downtown, a much smaller building than Nathan had anticipated. It was an old building, built low and squat from stone encrusted concrete, speckled with tiny, vaguely nautical, windows. Old-style Florida business architecture—ugly, but hurricane resistant. A solar marquee, much newer than the building itself, announced the Sunshine Network's presence. Well, what did he expect, Rockefeller Center? It was only a statewide show, high up there on the cable dial. Nathan was just old enough to remember television dials.

Kelly, he needed. She was a production assistant or something like that. He parked his groaning truck, entered the building and was relieved to see a high desk, manned by an officious looking black fellow, a solar patch emblazoned on the lapel of his navy sports jacket. The man nodded wordlessly upon Nathan's query and picked up his phone. "Kelly," the man uttered into the receiver. Nathan could smell cinnamon on his breath. "Your appointment is here."

"Thanks."

The man nodded again and returned to his crossword puzzle, which Nathan just noticed. In mere seconds, a trim young woman with disciplined blonde bangs burst through the wooden door to receive him.

She wore aggressively pleated khakis and a denim shirt, the Fishing Report logo stitched above one small breast, the Chevrolet automobile emblem on the other side of her chest, an emblem that always struck Nathan as vaguely Christological and off-putting.

"Good, you're here," she exclaimed. Her crisp, efficient voice seemed designed for punchy, mostly monosyllabic, words. "Mr. Pray, right?" Nathan nodded. She threw a tiny hand at him, which he shook. Nathan followed the bumblebee through the door and into a long dimly lit hall toward Wardrobe. It became real to him, suddenly, halfway down the linoleum hall. He tried to control his breathing.

They passed several employees, most of whom wore laminated tags at their chest, a few of whom nodded toward Kelly as she led him through a series of side doors through various cubicled rooms. Finally, they entered a large open space, clothes dripping from hangers on simple carts with rollers. The sight of the eight or so carts rocked Nathan as it reminded him immediately of Pray Clothiers, his grandfather's Miami Beach factory.

"What size are you?"

It was kind, or at least politic, of her to inquire. His size was clear.

"Uh, small," he confessed.

"Like Chip."

"I guess so. Sure."

"You're a little taller than him I think."

"A little, maybe."

Kelly reached toward a hanger and plucked a denim shirt, then handed him the swatch of blue fabric to hold.

"Waist?" she asked, springing to a separate rack.

"Twenty-eight."

"Serious?"

"Afraid so."

"You ate something today, right?"

"Yeah," he lied. Upon waking, he was too nervous to eat.

"Here," Kelly exclaimed, thrusting a pair of khaki shorts down at Nathan's crotch, which made him flinch. "These have an elastic waist. Folks at Columbia gave us a whole bunch of these hoping we'd wear them. Try them on. There's a curtain." She lifted a freckled nose toward the makeshift dressing room at one corner. Nathan obeyed. The shorts seemed a bit loose, even with the elastic, but they would do.

"Perfect," Kelly appraised him once he emerged, and then glanced downward. "You've got totally big calves."

It wasn't so much a compliment, just an observation innocuous enough that she needn't bother suppressing it.

"Yeah," Nathan said. "I guess so. All that hopping up and down on the boat and dock."

He decided that he didn't much like this perfectly pleasant looking, perfectly chipper, perfectly ordinary girl. Probably a recent Communications graduate from UCF, the state university nearby, biding her time here until something better came along. Maybe this was just an internship.

"Let's get you to makeup."

"Makeup? You sure I need makeup? I–"

"All you guys say the same thing," she interjected, coquettish now. "Trust me, Mr. Pray. It's TV. You need makeup."

**

There they sat. The Fishing Report cast. Bryan Dossett, the tall, telegenic network broadcaster, the show's everyman who routinely asked follow-up questions of the captains, or simply requested clarification when their vernacular lapsed into inscrutable jargon; Mark Sargeant, the garrulous editor of *Billfish Magazine*, who hosted the short segment each week devoted to new products: lures, boat wax, deck shoes, whatever; and Chip Holiday–the king of sting, as Frank joked. The men sat on their barber shop stools before lighted mirrors, paper bibs billowing from their necks. Mark slouched, visibly bored in his seat, waiting his turn for what appeared to be the sole make-up artist on call. Bryan sat higher, his chin lifted toward the mirror, appraising himself, not the least bit bored with his reflection.

"Okay, I'm leaving Mr. Pray with you, Zev," Kelly declared. It sounded like a threat. The man looming over Chip in his chair, who must have been Zev, nodded. "Break a leg," Kelly chirped as she turned heel.

"Is that the Snookmaster in the house?" Chip greeted him, but couldn't turn to face him, or even open his eyes quite, on account of Zev–who was probably Israeli judging by his name and swarthy look– plying Chip's face with what appeared to be a small air-pressure gun.

"Hey Chip," Nathan greeted his host, lifting his hand in a lame wave. Chip slipped a hand through his bib to shake, but still didn't turn his face. Nathan wasn't sure whether to look at Chip directly or through the mirror as he approached and shook. He settled on doing both, having jockeyed around the makeup artist, who couldn't quite disguise his mild annoyance. Chip's painted pallor seemed an odd yellowish brown up close. Stray paint-flecks adhered to some of the gray bristles of his goatee. The makeup made the shallow water angler seem older to Nathan, somehow. He *was* older, despite his puckish demeanor. Mid-fifties or so. Maybe sixty. His fishing proclivities, which Nathan appreciated, also betrayed his ripe age. Like Nathan, Chip still seemed to favor the hard stuff–stick baits, spoons, and plugs–over the multi-hued menagerie of soft, scented plastics. He didn't even douse his Parabolas with Carolina Lunker Sauce, far as Nathan knew. That's one of the reasons that Nathan respected the show. It mostly advocated artificial bait and techniques for actual anglers. It didn't cater to the bait-slingers dragging their knuckles across the ground. Chip also touted environmentally-friendly principles on the show, encouraged catch-and-release plus responsible line-management and anchoring practices; he sometimes decried the overly permissive regulations governing the commercial fishing industry.

"Well hello Captain Pray," Bryan sang from his chair, still half-gazing toward the mirror, his tongue testing the elasticity of his cheek. "Long time no see," the tall host alluded to their meeting at the Caribbean Café, swiveling in his chair now and offering his soft hand, which Nathan shook.

"Welcome to the big leagues, Captain Pray," the billfish mag editor uttered from the next chair, extending his larger, rougher hand. "Heard you really slay those snookies down there along the gold coast."

"Not so much these days, Captain Sargeant," Nathan admitted, releasing his grip.

"Yeah, that big die-off down there. Shit, they'll come back to your coast. Gulf coast guides are the ones in real trouble, red tide bad as it's been."

This was probably true, Nathan thought.

"Sit over here next to Captain Holiday, sweetness," Zev told Nathan, who obeyed, unsure whether there was some performative irony in Zev's *sweetness* remark or if this was just how he talked.

"You got my script, right?" he asked Chip.

"Yeah, yeah," Chip assured him. "I had to make some changes. Way too much info on there."

"Oh?"

"You'll get to practice on the teleprompter. No worries."

"Are you going to be nervous?" Zev asked Nathan once he finished with Chip, his hand hovering above various canister attachments to his airbrush.

"Uh, I don't know? Does it matter?"

Zev rolled his eyes. "Sort of." He crouched before Nathan and studied his countenance, while Nathan studied Zev. His coal-black eyebrows seemed to have been aggressively manicured just shy of feminine proportions. His strong cologne made Nathan shrink. "I'll have to go a step down," Zev said. "You're really white."

"I am?"

"You know what I mean." The Israeli smiled here for the first time that Nathan noticed and cracked his chewing gum between his teeth as if to punctuate the gesture.

"You make him pretty," Mark joked, rising from his seat. Bryan and Chip had risen too. "We'll meet you in the studio," Chip said. He slapped Nathan's shoulder, fraternally.

**

"Here, come help me with this, Nate," Chip proposed as soon as Nathan arrived at the studio, his face newly painted. It felt funny. Hot and tight. Nathan didn't like it. "You'll get used to it," Chip said. It was a hopeful thing to say, which lifted Nathan's spirits. Chip was leaning over Mark Sargeant's products table, pinching a barbed lure between his forefinger and thumb for a cameraman, who poked his giant lens awfully close to the offering. Nathan recognized what Chip was doing. They often cut away to the taped close-up of a particular lure–tantalizingly rolled between the pincers of Chip's paw–whenever it was mentioned in one of the captain's reports. Nathan made his way beside his host. The studio, like the building itself, was smaller than Nathan had expected, the square footage diminished by the two large cameras on their rolling tripods.

"Oh the glamor, eh?" Chip teased. "Gotta push that merchandise, though. Keep the sponsors happy. But don't worry now, Nate. You don't gotta hold none of the Parabolas. I'll do that. I know you're probably still sore at them, right?" It didn't surprise Nathan that Chip knew about his dealings with Parabola, the way they screwed him, stealing

316

his silver mullet stickbait design, but it did surprise him that it was something Chip thought to remember. It was a long time ago.

"Ancient history now," Nathan said, feeling sort of good to strike a magnanimous chord, more magnanimous than he felt toward Parabola. Chip nodded.

"Just grab one of those Yo-Zuris." Chip lifted his sunburnt nose toward the pile of artificial fish designs at the far end of the wide table.

"Sure you want these hands on camera?" Nathan lifted his mottled digits for inspection.

"Shee-it, Nate. Those hands ain't no worse than these old paws here."

Nathan plucked a Yo-Zuri stickbait from the pile of artificial baits.

"Now just hold your hand down there," the cameraman instructed. "Kinda curl it between your thumb and forefinger a bit . . . not that much . . . good. . . . Yo-Zuri Two-Inch 3-D Minnow with Flash Foil," the man intoned slowly and clearly for the microphone as he began filming.

Nathan could feel the heat from the camera's light against his mottled hand. He was glad that his fingernails were mostly clean. It was a test, of sorts, Nathan suspected, Chip's way of ascertaining whether or not Nathan was as big a prig as he'd likely heard out and about. As "Jew-sensitive," as Manny put it recently. Nathan felt sort of silly twirling the artificial minnow between his fingers, a hand model for all intents and purposes. But he didn't have much problem endorsing these stickbaits for the show. What was the crime? This was the world he lived in. He'd make an attempt, at any rate, to live in the real world. Why else was he here?

The second cameraman rolled his equipment over and began shooting Chip again, just down the table holding up a separate artificial offering.

"Now the MirrOlure," Chip instructed. "The Catch 2000 over there," he gestured with his goatee. "They got cool eyes on that new one, don't you think?" Nathan nodded mildly, clutched the glimmering bait and curled it between his fingers for the camera.

"MirrOlure Catch 2000 Suspending Twitchbait," Nathan's cameraman intoned for the microphone, then began filming again.

"Your artificials work better you think, right Nate?" Chip asked. Chip knew that he still constructed his own wooden lures. "What's your theory again?"

"Well, these babies look nice," Nathan answered, curling this larger plug between his fingers. "But the weight's all wrong. It's the most important thing, I think. The weight. More important than smell or sound." Nathan shook the plug next to his ear, which rattled.

"Hey hey hey," the cameraman complained. Nathan lowered the lure again for the camera. "They add these beads for sound, but now it's too heavy. Baitfish make a distinct wave when they swim, right?"

Chip nodded.

"It's the wave I think that matters most, the wave that snook detect with their lateral line before they even see or smell the pilchard or greenie. Lure like this, I can feel it's too heavy right off. You can cast it farther, I guess, but it'll make too steep a wave, one that won't travel as far."

"Damn, Nate."

"I get a flatter signature with the dogwood lures I build on the lathe. The vibration travels farther and registers against the snook's lateral line closer to an actual baitfish. It's closer to real. You want to be as close to real as possible is the thing. Plus . . ."

"Plus?"

"Plus it's not cheating. Those juiced baits. I won't use them. Worse than live."

Chip nodded, silent. Nathan didn't like the sound of his last words, which probably made him sound like a jerk. Here Chip was, giving his fellow shallow water angler a shot, which he didn't really have to do. They were competitors, after all, despite Nathan's recent uncompetitive performances at the Flatmaster's tourneys along the gulf and in the Glades.

"You know, however this works out, Chip, I appreciate the opportunity. I really do. Should've thanked you already. I've just got a lot going on."

"Shit, I know you appreciate it, Nate. Don't have to tell me that."

"I just wanted you to know. In case it turns out I suck at this."

Chip chortled here and bobbed his shoulders to complement the small laugh. "We'll just give it a whirl. What do we got to lose?"

Once they finished modeling about $1000 worth of gleaming baits, a preternaturally young man wearing a headset and microphone approached Nathan. "Luke," the sandy-haired boy introduced himself. He was Nathan's handler, he said, his teeth gleaming beneath the studio lights. He would take care of him, he promised, then led Nathan to his mark, just beyond the Sunshine Network logo painted on the floor, so that he could practice reading from his revised script.

The cameraman offered some preliminary instruction and Nathan was off. Every few sentences or so, Luke, standing behind the cameraman, flashed him a thumbs-up, as if Nathan were a toddler in desperate need of positive reinforcement.

Their director, whose name Nathan didn't absorb, interrupted him at one point to introduce himself. He was bald and heavy and moist with sweat. A swatch of button-down shirt fabric hung out of his waistband like a flag. "I'm just going to watch you for a few takes, captain, if that's okay?"

"Of course," Nathan said, surprised by the odd deference.

Bryan, Mark, and Chip, along with the director, lurked in the background, talking mostly amongst themselves, but glanced over from time to time, as well. Anonymous members of the production crew milled about.

Nathan thought that he was doing okay–and was cheered that Chip hadn't edited his language down too much–but the moist director, for his part, seemed dissatisfied, exhaled audibly out his nostrils. The cameraman finally flicked off his light, whereupon the director approached to offer instruction.

"Try, captain, not to scan the lines from side to side so much."

"Huh?"

"You look sort of cagey. Know what I mean? Even though viewers know that you're reading it from the teleprompter, you don't want folks *thinking* that you're reading it from the prompter. Get it?"

"I guess so."

"And try not to go so fast. Did you drink coffee this morning?"

"No."

"Good. Did you eat something? You look a little green around the gills."

"Yes," he lied. "I ate."

"Do you have to use the bathroom?"

"No."

"You're not too nervous, are you?"

"No, not really," he lied again. That was the funny thing about lying. It got easier.

Nathan practiced, and practiced, and practiced. "Okay, clear the set!" the director shouted in the middle of Nathan's fourth go-around or so, at which point various members of the crew scurried off the stage with their clipboards and headsets. One fellow finessed various cables about on the floor, ushering them out of the field of view. There were a couple lines in the revised script that Nathan didn't like. But he wouldn't be a pain in the ass. He'd leave well enough alone.

"Now you just wait here with me," his handler instructed. "You're not too nervous, are you?"

"No. Why is everyone asking me that?"

"You look kind of flushed is the thing."

"Oh?" Nathan lifted a hand to his face. He hadn't expected Luke to offer an actual explanation.

"Don't touch," Luke ordered, stern for the first time. Then

softer: "You don't want to mess up the makeup. Don't worry, Mr. Pray. It's not a live show. We can tape it a hundred times if we have to." His boyish handler said this as if the prospect was a good thing.

It took an ungodly long time to arrive at Nathan's segment. He was weary of standing for so long and hot from the lights, even though they weren't shining directly on him anymore. His painted face, particularly, felt hot and red. He was nervous. He should have eaten something.

After they taped the Panhandle report via phone–which only took Captain Pierce, a chicken-rigging red snapper specialist, two takes–Luke led him to his mark, while various crew members, wearing headsets and gleaming white sneakers, shuffled props, cords, boom microphones, and cameras about the small space. "Okay, just stand here," Luke said. "Wait 'til Jeff gives you the go-ahead."

"Huh?"

"The director. Jeff."

He stood there on his mark, positioned snug between Chip and Bryan. He felt heavy, somehow, in his shoes. And hot. Chip reached behind Nathan and tapped the back of Bryan's head. "Hey, watch the hair," Bryan joked, in better humor than he had thus far displayed. Chip laughed, nudging Nathan. They were both trying to put him at ease, Nathan knew, which was nice. But Nathan couldn't quite reciprocate. He felt hot still in the face, vaguely oxygen-deprived. It had been a long day, already. It was terribly warm in the studio, wasn't it? And stuffy. What was the matter with the ventilation?

"You're not nervous, Nathan, are you?"

"No, Bryan. I don't think so."

Bryan and Chip both cleared their throats, as if on cue.

"All right, action!"

We're trying something a little different here on the Report, Nathan heard Chip announce into the camera. *Lots of you in upper Broward and lower Palm Beach County been telling us that you'd appreciate a little southside of the southeast report. No offense to Cap'n Goddard up there in Stuart, but the boys at Lighthouse Point rightly enough want the 411 down in their local waters. We aim to please, ain't that right, Bryan?*

It certainly is, Chip, Bryan sang in his milky television voice.

We don't want y'all down in Boca and Deerfield feeling like red-headed stepchildren–here Chip leaned over and grasped both of Nathan's shoulders–*so we got ourselves a red-headed stepchild from your waters to represent!*

Suddenly Chip sounded like Miles. Standing there in Chip's good-humored grip, Nathan tried to look amused and loose, but suspected that he was failing miserably. He had never felt so self-conscious over his bodily presence. Before the camera now, he wasn't sure how exactly to react to Chip's quip, how to arrange the features on his face, tight from all the makeup, and whether or not to show his soft teeth.

So, without further adieu, Bryan picked up the thread, more sober and ceremonious now, *let us introduce Captain Nathan Pray, who fishes out of the Boca and Hillsboro Inlets–*

Fishes more inside the Boca Inlet, tell you the truth, brother, Chip interjected, off-script it seemed. He had released Nathan's shoulders. *A skinny water skippa' like myself.*

Very well, Bryan continued in his television voice. *Correction noted. Inside the Boca and Hillsboro Inlets, though he has friends in high places, we hear. Well*, Bryan opened his shoulders to Nathan now, sharing the stage, tapped Nathan's forearm with a rolled magazine he held as a prop. *Welcome to the Report, Captain Pray. What do you have for us, good sir, southside of the southeast? Take it away.*

The moist director threw an index finger at Nathan, and then wound his hand in terrific circles, urging him along. He had tucked in his shirttail at some point.

Well, Bryan—

"Cut!" the director barked behind the lights.

"You picking up that shine on his nose, 2?"

"Yep," the cameraman answered.

"Makeup!"

"Are you nervous, sweetness?" Zev asked, having rushed from out of nowhere to his side.

"For god's sake, no!" Nathan answered. "I'm not nervous." Zev looked perplexed as he powdered Nathan's nose and cheeks. Not with the gun this time, but with a round cloth pad.

"You have Rosacea or something?"

"Rose-what?" Nathan asked.

"Nevermind. Break a leg."

"All right, we can pick it up with you, Nathan," the director declared. "We're good with the lead-in, right Bruce?" The cameraman nodded.

"All right . . . action!"

324

Well, Bryan—

"Cut! Let's take five, everyone! Get him some ice water or something, Luke, would you please?" the director ordered, audibly annoyed. "He's sweating for Christ's sake."

"Yes sir!"

Luke was suddenly at his side with two paper-cone cups of cold water. If only Nathan could inject the cooling substance into his veins. "We're out of the bigger cups, I guess," Luke said. Nathan downed the first cup in two gulps, then sipped the second cup more slowly.

"You ate something today, right?" Luke inquired.

"Yeah. Sure."

After the five minutes were up, after Zev besieged him with another dose of powder, Nathan returned to his mark. The water had tasted good and cold, but he still felt the heat in his face and the odd weight in his legs.

"Sorry," he said to Bryan, whom he thought he heard sigh.

"No worries, cap."

"Yeah, no worries, Nate," Chip said. "It takes some getting used to."

Well, Bryan, Nathan began once the perspired director pointed toward him once again and wound his finger in those terrific circles, *despite the cold snaps, January is shaping up to be a relatively fishy month for us offshore. Those cold fronts and brisk east winds are pulling in prolific schools of mutton snapper to the thirty foot patch reefs just off Spanish River Park and the Deerfield Peer. We also—*

"Cut!" Nathan heard. He thought he knew why. He had gone

too fast, had slurred over some words.

"Jesus H. Christ, Jeff!" the billfish mag editor complained off camera, his elbows leaning against his products desk. "How about you stop interrupting and just let him shoot his wad for crying out loud. That'll settle him down."

"You catch that 'prolific' word he used there?" Chip asked of no one in particular, probably to lighten up the mood. "Anyone use that word here before? We might have a show first fellas!"

"What's it mean, that big word?" Mark called over.

"Plentiful," Bryan said.

"I know what it means, Bryan, you pretentious A-hole. I was just joking."

Chip laughed. Mark laughed. Even Bryan laughed.

"He's got some other doozies in there too," Chip said. "Just wait."

The director, per Mark's advice, allowed Nathan to run through most of the report, which Nathan thought was going okay up until the part about Del's three-way swivel rig, when the potency of the cool water seemed suddenly to expire. The words felt thick in his throat. Heavy. The lights felt ungodly hot in his face. *Captain Del Rodeffer out of Lighthouse Point rigs a three-way swivel with his charters when he fishes for grouper on his sportfisher, A-Salt Machine. He starts with 100-pound test braid on a variable speed conventional Avet reel. He creates about 6 feet of double line by tying a bimini twist at the top end, then a 12-twist no-name knot at the bottom . . .* Nathan managed to read the words he had transcribed, and lightly edited, from Del's notes, but they only made thick nonsensical sounds now to his own ears . . . *to another 6 foot span of 120 pound mono,*

tied to an 8-aught, 3-way swivel . . . Was he still standing, speaking? . . . *You*

tie a four-ounce pyramid sinker . . . on three feet of . . . mono to one eyelet, then a

full 50 feet of 100-pound fluoro . . .

He felt himself slipping, slipping. "Captain Pray! You okay!?

You okay, Mr. Pray? Someone help him! He's gonna–"

Nathan had just enough time to curse himself for not eating

breakfast before slipping away.

Nathan wouldn't sit by the phone to wait for it to ring with prospective charters. But it was a bit too early to head out to the reef, and Kati (they were taking it slow) was likely busy with her daughter's homework, and Miles (Nathan glanced down at his Timex) was between Hebrew School and swim practice, and there really wasn't anywhere to go in the Efficiency to escape the immediate sphere of the lazy telephone, slumbering on the breakfast table. So he sat there beside it, studying his log instead of listening for the phone, ignoring the unintelligible bass notes of his anonymous neighbors seeping through the shared wall as he flipped through the last twenty-two coastal years of this single night. Quite a night, as it happened, in his record of nights.

When the phone sounded, finally, it was Terrance.

"Need a partner tonight, Cap'?"

"You don't have to go out, T, just because . . . you know."

Terrance, Nathan suspected, felt guilty about the whole police station business, what he had said about Miles, about Devon. *We just can't risk Devon getting into any of this. It's different for him. For us.* Terrance, ever the peacemaker, didn't want any bad blood between them. Or maybe he caught the Fishing Report last night and felt sorry for him. It didn't turn out quite so bad, anyway. Luke had managed to revive him. He got through the rest of his script in yeomanlike (if not scintillating) fashion. Only the most discerning viewer would have noticed the odd, mid-segment color shift in his countenance from rosy to pallid, his fainting jag precipitating this odd before-and-after effect, impervious somehow to the makeup.

"Goodness gracious, I know I don't have to go out, Nate," Terrance declared in astonished falsetto. "Owen's clawing at my feet here. And 'milla's sick of chicken."

Nathan chuckled.

"And I feel like fishing's the thing. That report of yours on the tube got me jonesin' for some action."

"Well now I know you're lying."

"You could have told me about the show." Terrance spoke these words in his natural voice, which pierced Nathan.

"I know. Sorry, T."

"You were a bit stiff maybe, but–"

"All right, all right–"

"I could have given you some tips is all. Some exercises . . . you know, on public speaking. Least they could have done is give you a prop to hold. Magazine. Newspaper. Like that other guy. Something."

Nathan exhaled. Terrance was right. He should have confided in his friend, who might have helped him. "Boat's tied up at the marina, T. Let's just meet there in an hour."

**

Daylight hadn't quite surrendered to nightfall by the time the fishermen boarded the *Pray Fish* and motored toward the inlet. Larry, the most scrofulous of the dock pelicans, balding, his dark legs scaled, betraying his reptilian origins, bummed a ride with them on top of the Merc along the no-wake. Why bother flying all that way?

"Look dopey at me all you want, Moe, or Larry, or Curly, or whoever you are," Terrance declared as he sorted through their frozen bait at the stern. He pried loose a frozen, congealed block of four whole sardines and began slicing them up for chunk, near wafer thin, tail to head. "Stare away, Curly, I'm not giving you a sardine!"

"I think that's Larry," Nathan announced from the helm.

"I don't know, Nate," Terrance leaned back from his cutting board labors. "Should we give him just one?"

"Sure. One. No more. Or we'll never get rid of him." Nathan felt a certain kinship with Larry, yet he didn't much care for scraping off his copious white guano, which set like quick-concrete on the Merc's hood and smelled like ripe bluefish viscera.

"Now get, Larry!" Nathan heard, but didn't hear the accompanying beats of leaden wings. He glanced back and smiled to see the pelican, squatting still on his warm perch, his expectant beak dripping down at the end like a dragon's egg-tooth. Nathan wondered whether the warmth of the engine on this frosty evening was a draw greater than, or equal to, the free food and transport.

The Merc struggled some against the incoming as they neared the channel across from the hotel. The moon was almost full, Nathan knew from his log, though it hid now behind the lingering day-bright, or the hotel maybe. He glanced fruitlessly over Larry's head behind him. A lusty spring tide. Nathan studied the water's skin, rippling against the prow. They had chanced upon a strong incoming pulse. If a single snook survived, it would surely be here now, under the bridge somewhere, ambushing hapless whitebait at the water's throat.

A black skimmer troupe skittered low and far across Nathan's field of view as they neared the bridge. A good sign. Nathan watched as they keeled on sharp wings across the surface, corralling their prey. He listened to their faint barks. *Kaup . . . Kaup . . . Kaup.*

"Baitfish here," Terrance said, reading his partner's thoughts.

Nathan looked hard over the gunwale at port into the dark water as they passed under the A1A, groaning with traffic. He couldn't see anything down there.

"Hand me the twelve-footer, would you?" They had reached the inlet's elbow.

"Twelve-footer? You out to prove something?"

Nathan denied the charge.

His largest cast net. Heavy leadlines. Narrow, eighth-inch webbing. No picnic to throw. But efficient and beautiful when thrown properly. Terrance handed him the net from the back hatch, which Nathan wordlessly received. He grasped for selvage just below the horn with his left hand, then smoothed the netting down toward its middle with his right. Terrance wordlessly took the helm as Nathan, shoeless, mounted the casting deck at the bow. Clutching the generous folds of fabric now, tenderly, as if it were bridal taffeta, he lifted the heavy lead-line weights off the skiff's surface, watched the solid beads undulate at the hemline, finding true. He folded the twelve-foot net over his forearm, then threw a large wrap over his shoulder, grasped fistfuls of netting low near the leadline, bent his knees instinctively here, bobbed his head as if he were praying, which in a way he was. Nathan's prayer shawl gesture was familiar to Terrance, who offered no commentary. Only waited and watched.

"I don't see any," Terrance finally said.

"I see them." Nathan finally saw them. Vanishing silver commas. Deep.

"Those eyes of yours."

Nathan swiveled counterclockwise on his axis, dipped his knees and shoulders, extended his arms, and gaze, downward. A brief but palpable pause here in his crouch, his calves flexed, a magical spot of time, Nathan having summoned to the occasion the requisite potential energy, which huddled there within his embrace, awaiting its kinetic release. Swiveling back on his axis, extending his arms to the waters before him, opening his hands wide to release the net at its centripetal apex, Nathan rose. The net mouth yawned above for a split second, which seemed much longer, before bothering the still water below. *Tat-tat-tat-tat,* sang the leadlines. Nathan felt the rope slip slowly through his fingers as the halo descended. Baitfish liked this deep hole over which they hovered.

"Pull up now, Nate?"

Nathan nodded, but waited a moment more, then pulled the rope sharply, snapping the broad mouth closed deep below.

"Son of a gun," Terrance uttered, leaning over the starboard gunnel.

Silver dashes gleamed across the entire length of netting, well below the skin of the surface. Pilchards, sardines, minnows, greenies, pinfish.

Nathan, silent, felt more grateful than proud, as if he had received a generous gift. Not only the quivering pilchards and sardines and cigar minnows, and greenies, and pinfish, but his own back and legs and arms and hands, sinew and muscle and bone and flesh, which he had put to good use. This gift of his working body. Compact. Lean. Strong. Not everyone was drawn toward such tactile industry. It was a gift that most took entirely for granted these days. This great good thing. A working body. This artful outdoors labor.

"Good haul, Nate!" Terrance leaned over the bow and dipped both his dark arms into the water—"Freezing," he opined—to help lift the lead net bottom onto the boat, maneuvering it along with Nathan toward the stern, above the plashing livewell. Larry danced above on his lizard legs and duck feet.

"Shimmy all you want, Larry," Terrance said. "No way I'm giving you a livie tonight. No effing way."

Nathan smiled as he peeled the few gill-netted pilchards from the drapery, dropping them into the sloshing pool.

"I don't know, should we give him just one, Nate?"

"Sure. Go ahead and give him a couple. We've got plenty." Small wonder that Camilla did all the disciplining at home.

"Lucky son of a . . ." Terrance silenced his prospective curse as he underhanded the quivering silver cigars into Larry's bucketmouth. The pelican leaned his head back and swallowed, batted his wings.

"Another throw?" Terrance inquired as he shut the livewell hatch.

"Nah. Leave some for the skimmers . . . the snook."

"No point trying for linesiders, I guess?" Terrance asked from the stern.

"Maybe later."

"Perfect conditions."

"Last year this night you and I caught seven over-slot females right here edge of the jetty on spoons and my sinking eight-inch minnows. Tagged them. You don't remember?"

"Yeah, sure. I guess. That was a year ago? Exact?"

Nathan told him that it was.

"Gone for good, you think?" Nathan could hear Terrance folding up the net behind him, the lead *clacking* against the deck now and again, the skimmers barking above the surface as they made another pass. *Kaup . . . Kaup . . . Kaup.*

"They'll be back."

Terrance remained silent, nodded maybe.

"Wasn't quite so calm last year," Nathan said as he nudged the throttle into gear, having reached the end of the jetty. He gazed out across the expanse of open water and blinked back the frosty salt air from his eyes. "We had a strong southeast wind to deal with."

Terrance closed the back hatch, the cast net tucked inside like a secret. "Ready," he said, joining Nathan at the console.

It was one of those Lake Atlantic evenings, rare in winter. High pressure had washed over slow from the northwest, ushering in light winds and pacifying the ocean's seasonal temper. The water beneath the failing light of dusk lay heavy and dark. The thick ocean licked the

Pray Fish's hull audibly, yielding gently to the fiberglass. Most captains would have their vessels on plane immediately upon hearing their mate's "ready," grateful for the opportunity this time of year to exercise their engines full-throttle. Yet the placid night gave Nathan pause just outside the inlet. Time enough for a cleansing breath of salt air. Lingering below the salt, he could just detect the green smells of the sargasso rafts he couldn't see. Terrance, silent beside Nathan now, arms crossed, imbibed too. This preternaturally calm sea. Even Larry, still standing squat on the Merc, checked his grunts and groans. Nathan listened to the silence, the faintest echo of car traffic and, closer by, a gnatcatcher pair, wheezing unseen as they worked the seagrape clusters at the jetty just behind them now. The barking skimmers had moved on.

"Wreck maybe?" Terrance burst the noisome quiet, because one of them had to say something. "Go for some grouper slobs? Or maybe the third reef?"

Nathan considered his rotation on the reefs and wrecks. "Third reef I think."

Nathan opened up the throttle gradually in deference to their avian hitchhiker, who took the hint and took off southward on heavy wings, whereupon Nathan punched the throttle more purposefully and coaxed the skiff on plane. They headed northeast at thirty knots, Nathan glancing shoreward from time to time to check his bearing against the droopy Australian Pines, condos, and blinking cell-phone tower lights, just now visible against the purple twilight. He welcomed the Merc's quiet noise, erasing sound but sharpening his other senses. His heart thumped palpably within his chest. Every so often the skiff roused drowsy schools of flying fish. Nathan traced them with his eyes as they glided just above the surface before knifing beneath the sea's skin off the port and starboard. Terrance stood beside him, grasping the console rail for ballast. He lifted a lazy index finger toward the gliding schools from time to time. Nathan noticed the wind-teardrop creeping slowly behind Terrance's eye toward his small ear.

It was a good spot, Nathan thought, studying the now distant shoreline for his markers, slowing the *Pray Fish*, which lowered its bow, reverentially. It was near full dark now, the sky salted with stars. The skiff bobbed cork-like above the heavy sea before finding true. Nathan, an eye on the sonar now, motored slowly, leeward. He needed to anchor a bit inside, 110 or so he figured, to set up over the honey-hole. The west wind would push them out some. Terrance crept up to the bow and crouched over the anchor locker. The Danforth and its chain issued bright notes in his gentle hands as he rose.

"Just say when," Terrance said, which he didn't have to say, and usually didn't say. It had been a few weeks since they had fished together.

"Okay, T. Now."

Terrance threw the anchor.

Nathan turned off the ignition and unclipped the safety lanyard from his belt loop.

The two waited for the anchor to hold, hands on their hips. "There we go," Terrance uttered once the skiff shifted on its axis, like the hand of a clock, the stern settling finally northwest. A pretty good sign, Nathan knew. North current bucking the west wind. He tied off two blocks of chum, one to each back cleat.

"Big spender," Terrance said.

"Why mess around, eh? Anyway, no meatballs tonight. Didn't have time to make them."

Terrance nodded and smiled as he tossed fistfuls of his spliced sardines like flower petals. He studied the chunk bait in the water. So did Nathan. The sardine sheets drifted northward, steadily. "Hot-diggity," Terrance declared, reaching for his rod, dipping his hand in the livewell and sloshing it back and forth in blind pursuit. So many baitfish he needn't bother with the dip-net.

He heard Nathan tearing his fishing tape from the spool before he glanced up to spy his partner wrapping his digits.

"Blister or something?" Terrance inquired, hooking his quivering pilchard through the nostrils.

"Small cut," Nathan admitted. "Plus . . ." he continued to wrap his other fingers. Terrance noticed these additional wraps. He knew what it meant.

"Oh, mercy–"

"Don't start with me, Terrance."

"You know, Nate, they came up with a pretty cool invention last year. It's called a fishing pole."

Nathan smiled, silent. Having finished with the tape, he strode toward the bow hatch, where he kept his leader, swivels, hooks, and the plastic ring.

"Okay, so what's wrong? Let's have this out, Nate? What has you so upset? Snook'll probably come back, like you said. And if it's that Fishing Report show, I think it was–"

"It's not the snook. It's not the show."

"Well you're not sore at me about Miles, are you? Just want to give the boys a break, is all–"

"It's not that, T. It's not anything. Except the live bait, anyway."

Terrance, in place of words, conducted his fishing rod symphony with pugnacious verve, practically throwing his pilchard down to the reef. For whatever reason, he just couldn't accept the yo-yo rig as a legitimate angling tactic. Nathan only reverted to the yo-yo when he was upset about something. That's how Terrance saw it, Nathan knew. All the same, he proceeded to rig his thirty-pound mono to the plastic ring–he stepped up to heavier tackle when he freelined–the pinball weight tucked inside. Then he rigged the fifty-pound fluoro leader, a good eight foot stretch or so. Muttons were the smartest snappers. He snelled a uniknot with the leader to a long-shank 3-aught circle-hook, a size up from the 2-aughts Nathan usually preferred. He figured Terrance would approve of the bigger hook, anyway.

"Got a 'tail!" Terrance announced, tightening his drag some and reeling. "They're down there." Nathan watched as Terrance brought the gleaming yellowtail snapper up over the gunwale. It was a solid fish, if not a flag, its head thick and bullish like the bigger ones, the tail deeply forked.

"Good job, T."

Nathan netted a pinfish in the livewell. He hooked it under the dorsal. He tied the end of the line to his belt-loop and dropped circles of loose line onto the deck. He tossed the pinfish overboard along with the plastic yo-yo and felt the line drift across the taped pads of his fingers on its descent. It wasn't the safest thing in the world, freelining old-school this way. Even with the tape. An unexpected strike by a bull shark or hammerhead when you weren't managing the line properly, even a smoker king. . . . It didn't happen often, but fishermen lost fingers clean at the joints this way, where bone gave way to mere ligament and cartilage.

There wasn't much holding us together, Nathan reflected, when you got right down to it.

The weighted plastic ring sounded through mono against the tape-calloused pads of Nathan's fingers. It had reached bottom. Terrance threw another tassel of chunk off the stern. Then he reached over the gunwale and bothered the chum bag in the drink. Good. Splaying all his fingers, Nathan brought up some line with broad staccato gestures before his chest, propping the livie just over the reef, meting out perfect wet coils at his feet. Nice north current, Nathan could tell now, his line taut off the stern beneath the red beam of his headlamp that he couldn't quite see as red. Nathan bowed, then rose, flashing the bait above the reef. Terrance glanced over, then glanced away, scratched his scalp and squinted to offer his mild disapproval.

Nathan heard Terrance's drag *zippp* beside him. "Another one," Terrance announced, reaching down to tighten the drag some. "Might be a mango. Come on now, switch up, Nate!" he exhorted as he reeled. "At a hundred feet it'll be a pain in your butt anyway bringing up a snapper freeline."

"Gotta go slow to go fast sometimes," he retrieved Miles' expression for swimming.

"What's that supposed to mean?" Terrance asked just as the slow steady tug pulled Nathan's shoulders clear over the transom.

"Whoa—"

"Need help!?" Nathan felt Terrance's grip clutch a fistful of his jeans at the beltline.

"No no. I got it, T. You can let go my pants." Terrance released him to his labors as Nathan ushered his own core muscles, biceps, and flexed fingers to the fight, leaning back.

With five practiced pivots of his splayed digits before him, Nathan set the hook and turned the creature's head, then frisbeed down a clutch of perfect coils to the deck. He couldn't let the snapper descend into its rocky grotto.

"See, that's why I don't like that yo-yo, Nate." Terrance continued his own retrieve as he spoke. "Hands all bound up like that. Line taking up all that space at your feet. . . ."

Nathan heard Terrance's line peeling off the reel in short bursts. His partner had a decent mangrove or yellowtail, he thought. Else Terrance had the drag set too loose, which wasn't like Terrance at all. He always set it tighter than Nathan, lost fewer to the tax collectors that way—those lemons, bulls, and black tips—but Terrance lost more from knot-failure and tenuous hook sets.

"Tying off to your belt like that's just hot-mess crazy," Terrance continued, a smooth retrieve now, his prize spent, apparently. "Asking for trouble. You go overboard, don't think I'm diving in after you."

"Come on, T. Steak dinner. Remember?"

This was their longstanding deal should one of them be forced to save the other from drowning. Steak dinner.

"Yeah yeah."

Nathan continued his own retrieve, his splayed fingers dancing before his chest. He cast down the monofilament spheres at his feet every fifth gesture, making near perfect circles on deck, a steady but unhurried retrieve, bowing to the creature time to time as it bucked, affecting his makeshift drag.

"Yep, mango," Terrance uttered, throwing his own newly captured fish in the cooler after stunning it with the bosher. "Nothing to write home about. But decent."

Nathan heard Terrance's hand sloshing louder than necessary in the livewell, issuing this mild reproach rather than pause to pay him heed.

Nathan's still-secret fish was a solid one, he knew, but he wouldn't say anything. Terrance threw his baited line overboard, conducted his symphony anew. Then, finally: "Well, what is it, Nate!? Cheese 'n crackers, you're impossible!" Nathan smiled at Terrance's familiar non-curse. Nathan knew it was a mutton, could tell by its hybrid grouper-snapper song through his fingertips.

"Mutton, T. Relax."

"Good one? Need a net? Gaff?"

Nathan declined.

"Goodness gracious!" Terrance uttered moments later, abandoning his post to inspect Nathan's prize, pounding the deck with heavy blows. He flicked his headlamp on to its brightest setting. They both studied the creature a moment. Its sloping brow and large liquid eyes did, in fact, look sheep-like.

"Shame you don't see that red at the belly, Nate. Beautiful."

"I see it some. I see those green stripes too."

"Blue."

"Whatever."

Terrance nodded. The beam of his light bobbed to and fro on the deck. "Fifteen pounds, easy."

"Thirteen, I'd say." Nathan performed a silent calculation. "Doc'll be happy." He lifted the creature from its thick belly with a towel, popped the circle hook loose with the padded pincer of his thumb against the side-knuckle of his forefinger. Terrance asked him if he wanted the bosher, but Nathan declined. Instead, he reached for his knife at the console and dispatched the snapper with a practiced incision through its spinal column.

"So you'll do this for a bit more, even without the snook," Terrance stated more than asked as Nathan maneuvered to the cooler. The bustle about the boat had somehow encouraged Terrance to broach the freighted topic.

"Yeah, T. Think so." Nathan slapped his hands clean as he returned to the stern.

"Good," Terrance said. "That's good I think. Really."

"Charters'll pick up, maybe, now that I did the show, even if Chip doesn't ask me back. And I fished with Nguyen the other night. Might do it some more, time to time. We did pretty well with the kings." Nathan felt as if he had admitted an affair to a spouse. It was stupid to feel this way.

"For real?"

"Mmm-hmm."

"Well, he knows what he's doing, anyway. And since he targets kingfish 'least you'll be diversifying. Makes a lot of sense."

It was good of Terrance to say all this.

"You're like the last of the Mohicans, Nate."

"Yeah, that's me. Uncas. That was his name, right Mr. English teacher?"

"Chingachgook," Terrance said, chuckling. "Uncas dies."

"Oh. Guess I'll be Chingachgook, then."

They lowered their lines, each in their own fashion. They didn't catch very many fish under the obnoxious eye of the risen moon, that northeast bully, but they caught enough to keep at it well past midnight without pulling up the Danforth to try a different spot. Mostly mangrove. A bit cold still for the yellowtail. Nathan caught two more muttons before spooking the rest. They were just about to pack it in when something spoke strangely through his fingertips.

"Have some prime Florida real estate there?" Terrance inquired, his egg-sinker *clicking* against his rod-blank.

"Maybe. But . . . whoa–"

"Another mutton?"

"No." Nathan flashed his splayed fingers before him, turned the creature's head, meted out the wet coils at his feet.

"Big mangrove?"

"Don't think so." Nathan continued his retrieve.

"Grouper?"

"Probably, but . . . it could just be a big glass-eye. Or small shark. Tough to tell."

"Tough for *you* to tell?" Terrance asked, incredulous. He threw his rod butt into a holder at the console and approached Nathan's side.

"Watch your feet, T." Terrance, glancing down, retreated to keep his big feet away from the loose circles of line on deck. Nathan bowed to the strong creature, leaned his elbows on the gunwale to rest a second. Why couldn't he catch this slob at the beginning of the night, when he still had most of his strength?

"Net?"

"Yeah. Better get it." Nathan rose, continued his retrieve, meting out perfect salty coils on deck every five pulls, lathering his arms and sweatshirt and tattered jeans with frothy cold.

Terrance returned from the bow hatch with the net, keeping a safe distance from the loose line between them.

"I can always take over," Terrance proposed. "I can grab the line below."

"Almost got it. . . . My god!" the knowledge struck Nathan like a blow just before he glimpsed the copper silhouette, deep, beneath his headlamp's halo.

"What? You see it?" Terrance asked, leaning over the gunwale with his net.

"Forget the net." Nathan feared injuring the creature.

"Is that a–"

Its lateral line glistened as the fish listed sideward against the ocean's skin, a black scar beneath the bully moon.

"Yeah." Nathan leaned over the gunwale on his knees, cradled the snook at the abdomen with one hand and popped the circle hook free of its lip with the other, taking care to avoid the barbs on the limp pinfish bait, stripped of its scales. Terrance clutched a fistful of Nathan's jeans at the waist as Nathan leaned over into the drink. The heavy creature remained frightfully still.

"Big one, eh?"

Nathan clutched the snook by the lip now, bass-style, felt its sandpaper lips where his tape gave way to skin at his thumb's second joint. He pointed her head downward some into the drink, worked water into its gills by sweeping its sloping head side to side. He probed the creature for parasites, abrasions, sheered fins, happy to see that she was sound and fat. He felt the creature return, quivering now against his grip. "Easy, girl."

"Tag it for Mote, Nate? You got the tags on board, right?"

"Yes. But . . . no. Let's not stress her anymore." Nathan could feel the fish gather itself. He released his grip from its chin as the snook clamped down on his thumb, fisherman and fish joined now on the creature's terms. "I just want to let her go, Terrance. We'll let her keep her secret. She's almost ready. Any second now she'll give me my thumb back."

"We've never caught one out here, have we?"

"No. Never. Not this far from the inlet. Not over the third reef." And then she was gone, her sulfur tail smacking the surface with surprising vigor.

Nathan remained on his knees, both elbows over the gunwales still. He gazed into the black water and gathered his wind. He knew the theory–snook schools sought out deep reefs for shelter against the cold–but never gave it much credence. It didn't make sense to him. During cold snaps, they headed inshore to more deeply stained shallow water, the tea-stains and shallows absorbing and holding heat. All his experience told him this. Yet apparently the deep reefs offered their own succor. A snook school, or maybe just a few, had found a way to survive. Had shifted strategy. Gone deep. There was something here to extract, maybe, the snook's sphere lapping against the broadening borders of his own circle.

"Well, at least there's one linesider still fighting the good fight."

"Yeah. One." Nathan rose from the deck, wiped his slick hands against his jeans. "Let's just hope she's not the last of the Mohicans."

Nathan's thoughts drifted . . .

Chaim Schuss was weak from the long passage, the cold, his stomach

346

sick–too weak, too sick to challenge the irate immigration officer at the Port of Galveston?

You telling me to shut up my mouth, son?

No, Mister. Sir. My name you ask.

So come again?

Schuss.

Silver? That what I hear? Silver'll work.

Schuss. No Silver. SCHUSS, Chaim declared, reaching deep in his lungs to locate the volume, deep enough that it hurt.

Well there you go again, son, giving me the business. You gotta be the dumbest durn snook I seen this week.

The sudden *(if mispronounced)* Yiddish surprised his great-grandfather. How did this *goyische* immigration officer–perspiration beading on his rubicund forehead, tobacco bulging beneath his lower lip like a malignancy–know enough to call him a shnook? Someone, a fellow passenger, prodded Chaim from behind, in warning or complaint. Someone from the Jewish Immigrant Information Bureau was supposed to be there to help. Where was he!?

Seems to me you been hoodwinked, Mr. Kai-yam. You don't have no job. No family. Can't be more'n ninety pounds soakin' wet. No prospects to speak of. Not even a respectable name a God-fearin' man can write down in English. I can't see my way clear, some days. I just can't see my way clear, I say.

Anything there is I can do?

You can pray, Kai-yam. Kai-yam, you can pray.

Yes. Good. Chaim Pray. My name. Now good? Chaim Pray, he tasted the name again in his mouth as if it were his first orange.

And so it wasn't a Jewish name, Pray. Or else it was a Jewish name, depending on how you looked at it. Nathan's grandfather had improvised like the snook, maybe, created himself anew, found a way to survive and even thrive as an unwashed immigrant in his strange new world.

Texas!

**

Nathan's headlights swept over the human figure, swaddled in winter layers, as he swerved into the blighted parking lot. Kati. He had been looking forward to scrubbing up and meeting her at the restaurant. Yet it jarred him seeing her here. He had only mentioned his apartment complex once, maybe twice.

"Everything okay, Kati?" he asked as he approached, sounding more standoffish than he intended.

"Yes. Everything okay." She smiled awkwardly, her dog tooth flashing beneath the still-bright moon. Her dark shock of hair was mostly hidden beneath the cap he knitted for her months ago, long before they started in together, when the subtropical summer heat made it seem a ludicrous offering. "Sorry I come here." She lowered her kohl-rimmed eyes, and then raised them. Crossed her jacket-padded forearms, and then uncrossed them. He noticed her slender olive hands, her clean, quarter-moon nails. "Your house is on the way to restaurant. So I knocked on the door. Then you come."

"That's okay," Nathan softened.

"I saw the show. You were so good!" She seemed genuinely impressed. More, she was excited for him. "And I want to see you before the restaurant."

"You don't have to explain. I'm sorry. I'm just surprised. I'm glad you came. It's good to see you."

He was glad that she came. It was good to see her.

She narrowed the distance between them on the parking lot macadam and kissed him on the lips, making contact just long enough for Nathan to taste the wet. He shrank some, aware suddenly of the sardine stink rising from his mottled hands, his soiled sweatshirt. He grasped her elbow to keep her from shrinking from his shrinking.

"I'm not backing away from you. It's just I stink. I need to wash up."

Kati laughed and scrunched up her nose. Yes, he stunk. Nathan liked that she didn't try to pretend otherwise.

They ascended the stairway beneath the dusky security light.

"It's just temporary," he warned Kati, unlocking his apartment door. "I'm sort of in between places."

He paused once they passed the threshold and allowed her to complete her short scan of the room: Formica table and two chairs, bed (made, thankfully), small TV, pull-out sofa, linoleum floor an unfortunate mucous hue, the rust-stained popcorn ceiling. He noticed the digital display on the telephone's answering machine, flashing an unprecedented double-digit number. He'd check the messages later.

"This is where you live," she uttered, as if to convince herself, handing Nathan her heavy jacket and knit cap, which he laid on the bed.

"Yes. It's where I live. For now."

"It's okay."

"I'll make you a quick breakfast, Kati." Her eyes widened. He'd fry up two small yellowtail fillets in olive oil, he thought. Dredge them in cornmeal, lots of pepper, just a bit of flour. With poached eggs. He'd crack the brown shells over boiling water, the rich orange yolks a sauce of sorts for the mild white fillets.

"First let me shower," he said, grabbing a lemon bulb from the bar. "I'll be right with you."

"Can I come?"

"To the shower?"

Kati nodded.

"You sure?"

"We're not children, Nathan. You go first. Then I come. Then we have breakfast."

Nathan obeyed, pensive. This is what you did, he supposed, when you were a single woman with a young daughter and mother at home, when you worked an odd shift then walked your child home from school, when, in short, you had a life chock full of obligations. You stole a moment here and there for yourself. His heart swelled.

Nathan twisted the creaking knobs so the stubborn water would warm, then yanked the short beaded cord to the sizzling incandescent bulb. He undressed quickly, then contemplated the heap on the floor. He couldn't leave his stinking clothes there in the small bathroom, so he cracked open the door and tossed out the garments. Kati, outside the door, laughed at the sight of his naked arm, discarding the heap.

He sheared the lemon bulb in two with his fingers, then

scrubbed his hands with the acid juice over the basin. Setting aside the spent bulb halves, he entered the stall, shrinking from the still-cool torrent of water that tattered his feet with stinging blows. Thankfully, he had recently scrubbed clean the mildew, using the same Simple Green he also used on the skiff. The old soap on the ledge, however, was a problem. He scooped up the nebulous mass best he could, drew back the curtain and lobbed it into the sink, then reached into the cupboard below for a fresh golden cake. The bathroom was small enough that he was able to perform these errands without leaving the stall.

"You okay?" Kati asked from outside the door. She must have heard the curtain screech, the frenzied opening and shutting of the cupboard. "Yeah. Just give me a sec." He forced his head under the luke-warm stream, shampooed and lathered quickly, hoping to remove the outmost layer of fish-smell before Kati joined him. There. He calmed some as the water heated, the steam rising now.

He heard the door open, and then heard the chain pull before seeing the new dark, which wasn't dark. The moon bully penetrated the high hazy window, throwing up a languid steam-cloud of light. He heard the curtain draw open behind, then started to turn.

"No no. Stay. Hand me soap."

She touched him with a single hand, slender and soft, pressed the lathered hand on his shoulder and kept it there for a moment, as if she were testing the heat over an open flame. They had kissed on the pier, but it had been a long time since someone touched him like this.

She placed her other hand on his other shoulder, as if to gauge his breadth. Then she proceeded to lather his flesh carefully, slowly, in small circles, starting at the shoulders, only slightly higher than her own. She made her way down his biceps to his forearms, then scrubbed his ginger chest and stomach, drawing closer, her breasts soft between the blades of his shoulders. She reached for the fur under his arms, which made Nathan flinch–"ah-ah-ah," Kati said–before he relaxed again. She made small soapy circles across his chest again, then across the tight cords of his abdomen, and then lower, reaching his center.

She lingered there, which simultaneously humbled and aroused Nathan.

"Okay," she said. Nathan turned.

Book Four

Chapter One

Spring. The sun vaulted higher each day across the southern horizon. A certain slant of light betrayed the season to the discerning eye. As February gave way to March, the relentless succession of strange cold fronts finally subsided, restoring the subtropical warmth and restoring a greater level of the human familiar to Nathan. Adolescents bounced shoreward on sidewalks again, scruffy boys and neater girls, bikini-top strings dangling out their tank-top necklines. Retirees in pleated Bahama shorts and necktied office workers on lunch break lined the restaurant patio frontage along Palmetto, nursed their ice teas and lemony waters. Brighter murmuring from crusty regulars and pleased tourists punctuated the early morning atmosphere of the Caribbean Café. Maintenance workers and contractors redoubled their efforts downtown, the distant chirping of jack hammers, drills, nail guns, and band saws curiously pleasing to Nathan's ears despite the implications of overdevelopment. The human inhabitants along this tenuous coastal ridge, this barely terrestrial toe-tip of the continent, had slept through the winter, perhaps–bitter by Florida standards–but had finally arisen.

As March yielded to April, April to May, Nathan cast sideward glances all about town at the trees he couldn't see. Even though the fiery blossoms eluded him, he knew when the royal poincianas bloomed each year. The sprawling feathery specimens–the foliage still pretty much all dark green by Nathan's lights–took on a fuller, less wispy profile. Yet he wasn't sure he wanted to see these trees heap on their more substantial clothes this year. The invisible red blossoms heralded the return of the snook from their secret inshore haunts to the intracoastal, the inlets, and the beaches. These heady spawning days. But this year? He had only found that one with Terrance. Deep.

So when Nathan, who finally couldn't deny the recent poinciana blossoms, told Nguyen to hold up at the jetty's edge one still-bright May evening, the incoming tide whipping in from the mild sea, and Nguyen said, "Wha' fo' Nate," and Nathan, leaning over the bow without a rod, grasping the rail, said, "Just give me a second Nguyen, right here's good, hold the spot here, nose to the current if you can, nobody's behind us," and Nguyen exhaled and said "okay-okay," and a kingfisher giggled overhead, and the gnatcatchers wheezed in the nearby seagrape foliage, and a lone car rumbled across the inlet bridge, Nathan could hardly believe his eyes and blinked several times to clear his mental screen, which wouldn't clear of those copper silhouettes through the silt, brooking the current in a parenthesis about the jetty, ambushing gleaming silver dashes. "Here, look!" he cried. "See 'em down there!? See 'em all!?" Nguyen leaned his potbelly over the gunwale and nodded his head at Nathan's discovery.

Nathan had braced for disaster this spring, snook-wise, as everything else had lately worked out too well for his comfort. That first calamitous night on the Fishing Report led to eight charters, and while Chip hadn't selected him to represent the southside of the southeast on a weekly basis, he tapped Nathan to create and host an occasional segment, the Environmental Angler, taped on location rather than in the studio. The segment inspired a steady stream of quality charters and maybe did some good in the bargain. Nathan wasn't sore that Chip had chosen Manny over him for the regular report. Turned out Manny wasn't up to any funny business, after all, with his midnight jaunts along the canals in his panga, or at least no funny business, fishing-wise. He wasn't poaching snook, or anything else with a seine net, as Nathan had feared. It was a woman he was meeting under the cover of darkness, a married woman whom he'd met on a charter with her sugar-daddy husband. Manny and she had taken to late-night rendezvous on the canal behind her swanky home, up until the time they idled back to the dock to find the husband waiting for them in his bathrobe, which put an awkward halt to the liaison. Once the jig was up, Manny disclosed the salacious affair to his fellow captains in the café, crafting an entertaining and self-aggrandizing story out of the whole thing that didn't keep his fellow captains from ribbing him about it time to time.

In any case, Manny was better at the weekly television reports than Nathan was, more naturally expansive. It freed Nathan to fish more, and kept Manny off the water some also, which might have explained Nathan's superior performance at last weekend's SnookeRed tournament. Strange, how losing could translate into winning. His charter business picking up as it had, Nathan needn't mess with the commercial harvest at all. Even so, he fished the reefs and wrecks with Nguyen one night each week, answering inmost summons.

And then there was Kati, preparing now for the arrival of Nathan's peers and their rigorous caffeinating. Here she was behind the bar, tamping out depleted Bustelo grinds with practiced blows, glancing up intermittently toward the TV to track the progress of her telenovela, stretching on toe-tips to feed sugarcane down into the mouth of the behemoth processor, which issued great digestive rumblings and much smaller nectar doses upon consuming the fibrous stalks. Here Nathan was, enjoying these final moments of shared solitude with Kati, working his needles. Rapt as he was in tactile employment, in the pleasant hum of Kati's industry, he didn't even notice Manny's approach.

"Not a frickin' word about the tourney, Nate. You hear? Not a frickin' word."

Nathan's goateed competitor frisbeed a soft pack of Marlboros on the Formica bar and plopped down on the stool just beside Nathan rather than one seat down, as if he had decided ahead of time to tackle matters foursquare.

"What did I say?" Nathan splayed his mottled hands above his tea, but couldn't keep his smile from dawning. Kati, smiling now too, set down Manny's Café Cubano.

"You don't have to say a frickin' thing sitting there with that shit eatin' grin. Look at you. Just look at you for Chris'sake!" Nathan laughed. Kati laughed too, then cleared her throat to disguise her laughter and turned toward the pass-through to place Manny's order.

"What's all the ruckus about?" Frank asked upon his arrival, bedecked in his garish sponsorship attire. Kati, glancing up at the TV, tended the Rancilio to prepare his café con leche.

"It's not like Chip didn't whup your ass, anyway," Manny continued, ignoring Frank. "Second place. Big deal."

"Oh, that," Frank uttered. Taking his seat beside Manny, he bobbed his shoulders in mildest morning laughter. Then, leaning to one side, he extracted his chain of keys with its cumbersome flotation fob from a hip pocket and cast the load on the Formica bar. "Maybe, Manny, you ought to take on your fancy girlfriend as a fishing partner," Frank prodded. "Hear she likes boats, right?"

Frank laughed at his own joke. Nathan struggled not to join in as Manny reddened.

Nathan didn't win the SnookeRed tournament, as Manny had reminded him. Chip and his partner had edged Terrance and him on the second day, landing and photographing a snook with shoulders just a mite broader than Nathan's 42-inch specimen from the first day. Even so, second place in the SnookeRed tournament was Nathan's strongest showing in ten years. Manny hadn't placed. Which wouldn't have been such a big deal were it not for the manner in which Manny had failed. Word was out soon as Nathan and Terrance arrived back at the dock the first day. The fish didn't skunk the young captain. Far from it. Rather, having accepted Wolf's sponsorship, Manny's assortment of juiced plastic baits worked too well, summoning every jack, grunt, ladyfish, trout, barracuda, catfish, sand perch and sheepshead within sniffing distance. For the entire tourney, Manny and his partner were inundated with non-snook and non-redfish strikes. These less prized piscine creatures mobbed Manny's reeking plastics, fairly chasing off the skittish snook and redfish. Nathan might have glimpsed this essential weakness of Wolf's juiced baits that night out with his cameraman, Simon. But he hadn't. The juiced baits failed to make distinctions. Here was the challenge of the perfect bait, it seemed: to offer the most irresistible enticement, yet still make fine distinctions.

Wolf's aquaculture scheme, however, still loomed, still threatened to domesticate the wild snook. Nathan had researched matters at Mote while scouting for one of his Environmental Angler segments on the Fishing Report, which reaffirmed what he already knew. A costly and wasteful enterprise. Hardly fit for commercial scale. Interventional, intermediary aquaculture–from frothy egg-milt to the larvael stage– might prove vital for stock enhancement down the line, Dr. Kathy Briggs claimed. The cold spells, plus red tide on the gulf coast, nearly depleted them this year, after all. But it would take pounds upon pounds of wild mackerel, menhaden, herring and sardine–less tantalizing morsels, apparently, for the finicky American palate–to fatten up a single finicky snook. And nothing could shake them from cannibalizing themselves in close quarters, which sort of defeated the purpose. Aquaculture didn't make much sense from an environmental or financial perspective. Dr. Briggs doubted a commercial interest could make a go of it. Still, Nathan would remain vigilant. He had alerted his snook working group, had spearheaded their working paper for the South Atlantic Fisheries Management Council and the Florida Department of Environmental Protection. If Wolf persisted, Nathan would fight him tooth and nail.

He'd lambaste the project in a series of Fishing Report segments, muster the whole charter community and weekend warrior hangers-on to the cause, put his modest media renown to good use.

"Hear some congratulations are in order," Hollis announced upon his approach, slapping Nathan between the shoulder blades with stinging vigor. "Second place ain't bad."

"Morning," Del uttered next, to Manny alone it seemed, checking the young captain's temperature as he negotiated his girth past his stool. Their leader descended gingerly into the last available seat.

Ceramic mugs bucked against their saucers as Kati set down Frank's, then Hollis', then Del's coffee concoctions. Silence. The bouillabaisse slowly simmered. Then boiled over.

"Oh hell," Manny said. "Frickin' Nathan." And then Manny finally laughed, acceding to the prevailing tenor, smacking his Marlboro soft pack against the heel of his palm. "Fine. Congratulations, Nate. . . . I call the Corey & Chris this morning." The laughter at his expense entitled him to first dibs on the wreck, apparently.

"I call?" Frank teased. "What is this, fifth grade?"

The bouillabaisse boiled again.

"No problem, though," Frank declared, raising his palms in mock surrender. "It's all yours, Manny. Wrestle with reef donkeys all you want." Manny nodded, slurped the dregs of his first café Cubano.

"I'll drift the Rebel, I guess," Hollis said.

"I'll head north from thereabouts." Frank. "Scout for weedlines. Sure you want to anchor up, Manny, all the bulls out there, lately?"

"Think so. Least to start. Don't feel like running all around today. Gotta show to tape tomorrow."

Frank rolled his eyes. "Well can you check for weeds deeper, Del?"

Del shook his head. "Fast trolling for wahoo, Frank. I'll let you know about any color changes or rips I see, anyway." His elbows crossed and braced on the bar, Del shifted his oversized posterior on his seat. "Finally had that prostate checked," Del said, as if to explain his squirming.

"Good. 'Bout time," said Hollis.

"Yee-haw," Frank said, affecting a cowboy smack to his rear.

The bouillabaisse simmered.

The captains, bolstered by the caffeine, were feeling loose and fine. The prevailing weather these days. Their charters had picked up, mostly on account of Manny's localized fame, and Nathan's to a lesser extent. Fishing all around had picked up, along with the water temp. The winter sailfish catch and release bite was over, but the warm spring waters had ushered back voracious patrols of mahi, wahoo, and blackfin in the deep bluewater, while snapper, grouper, and amberjack on the closer wrecks and reefs stopped being so fussy, their gonads driving them toward spawn. Nathan's snook too had returned to provide catch-and-release memories inshore, mostly to vacationing fathers and their young sons and daughters. Still a fair bit of Florida coast left, after all. They hadn't loused things up quite yet.

Kati returned with their steaming platters of eggs and congris and oiled Cuban bread and flap steak. Nathan, who had mostly finished

eating, returned to his needles as his colleagues devoured their break-
fasts, their cutlery clinking against the ceramic.

"Stay on 73 today, boys?" Del uttered, wiping rice and bean
specs from his beard with a paper napkin.

The captains nodded.

"What are you up to today Nathan?" Frank asked, leaning
forward around Manny to peer toward Nathan. "Mr. Quiet over there."

"Taking the day off, fellas. Picking up my brother from the
airport."

"Brother?" Del asked, mopping up yolk with his toast.

"Yeah. Brother. His name's Jake."

**

Later that day, as he distractedly planned his next Environmental Angler
segment (venting barotraumatized fish), Nathan fielded a call on his cell
from his father.

"Sure I can't drive down with you?"

"I'm okay, pop. They'll be exhausted, I'm sure. It's, like, a thir-
teen-hour flight."

"I know how long the flight is."

It was at least the third time Nathan had had to fend off his father's advance, but the mild retort this time—if that's what it was—gave
him pause. Why didn't he want his father to tag along? It had nothing to
do with Jake's and Hannah's probable fatigue, as his father likely intuited. Nathan, instead, was nervous about seeing his brother after so long
(it had been nearly twenty years since he had accompanied his mother

for a visit to Jake's moshav, after the first intifada). He didn't want to take on the additional burden of negotiating his father's more complicated reunion with Jake at the same time.

"You'll see Jake and Hannah tomorrow for lunch at the Mandarin Wok, remember?

His father remembered, but wanted to make sure of one thing. "Hannah's the oldest one, right?"

"Yes," Nathan replied, filling his father in on a few additional details. She was almost nineteen and had just completed the first year of her military service. She was a medic. Her little sister was almost sixteen. A talented ballet dancer. She lived and studied at a special school in Tel Aviv. Her name was Yael. Ephraim, the youngest, was fourteen and had undergone a surgical procedure of some sort to repair a lazy eye, or something like that.

And there was another thing his father wanted to know, apparently. "So why aren't Yael and Ephraim coming? And Jake's wife, Sheva? Seems strange."

"Something about one of Yael's performances, maybe. Jake might have mentioned that. Plane tickets aren't cheap, either. I don't know. You can ask Jake tomorrow." Nathan thought about this for a moment, and reconsidered. "On second thought, pop, don't pester him about this." His advice elicited a low chuckle from the other end of the line.

"Drive safely," his father advised.

**

Nathan couldn't remember the last time he'd been to the Miami International Airport, or whether it was fair for him to think, as he thought now—wending his way past the narrow corridors lined with plywood, his eye out for the temporary signage directing him toward Customs on the first level of the north terminal—that the beleaguered facility was in a constant state of disrepair and hasty, shoddily-conceived renovation. He finally made it to the dingy linoleum space where a human throng beneath strangely vibrating fluorescent light waited to retrieve their significant others. A high wall of glass—bulletproof? Nathan wondered—separated the waiting area from Customs beyond. Most people on Nathan's side pressed toward the invisible border to catch the earliest glimpse of their loved ones, guarded half-smiles or worried frowns frozen on their faces. The few vinyl bench-seats scattered about were occupied mostly by elderly women and fewer men of various ethnic origin. One woman worried the beads of a rosary in her lap, a colorful scarf covering her hair. A younger family that struck Nathan as European, or South American maybe, sat and stood in a cluster nearby, the father wearing designer jeans adorned with visible golden threads, an expensive-looking silver watch wrapped around his furry wrist, his two teenage daughters (Nathan presumed) sporting low-slung velour sweat pants, their bejeweled navels bared. A twenty-something black man paced as he spoke into his cell phone, a bright orange baseball cap with a high crown perched at a fastidious sideways angle on his head, its tag dangling as some sort of fashion statement. Children scampered this way and that underfoot, ignoring the discipline issued their way in harsh glottals, mostly Spanish. And here was Nathan, too, part of this

American tableau. A great tenderness for his home place rose in him, thickening his throat.

Nathan made his way to the closest Arrivals screen and was pleased, and somewhat surprised, to see that his brother's flight had just landed. He made his way back to the edge of the glass partition near the guarded gate to keep a lookout for Jake and Hannah. He waited there longer than he expected and observed the reunions of several other parties conducted at various emotional tenors. A young south-Asian couple surprised him with their amorousness, causing him to avert his eyes. After half an hour passed, then forty-five minutes, he worried that he might have failed to recognize Jake and Hannah, that he had missed them. He checked the screen of his cell phone for the tenth time. Nothing. He wasn't certain whether Jake's phone would work in Florida. He approached the Latina TSA officer at the gate to ask whether he was waiting at the right location—there was a separate Customs area on the third floor of the south terminal, he knew—but just as he was about to say something, just as the TSA agent lifted her head to listen, he spotted Jake beyond the woman's shoulder, or, rather, spotted Jake spotting him, raising a broad palm and smiling as he dragged a suitcase behind. Nathan raised his smaller hand. His brother's modest dark beard surprised him, but he would have recognized Jake, anyway, even if Jake hadn't recognized him first. It was a comfort, this knowledge. Hannah walked beside her father, nearly as tall, her curly shock of red hair dancing about her broad shoulders. She looked over toward her father and said something to him. *Is that him?* Nathan guessed.

He backed up a bit to allow some other passengers through the gate. The TSA officer on her padded stool was fielding a question from a black woman burdened with too much luggage. As Jake and Hannah drew nearer, she placed a hand at the small of her father's back as if to shove him along toward his younger brother. Hannah had accompanied her father, Nathan had presumed, to see some of her relatives and represent the Israeli Pray contingent for her cousin's important day. And to see Florida. But also, it only now occurred to him, to offer her father ballast and see him through what might be a difficult time.

Nathan wasn't certain how he would greet his brother, exactly. Somewhat un-Jewishly, they had never been demonstrative with their affections. As adults, Jake and he carried out their intermittent phone conversations in businesslike fashion. So he was grateful when Jake slipped past the black woman and the TSA officer and stretched his broad arms to fold Nathan into a hug, patting his back a few times for good measure.

"Hey bro," Jake said, an expression right out of the 1980s that made Nathan's eyes blur some. Or maybe it was just the voice that moved him, Jake's voice of old yet an octave or two deeper and accented now by the faintest Hebrew timbre in that *bro*. Trailing just behind the sound of his voice was the smell of stale smoke and the stronger wintergreen of a recently consumed mint.

"Hey," Nathan said, hugging back. Jake's frame felt solid, a bit beefier maybe on account of both muscle and middle-aged fat around his middle. A ripe odor rose from him. Jake's new smells were unfamiliar and saddened Nathan some. Jake ate different food, breathed different air, smoked cigarettes, apparently. So, sure, his breath and body exuded different smells now. His voice had grown deeper.

"Skinny as ever," Jake said, releasing him, still gripping his shoulders. It seemed like a compliment, mostly, given Jake's modest spread above the beltline of his trousers. He had felt his brother's soft belly when they hugged. Jake's straight hair was still dark and parted on the right, but had receded some around the temples. A complex network of branched wrinkles marked his olive flesh all about his dark eyes. A distinctive frowning crease now connected his eyebrows, remnants of too many angry expressions over the years. He looked even more like their father now, it occurred to Nathan with a start, keeping the knowledge to himself.

"*You* look well," Nathan declared, instead. His brother thanked him and then told Hannah to give her uncle a hug. She smiled and hugged him. Nathan scanned her features for signs of Prayness. There was the hair, of course, from their mother's side.

"I see where I get my hair," Hannah said, as if reading his thoughts. Hebrew vowels inflected her English speech more dramatically than they marked her father's voice. "Everyone called me Gingy when I grow up."

"It looks better on you," Nathan assured her. "Anyway, let's get you both out of here." The harsh fluorescent lighting. The human crush. It wasn't a space that encouraged one to linger. Nathan offered to carry her green duffle as they made their way to the car and was pleased that she let him. He wondered if it was military-issue, her duffle, but didn't ask, just swung the thick canvas strap around his shoulder. She rolled a small suitcase behind her as the three of them made their way through the labyrinthine garage, tires and brakes squealing against the hard surfaces as they zipped past. "5J," he announced, relieved that he remembered the general locale of the car. Finally, they found it. Hannah admired the gleaming sedan and Nathan told her that it was her grandmother's, vaguely embarrassed by the opulence of the car he was forced to borrow to pick them up with all their luggage.

"So mom's doing well I see," Jake declared, taking in the gleaming sedan, mostly just to say something, Nathan decided, having decided not to infer an insult in the remark.

"Fish biting, too?"

Nathan told him that they were biting as a matter of fact. He did most of the talking as he navigated his way up the interstate, but he didn't want to talk about fishing. He asked whether Ephraim's eyes were still doing well after his surgery (they were), whether Yael was still enjoying the rigors of dance (she was), whether they were exhausted from the flight (they weren't), asked why it seemed to take so long for them to get through Customs (passports from the Middle East made Customs officers nervous), whether the Miami skyline looked familiar to Jake (it didn't). Nathan assured them that it would only take an hour or so to get up to their mother's house. It was a good thing their flight got in at night, after rush hour. Jake wouldn't believe how bad the traffic had gotten over the past twenty years or so, how many people lived here now on this narrow strip of coastal ridge, how much the place had changed.

Nathan finally controlled his banter, embraced the silence and tried not to stare at the blinding headlights flashing past. He could hear Jake's heavy breath beside him, Hannah zipping open her duffle that she had set in the seat beside her, rifling through it for something, he supposed. Her smartphone? A breath mint? A tissue? She sighed, leaned her ginger head back against the headrest, Nathan noticed though his mirror. He wondered whether they were more tired than they had claimed. And then it occurred to him that there was something he had forgotten to say to Jake and his niece, something that he ought to say before they drifted off to sleep in the car.

"Thank you," he uttered above the engine's hum, the words sounding loud and abrupt to his own ears.

"Huh? What?" Jake asked, coming to.

"Thanks for coming. To Miles' Bar Mitzvah. I appreciate it."

Jake sort of chuckled through his nose, the amused and vaguely condescending chuckle that all older brothers, perhaps, issued toward their younger brothers, no matter their ages.

"You're welcome, Uncle Nathan," Hannah answered for the both of them. "Thank you for inviting us."

A crisis was well underway by the time Nathan called his mother's house the next morning.

"You're not going to believe this, Nathan. You're just not going to believe it." His mother's voice rose above some background chatter and less descript sounds, as if he had caught her out in public, at the grocery store, maybe. In addition to the sheer volume of her voice, it lilted at a high register that he couldn't remember hearing for a long time. Hannah, his mother explained, had packed a few small bottles of a hair product. The liquid contents of one bottle had spilled, staining the dress she had planned to wear to the Bar Mitzvah on Saturday. "The only thing it touched, of course, was the best dress in the suitcase," his mother was saying. "You just have to laugh. I tried all last night to get it out, but's it's a lost cause. You just have to laugh, Nathan."

"I guess so," he agreed, amused by his mother's buoyancy. She didn't seem very upset by the crisis. Truth was, she couldn't have scripted a better predicament for the occasion. Now she wouldn't have to worry about occupying Jacob and Hannah all morning at the house, whether her neighbors at the pool or spa or clubhouse would offend Jake or her granddaughter with their Philistine ways, real or perceived. Now there was an important task to perform. Finding Hannah a new dress, Nathan presumed. Now she could snap into action. And she was enjoying this time alone with her granddaughter, Nathan figured.

"We're at Nordstrom's now," she continued. "Already looked

at Bloomingdale's. It's going to take us all morning. You don't just buy the first dress you see." She paused, lifted her wrist to scan her watch, Nathan imagined, or maybe exchanged a conspiratorial glance with Hannah.

"Of course, mother," he agreed. He told her not to worry and to do what she needed to do with Hannah. He'd drop by later to pick up Jake for lunch with their father, or come by whenever Jake wanted him to come by. He'd call the house now.

"You're so good," his mother said, as if she expected him to obstruct her plans, somehow. "Thanks for being so good, Nathan. For making this so easy." It was a strain on her, clearly, this visit with Jake and Hannah on her home turf. Miles' Bar Mitzvah. She wanted desperately for it all to go off well.

**

Jake told Nathan over the phone that he just wanted to relax until lunch with their father, stretch his muscles in the small backyard pool. He hoped that Nathan could come by early if he wasn't too busy with the Bar Mitzvah meshugass (the Yiddish word sounding strange out of his brother's mouth), hang out with him (which sounded more familiar). So Nathan met his brother over at his mother's house and watched from the chaise lounge as Jake finished a series of short laps, his freestyle strokes short and deliberate, but strong. A bald spot Nathan hadn't noticed at the airport last night was visible toward the back of his wet crown. He wondered when his brother had picked up swimming for exercise. Neither of them swam much as youngsters, despite growing up in Florida.

Nathan listened to the *plunk* of his brother's heavy kicks, the sporadic tinny sound of metal clubs striking golf balls (poorly) on the fairway beyond the ficus hedge, the distant curses of alter kockers displeased with their efforts.

Jake rose from the pool, the water slapping against the pavers as he reached for his towel. His torso was huskier than when they were young, his abdominal muscles obscured beneath the salt and pepper fur and fat.

"Beautiful morning," Jake said, worrying an ear with his towel as if there was some water trapped inside. It *was* a beautiful day. A modest breeze made leaf-shadows dance across the pavers from the tall banyan over the hedge.

Spring had summoned this dry Florida warmth. Along with the snook. Along with Jake.

"You're lucky," Nathan replied. "The winter was brutal. Polar vortex they were calling it." Jake's eyebrows knitted together in disbelief as he dried his back, jutting out his chest. "I mean, brutal for Florida," Nathan added. "You're a good swimmer, by the way." It felt good to offer this simple compliment, which seemed to amuse his brother.

"You kidding? I stink."

Inside, Jake disappeared for just an instant to change into dry shorts and a V-neck undershirt that seemed old-fashioned to Nathan, or maybe just old. His salt and pepper fur spilled out the top and looked like it might travel all the way up to join Jake's beard if it weren't for his brother's efforts with a razor. They plopped down on separate branches of their mother's L-shaped sofa, where Nathan had never seen her sit. The years between them contained far too many gaps to know which ones to fill. But they tried. Nathan told Jake about his fishing travails and his more recent good luck, and told him about his new lady-friend, Kati. Jake listened with interest and offered clipped but sincere verbal encouragements. Upon Nathan's inquiries, his brother explained with greater thoroughness than ever before the area of his expertise, vis a vis plants. He had studied agronomy at the Volcani Center in Beit Dagan, conducted research for the government and for the moshav that he and Sheva had joined years ago in the Jezreel Valley. He and other researchers had optimized, most recently, the cultivation of baby's breath flowers, which their moshav and others supplied to the European flower market. It seemed like an awfully feminine plant to have commanded his tough brother's expertise. Nathan had thought, from a previous conversation years ago, that his brother focused on a hardier, more functional crop. A food staple. Wheat, maybe. Or some other cereal grain.

"Remember . . .?" Jake began to ask, his voice rising, then falling away. A dreamy look washed over his face. It seemed as if there was something specific he had recalled, but had just as soon forgotten.

"Yes," Nathan answered. "I remember."

Nathan's cell phone vibrated against his thigh. It was their mother. As she had sort of warned him earlier in her circuitous way, they weren't finished shopping for Hannah's dress, even though they were "making progress," whatever that meant. Was it okay if Hannah skipped lunch, spent time with her grandfather tomorrow or after the

Bar Mitzvah Saturday? Nathan, checking first with Jake, not quite knowing where to put his hand on his antiquated flip-phone to mask their voices, told her that it was fine. Maybe it was for the best, Nathan figured, not to overwhelm their father with too many reunions at once.

So Nathan and his brother headed to the restaurant to meet their father. Jake propped his thick arm out the open window frame, clutching a cigarette behind the side mirror to shield it from the wind. (He hadn't dared light up in their mother's house.) The cigarette smoke infiltrated the truck's interior, anyway, and burned Nathan's throat, but he didn't say anything. They didn't speak much in the truck, the gravity of the occasion banishing small talk. Or maybe Jake was only tired still from his flight or from his exercise in the pool. He mostly peered out his window and studied the new buildings on Federal, it seemed to Nathan. He wondered what his brother was thinking. Probably nothing good, the once lovely horizon to the east and west now blotted out by too many mid-rise glass buildings standing shoulder-to-shoulder holding brokerage houses, banks, and other financial interests, plus various medical suites, including more than a few plastic surgery centers. He thought he heard his brother issue a disapproving cluck with his tongue, which reflexively peeved Nathan, even if he didn't much like the way their hometown had grown up, either.

"So how bad *is* he?" Jake finally asked over the engine's rumble and the wind. Maybe he hadn't been thinking about their hometown, after all, or its overdevelopment. Of course he hadn't. What did it matter at a time like this? Nathan shifted to a higher, smoother gear before answering Jake's question about their father.

"It depends. You might not be able to tell much at all if he's having a good day."

"And if he's not?"

"If he's not, well, then you *will* be able to tell. He might stumble over his words, or space out, or lose his temper, because he can't find the right words or keep himself from spacing out. That sort of thing."

"Dad's temper," Jake said, as if it was something he had forgotten.

Nathan downshifted and then stopped at the red light at Spanish River. He glanced over at his brother. Jake seemed pensive, nodding slowly as he flicked his thumb against the filter of the cigarette, sending flecks of ash off into the mild ocean breeze.

The aroma of Hoisin sauce and some sort of deodorizer beneath (carpet cleaner?) greeted the brothers as soon as Nathan swung open the glass door to the Chinese restaurant. "Looks like he's not here yet," Nathan said beside the old metal cash register, scanning the round tables for their father. He had to stand on his tip-toes a bit to peer over the long goldfish tank, which divided the dining space roughly in half.

"Smells the same, anyway," Jake said, flashing a yellow smile. The restaurant was one of the few surviving eateries in town that dated back to their childhood. The shrunken sushi bar in the corner was the only significant upgrade, which Jake must have noticed upon entering but decided for whatever reason not to comment upon. Nathan had suggested the Mandarin Wok because it was close to their father's condo and Nathan thought of it as a sort of neutral territory. But it was anything but neutral, it occurred to him only now as he took in the tacky décor, which seemed not to have changed at all over the years: the fish tank with its chintzy castles and neon blue pebbles, the off-white table linens, the tall vinyl chairs, the wallpaper design of willowy golden reeds meant to recall the Orient, Nathan supposed. The familiar look and smell of the place summoned charged memories that Nathan, for whatever reason, hadn't anticipated.

"Hope they still have moo-shoo chicken," Jake said. He'd been courting his own memories.

A few minutes passed. Five. Ten. They probably should have just picked up their father at his high-rise across the intracoastal. Nathan apologized for the snafu. But their father insisted that he'd meet them, that it was just as easy for Louna to drop him off. Jake told him to relax, that there wasn't any hurry, was there? As if to distract Nathan, Jake commented on the magnolia trees in the courtyard outside the tinted, and somewhat blurred, windows, how tall they'd grown, the pretty painted sky beyond. Nathan smiled at this new brother of his. Since when had Jake been the patient one? Since when had *he* noticed trees and painted skies? As kids, Jake never seemed particularly moved by nature. The few times the brothers spoke over the long-distance wires as adults, he couched his horticultural work in the most clinical terms. So it only now occurred to Nathan that Jake had developed a strong connection to the land in Israel. Of course he had. They likely shared more in common now than Nathan had dared to fathom. For whatever reason, this made Nathan sad rather than happy.

He finally glimpsed Louna's small coupe pull into a spot in the parking lot facing the smoky window, was about to announce *There they are* but held his tongue as he watched his father pull himself to vertical from the low vehicle, gripping the doorframe and roof with both hands, as he watched Louna rise from the other side, his father fending off her advance with a palm and whatever words he spoke. Jake hadn't spotted their father yet. He still seemed to be studying the trees outside the west-facing window, or maybe those pretty purple clouds.

"Here he comes," Nathan said only after Louna lowered herself back into the driver's seat and shut her door. Jake turned from the magnolias and purple clouds and watched with Nathan as their father walked toward the door. Nathan reached for it and swung it open with one arm, leaving plenty of room for their father to slip inside past him.

Upon recognizing his elder son, their father seemed to lift his woolly eyebrows higher on his forehead, but he didn't say anything right away, just thrust his hand forward. Jake grasped it. The two stood eye to eye and shook with two vigorous pumps. Their father's complexion was smooth and pink. He'd given himself a fresh shave. Wispy white remnants of a cotton ball or swab adhered to his skin near a few visible specs of dark dried blood at the corner of his still-strong chin, which was how Nathan knew that he'd shaved on his own. Louna would have done a better job of it.

"Jacob," their father finally uttered.

"Father," Jacob replied, his voice a tad lower than their father's voice.

It seemed a stiff standoffish greeting, but it was civil anyway. What did Nathan expect? He suddenly felt shrunken beside these larger, darker men. The restaurant seemed too bright, middle of the day, between the natural light and the overhead fluorescents. The owner might have sensed the awkwardness of the encounter, or else she simply wanted them out of the way, because she ushered them all to their table in the mostly empty dining room, the menus in her hand dwarfing her slight frame. She seated them at an oversized round table near the fish tank, probably to leave ample space between them and the young couple with their baby over at one of the booths.

"Let's look at the menu first," Nathan suggested, not really knowing what he meant to imply would come second. Jake and his father silently obeyed. The laminated menu was several pages long and contained two paper inserts, as well, mottled with soy sauce stains, advertising Lunch options and costlier Specialties of the House (e.g., Crispy Whole Fish, Lobster Two-Way, Giant Prawn in Hunan Sauce). Nathan fumbled dazedly through the offerings, figured he'd just let Jake or their father do the ordering, but took note of an eggplant dish just in case.

The baby's unignorable wail suddenly pierced the relative quiet of the room. Nathan looked up toward the cry, noticed the parents laboring in the booth to pacify the child, a boy looked like, now smacking the cloth tabletop with both hands. The family was close to finishing their meal, it seemed. Strewn about their tabletop was the wreckage of troubled dinnerware: aluminum covers propped helter skelter against plates and platters, tiny teacups on end, crumpled napkins. The tyke had made a mess of his rice, Nathan noticed, which lay like snow against the mint green carpet beneath his wooden high-chair.

"They should take the baby outside," their father opined.

"Babies cry."

Now here was the familiar Jake, instinctively bristling against their father, not bothering to lift his eyes from the menu. He wondered whether he ought to have emphasized their father's debility more strenuously in the truck rather than downplay it, as he'd pretty much done. It might have encouraged Jake to offer their father a wider berth. In any case, their father had registered the rebuff. Nathan could tell by the way his muscles worked in his square jaw behind the menu, the way he flipped the laminated page making it go *snap*. He worried over his father's next words. His cheeks seemed overly pinked now under the harsh lights.

"So what do you boys think, should we do this family-style, get two orders of the spareribs?"

Nathan exhaled, then realized he'd been holding his breath.

"Sure dad," Jake said, setting his menu down, wearing a softer expression. "Good idea, two orders of ribs. We'll eat everything family-style." Nathan echoed the sentiment, even though he didn't eat ribs anymore. It just felt good to agree.

Their father, Nathan was certain, had been a hair's breadth from lashing out at Jake. That clenched jaw. Those pinked cheeks. Yet he had checked the impulse, chosen a different course. Time was too precious to pick at their scabs. He and Jake would never fully resolve their ancient grievances—ever somewhat murky to Nathan—nor could they retrieve the lost decades between them. But what they could do, anyway, was eat this trayf meal together in peace. That's what their father seemed to recognize, anyway.

When their waiter greeted them, lifting his pad and pencil awfully close to his nose, Nathan and Jake deferred to their father, who issued the official order to the waiter after querying them on their preferences. As they ate the ribs (Nathan nibbled on one), their father asked Jake some innocuous questions about their flight, whether El Al served decent food, how crazy the Miami airport was last night. Over the soup, Jake asked their father about his "condition," how he felt on a "typical day," sifting carefully through his broth with the broad white spoon for the proper words. Their father described his symptoms and put the sunniest clinical spin on his prognosis ("I can remain high-functioning for years, no one really knows"), while Jake nodded slowly, thoughtfully. As they enjoyed their entrees (the eggplant, kung pao chicken, and, of course, moo-shoo chicken), their father asked after Sheva and the children—taking special care to pronounce Hannah's and Yael's and Ephraim's names to prove that he knew them—then asked some technical questions about agronomy, about the moshav, how its structure differed from Jake's first kibbutz up near Lebanon, pressing for a bit more financial detail than Nathan thought was advisable. Yet Jake, to his credit, answered his father's questions without growing defensive.

Soon, they were done with their meals. An awkward silence settled in as they nursed their tepid tea. Whose turn was it to speak?

The waiter suddenly appeared and set down the small tray holding the check and too many fortune cookies. Their father plucked the check from beneath the cookies, as if it were a magic trick. Nathan and Jake let him take it.

"Jacob, you can help me with this I bet," their father announced brightly, as if he had just remembered a topic he had planned on broaching all along.

"Oh?" Jake answered, reaching for a cookie. Nathan asked for one too and Jake passed it to him.

"I planted impatiens and vincas and mandevillas in pots out on my balcony. But they don't look so good anymore. They've dropped nearly all of their flowers and they seem too tall and, uh, leggy. Now if I prune them back, I have a pair of pruners, I can do it, will this help them, will it . . ." he lifted his gray eyes to search for the word somewhere above his eyebrows, "*revitalize* the plants, encourage them to put out new flowers, maybe, or will I just end up killing them?"

Just months ago, Dr. Joseph Pray, King of the colonoscopy, was conducting important lifesaving work, leaning over anesthetized patients, scanning their X-rays, scribbling out scripts. And here he was now, worried over a few lousy plants on his balcony—impatiens and vincas and mandevillas—visibly proud to have summoned all on his own the appropriate word, *revitalize,* to the occasion.

Jake glanced toward Nathan, held his gaze for a protracted moment as if he was hoping to convey or receive silent knowledge, and then looked back toward their father. "Yes, I'd try pruning them, dad, like you were thinking. It might encourage new shoots. I can take a look at them if you'd like. We have time, right Nathan?"

"Of course."

And so maybe Jake too—maybe only now, crunching down on his flavorless fortune cookie—recognized that time was precious, too precious to pick at their scabs.

**

Later that afternoon, Nathan met Miles and a very pregnant Sam at the synagogue for their rehearsal with Rabbi Plotnick and Cantor Rachel, and walked through the service in the echo chamber that was the empty sanctuary. Miles, before the closed wooden ark, chanted the *Bar'chu*, the *Yotzeir*, the *V'ahavta,* and the other prayers without pause. From time to time, Nathan lifted his gaze above his son and the ark to the vertical panels of stained glass against the wall, the foliage outside lashing the glass with its shadows. Miles stumbled a bit, but not much, over the last lines of his *Haftarah.* He was ready. They sorted out one last time the few special readings in English for their relatives, the order of the *aliyot* at the bima, paused to acknowledge the place for their speech to Miles and for Miles' speech on his Torah portion. His son's *drash* would be fine, Nathan knew, whatever genealogical notions on Moses he decided to share. Miles, more importantly, would be fine, would invent himself as he saw fit, as Jake had done, as Nathan had done. He felt his son's solid personhood, above all, as Miles recited the Hebrew prayers, as he nodded toward the rabbi and the cantor upon their encouragements and mild suggestions.

"And as you know we close the service, Miles, by blessing you,"

381

Rabbi Plotnick was saying now. "So let us bless you."

"Chill," Miles answered, which made Plotnick smile behind his beard. Miles lowered his head as the rabbi splayed thick fingers atop his dreadlocks, as the young cantor reached for a separate patch of ginger fur. The rabbi summoned Nathan and Sam to draw closer, the two of them reaching toward Miles, as well, completing the circuit. Nathan felt the warmth radiating from his son's scalp, smelled the rich odors of Miles' tousled hair rising against the rabbi's citrusy cologne. "*Y'simcha Elohim K'Ephraim v'che-Menasheh,*" Plotnick chanted. "May God make you like Ephraim and Menasheh. *Y'varachecha Adonai V'yish'm'recha.* May God Bless you and guard you. *Ya'er Adonai panav eilecha vichuneka.* May the light of God shine upon you, and may God be gracious to you. *Yisa Adonai panav eliecha v'yasem l'cha shalom.* May the presence of God be with you and give you peace."

She was turning out to be a tough nut to crack, Alicia. It was one of the reasons that Nathan encouraged Miles to tag along this afternoon. He figured that someone associated with him, but closer to Alicia's age, might lower the girl's defenses. Miles lived with Nathan half the time now, as the custody agreement stipulated all along, and as Nathan's new condo (brokered by his delighted mother) finally made practicable. He was glad that Sam, a new mother to a baby girl, seemed to appreciate rather than resent the uptick in his fatherly efforts. Glad, too, that Miles liked his new room in the new condo, which had its own bathroom, and that he offered to skip swim practice this afternoon to meet Alicia after school. There were all those knock-knock jokes Miles used to tell. Maybe he'd win her over with those jokes.

They walked the few blocks from Kati and her mother's apartment to the El Rio, Nathan and Kati up ahead, Alicia and Miles bringing up the rear. Nathan could hear the folding chair Miles carried *thwacking* against his legs a bit as he walked.

"Can I carry my pole?" he heard Alicia ask Miles.

"Sure, Alicia," Miles said. It was the first time Miles addressed the girl by her name and it gave Nathan a start. It was quite something, really, to address someone by name. He wondered if it seemed as strange and new to Alicia, or to Kati, or to Miles. He turned back in time to watch Miles hand the old Zebco to the girl, which she grasped in her seashell fist.

They reached the familiar dusty edge of the El Rio just north of the spillway, where Jake had fought the big black boy who'd tricked Nathan, where Nathan for years afterward used to fish with Terrance, where freshwater from Lake Okeechobee gave way to brackish, where bass and Mayan cichlids on one side of the spillway gave way to snook and small snapper on the other side. Nathan leaned over the edge and looked up and down the canal. "What are you looking for?" Alicia inquired a few feet behind, raising her voice to be heard over the tea-stained water that toppled over the spillway.

"Alligators."

"Alligators!?" Kati asked.

"Most of them are only six feet long," Miles joked to Alicia and Kati, "you guys don't have to worry."

"He's just teasing," Nathan said, turning back to make sure they understood.

"I know," Alicia said, shooting a look up at Miles that came awfully close to a smile. Nathan half expected her to stick her tongue out.

"No alligators," Nathan said, studying the shoreline again.

Kati drew closer to her daughter, unconvinced. Nathan walked back a few feet from the bank where they stood, set down his light rod, his tackle box, smiling as he reached inside for the mayonnaise jar, flecks of the Hellman's label still clinging to the glass. Red worms in their briny bath. Miles made himself useful by standing up the two chairs. "Don't worry, Kati," Nathan said. "I'll keep a close eye."

Kati, appeased, sat down on one of the chairs as Nathan and

Miles led Alicia to the bank with their bait and gear.

"What are those?" Alicia finally asked. "In the jar?"

"Red worms. Bass candy." Nathan, on one knee, held the jar up for Alicia's more concerted inspection as he inspected her. It was hot in the sun. Tendrils of hair that had escaped the girl's braided pony-tail adhered to perspiration at her temples, slicked their way down below her tiny ears.

"They dead?"

"Yep. Already dead."

"That's good."

Nathan and Miles exchanged a pregnant glance. Years ago, Nathan had euthanized red worms in briny water to dispatch them, too—for Miles, who thought it impossibly cruel to impale living writhing worms, and who apparently remembered these mayonnaise jars of brine and bait.

On one knee still, Nathan grasped his own rod and wetted the end of the monofilament in his mouth. This seemed to spark the girl's interest. "Now this is how you tie a knot, Alicia. A clinch knot. That's what it's called. A clinch knot." Miles, on the other side of Alicia, began tying his own knot to his hook, showing off a bit, maybe, with his silent progress. Nathan was pleased to glimpse Miles make the requisite wraps. He wasn't so sure Miles would remember how to tie a clinch knot, or any knot. "Only a few knots you'll ever need to know," Nathan continued. "Trick is knowing them well. There's a right way and a wrong way." Alicia nodded. "Now this is your hook. A number four offset long-shank bronze hook." Her eyes widened. "You don't need to know all that now. It's just a hook for now. First, you thread the end through the eye like so. This is the eye. This is the shank that I'm holding."

"Your hands look funny."

"Alicia!" Kati called down from her chair.

Miles chuckled.

"I know they look funny," Nathan said, grinning.

"Like a cow, sorta."

"Alicia, be nice!" The girl chuckled too now, in two lazy syllables as if imitating Miles. "What?" she asked, turning toward her mother, showing oversized teeth for the first time. She'd need braces, Nathan thought.

"You have to remember to give yourself plenty of line past the eye to work with," Miles chimed in. "Like this." He held up all the extra monofilament past his knot that he'd have to trim off with Nathan's nail clippers. "That's the trick."

"Miles is right," Nathan said. He lifted the shoelace loop attached to the nail clippers over his neck, handed the necklace and charm over to Miles, who set about trimming the line. "Then after you pay out enough line you hold the pieces either side of the eye and twist the hook five times. Count for me?"

"One . . . two . . . three . . . four . . . five."

"Good, Alicia. Then–you gotta pay attention here; it gets just a little tricky here–you thread the end of the line back through the gap here next to the eye. Here, watch me again. Got it?"

Alicia nodded.

"And pull." Nathan pulled the knot taut. "See. Simple knot. No need for fancy shmancy. Now you try on your hook."

Nathan handed her a small, long-shank hook. The long-shanks, he knew, would make it easier to tie knots and to remove the hook from the cichlids and bass once they caught them. She poked the line through the eye, curled pink lips over her teeth. Perspiration beaded above her lip and across the bridge of her flat nose.

"Good."

"You're doing so nice, Alicia," Kati called down from her chair.

"One . . . two . . . three . . . four . . . five," Alicia said, ignoring her mother's praise. "Wait, what do you do next?" She slumped her shoulders. Nathan showed her, while Miles assured her that it took a few practice-tries to get it down.

"Okay," she said. "Let me try again." Nathan unraveled the loops and she started fresh, made quick progress.

"Presto," Nathan said once she wrapped and tightened the clinch. He trimmed the excess line with the nail clippers that Miles had silently handed back to him. "Here, I'll bait your hook."

"I can do it." She reached for the limp red thread, which Nathan relinquished.

"All right, expert." He held up his hands in mock surrender. The kid had moxie. He watched, and Miles watched, as she pierced the bait, squinting some despite her best efforts to look nonchalant. "Good," Nathan said. "Now one more time through the body, lower."

"Like that?"

"Perfect."

"Better than I ever did," Miles said.

"Now here's how you cast," Nathan continued. Rising to his feet, then bending at the waist, he wrapped his arms around her tiny frame, placed a mottled hand over her tiny paw at the close-faced reel.

"Now, pay attention. It's simple, but you have to pay attention. This is your reel. A close-faced spinning reel. A good reel to start with. You grip the rod like this"–he wrapped her small hand around the handle–"and hold your thumb down on the button like this." Nathan placed her small thumb on the cream-colored button and pressed it down. "Now if you let go, look what happens."

"Oh. Okay."

"So let's reel in again." She reeled. "Trick is to let go your thumb just when the rod tip's pointed where you want your bait to fly. So here goes. I'll help, but you do the button."

Nathan framed Alicia as she cast back, then snapped forward, releasing her thumb a tad too late, the red worm going *kerplunk* in the murky creek just a few feet off the berm.

"Oops."

"Like this," Miles said, casting his line that he'd just baited. "See?" He reeled it back in the moment it splashed down in the water, not wanting to catch the first fish, maybe.

"Try again," Nathan suggested. She retrieved her line and tried again, sending the bait a good ways out, beneath the shadow of the cabbage palm clear at the other shore. Lucky cast, Nathan thought, but didn't say.

"Beautiful!" he said instead.

"Way to go!" Miles.

"Good job!" Kati uttered from the chair with her squishy j. No squishy j's from Alicia.

"How do I know I have a fish?"

"You'll know, Alicia. You'll feel it."

"He's right," Miles said. "It's pretty cool, the first time. Way it feels." Nathan glanced over at Miles, who was looking into the water after his line, then looked back at Alicia.

"No other feeling like it in the world," Nathan said. "Brace yourself."

And so Alicia learned how to fish.

Acknowledgments

Thank you,

Tim Lenz, for introducing me to Florida's nearshore waters at night, and the entire fishing crew: Jeff Galin, Craig Sartori, Rama and Rohit Ramasamy, and Blaine Dickenson.

Laura Strachan, for believing in this book from its earliest draft.

Roger Drouin and his team at Little Curlew Press, for their ecological and literary vision that helped make this book a reality.

David M. Tripp, for his artwork that graces the cover of this book.

Mote Marine Laboratory & Aquarium, for the good work that they do.

Vanessa Coto, for the Spanish lessons.

Colleagues and students at Florida Atlantic University.

Coach Phil Lustig and my noontime Florida Atlantic Masters Swim group.

Friends, those listed above and those who know who they are.

Family.

Florida.

An excerpt of the first chapter of *Jewfish* was originally published in *Jewish Fiction.net.* Gratitude goes to the Editor, Dr. Nora Gold, for supporting my work and the work of fellow Jewish writers.

CPSIA information can be obtained
at www.ICGtesting.com
Printed in the USA
LVHW040408290720
661665LV00002B/45